DAVID ALBERT

TENTACLE : CHAMELEON 2012

AMANDA ROBINSON PUBLISHING
LONDON

First published in Great Britain in 2010 by

Amanda Robinson Publishing

Suite 265
10 Great Russell Street
London
WC1B 3BQ

ISBN 978-0-9565109-2-1

DEDICATION

This book is dedicated to my Father and Mother.

ACKNOWLEDGEMENTS

To my wife for bearing with me during my periods of solitary confinement in front of the PC.

To Carly, our now departed Golden Retriever, who lay by my feet at all hours and gave me the inspiration to face the next blank page.

To Stephen Allen, whose chance meeting whilst walking our new 'Goldie' led to Amanda, my publisher.

David Albert

CHAMELEON : 2012

the first in the Tentacle Series

PREFACE

'The future belongs to those who prepare for it'

Malcolm X, June, 1963

'Beauty is skin deep, until you scratch it'

Professor Lang, July, 2012

INTRODUCTION

The elderly man stood in his windswept garden, looked up to the sky and smiled to himself. His grey eyes followed the billowing clouds being chased by the wind to the west and, feeling the chill of a late spring day down his back, turned and trudged wearily towards his lonely, ragstone cottage. Inside, with the oak door shut firmly behind him, was a warm, friendly living area which had as its centrepiece a roaring log fire within a huge open chimney breast. Several dusty photographs of fish and fishermen hung on the near barren walls at obtuse angles interspersed with a mixture of brightly coloured fishing rods, reels and nets. Beyond an open doorway leading to the small, masculine, kitchen stood a massive green Aga, its warm oven gently heating a traditional Scottish loaf while atop the stove sat a bubbling pan of hot lentil soup wafting its vapours around the small abode. He eased himself onto one of the large stout chairs in front of his bureau, slipped his shoes off and, after sipping some fortifying whiskey, lifted his pen and began to write.

The following morning out of a clear blue sky, a RAF jump helicopter clattered noisily to a dusty landing amongst the tall pine trees and lush undergrowth situated around Loch Muick, ten miles south of Balmoral Castle, the Queen's Scottish retreat. Exiting the aircraft were two plain clothes officers of S015, Scotland Yard's elite Counter Terrorism Command and a senior, uniformed, army staff officer, wearing the distinguished emblem of the Parachute regiment above another displaying the famous winged dagger of the SAS. The three men strode purposefully beneath the vast canopy of thick foliage shadowing the early morning Sun's rays from the thick carpet of pine cones that crunched under their impatient feet as yard by yard they approached the old man's cottage. Cautiously they skirted the perimeter before breaking cover from the clearing surrounding the solitary abode and entered the humble lodge.

'Professor?' called the uniformed man, peering into the gloomy interior, his service revolver drawn and ready for use.

His two companions silently eased their way past him and opened the heavy wooden internal shutters around the windows, exposing the daylight to the musty vacant interior. They carefully picked their way through the sparse personal belongings that lay strewn around the cabin particularly taking note that the Aga was barely warm and the bed unmade. All around them was the scene of a casual exit many hours before.

The staff officer holstered his revolver and stepped in to join the other two. 'What do you think?' he posed the question in his clipped, public school, superior accent.

Only one of them spoke, the other just stared as if mesmerized by the staccato voice. 'Well. If I didn't know better' he replied in a broad Cockney accent, 'I would say he's done a bunk.' He scratched his chin thoughtfully and looked around. 'What dy'a think, Harry?' he looked across at his partner still staring at the educated portal that was the officer's mouth.

'Yeah. No struggle. No displacement' the silent one retorted mechanically. 'He's fucked off. Thing is' he briefly stopped, starting to get a flow going 'has he taken any secrets away?'

The question was rhetorical, but the uniformed man replied anyway. 'His research had a particularly dark side! If any radical group got hold of it we could have a living nightmare on our hands! He carried all his research in here' he tapped his head 'and only he and his assistant knew the genetic make up. This way he could have complete control of the code.'

'What about papers, documents. Surely he must have kept them somewhere?' asked the Cockney.

'Nope' said the officer 'he burned *everything*. There's no trace of his work. If we don't find him soon we may have to go public and my masters definitely don't want that! The clock is ticking gentlemen. We don't have much time!'

A few days later, buried within the normal daily bulk mail that was an everyday occurrence at the Science Museum in London, a scraggy and forgettable large brown envelope landed quietly on the dusty heavy oak desk of one of the Oxbridge research assistants that walked these hallowed corridors within this edifice, dedicated to the triumphalism of British Victorian Empire.

Simultaneously, but five hours earlier due to New York being geographically positioned three thousand miles behind Greenwich Mean Time, the underpaid and overworked staff of the mail room buried deep in the bowels of the United Nations Building started sorting the early morning post. The job was very physical and extremely boring and only alleviated by the slick comments on the previous night's football game among the muscled workers, intertwined with the dulcet tones of WNYE music screeching from badly positioned speakers placed high above the sorting bays on the exposed metal beams. Jonah's job today was to sort the mail for the African delegates and ensure that they were in their slots before seven. He, like the majority of the other postal sorters had been 'toiling' as they called it for several years and, apart from an occasional security scare involving suspicious packages at times of increased political tensions, the job was just that, a job. Nothing brightened his day except the sure knowledge that by ten am he could leave the building and head home to Harlem, take his shoes off and relax with his pretty girlfriend who loved him for his personality and not for the colour of his skin. But that was later. Right now he mechanically distributed the mail into the large, white, suspended sacks around him in alphabetical country order and placed the 'unknowns' into a separate bag for further investigation later. For a split second he noticed the same handwriting on a large batch of incoming mail with franked Edinburgh postal marks. The writing for each letter was individually crafted and looked as if whoever had put pen to paper was thinking seriously about each addressee. He sighed, put them into their respective sacks as the large twenty- four hour clock above his head moved its minute hand inexorably towards the vertical position.

By seven all the addressees had received their deliveries and the junior staff in each of the nation's offices were busy at work opening their respective inbound letters and parcels, secure in the knowledge that the UN postal workers many floors below them had scanned and screened all packets for explosives and dangerous objects. The majority of the First Secretaries and Ambassadors did not arrive until about eight, leaving their minions to prioritize the correspondence into high priority, urgent and standard responses. The white neatly addressed envelopes that Jonah had seen some hours before now began to be opened by various staff members. On reading the contents, the reactions ranged from disbelief to abject horror as the political ramifications started to sink in. In the Zimbabwean office the Ambassador had arrived early and almost without protocol, his senior aide being so concerned by one hand-written document that had been passed to him took the letter into his superior before he had even had a chance to remove his coat. Only a nuclear war or possible coup d'états would be brought so urgently to his attention and he took heed of his trusted aide's worry. With a cup of frothy cappuccino in front of him and his confidant shuffling nervously from foot to foot in front of his desk, he calmly read the letter, lowered it and re-read the contents again to make sure that he had not missed anything.

'What do you think Samuel?' he looked up at his aide. 'Is this Professor mad or what?' he continued, his voice became shriller and more paranoid with every utterance. 'Does he *really* think his formula can save anyone? Can he seriously expect us to squander millions of dollars feeding and ministering our divided nation just to have the rebels overthrow us when they recover? In any event I can see no financial benefits. No. The downside is too bleak and completely unacceptable. Well?' He stopped and fixed Samuel with a menacing glare. 'What do you have to say?'

By now Samuel was motionless, but sweating, as he felt the Ambassador's eyes drilling into his soul carefully looking for a reaction, while his large manicured fingers drummed slowly on the mahogany desktop awaiting a response. 'It *could* alleviate the disease' he blurted out quickly 'but we could be cutting our own throats as there would be more to feed as more survived. If he's wrong, any side effects would be unacceptable as we become a 'changed' nation leading to insurmountable debts and insurrection. Anyway we have other highly profitable sources for our funds. This cure is a pipe dream from a crazy scientist and we shouldn't get involved.'

For a moment there was a deafening silence between them as Samuel prayed he had answered to his master's liking. An imperceptible fine line of sweat ran off his furrowed brow, down his cheek and settled across his large rolling lips. The fingers stopped drumming and to Samuel's relief the Ambassador's demeanour softened.

'Thank the Professor for his input, but advise him *we* will let him know if we need his help. That should be the end of that. Let me see the draft before you send it and Samuel?'

'Ambassador?' he turned facing his superior.

'Do not tell anyone about our response. I mean *anyone*. Do I make myself clear?' The tone was sharp and so was the underlying menace beneath it.

'On my life' replied the aide, breathing deeply as he went out to prepare the draft, closing the door quietly behind him. Sitting alone and sipping his coffee, the Ambassador looked out of his window and fleetingly caught his reflection in the bullet proof glass. 'Fancy trying to get us to agree to this madcap scheme?' he thought, studying his palms carefully. 'I wonder how I would feel to be white like the Professor?'

Within the hour similar decisions had been taken unilaterally throughout the building by many member states. Most had not even bothered replying and had rejected the old man's proposals out of hand.

The Vice President of the United States of America quietly entered the Oval Office and stood calmly and patiently in front of his long time friend the President, Barack Obama. Under his right arm he carried a manila folder containing details of the forthcoming trip to London and the schedule for the upcoming Olympic Games opening ceremony. The first Negro ever to hold that coveted office lowered his pen, smiled and walked slowly around the famous Resolute desk, greeting his friend with a formal hand-shake followed by a long affectionate hug. They stood patting each other and then, without a word between them, walked through the open French doors leading to the rose garden, so loved and maintained by all the First Ladies since Jackie Kennedy first brought art and fashion to the previously dour look of the White House. The silent, but warm, early morning rays of approaching mid-summer combined with the floral scents and occasional buzzing of large bumblebees sourcing their honey-giving nectar, gave the garden a slightly surreal feel especially in the light of the recent troubles on the African continent. They strolled quietly through the shaded paths, exchanging personal confidences regarding their wives and families, the suited secret service agents just out of earshot but close enough to put their lives on the line in the unlikely event of an assassination attempt on either man.

'Ok' the President said, standing by a small open-mouthed fish fountain, the water cascading vertically below into a large goldfish filled pond covered with floating lilies. 'You never normally call me unless its urgent. What's up?'

The Vice-President adjusted his Benjamin Franklin spectacles and looked upwards at his friend. 'I understand that you are considering *not* attending the upcoming Olympic opening ceremony in London?'

The question was rhetorical, but the President answered anyway. 'Yes. You're right. I am considering *not* going. The resurgence of hostilities on the African Continent is deeply troubling. I can't afford to be away.'

'If you don't go' his friend said 'then you will definitely miss the opportunity to get the warring parties in one place and deal with them in one fell swoop. I think that if you read this' he handed the folder across 'you will see that *all* the leaders and their subordinates will be at the Games opening ceremony. I honestly believe you should reconsider. It'll improve your re-election chances. I'll hold the fort here and call you if anything comes up. You can rely on me.'

The President studied the typewritten sheets and slipping them back into the folder, handed it back to his friend. For a moment he said nothing, but bent down to smell a brilliantly blooming red rose. 'You of course are right!' he said straightening up and slapping his old Harvard friend on the back. 'Set it up will you? Let's have some breakfast. What would I do without you? You always did have the gift to persuade me!'

As they strolled off re-entering the Oval Office through the French doors, the beefy suited security men sauntered two paces behind, taking their pre-ordained positions either side of the bullet-proof windows. Imperceptibly, the Vice-President glided an envious finger across his Commander-in-Chief's Victorian desk, knowing that the days of the office of a black President were numbered, if the Professor's predictions proved correct.

U.S.A.

Joe Williams lowered his large, white body into the Executive chair of Williams Inc atop the Chrysler building high above Manhattan, his cold blue eyes focussed below on the swarms of dots that were the populace of this great city. He hated them all. He abhorred the cookie-cutter homes and the neat compact lives that they all seemed to aspire to without regard for others around them. It was the stereo-typical rat-race. There was no *real* challenge. Everything was of uniform proportions. The majority had to accept what the minority wanted. You couldn't even pray to your own God without being branded a racist. It was supposed to be a white Christian nation and look what it was now. A cosmopolitan blend of multi-racial diversity encroaching into every aspect of his and his family's life. He had ringed the changes, slight, but noticeable especially from his vantage point. The appointment of what he considered to be uneducated immigrants who could not speak the language and employed under the flag of political correctness really annoyed him. He knew that not all his employees fell into this category, as his number two, Kino Sato, was anything but untypical for his position, speaking four languages fluently and holding two First's at Oxford and one at Cal Tech. But he was one of the exceptions and Joe as its founder and President could live with that for now, as his company being the largest global call centre group had to set an example of racial multilingualism and tolerance.

Joe thought back to the day when he started the company thirty years before with no money in a dingy rented office overlooking Brooklyn. He had employed Catherine whom he had just married and whose father violently disapproved of his new son-in law, 'a man with no prospects' he had warned her. 'If she married Joe' he had said gruffly 'she would be cut off from the family with no inheritance' despite being the sole child from a traditional shipping background with an estimated fortune at around fifty million dollars. It was a decision that she had taken freely as she adored Joe and no money on earth could sway her. She was, after all, made in her father's tough image. The first couple of years were hard with Joe away bidding for business while she ran the office. When her mother unexpectedly called to see her one day, she was shocked to see Catherine scrubbing the floors in front of a single bar electric fire.

'Don't worry Mom' she said. 'Things are looking up and soon we'll be better off. But don't tell Dad.'

Her mother pushed a hundred dollar bill into her daughters hand and walked down the rickety stairs wiping her tears away only when she was out of sight. Things did improve and over the next few years the company expanded with contracts being gained from the US military and it's satellite agencies. Very quickly overseas governments lined up for business and Williams Inc started to develop into a household name nationally and globally. Joe also had cultivated and developed political and industrial links at the highest levels never asking for favours, but building IOU's that he could call on and collect some day in the future. Years passed and when one day, Catherine's father, now retired, showed up unannounced at Joe's office, the younger man was taken aback as he knew his father-in-law would never admit freely that he could be wrong about anything regarding business. The old man held out his wrinkled, but strong hand and staring into Joe's face with his cold grey eyes nodded slightly.

'I was wrong about you. If I was not so stubborn I would have seen you alright a long time ago.' Then, for one of the very rare times in this stubborn and powerful old man's life, he was suddenly overwhelmed with an uncomfortable sense of emotion. He knew, contrary to all of his deeply held convictions, that his guard was down leaving him ashamed and vulnerable. Involuntarily as if in a dream sequence he reached out and for the very first and last time hugged his son-in-law. 'Joe' he whispered 'look after Catherine and take care of this nation.'

'What do you mean? I'm not a politician' Joe said surprised.

'You're right. You are better than them. Get the country proud again. When the time comes someone will contact you. Promise me that you will honour my name.' The old man pushed Joe back, smiled and left. Two month's later he died, the funeral attracting the great and the famous. Among the many mourners, a small bald man shook Joe's hand silently and slipped a card into his palm. He smiled, turned and disappeared. Joe looked at the card. There was no name, no details, only a picture of a Chameleon and a cell phone number. Later that night, alone in his office, he inquisitively called the number. When twenty minutes later he had clicked off the call, he finally understood what Catherine's father had meant in the brief time that they had had and for the first time in his life he felt alive and totally committed to a cause that he knew he could win.

The next four years saw his business rapidly expand, contrary to the trend of the financial markets, particularly in the face of the crippling global credit crisis and the disastrous housing slump of 2008 and crash of 2009. By the spring of 2010 he was not only appearing in Forbes and Millionaire magazine regularly, but had also been tipped as a future Senator and maybe, some said, even higher. He had even been compared to Obama and Clinton in his style and rhetoric although he hated the first being black and loathed the second as having very low morals. With all the glitz and public appearances, he was secretly amassing a war chest and a global network of like thinking people who would one day trigger the biggest racial revolution the world had ever seen.

Therefore, by the summer of 2012, his secret and well laid plans were fully formed and ready to be implemented. He flicked the new daily picture over on his Golden Retriever desk diary and silently smiled remembering Carly, his faithful dog who was taken from him when she was an old lady of fourteen. She had been his doggy, his puppy, Daddy's little girl and even though they had a beautiful little 'Goldie' puppy four months after her passing, he could never quite get over her dying in his arms and begging with her eyes for him to save her. He had gone onto the lonely common that cold October night and uncontrollably cried and screamed at God for taking her from him. It seemed so unfair to him that nasty evil bastards were allowed to live, while his innocent little girl who had not an ounce of enmity in her entire body was not here now by his side anymore. The contrast between good and evil that night four years before, together with his honour bound promise to Catherine's father had propelled him along a wild roller-coaster ride that would end with either triumph or death. Breathing heavily, he stood up and strode across to the ornate, large whiskey dispenser given to him as a parting gift from one of his close business contacts in Tokyo the previous year. As soon as the Johnny Walker splashed into the cut glass, he tossed it quickly down his throat, the crystal reflecting every shimmer of the pungent liquid. Greedily he gulped two more down in quick succession and running his manicured fingers through his well groomed hair slumped heavily onto a leather buttoned green sofa and shut his eyes.

'Whew!' he muttered loudly to himself trying to regain his composure.

'Is everything all right Mr Williams?' crackled Carole's voice through the intercom.

'Yes, everything's fine. Could you come in? I've got something I want you to do.'

Opening the double wooden doors, she stepped in and strode purposefully across to him, her long blonde hair cascading down the figure hugging red Calvin Klein dress. His eyes followed her every move and she knew it, teasing him with her seductively swaying hips as a cobra does before spitting out its lethal venom. She stood in front of him, waiting.

'Eh. Eh!' clearing his throat. 'I want you to arrange a video conference for 10am. Here are the contacts.' He passed a note to her.

'Yes' she smiled. 'Leave it to me. Anything else?'

'Yes. Just let me know a few minutes beforehand that they're on-line. Cancel all my meetings and hold all my calls. I'm not available to anyone and you don't know where I am.'

'No problem.' She left the suite, closing the door silently behind her.

He sat back, closed his eyes and tried to focus. In what had seemed hours, but was in fact only fifteen minutes she called him.

'Mr Williams? They're both on line and waiting.'

'Thanks Carole. I'll pick it up in a minute.' He stood up, stretched and walked over to his wall safe, removing a clear plastic wallet which he placed on his desk, eyeing the coloured capsules within. With one click on his remote, his office was electronically sealed, while at the same time scrambling the upcoming call. He poured a glass of water from the decanter on his desk. There would be no need for notes. Leaning forward he touched the screen activating the split images.

'Good day Nandi. Good day Hardeep. Before we begin, can you make sure your scramblers are on? We don't want anyone outside eavesdropping on this call. Can you confirm by sending the signal?'

On a mini display next to his main screen, two red lights illuminated against each colour image. 'That's fine' he said.

'Hi Joe. Nandi here'. A stunning, black young woman with a distinctive South African accent smiled out of the top right split screen at him. 'What's the weather like in New York?' she asked coyly.

'Hot and stuffy. Typical Big Apple weather. And Joburg?' he asked, smiling back at this slim Zulu girl. He looked admiringly at her polished cherub features and remembered her 'perfect 10' figure. To see her in the flesh, as he had done on several occasions, one could easily have mistaken her for a super model, such was her grace and poise. With long legs that seemed to go on forever, the comparison could not be easily avoided.

'It's thirty Celsius, warm and sticky, just like the last time you visited me in Natal!' she winked at him seductively.

'Ok. Ok' he smiled back at her cheekiness. 'Let's stick to the agenda.'

'Hi Joe' came Hardeep's voice and image from Delhi. 'Like Nandi, the heat here is hot as we approach our zenith in August.'

Joe looked serious and leant forward so he could see their images that bit clearer.

'This is probably the last time we will talk before the Olympics kick off in a few weeks and I want you both to know that I appreciate all your hard work to date. However the final push is the most important and I need you tell me that you both have everything in hand? This is a top to bottom operation. We are all interlocked and if any part of this fails, we all fail. I have other operatives in place and they are waiting for my signal. The global population has now hit 9 billion and most of the extra 2.5 billion will live in the so called *3rd world*, undernourished with life expectancy dropping dramatically.' He paused. 'We can't wait for the civilised western *'leaders'* to act. The UN and other NGO's have just become talking shops with no teeth, while people suffer and starve. Therefore we have to take affirmative action now against the tyrants on your lists. Just make sure that all the targeted leaders and their cronies are in London so we can deal with them there. You two are in a unique position to use your contacts and ability to shepherd not just your own politicos to London, but other countries leaders with whom you are actively in contact with. Please liaise with the London team as to flights and hotels. Once all the people on your lists are there, they will deliver the *coup de grace.*' He paused and smiled at them both. 'Do we have a green light guys or are there any outstanding issues that we should deal with now?'

'I'm fine' said Nandi.

'Me too' added Hardeep.

'Actually there is one question' said Nandi.

'What is it my friend?' he smiled at her.

'Are we going to see you in London?'

Joe sighed and smiled at them both. 'I honestly don't know. I have a lot to do here as well. I might even surprise myself! As I said earlier, this will be our last contact until it's all over. We won't talk again until then. Good luck to you both and may your God go with you.' Smiling at his lieutenants and wondering if he would ever see them again, he leaned forward and shut his screen off. He reached across the green leather-topped desk and pulled the silver photo frame towards him from where Catherine and the kids smiled back at him from the hammock on the wooden porch. 'How quickly they've grown' he thought, noting how Scott gently hugged Carly, their first Golden Retriever puppy in his arms, her sad brown eyes and large floppy ears still melting his heart after all these years. Twisting sideways in his chair, he removed a large Winston Churchill cigar from the second drawer down on his left and expertly rolled it between his index finger and thumb, removing the tissue to expose a brown potent leaf which he ran seductively under his nose. The deep aroma of expensive tobacco really came alive when he expertly snipped the end off with a professional cutter and kindled the flame from a sulphur match. A plume of smoke rose from his lips into the air above him and shutting his eyes, he savoured one of the only vices he had left.

After five minutes he released the electronic lock of the suite and strode purposefully through the double doors, to the outer office surprising Carole and her PA in conversation. 'Sorry Pauline, but I need Carole now!'

Pauline mumbled an apology, but he was already inside by his desk waiting. Carole, taken aback by his abrupt and out of character summons, ran in and sat down opposite him notepad at the ready.

'Book me a flight to Chicago. Contact the MD of the Jardine Water Purification Plant and tell him I'm coming. He'll be expecting me. I am not available or contactable by anyone and you do not know where I've gone or what for. Understand?'

'No problem' she quickly retorted, surprised at his aggressive style. In five years of working with him, she had never seen him this animated.

'And have your Blackberry on all the time I'm away. I may need you at a moment's notice. Clear your desk. Give all your work to Pauline. Carole, I'm relying on you.' He walked round, bent down and looked into her eyes.

'Do you trust me?' he said softly.

She smiled back at him sheepishly. 'You know I do. I always have.'

He straightened up and smiled back. 'That's what I wanted to hear!' He patted her hand affectionately as she stood up and seductively walked back through the double doors to her outer office.   As she closed the doors behind her, a worried frown passed across his face. He strode over to the tinted floor to ceiling windows and viewed the 'ants' moving far below him.

HARDEEP

For a twenty first century nation and a member of the 'Nuclear Club', India still had a vast and poor population to feed while trying to shake off its image of still being the British Empire's 'Jewel in The Crown'. Even though its GDP growth was a staggering eight per cent, it still had the largest number of poor people in the world and its death rate of forty eight per cent was second only to Africa. Not since the revolutionary days of Ghandi and the partition of Pakistan had there ever been such economic and political activity in this country which was actually a continent in its own right. With expansion came dreams of economic growth leaving the leaders at odds of how to deliver the benefits of a western economy while keeping traditional values firmly at the front of the secular versus religious divide.

Among the new celebrity intellectuals was Raj, a twenty eight year old genius with two double Firsts in Molecular Science and Bio Fuel Agronomics. Standing tall at well over six feet, his athletic frame of square jaw, broad shoulders, slim waist and a 'six pack' of powerful stomach muscles balanced comfortably with a body weight of fourteen stone. With perfectly groomed shoulder length jet-black hair, dark eyes and an upwardly mobile playboy lifestyle to match, his rich, single status always meant that he was never seen without a stunning girl on his arm. He enjoyed fast cars and fast women while being a regular at all the cream of society and sporting events. His other pastimes and attributes were gambling, karate, piloting his own plane and he was an accomplished motivational speaker. All this led to him having a strong iconic and almost hero status among the teeming masses of India while others suggested that he was more popular than many politicians. This, in turn, created envy and fear within the Indian establishment as to his popularity and many felt threatened by his demands for legalized birth controls. In particular, Raj was constantly using a quote from Thomas Malthus; a British political economist at the beginning of the nineteenth century who predicted that population had the potential to grow much faster than food supply. His rhetoric scared the politicians and plans had been forged to silence him before his oratory became inflammatory and rabble rousing.

His friend Hardeep, however, although possessing this same zeal and passion for reform, was a political bureaucrat by profession and consequently came across to all he met for the first time as a boring intellectual. Measuring five feet nine in height and just over ten stone in weight, his bony frame supported a small bald head displaying bright blue eyes due to the coloured contact lenses that he slipped in every morning. And yet for all the qualities that Raj possessed, this boring little civil servant from one of the lowest castes that India still traditionally clung on to could be a formidable enemy and a man to avoid upsetting at any cost.

Hardeep had recognised in Raj a man with similar ideals which he strove to carefully cultivate via subtlety engineered social encounters. Over time they had developed a strong relationship, upon which the government man slowly revealed to his friend Chameleon and Tentacle's real involvement. Hardeep realised that together, they held the key for political agitation and revolution. It therefore came as no surprise to Raj when he received Hardeep's call at home a few minutes after the latter had clicked off from the conference call with Joe. The phone rang several times identifying Hardeep on the caller display before being answered by a female voice he didn't recognise.

'Raj?' said a wary Hardeep, always on his guard against the security services intercepting his calls.

'No. Who wants him?' came the same sleepy, but sultry, female voice again.

'Can you put Raj on please? Tell him it's Hardeep.'

There was a soft whispering and frantic rustling of sheets.

'Hardeep, old friend. Do you know what time it is?' said Raj, rubbing his eyes with his left hand and jamming the receiver between his chin and right shoulder. 'It's eight in the evening' his bald friend said looking at an illuminated Rolex.

'This better be worth it!' Raj said sitting cross-legged while plumping two large pillows up behind him as a back support.

'Can you talk confidentially?' asked Hardeep, drumming his fingers impatiently on the heavy Victorian bureau ceded to him by the last incumbent of this prestigious government office located in the very heart of New Delhi's diplomatic enclave.

'Hold on' Raj said. 'I'm going to scramble the call' and depressed a black button next to the phone by his bed. He looked across the massive four-poster bed at the beautiful tanned and semi-naked body of Shakira. As much as he admired Hardeep, this was definitely not the right moment for him to call. He shook his head in abject disbelief.

'Who is that?' Shakira mumbled, half asleep, rolling face down into the soft duvet that gently supported her curvaceous figure.

'Go back to sleep' he whispered in her right ear, nibbling the lobe tenderly.

Sighing sensually she mechanically reached for him, brushing her milk-soft skin against his muscular body.

He moved away from her and grabbed a white sarong from a nearby chair wrapping it around his slim waist and tip-toed across the marble of the palatial bedroom within the penthouse apartment in Connaught Place high above the main bustling shopping centre of New Delhi. Quietly closing the bedroom door he crossed through the hallway and stepped into his study settling himself into a large executive chair and flicked on the large fan, even though the million pound apartment was fully air conditioned. He picked up the phone.

'The scrambler is on. You there?' he asked leaning backwards, letting the breeze from the fan gently play through his hair. 'What's up? It better be important' he repeated. 'I've been chasing this girl for weeks!' he said referring to the temptress waiting for him on the bed.

'Forget the girl! It's on!' replied Hardeep excitedly.

'You mean Chameleon?' Raj asked in astonishment. 'Wow! Are you sure? I mean. It's come so fast!' blurted Raj.

'Yes. I've just got off the phone' said Hardeep. 'It's already started! I don't have all the details, but apparently some people have already been affected, even before the games themselves have begun!'

'My God!' exclaimed Raj. 'I just thought because I hadn't heard from you in months that it all died a death.'

'No chance! We were just waiting for the signal and now we're ready to roll. Are all your contacts in place?' asked Hardeep.

'Ready and waiting. I was only talking to them last night and they were all asking what was happening. Now we can really make a difference! It's amazing that we can change so many people's lives in such a short amount of time and get rid of some of the unscrupulous arms dealers and corrupt politicians who are sucking this country dry.'

'Yes. And for the better' said the government man. 'When this call is over, you know what to do, but target especially the purification and drinking plants. Don't forget the soft drinks industry and all the transport networks. We must be able to create the short term panic that will give our people enough time to control all the media and food outlets. Our friends in the military will start their moves in twelve hours as the panic sets in. Keep me posted.'

'No problem' replied Raj now fully awake and ready to go. Hardeep hung up and walked over to a large sash window draped on either side with floor to ceiling red velvet curtains and deep plush carpets. He looked whimsically out over the immaculately tended lush lawns and Imperial fountains of the Rashtrapati Bhavan, sitting proudly atop Raisina Hill in the heart of New Delhi, better known to outsiders as the President's official abode. This magnificent and imposing palace is located in Prakash Vir Shastri Avenue, itself only a quarter of a mile from nineteen foreign embassies located on Shantipath or as the Hindi's say 'Path of Peace.' The most prominent and distinguishing aspect of Rashtrapati Bhavan is it's architecturally breathtaking dome, emulating the ancient Pantheon of Rome on its vast, multi-dimensional structure of four floors and three hundred and forty colonial rooms. To its front sits an enormously wide stately mall projecting over half a mile in length and having at its centre the Jaipur Column, 145 feet tall, topped by a bronze lotus from which rises a six-pointed glass star. This area in the coming days was to be Hardeep's 'hunting ground'. Being cleared at the highest levels within the President's Secretariat gave him unrestricted access to all national and foreign dignitaries including their movements in and out of the country. In particular, he knew the travel plans of all the key politicians before, during and after the Olympics and had already organised his timetable to deal with them accordingly.

Knowing that Raj and his team would handle all the domestic targets, Hardeep now felt free to concentrate all his efforts on the overseas operation with particular emphasis on London. Although the time was fast approaching nine, he had no time to lose and set to work at his computer terminal, identifying the latest location of all those on his target list. Within a couple of minutes he had several print-outs, all cross referenced against one another displaying name, job and travel arrangements. Taking a red highlight pen from his drawer, he started to mark and prioritise these lists and re-enter them back into the computer. When he had almost finished, it was nearing midnight and only a massive surge of adrenaline was keeping him going to finalise the draft. Still, he knew that this task was critical if their overall plan was to succeed and so he persevered, finally finishing at one in the morning. From the lawns outside the buildings, his office light was the only one burning bright as he leant forward and sent the relevant encrypted message to his contact in the Ramada

Hotel London, who had been anticipating it since receiving a call from Morgan Ibotu. His overseas connection now made, Hardeep proceeded to pinpoint the location of any other individuals still in India who were staying put or were about to travel in the next few days; the former names being forwarded onto Raj, while he personally would deal with the latter group. No one on the list was to be allowed to evade Tentacle's far reaching limbs. Although the numbers that he had to account for amounted to over three hundred, there was no reason to pursue them at this hour as they were all bound to depart on the same flight for the London Olympics in two days.

He gingerly stood up and rolled his head through three hundred and sixty degrees while attempting to restrain a tired, but necessary yawn. Leaning over the desk he shut the computer down, picked up the printouts and left the office, killing the lights as he went. The security guard on duty by the main door bid him a pleasant morning as he exhaustedly descended the external floodlit stairs leading to the private car park and the twenty eight kilometre drive home along the eight lane expressway to the booming mini-city of Gurgaon, south west of New Delhi. The next day he worked from home. This was not unusual as he had done this many times before and therefore did not draw any undue attention to himself. In any case he was a departmental head and had almost complete autonomy over his own work schedules. Within his luxurious villa set amongst broad tree-lined roads, flanked with lush open planned lawns and whirling sprinklers, he put the final touches to his part in Tentacle's plan. Using his authority to by-pass the security of the passenger check-in database, he double checked that all those on his list had confirmed their flight. Because of the numbers involved, he noted that the plane had an exclusive charter and this fact alone allayed any fears he might have had of any other parties being on board when affirmative action was taken. Today he sat outside on the shaded patio, beneath a large green awning that covered almost eighty per cent of the wooden decking and watched a small bird, resplendent in its tropical blue plumage bathe itself under a cool cascading waterfall within the shadow of his affluent residence. Dinesh, the senior maintenance engineer at Indira Ghandi International Airport, his gleaming bald head and baby face appearance masking his thirty one years sat next to him.

'What flight are they on?' he asked sipping some iced tea.

'Air India departing at 0700, tomorrow terminal three, into London Heathrow' replied Hardeep, passing the printed flight details across to the engineer. 'I've checked that they're all coming. If any do miss the flight, Raj can deal with them separately.'

Methodically, Dinesh ran down the list, a red highlight pen in hand. Now and then he marked a name then continued until he had exhausted the printout, repeating the process again, this time with a green pen. When he had completely finished he looked up at Hardeep.

'Almost seventy per cent are corrupt local and foreign dignitaries, the balance mobsters, terrorists and crooked businessmen. What a contemptuous grouping!'

'Exactly' agreed Hardeep. 'The sooner we deal with this lot the better! Can you envisage any problems?'

'None that I can think of. The panic will be on British soil and we can then literally wash our hands of them all. Anything else?' Dinesh furrowed his forehead deep in thought and shook his head. 'Nothing of importance, except' he looked up at his old school friend 'what the hell will you be doing while this performance is going on?'

Hardeep smiled knowingly and looked up at his friend. 'Why. That's simple. I'll be watching the games begin and history unfold before my eyes.'

'What!' the engineer exclaimed in total surprise. 'Do you mean to tell me you're actually travelling to London?'

'Well of course. Do you really think that I'm going to miss this? Not in a million years!'

'But when are you going?' Dinesh asked, taken aback at this new revelation. 'I mean, won't it be dangerous for you?' he stressed quietly.

Hardeep leaned forward and bade his friend do the same. 'Actually, I'm on the same flight and no it won't be dangerous, as I know what's going on and will keep well out of the way. In any case I want to make sure that everything runs smoothly and I even get a chance to see London and the Games as well!'

'As long as you don't get caught!' emphasised Dinesh sternly.

'You don't have to worry there' said the government man. 'There are only a few people who know that I have any connection to Tentacle and they won't say anything. Anyway, I'll be travelling under my own name and with diplomatic immunity, so I'm untouchable.'

'But I didn't see your name on the passenger list!' stressed Dinesh looking carefully again at the papers in his hand.

'You're right' said Hardeep, stretching out and taking back the print-out from his friend. 'I'm *not* on the passenger list. I'm on the *crew* list' he smiled confidently.

'Whoa!' exclaimed his friend. 'You really have thought this through. There are no flies on you as the British say!'

'For all our sakes, let's hope that's true. I think that's it now. Let's have some lunch. I've made a vegetable curry and to top it off I've got some cold Cobra to pre-celebrate with.'

RAJ

Two miles away, Raj lowered the Bang & Olufsen Serenata mobile onto the desk ahead of him and then sauntered over to the glass tank by the window containing his green Two-Horned Tanzanian Chameleon. The lizard sat motionless as he crouched down and gently tapped on the glass trying to get its attention while considering and dispelling in an instant the ethics of his upcoming actions. Moving quietly so as not to wake his partner, he tossed the sarong to one side and stepped across the hallway naked into the shower room, emerging a few minutes later, dripping wet but invigorated. He quickly towelled down, changing into blue denim jeans, hiking boots and a Cambridge University sweatshirt given to him some time ago by a visiting Professor from that esteemed place of learning. After scribbling a brief note to Shakira, which he attached via a fridge magnet to the upright freezer door, he removed a sealed plastic container from the ice box and carefully placed it into the external zip pocket of a pre-packed emergency travel bag. Picking up his keys and wallet he furtively stepped out of the front door and headed down the internal stairway to the underground car park. He opened the boot and slung the bag in between a large black Maglite and a full emergency petrol can. It was too dangerous for him to travel by air. There were spies everywhere. The warm leather seats and walnut trim of his steel blue Jaguar XJR with the air con streaming around him delivered a satisfied feeling of security and calm as he slowly moved out through the security gates turning east across the still silent city. He quickly joined the empty ring road near the national zoological park, turning south out of Delhi and onto the NH2 to Agra and ultimately Bangalore some 1200 miles to the south of Delhi and ten degrees north of the equator. The luminescent green lights on his dashboard could have been confused with a fighter pilot's head up display, but at this moment only one indicator was of importance, the fuel gauge. It was low and the long run would need at least two complete fills. A large blue sign indicated services at two miles which the Jaguar made in minutes as it sliced through the humid night air temperature of 28 Celsius. The glowing red lights of the petrol station and its facilities came into view and Raj swung the car in next unleaded pump. As he filled the tank, a white Delhi Police jeep with the symbol 'with you for always' drew up on the opposite side, its two officers dressed in white summer uniforms and dark glasses exiting the front doors. One proceeded to fill the jeep, the other walked over to the mini supermarket and disappeared into the shop. Watching the gauge, his hand gripping the pump, he felt the nearest officer staring at him from behind his dark lenses. Avoiding eye contact, he altered his stance so that he was now filling the car with his back to the prying eyes. Raj had now built up a nervous sweat and felt distinctly uncomfortable in their presence. As soon as he could, he finished the fill and strode easily over and through the automatic glass doors into the air conditioned mini market. At the counter he saw the other officer and turned away to the magazine rack picking up a copy of 'The Times of India', burying his head within its pages until the man had departed. He walked over to the drinks cabinet and picked up a cold bottle of milk, avoiding any of the soft drinks and paid the cashier with his credit card, telling him to keep the bonus points and casually exited the store. The heat hit him like a slap in the face as he stepped out and paced over to the Jaguar, keeping his eyes low and avoiding any form of contact with the officer who still stood by his vehicle talking with his partner. Raj 'beeped' the lock and eased himself into the car, putting the milk and paper on the floor behind him while switching the engine on. A cool blast of air caressed his face, visibly relaxing him and he sat for a minute composing himself. Suddenly an urgent tap on his driver's window jolted his senses and, cautiously, he lowered the glass an inch only to see the dark mirrored glasses of one of the officers staring in at him.

'Excuse me sir, but could you step out for a minute?'

'Is there anything wrong officer?'

'Please sir. If you don't mind?' The officer stood back, his partner another step behind him. Their demeanour was cautious but mechanical, the stance well practiced through years of dealing with violent thugs and religious fanatics. The holsters containing the guns were unclipped and ready for action.

From his seat Raj noted that the nearest man was sweating slightly beneath his cap, while his partner casually rested his right hand on the large gun handle. He thought of the plastic box in the boot and quickly ran through his options if he had to explain its contents to these notoriously trigger-happy traffic cops. Taking a deep breath, he turned the engine off, opened the door and stepped out. He was taller than both officers and bigger built, but noticing they both carried guns decided that in any confrontation he would probably lose, his intention was to play innocent.

Smiling and leaning casually against the car he opened his arms wide. 'How can I help you?'

'It is him. I'm sure' turning behind him to his partner.

The other officer took off his dark glasses, rubbed his eyes and looked at Raj. 'You're right! It is him!'

'Is there a problem?' said Raj slightly concerned.

'I'm sorry sir' said the first. 'You are Raj. The guy in the papers, on TV etc?'

'Yes. That's me. Guilty as charged' he said cautiously. 'Is there a problem?' he repeated.

'No problem sir. My colleague thought that it was not you and I thought otherwise. We had a small bet. I won!' he smiled.

Raj visibly relaxed and breathed easily. 'I thought I had done something wrong' he laughed. 'How much was the bet?' he enquired.

'Fifty Rupees' they both said in unison.

The second officer handed over a fifty Rupee note bearing the Ashoka Lion to his partner who immediately handed it to Raj. 'Could you sign it? I would be much obliged. My kids will love it. They don't stop talking about you. You are their hero!' he smiled and handed over a pen.

Raj took the note and leaning on his roof, signed it, passing the pen and note back.

'Thanks Raj. You've made my day' and held his hand out.

Raj shook his hand and that offered by his colleague. 'Thanks guys. You've made mine as well' and got back into his car and for the second time in five minutes, started the engine and let the air-con cool him down before he moved off.

To his left an auto rickshaw stopped, its swarthy driver looking decidedly out of place at this hour and now starting to receive the full attention of the two officers, one of whom had replaced his dark glasses and was giving the driver the third degree, especially as India was on a constant terror threat and anyone out of the ordinary was a suspect. Now cooled off and refreshed from the milk, Raj opened the throttle and rolled the car past the officers, waving his hand out of the driver's window as he sped off into the night and southern India. The journey south was uneventful apart from the continuous attempts by truck drivers to undertake on the left and force him off the road with sheer brute strength when legitimately overtaking. Luckily Raj was used to these normal driving practices by the truckers and anticipated their every move, using the power and speed of the 4.2 litre V8 engine to out manoeuvre them. By nine he had by-passed Agra, the seat of the imperial Mughal court in the 16th and 17th centuries, now home of the world famous Taj Mahal, and had swung south west joining the NH3 to the busy port of Mumbai, some 800 miles distant on the coast of the Arabian Sea. As the miles passed and he drew further away from the populated cities and their humid atmospheres, the night skies opened up revealing a star studded heaven full of twinkling, but silent bodies. Travelling at over 100 mph along the unlit roads soon started to strain his eyes especially when faced by onward coming trucks, their headlight beams set on high causing temporary blindness for a split second or two. This in itself was not that bad, but after passing Indore at 3am he was forced to a stop in a queue of vehicles, one of which had decapitated a wandering cow that had unfortunately strolled across the road in the dark, he decided to take a break and pull up for a while. Five miles after clearing the carnage, he spotted a lay by and pulled off the main highway easing into the bright forecourt of a petrol station where he filled his tank again. Then, seeking the dark, he trundled towards the shadows at the rear of the facilities. Here he turned his engine off and made a few calls to his operatives in various cities around India, mainly in Mumbai and Bangalore. He needed sleep like a thirsty man needs water and with the sky lightening by the minute as dawn approached, he decided that a few hours sleep was not just a luxury, but a necessity. He set his watch alarm for five and closed his eyes, dropping off quickly into a slumber and then descending into a pit of darkness and gentle oblivion.

At five minutes before five he woke with a start. It was not his watch that made him sit up awkwardly with a crick in his neck. It was not even the bad posture of the Jaguar seats that could be blamed for his sudden arousal. It was the rain. The slow 'pitter patter' on his glass roof vibrated slowly and then increased rapidly with the intensity of a snare drum on a military parade. He looked up to see liquid pods plonking heavily down on the roof and the dirt around him. One moment the vehicle was sitting amongst dry scrub bushes. The next, giant pools of water had been created, overflowing and forming raging torrents in minutes. Although the vibrator on his watch trembled in combination with a loud shrill, he just about felt and heard it above the now thunderous impact of the opening crescendo of the monsoon that seasonally visited the sub-continent at this time of the year. The air being oppressively humid meant that he had to start the engine while bringing the wipers and the air-con on to see through the misty windows that now surrounded him. Quickly the windows cleared and he watched as if mesmerised by the rapidly changing landscape around him. For a moment he thought of Noah and the Great Flood and could almost visualise that biblical scene happening now as he sat, a spectator to one of the world's great repeat performances. Dropping the gears into drive he eased the vehicle forward until it stood directly outside the main doors of a small supermarket and almost in one movement jumped out, locked the door and ran inside avoiding the large, deep puddles that barred his way. Although it was only a distance of some six feet from the car to the doors, it was enough to get thoroughly soaked under the intense rain that now hammered down on the tin roof of the building. Breathing heavily, he wiped away the rain from his face and stood sodden and dripping as the large fan to his left tried unsuccessfully to dry him down. Then, like a dog after getting soaked, he shook his body violently, spraying droplets of water over the surrounding counters to the verbal displeasure of the owner. Raj tried to pacify him with the traditional pressed palms greeting of 'namaste' at the same time as enquiring where the toilet was placed. The disgruntled man pointed to a darkened doorway behind him and stood aside as Raj stepped by. After a few minutes, when he emerged again, his first response was to place on the counter two five rupee coins for the service and also purchase a small box of biscuits to which the owner merely grunted begrudgingly. By the time he had looked up, the Jaguar with a wet Raj in it had already moved down the torrid embankment and was en-route for Mumbai.

Through the flailing wipers he could just about make out the national highway signs which placed his destination at just over four hundred miles. Because of the treacherous weather, he had to reduce his speed to just over fifty and re-evaluate his arrival time to one pm. This was, he thought, ok as the Tentacle clock, although ticking, had flexibility in it and the massive support amongst the indigenous population for a halt to water-intensive units from multinationals was at such a pitch now that another day or so to take action would make no difference at all. All the same, he wanted confirmation that all was ready to roll on his arrival and made a mental note to call his operatives at eleven. Leaning comfortably back into his seat, he listened to the early morning national news in Hindi and, after gleaning the information he required, flicked over to BBC World for an international perspective. As if in a time capsule he was unaware of the hour until the reporter announced with a cultured Oxford / Delhi accent that it was now seven and although the rain was still constant the sky had lightened enough to allow an increase in speed to sixty. Although he had not seen any vehicles in hours, as the distance closed on this of India's most dynamic, cosmopolitan and crowded city with a mass of some fifteen million people, from billionaire tycoons to homeless pavement dwellers, the traffic started building up. By eleven, when he pulled off the road to make his calls, the traffic was growing in intensity with minor hold up's turning into major jams as traditional hay- carts pulled by oxen vied for road space with yellow roofed taxis and red double-decker buses on their way to Marine Drive and the waiting tourists. Not wishing to be harassed by the constant beggars that descend on any vehicle, especially those that appear to be tourists, he parked the car out of sight behind a large warehouse. The dark skinned porters were totally oblivious to his presence, their only focus being on lifting back-breaking white sacks of strong scented spices onto low backed lorries ready for the onward trip to Crawford market lying to the north of Victoria Terminus, itself centrally positioned within the city and handling over 1000 trains and two million passengers daily. He made several calls, all preceded by his portable scrambler being activated. The last one with Ibrahim (his main contact in the south) was that all the leaders attended a final briefing at the stately, red-domed Taj Mahal Hotel the next day at ten am in Raj's suite, booked in the name of Mr Singh. The irony of this particular meeting place was not lost on Ibrahim, a devout Muslim and fanatic of Tentacle since his inclusion about one year previously. Through his grandfather he had learned of the British Victorian policy of allowing 'Whites Only' into the Watsons Hotel and when Jamshedji Tata, a prominent Parsi industrialist, heard that he had been barred, he decided to construct the Taj in protest. As the Taj, with its stylish Moorish arches and columns, majestic stairways and galleries, flourished as one of Asia's grandest hotels, Watsons became a dilapidated, sad, building and subsequently fell into a state of disrepair, shutting down as the British Raj came finally to an end.

Even though the calls had taken about thirty minutes, it was, he thought, time well spent. All the participants, who in the majority of cases were security cleared at the highest level, had hundreds of people ready to act at a moments notice. Only one or two had any serious questions and these he answered quickly and clearly putting their minds at rest and into a 'we can do it' positive frame of mind. Leaning forward so that his head jammed into the narrowing space between the dashboard and the windscreen Raj was just able to peer around the corner of the warehouse into the dirt track that he had recently driven up. The traffic build up had continued unabated but now in addition to the cars, trucks and buses heading for Mumbai, the number of pedestrians had also swelled dramatically, as people from the villages of Maharashtra and neighbouring states converged on this very affluent port in search of work, many of them arriving from squalid slums like Dharavi where more than 300,000 dwellers heaved in shanty towns extending to less than 500 acres.

'These poor people' he thought 'would be the beneficiaries of my actions' and for the first time since his father died some years previously, tears ran down his cheeks and he sobbed uncontrollably. After a few minutes he regained his composure, wiped his eyes and started the engine allowing the car to roll down the track to join the noisy hubbub created by these teeming masses all heading in the same direction, like soldier ants on a vital mission. Although the journey was now much slower due to the throngs of this mass populace on the move, he was still closing in to his destination at every humid mile. Sometimes as intermittent cloud bursts and driving rain forced his wipers to protest loudly as they battled against the elements, the massed crowds magically just melted away allowing him to pick up speed and lost time.

Using his 'Tom Tom' he asked the satellite navigation system for his 'geo-position' and the best route to his hotel. The computer generated voice advised him to keep to the NH3 all the way in, his ETA being 2pm. He eased back into his seat, selected a jazz CD and surged forward to the south west, the sky brightening ahead of him. Two hours later Raj had left the national highway and was entering the long narrow promontory of downtown Mumbai, its tip jutting gently into the Arabian Sea. As he stopped to allow a multitude of Indian built Ambassador taxis to cross his path at the junction of Sardar Patel and P D Mello he watched one of the many daily ferries from Elephanta Island and Mandwa slowly dock, its rainbow clothed passengers shuffling down the gangplanks to be quickly immersed like quicksand amongst the throngs of vocal portside traders. The 'geo navigation' advised him to continue straight ahead passing the General Post Office, its classical combination of minarets, domes and arches standing proud at the northernmost point of the neat tree-lined and broad pavements of the Ballard Estate, Mumbai's business centre. Suddenly he saw a sign for the 'Gateway of India', a colossal building with a giant archway set on Mumbai's seafront, welcoming travellers to the Indian shores during the heyday of the British Raj. Knowing that the hotel stood just behind it he followed the road, passing the Royal Mumbai Yacht Club on his left and swung the Jaguar into the afternoon shadow of its large red domed roof that overlooked the harbour. The car park was not only full of cars, but also hundreds of CCTV cameras installed after the bloodbath of the terrorist attack in 2008. He stepped around to the boot, carefully removing the holdall and almost as second nature electronically locked the doors while checking the time on his watch. One thirty.

The immaculately dressed, red turbaned, white coated head porter stepped out to greet him, bowing slightly with his hands pressed together in the traditional greeting of 'namaste'. Raj responded in kind and, after some brief words, entered the sumptuous lobby of one of the best known five star hotels in the world. At the desk he checked in under the name of Mr Singh and was escorted to the old wing with its elegant turn of the century atmosphere. After tipping the porter he closed the door and hung up his clothes from the holdall. The air conditioning was just right and with the almost total silence and soft lights of the suite, he stripped off and swiftly showered, feeling totally relaxed for the first time in twelve hard hours on the road. Emerging ten minutes later, a white towel wrapped around his slim waist, his bulging muscles dripping with water, he eased himself between the cool cotton sheets of the Maharaja four-poster and drifted off to sleep.

When he awoke the room was dark, the gentle hum of the background air conditioning the only discernable sound. He rubbed his eyes, sat up and looked at the luminous date and time on his Rolex. Six am. Sixteen hours asleep! Feeling a locked neck muscle, he rotated his head and then easing the sheets back, swivelled off the bed, his feet cushioned by the deep soft pile of a luxurious Persian carpet. The coffee percolator stood a few paces away in the lounge, its orange mains light glowing in the gloom, beckoning him to join it. Slipping on the white towelling robe provided by the hotel, he refreshed himself in the bathroom, then walked easily over to the waiting appliance and dispensed the Nescafe into the black orifice that together with the scorching water to follow, would give him the shot he needed to begin this historic day. Holding the remote in one hand and his coffee in the other, he flicked onto BBC World and curled up into a deep and comfy armchair similar to the other four that were strategically placed around the suite. The main news appeared to be about the Olympics and the scrabble that had occurred four years before, when the Olympic torch was paraded globally in the run up to Beijing, bringing vehement objections to the Chinese record on human rights, particularly their actions toward Tibet. Even the 2008 global financial crisis that almost bankrupted the world's economies would be of little comparison in relation to the unleashing of Chameleon. After all, money can be replaced, but overthrowing governments and cleansing society was a different story. 'That' he thought 'was a children's tea party compared to what was about to happen now.'

'Is the pool available?' he enquired on the phone to the concierge.

'Yes sir. It opens at six am and closes at nine in the evening. Towels are provided by the entrance.'

'Thanks. Could you have a Continental breakfast delivered to my room for seven? I prefer fresh orange and two, six minute boiled eggs. I also need copies of the International Herald Tribune and the Indian Express.'

'Consider that done Sir. Is there anything else?'

'Actually there is. I am expecting some visitors for ten. Could you arrange for them to be shown directly to my suite and could you also provide twelve bottles of Himalayan still bottled water at the same hour, together with a selection of your best cakes?'

'No problem sir. Is that all?'

'Yes. Namaste' expressing the traditional parting.

'Namaste' repeated the concierge.

Reaching to his left he yanked the leather holdall towards him and unzipped the remaining contents. The plastic box fell out onto the deep carpet by his feet, followed by a selection of odds and sods that he had pre-packed just for this type of emergency. Picking the box up he placed it together with his wallet, passport and a small handgun deep within the confines of the mini-safe that nestled comfortably just behind the entrance door to the suite. He closed the safe door and tapped a code into the keypad which responded with a red light indicating that it was now locked. He deposited all his soiled clothes into the hotel laundry bag for collection that day in the hallway. Stepping into the white marble bathroom he shaved off the overnight stubble, gargled and splashed Brut Original over his deep tanned muscular frame. After donning a pair of jeans, tee-shirt and blue canvas shoes he headed to the pool three floors below carrying his shorts in a gym bag. The changing room appeared to be empty, save for the old and deeply lined janitor who swung his mop around like a philharmonic conductor quite oblivious of Raj's presence. The old man suddenly looked up from his chores only to see a departing figure sloshing through the hygienic foot spa to the blue shimmering water of the aqua dome. Sighing deeply he continued his monotonous job unaware of the series of events that were about to unfold and the effect they would have on his and his families lives in the next few weeks. Raj picked up a white fluffy towel from the freshly laundered pile adjacent to the unmanned registration desk and plodded over to a wooden sun lounger still shaded in the early morning light and waited. It was just after seven that the man entered, his tall lean physique, dark thinning hair and extremely light tan belied his age and his background. His black 'Speedo' shorts topped by a narrow white belt gave the impression that he could have been a catwalk model save for the long red scar that zigzagged across the lower part of his left arm, a 'trophy' from a street fight years before. To a neutral observer he could easily be mistaken for a gentleman of military rank such was his bearing and commanding posture, but to the select few that really knew him, Ibrahim was cold, calculating and every inch the religious fanatic that the establishment feared most.

'Adaab' said Ibrahim, raising his right hand to his forehead in a traditional Muslim greeting.

'Walikum salaam' replied Raj, indicating that Ibrahim should sit next to him.

They shook hands and for the next few minutes sat in silence, the suns rays stroking their faces, the gentle lapping of the pool water bringing serenity and a type of karma to them both. Eventually Raj rose and stepping over to the glinting water steps, lowered himself into the pure blue liquid. Submerging, he gently glided off at first then power swam to the far end and back, only easing up as he touched the pool's edge where Ibrahim was crouching down to meet him.

'Very impressive' he said smiling at his friend. 'You should take it up professionally. You might make it to the *next* Olympics!'

They both laughed, knowing the implications of the joke.

'Out of the way! I'm coming in!' And with that he dived full stretch over the top of Raj, entering the water seamlessly. Like Raj, he was an accomplished swimmer and within seconds he was back, exhausted but also exhilarated. They stood together, towels draped around them and furtively ensuring nobody else was in the pool spoke briskly, re-confirming their original plans.

'What names are you booked under and what's the number?' asked Raj.

'Sevki Mehmet. Suite H, the one across the corridor from you.'

'Has everyone confirmed their attendance?' Raj asked.

'Yes. No problems.'

'Anything else I should know?' Raj probed.

'No, that's it.'

'Good. Get them all there for ten. In the meantime, I'll race you there and back' indicating the far end of the pool.

'You're on. But I am not allowed to bet. Allah forbids it. Blessed be his name!'

'Agreed!' said Raj diplomatically.

Standing together, tensed like wound up coils, the two men from completely different backgrounds leaned forward, took deep breaths and focussed on the water ahead of them.

The minute hand on the pool clock jumped forward. It was seven forty five.

At the colonial reception desk, set to one side of the vast air-conditioned lobby, the immaculately attired Mr Sudah, head of reception, picked up a small hand-bell and, with the deftness acquired over a lifetime of experience purposefully, but gracefully, rang the instrument, its peal reverberating past the tea lounge, while just penetrating the high class shopping arcades further into this oasis of luxury. Within seconds the desk was besieged by several young boys all dressed in starched white uniforms and shiny black shoes, their heavy breathing concealed in this prestigious of all jobs, where ten thousand applications for each available position is the norm. Mr Sudah picked the two boys closest to him and dismissed the rest with a flick of his hand, who promptly vanished from sight as quickly as they had come. Handing one of the boys a memo he instructed that he show the assembled quartet of guests to Mr Singh's suite and sharply return as others were due at any time. Mr

Sudah requested the guests to follow the liveried boys and watching them arrive by the lifts, picked up the house phone and called Raj advising him of the same. No sooner had this first group entered the lift, than three more arrived for the same destination, Mr Sudah repeating his instructions to the eager second boy and the call to Raj.

'Will there be any more guests?' he enquired.

'Please hold' checking with Ibrahim by his side. 'Yes, thank you. I am expecting two more. If you can be so good to show them up, I would be much obliged.'

'No problem, sir' replacing the receiver on its Victorian holder while assuming his calm demeanour behind the busy, but smartly dressed reception team.

In Raj's suite, the large oval table accommodating eleven had at its centrepiece cold bottles of Himalayan water, the condensation dripping slowly down their blue shoulders into a colonial presentation bucket. A knock at the suite door had Ibrahim acting as the greeting host, while Raj stayed out of sight behind the now closed dividing doors. The guests, some of whom knew each other, sat where requested. No sooner had the foursome sat than the following three arrived, Ibrahim again acting as host. Some small chatter emanated from the gathering, all of it concerning the weather and the rigours of their respective journeys. Drinks were poured with Ibrahim acting as a waiter walking round the multi-tiered and lavishly assorted cake stand to each seat. He glanced casually at his watch and mentally noted the missing two places knowing that Raj through the slightly open slats could also see the unoccupied seats. 'Still' thought Raj. 'It was only nine fifty eight' and knowing that these last two were always punctual, he calmly finished a cappuccino while watching the latest BBC World news reports.

Through the double-glazed panoramic window set behind four of the guests, the 'Deluxe' ferry and the cheaper Ordinary ferry packed to the brim with noisy day trippers trumpeted their deep horns pending their hourly departure for Elephanta Island. As last minute stragglers leapt in near suicidal bids to catch the densely packed boat from the harbour steps, a sharp but loud double knock halted the polite conversation as all eyes swivelled to watch Ibrahim open the door to the last two guests. A quick, but hardly discernable few words were mumbled at the door after which the last two invitees stepped passed Ibrahim, taking their seats adjacent to each other and at the far end of the table.

'Gentlemen' said Ibrahim. 'Thank you for coming. I hope your journeys here were not too stressed' he motioned to the sea of humanity around the harbour steps. 'You are not here to meet me, but the gentleman you all know as Raj. So without further ado, please let me introduce the man that has re-kindled my aspirations and hopefully yours.' With that he turned and faced the far end of the suite and, with a dramatic entry only second to the Bollywood blockbuster movies, Raj swept through the double doors resplendent in a white summer business suit.

'Friends' he beamed advancing on them, his hand held out in the western fashion, greeting each person in turn until he had walked completely around and sat down at the head of the table, Ibrahim on his left. 'Please help yourself' he indicated the water and cakes. 'If there's anything else you require as we move along please feel free to ask, but I would ask you to try and refrain until I have finished briefing you and hopefully most, if not all of your questions, will be answered. You will notice that there are no pads and pencils here. That is for security and as you all know the basic intention already, note taking is firstly unnecessary and secondly extremely dangerous bearing in mind what we are about to execute. You were all selected for this operation because of your ability to move quickly when required without question and also because of the influence you all have in the populace at large. There are some seated around this table that may know some of the others. For the purpose of this final briefing it is irrelevant whether you do know them or not as each person with the exception of these two gentlemen,' he indicated the swarthy bald-headed duo that had just arrived, 'will operate as a unique cell within the umbrella of Tentacle. In the last twenty four hours Chameleon has been delivered to our people at the Olympics in London. Our function here is to create panic in India and surrounding countries by the immersion of these,' he produced the plastic box containing the dissolvable capsules, 'wherever water is used. This will mean transport, medicine, food and of course all water treatment and processing plants. Remember though, that our time frame is only seven days, just enough time for the military to overthrow the current corrupt regimes in all the confusion that will abound. Your deliveries of these are taking place as we speak. Lorry loads, under the pretence of chlorine tablets, are being delivered to the locations each of you requested. You all have primary and secondary targets to hit. I think that's it.'   He looked around the table. 'Any questions?'

Professor J.M. Singh, head of the largest soft drinks consortium in the country raised his hand.

'Yes, Professor?' asked Raj.

'As you probably all know the international soft drink companies came here with a view of expanding their markets at the expense of the poor and illiterate. Unfortunately, I and others have been responsible for allowing our wells to dry up under intensive production methods and offer the surrounding farmers the residue of infected mud under the cover of fertilizer. This is causing tens of thousands of our people to go hungry and in many cases actually die in the name of globalisation. I just want to hear from you' he looked directly at Raj 'that this process will stop once we have a government that *really* cares for the people?'

Raj looked directly into the deep brown eyes of the grey haired, bespectacled and smartly dressed man. 'Let me tell you that upon my life this malpractice will be one of the first things to go. Does that answer your question?'

'Yes. Totally' said Professor Singh. 'I am now happy and confident to do my part. I just wanted to hear this from your lips, but I would further add so that the rest of you' he paused and looked around at the others 'have no illusions as to the general suffering of our people.'

'Listen' said Raj, looking round the table. 'I am very well off and frankly do not need anything more in life for myself. But' he paused and looked hard at every one of them in turn 'when I see some of the injustices, particularly affecting the poor and vulnerable that are going on around me, I get really mad. I'm not trying to be like Ghandi' he particularly addressed Ibrahim with this remark, being a committed Muslim who reviled the long deceased lawyer, 'but a human being. There will be those of you who even now are wondering what personal benefit you can gain from this exercise. For those that do think that way I don't blame you. All I can say is that the rewards on offer after all revolutions are there for the taking and this will be no different.' He looked this time at the two that came in last, knowing of their direct involvement with organised crime run by the notorious Don Chhota Rajan, who controlled Mumbai. The two men sat still quietly, their dark brown eyes fixed menacingly on Raj's face, guns just protruding from their open jackets. 'There will be no need for those' he indicated the large bulges under their arms. 'What we have here' he turned and addressed the entire table 'is a non violent method of revolution. We don't want and will not countenance the type of slaughter that occurred here, at the Oberoi and the Jewish Centre four years ago. That was a mad bloodbath which, if we get this right, will be avoided.' He dramatically paused, letting his words sink in. Churchill was the master of pregnant pauses in his day and Raj, having studied the man and his techniques, was determined to be *the* orator of the twenty first century. 'Anything else? Please, gentleman, don't hold back! What we are about to do will have implications not just for India but the whole world.' Again he waited. The silence was deafening. 'Good! Then let's begin! As I have said before, you all have your targets. The military are with us. As soon as the panic starts in London they will step in ostensibly to calm the populace and maintain control, but in effect will take over all the key areas that you have infected. You will not meet me again, but can liaise with Ibrahim.' He placed his hand on his friend's shoulder and smiled affectionately at him. Standing, he strode over to the door. 'I would suggest that for the sake of security you all do not leave together.'

They all concurred, the two 'heavies' leaving together first, followed at irregular intervals by the rest. Professor Singh was the last to leave.

'You know' he said looking at Raj and Ibrahim. 'It's a funny thing. I have battled all my life against the white British Raj, and now I will be responsible for changing millions of my countrymen into the embodiment of everything I have fought against. How can I justify that?' Briefly, the question hung in the air.

'Professor' said Ibrahim attempting to justify the moral dilemma 'you will not damage their souls. Only God can do that!'

'Very well put young man! That is very profound!'He offered his hand to both of them which they shook as he left the suite.

'Well!' Raj sighed 'we're on our way' he said quietly to Ibrahim. He picked up an unopened bottle of water, twisted the cap off and dispensed two glasses which they clinked together.

'To us!' Ibrahim toasted, holding his glass high. 'May the Prophet Mohammed, blessed be his name, protect us this day!' They sat down at the table and looked out through the window at the masses by the ferries.

'God help them!' said Raj motioning to the teeming populace swarming below them.

They finished their water. It was midday. Within a week chaos would start to erupt. For a moment he doubted the plan, but quickly snapped out of it as Ibrahim flicked on a special CNN report comparing the current global food crisis with the inept Burmese government's handling of the 2008 typhoon and Mugabe's failed efforts in Zimbwabe. The report also picked up on the earthquake and after shocks in Central China only weeks before the Beijing Games. It went on to add that the financial mess that the world got into in October of the same year would not bring total recovery until 2015. Raj stared painfully at the suffering portrayed before him and, like the Professor, felt morally inept. God help those who now got in his way. He had set the wheels in motion and nothing would stop the express train now!

Professor Singh, his mind now fully set on action, drove out from the hotel and headed for the rich environment of Marine Drive, locally known in Mumbai as the 'Queen's Necklace' reflecting the shimmering string of streetlights sweeping along a sea-facing promenade. He pulled up adjacent to the Hanging Gardens on Malabar Hill which, apart from providing a pleasant open space, also had excellent views of the city below. Stepping from his car he strode a few paces until he was by a vacant green and yellow ornate bench set amongst the perfectly trimmed lawns overlooking the Black Bay of Mumbai. Looking around, he saw that he was alone and took out his mobile phone. Within fifteen minutes he had sent out his text to the water purification plants and reservoir managers giving them the green light to start infecting the water immediately, in total disregard of Raj's instructions and well in advance of the Olympic opening ceremony.*'If necessary the irate local villagers consisting mostly of dalits (oppressed castes) should be utilised to assist. They are angry enough to stop the wells and aquifers being run dry and polluted. I have made arrangements for the youth wing in the Congress Party to work with you all. Call me when you are done.'* Still alone on the bench he took out a linen handkerchief and dabbed his brow and balding head repeatedly until he had regained his composure. 'That' he thought 'was the most traumatic instruction I have ever given in his forty years in business. I hope I don't have to do that again.'

He strolled back to his car and pulled out a local map of the area spreading it across the bonnet. Seeing where the nearest plant was he decided to head there first and trigger rampant chaos within the luxury hotels and private clubs before dealing with the slums of Mumbai. Folding the map up and putting it back, he opened the boot, exposing a large blue plastic box and patted it like a father does affectionately with his child. Slowly he closed the lid, stepped into the car and drove over to the Ballard Estate, turning into a small cul-de-sac within the city centre. Facing him was a tall green electronic gate topped with razor wire and displaying a sign 'KEEP OUT. DANGER OF DEATH! MINISTRY OF PUBLIC WORKS' combined with a silhouette of a frizzled dead man. Calmly he got out, walked over to the gate and swiped his e-tag over the electronic reader.   Then he re-entered his car. The gate slowly opened and he drove forward into the shadows of the parking bay watching it shut behind him with a heavy 'clonk!' Seeing that his was the only car there made him relax enough to open the boot and remove the box without breaking into a sweat. Swiping the card again, he opened and closed the two inner doors allowing him to access two large Microprocessor control systems adjacent to the glass-walled main control room. Next to these stood four two metre tall blue dealkalisers connected by a series of stainless steel blue and orange pipes. The gentle humming from the generators on the floor below together with a swishing of the demineraliser plant at the end of spotless corridor ahead stopped him in tracks as he again realised the enormity of what he was about to do. The heat outside was approaching 30C, but in here with air conditioning it was a comfortable 20C. He opened the box that he carried in with him and removed the capsules sealed in a large plastic bag. There were one hundred, enough to infect a quarter of a million from a population of some sixteen million. This plant, being the central hub for all the other subsidiaries in the city, was critical to his planning as it allowed him into every area unchallenged by the complex alarm system that he could override at will. As he headed off under the bright lights he watched a large rat scurry under his feet and disappear beneath the safety and warmth of the intricate pipe work. He turned a corner past the pressure filters containing suspended solids ready to be cleaned by sand, carbon or iron pressure and the emergency cut off room came into sight. Within a couple of minutes he had re-familiarised himself with the equipment and proceeded to shut the plant down, estimating that all power would be out for ten minutes in order for him to complete his objective. As the first of the ten generators ground to a halt, a strange silence ensued. The lights flickered for a second as the back-up system kicked in and the air conditioning re-phased itself, but more importantly, the water pumps stood silent. He electronically opened all the water input valves and carefully tipped all the capsules into the sluices, the permeable shells settling on the bottom of the giant pipe works. After almost ten minutes he had finished. He closed the water input valves and electronically sealed them. Overriding the emergency cut off he restarted the plant, the pumps kicking in and dispersing the foreign bodies throughout the entire system and, within minutes, flushing the effluent into the supplies of the city and beyond. As he now ran towards the exit several wall-mounted phones began to ring repeatedly. It would only be minutes before the first engineer appeared and he had to be out before then. Carrying the empty box he exited through all the doors, a 'clonk' following his every step. Finally, as the large green gate shut firmly behind him, he electronically swiped another card, wiping all traces of him being there. He calmly drove out of the cul-de-sac and turned into the heart of the Ballard Estate lowering his speed to a placid thirty as several police cars and maintenance vehicles sped past him, sirens blaring, dust rising from their spinning tyres. He disposed of the box by surreptitiously dumping it behind Anant Ashram, a tiny prawn and curry eatery within the old-fashioned and narrow by-lanes of Khotachiwadi, made up of low tiled roofed cottages with their open verandas and cast-iron balconies. The Professor, sweating again, finally headed through the massed sea of humanity towards the Royal Mumbai Yacht Club, of which he was an honoured member. Arriving just after two, he entered the cool shade of the bamboo dining room, a large rotating overhead fan churning the air amongst the large green plants and casual diners complete with their gin and tonics. He sat at a secluded table in the corner away from prying eyes. George, the white coated head-waiter, approached him.

'Good day Professor' he beamed, the gold in his lower tooth glistening brightly.

'Good day, George' the academic smiled back.

'The usual?' George enquired politely.

'Actually, I won't. I'll have Bells straight, no water.'

'No problem. What would you want for lunch? The steak is a cuisine special marinated in red wine with baby potatoes and good selection of fresh vegetables.'

'Sounds good to me' the Professor amiably replied.

He handed the Professor an ironed copy of The Times, his usual preference, while heading off to convey the drinks order to the wine waiter hovering just behind the cascading waterfall at the centre of the dining area. The academic sat back, holding the paper upright trying to calm himself. The quiet, monotonous, ticking of the large grandfather clock standing proudly in the reception area was suddenly broken by a short gasp followed by a loud scream from the table to his right. He lowered the paper just enough for his eyes to see Mrs Danni Shah, the speaker of the National Parliament lying on the floor by a chair, her male dining companion kneeling by her side on the deep crimson carpet. She had obviously passed out and had fallen face down in a contorted position, her arms buried beneath her torso. Her face was just visible to the Professor even though the remainder was obscured by a gaggle of waiters and other diners who had rushed over on hearing the crockery and cutlery crash to the floor. At first she showed no movement, but after George had applied smelling salts to her nose, she stirred and gradually sat up, her back against a chair, legs outstretched. For a moment or two she sat there gasping for air while the wine waiter brought her a glass of water which she sipped carefully, all the time gradually regaining her composure. It wasn't until one of the other guests mumbled something to his partner, followed by other whispered words and half glances from others standing around, did she remember what it was that led her to collapse. Again, she screamed, but this time nobody approached her. Even her partner stood back, frightened at what he saw was happening to her. It appeared to all around that she had been struck down by a form of leprosy, such was the effect as her skin changed by the second from deep brown through to lighter shadings. Holding the chair for support, she stood up and took a deep breath to assist in keeping her upright. Within a split second, however, she caught sight of her reflection in a large art-deco wall mirror and watched transfixed in horror as her face, arms and legs started to bubble and mutate, revealing a sickly, but patchy effect where only moments before had been a deep brown tone. Almost as soon as the mutation started other cries went up from the assembled diners followed by the same from the direction of the entrance lobby.

By the time the wine waiter had appeared with the Professor's whiskey, several others had succumbed to the same condition and were in a state of deep panic picking shreds of skin off their hands or face as well as those of their guest or partners. Either way the effect became cumulative, afflicting all those that had only just had consumed the tap water from either the restaurant, bar or even by the simplest action of gargling after brushing their teeth. Revolted and shocked by what he had just witnessed, the Professor screwed his eyes shut and buried his head deeply within the financial pages. If he had not known better he could have believed that he had entered

Dante's Inferno and that he was the Devil's stooge or Anti-Christ such was the despair on the other side of the paper.

'Sir? Are you alright?' shouted George, respectfully, above the din.

He lowered the page slowly making eye contact with the questioner. 'Yes George. I'm fine. What's going on?' feigning disbelief at the scenes surrounding him.

'I don't know sir. But I would suggest you finish your drink and we'll get you out of here quickly.'

'Yes. My drink' he muttered slowly as if mesmerised by the full glass on the table by his side.

When he awoke he was aware of the darkness around him and the cold. He knew he was fully dressed as he could feel the close fit of his trousers and jacket, but his shoes were gone. For a moment he tried to focus on his surroundings. They seemed familiar but in the gloom it was difficult and anyway his eyelids felt as if they had heavy weights attached, straining against the pulling power of the muscles of his retinas. Millimetre by millimetre, the muscles were gradually winning the tug of war until both eyes had a taught canopy pulled down firmly but securely over the exhausted eyeballs, the ultimate victor being sleep.

'Wake up!' the voice said followed by a violent movement that shook his inert body backwards and forwards until he felt a bit queasy.

'Ok. Just stop!' he held his hand up to indicate enough. Through his transparent eyelids he could see light and involuntarily he turned away from it to a less brilliant area beyond his limited vision. Gradually he opened his eyes seeing a close-up of a blue bed quilt on which he was laying followed by the ceiling as he rolled easily onto his back.

'Hello.' Raj's face stared into his just above him. 'Are you alright? Ibrahim was a bit worried when we got the call from George and decided to get over to the 'Club' and get you back to the Taj. It seems you passed out.' Raj smiled and gently patted his accomplice on the shoulder while helping him to sit upright.

'Did it all go well?' the Professor enquired. 'I saw the start in the dining room and' he paused looking for a moment, forlorn and lost 'did I achieve the results we had planned?'

'Did you achieve your results?' repeated Raj laughing. 'Professor. What you achieved was well beyond all of our expectations. I think you can give yourself an A+ for your vocational work!' and again patted the older man gently on the shoulder, while lowering himself down to sit next to him on the single bed. 'What you achieved was amazing. Not only was the 'Club' affected but also many of the hotels and restaurants frequented by the very people we have been after, including quite a number of the corrupt leaders we were targeting. In fact, Professor, large swathes of Mumbai are in chaos! I don't think even Bombay under the Raj created so much chaos! Take a look!'

They both looked downwards towards the heaving masses which appeared to be composed of a majority of infected people. To add to the total confusion, they were all fighting each other with cars being overturned, windows smashed and alarms triggered by looters. In the front of the hotel stood a phalanx of police and armed troops pushing the crowds back and occasionally firing in the air as a warning to disburse.

'My God! What have I done?' the Professor said reflectively.

'What we said we would do' said Raj. 'Although we have started this before the 'Games' begin, it doesn't matter. This is happening all over India as we speak. This is what Ghandi preached. A protest. Yes, it is true that some will die en-route. We knew that would happen. But just think. Those would have died anyway because of the corrupt governments that we have inherited since our independence in 1947. This time we will be able to defeat the Cancer, control the exploding birth rate, manage food and keep the grain prices at levels that we want. All this will be in addition to getting the multinationals out from parching our soil bone dry by indiscriminate water extraction. I know this may seem harsh, but it is absolutely necessary to demonstrate that we, in Tentacle, mean business.' He looked at the Professor and tried to read his mind. The academic stared out at the chaos below, slowly turned away and walked over to the bed, sitting down gently. 'Does anyone have my shoes?' he asked. George, who was standing quietly in the corner of the suite, picked them up and handed them over.

'Thank you' he motioned towards the Head Waiter. 'Do any of you know' he said levering the shoes on, 'what the Chinese say in regard to shoes?' He looked around from Raj to Ibrahim to George. There were only blank expressions on their faces. 'No? Then I'll tell you. They say that a journey of a thousand miles starts with the first step. Well. Gentleman here we go!' and he stepped forward to firmly grasp Raj's hand. Solemnly the two men from different generations embraced, while outside, down in the streets of Mumbai chaos ensued everywhere.

An hour later, after the Professor and George had left the building under the close protection of the police, Raj called Hardeep using carefully crafted words.

'Hardeep? It's Raj. How are you? How's the family, especially that snake in the grass lizard of a cousin of yours? What's the temperature in Delhi? I hear it's starting to hot up.'

'The family's fine, particularly my cousin' Hardeep responded. 'I think he's gone down with a bit of sunstroke or something in the water. It's the heat. It is getting hotter, but I think it will peak in a few days.'

'I'm glad to hear that' Raj countered. 'Give my regards to *all* the family and if you need anything call me.'

Hardeep hung up and watched the flames leaping skywards from the burning government buildings around Victory Square and the screams of the baying mobs as they hunted down like wild dogs all and any individuals that appeared to be from the government or civil service. He shook his head while below him three men hacked each other to death all calling each other 'lepors'. The tragedy was that they were all brothers and did not recognise one another in the half light of the coming dusk. All over Delhi and, indeed over all of India, chaos gripped the nation as racial tensions were inflamed in a pandemic similar to that experienced during the bloody independence of 1947. The minority of the unaffected watched in shock and awe at the butchery being played out in the streets of the nation and, genuinely fearing for their lives, either barricaded themselves within their apartments or, as many did, fled for the relative safety of their respective embassies.

That evening Hardeep made the call to Joe advising him of their success, even though this premature start was well in advance of the opening ceremony in London.

JOE

One hundred and sixty degrees longitude, eight hours earlier and six thousand miles to the west of Hardeep, the Senior Captain of the British Airways A380 Airbus en-route to Chicago from New York, gently pitched the plane's angle of descent ten degrees starboard, lining up the monster aircraft for its final approach over Lake Michigan. On the upper deck, amidst the grandeur of the first-class accommodation, the cabin director, dressed immaculately in her powder blue BA two piece suit, walked purposefully down the central aisle checking and adjusting, where necessary, the seat pitches and their attached safety belts. Her slim figure and elegant poise belied the years of experience she had gathered at this level of executive service for the 'world's favourite airline', having gradually worked her way up from ground based check-in assistant as her first 'real job' on leaving school some fifteen years previously. Now, as titular head of the entire cabin crew of the plane and directly responsible for the safety and comfort of over eight hundred passengers, her position and authority was total and only second to that of the Captain and First Officer in all operational matters.

'Excuse me?' said Joe raising his hand politely as he had been taught to do so from his early days at home with his strict father and even more so at the St Christopher's Catholic school where he ended up as head boy some forty years past.

'Yes, Mr Williams. How can I help you?' she bent slightly down over the back of his deep leather seat and smiled in that particularly quintessential English way that only the people from that ancient island race have with their elite and superior attitude. For a moment he smiled to himself, recalling the British surrender of Lord Cornwallis to the fledging Continental Army of George Washington, some two centuries previously and the total humiliation that followed for the British Crown and its Parliament. Yet for all that, he still preferred to fly with the Brits on their national carrier in a calmer and more sophisticated environment than that of the brash and hurried approach of his own US airlines.

'Could you arrange to get me a copy of Newsweek before we land? I would be very much obliged.'

'No problem sir. I'll just see if we have any left.' With that, she gracefully turned towards the central galley returning in less than a minute with a sealed edition in clear plastic.

'Thank you. That was very efficient' he smiled at her.

'That's what we are here for. Is there anything else? We will be landing in about ten minutes.'

'No thanks. But, if ever you need a job, call me' and unobtrusively slid his personal card into her palm.

'Thank you. I'm happy at the moment, but I'll file it under opportunities. You never know.' She placed the card into her outer suit pocket and stepped forward to the next row, her demeanour unchanged.

'What a woman!' he thought. 'Cool, calm and I bet, *very* calculating!' For a moment he felt guilty thinking about her like that. After all he was happily married to Catherine. They had a long, stable marriage without an indiscretion by either one of them. He loved her more than she would ever know, but .... he shook his head. Stop this. It's crazy! He wiped his forehead with one of the moist towels supplied with the lunch long since eaten, took a deep breath and stared out at the ground rushing up at breakneck speed to meet him. The slight rumbling and reverse G force applied by the Rolls Royce Spey engines told him he was down safely, the plane now trundling off the main runway into a series of turns, before finally lining up for its docking at gate fifteen which was especially designed to accommodate this condor of the skies. Thirty feet below the flight deck, and visible only to the Captain, a fluorescent attired batman complete with two large luminous paddles stood directly in front of the slowly rolling plane. Under his command, and with years of navy operations as a Landing Signals Officer aboard a Nimitz nuclear powered aircraft carrier, George Farley guided this leviathan's front wheels to the prominent white marker just two feet ahead of him and crossed his paddles high above his head, the plane rocking gently to a stop, the engines shutting down.

By the time the economy passengers had started to disembark and were streaming through the exit gangways in their hundreds, Joe, along with the other First and Business class travellers, had cleared through the fast track gates heading for the airport exits. There to meet him was Clarence, a huge American Negro chauffeur standing six feet nine and weighing in at almost two hundred and sixty pounds. Clarence had been selected by Joe's partners after Carole had forwarded his details from a short list of ex-marines on Tentacle's internal listings. The big man introduced himself and opened the door wide for Joe who settled back into the soft leather of the darkened window limousine while Clarence touched the accelerator and headed away from the airport for his passenger's first meeting. Moving with consummate skill through the busy traffic, Clarence used the intercom to communicate with Joe.

'Mr Williams. If you look in the pouch ahead of you, you will see a schedule that Carole has arranged. Please advise me if you intend to amend this as my other main function is your security.' Without turning round he held up a Browning semi-automatic for Joe to see.

At 1000 East Ohio Street, north of Navy Pier with the coordinates of 41.8947 degrees north and 87.6062 degrees west, sits the Jardine Water Purification Plant, the largest capacity water filtration complex in the world. Supplying one billion gallons daily to about five million Chicago residents and to one hundred and eighteen suburbs, it opened in 1968, drawing water from two of the city's cribs four miles offshore in Lake Michigan. Apart from the landscaping around the plant and the adjoining Milton Olive Park featuring a statue, *Hymn to Water* by Milton Horn, the production area is cold, grey and inhospitable. Security is very tight, with high fences, lights and cameras, backed up by alarms, guards and guard dogs. Anyone foolish enough to attempt a forced entry would also have to contend with a fully armed unit from the National Guard permanently on standby in the Navy Yard less than half a mile away.

From his third floor office Dr Dick James, the Operations Director of the plant, watched via video link the approaching limousine and put in reminder calls to the respective heads of the Chicago Board of Trade, the Kansas City Board of Trade and the Minneapolis Grain Exchange, requesting their immediate attendance at his office. The only other call was to General Weaver, Commandant of the National Guard in Chicago, only to be informed by his senior staff officer that he had already left for the meeting and should be arriving at any minute. Buzzing his intercom, he requested that Donna, his executive assistant of twenty years standing, to arrange for tea, coffee and biscuits for the attendees, followed at one pm by a light lunch in the dining room.

'Do you want me to take notes?' she asked.

'No thanks, Donna. This will be strictly off the record, so I will not need your professional skills, but please stand by in case I need something unusual.'

'No problem, sir. I believe your first guest is here. Mr Joe Williams. Shall I show him in?'

'Yes, thanks Donna. There will be four more guests after him. Just keep me appraised.'

He clicked off, standing motionless in the middle of his Victorian office, heavy with dark oak furniture, velvet green curtains and a musty smell of old leather.

The door opened and Joe stepped in smiling, his hand outstretched which Dick firmly gripped.

'Please come in' he motioned to the surrounding armchairs. 'Take a seat.'

'Thanks. Are the others coming?' Joe asked.

'Yes. I've put calls out for them and they shouldn't be long. Tea, coffee?'

'Green tea, please. No sugar.'

'Of course. How's the family. Catherine, the kids?' the Chicago man asked. He proceeded to be 'mother' in this tea ceremony, pouring the strained tea and placing it on a side table next to where Joe sat.

'They're fine and yours?' Joe politely responded.

'The same. Kids grow so fast don't you know!'

For a moment there was a silence as Joe lifted his tea to his lips and paused looking directly at Dick.

'Its ok!' blurted Dick grinning. 'Nothing's happened here yet to the water. That's what the meeting's for.' He smiled in a homely way at Joe who visibly relaxed, sat back and sipped the fragrant brew imported from the rich, volcanic slopes of Indonesia.

Within minutes they were joined by General Weaver, a big bustling man, full of confidence as indicated by the battery of campaign ribbons emblazoned over the left half of his immaculately pressed military jacket. This, together with razor sharp creases in his trousers and brilliant shiny shoes, made him a man not to be trifled with. He told you exactly what he thought and would stand no bullshit from anybody. The last resident of the White House, President George W Bush Jr and the current incumbent Barack Obama, had been careful not to push him too far, such was his plain speaking rhetoric. For all that, he meant well and was possibly one of the only Generals who could understand ordinary citizens, better than most politicians. Therefore his advice, when called for, was invaluable. He was a friend of the common man and also was held in high esteem by all ranks in the three services from the lowliest rating to his superior five star generals. Woe betides any politician that ignored his advice. General Weaver mechanically shook both men's hands, chose a deep brown leather armchair, and sat down comfortably, facing them.

'Tea, coffee?' asked Dick James.

'Thanks, but I'll pass' he growled, picking up a copy of USA Today from the table next to him and burying his head within the pages.

Dick and Joe smiled knowingly at each other, as the General completely ignored them. Within the next few minutes the three heads of the trading exchanges arrived, shaking hands with the assembled trio already there.

'Let me get you up to speed' said Joe, chairing the meeting. 'A few weeks ago a *request* by Tentacle was made to certain governments around the globe to immediately change their policies regarding their internal attitudes to their own populations. They were given a deadline of the start of the Olympic Games in London to comply or suffer the consequences. We made it absolutely clear that that there would be no second chances or delays allowed to their responses. To date not one of the addressed governments has replied. Therefore gentlemen, in order to show that we are serious, specified global leaders and their cohorts will be directly targeted at the upcoming Olympics. We will only use the blue capsules, which have a temporary transformation of one week, on the general populace to create panic if needs be. Our 'military friends' will take advantage of the ensuing panic to overthrow the incumbent governments while the chaos is rife. Once control has been acquired we will hand over control to truly democratically elected governments.'

There was a general mumbling of agreement from the other five, with the General in particular expressing his enthusiasm by bringing his fist down on the magazine table next to him .

'Easy General' Joe said. 'Let's do this step by step. So, gentlemen' he now addressed the three exchange heads, 'how do you all fit into this dynamic kaleidoscope as your expertise lies in grain, food and commodities? Well' he leaned forward on his chair to make a relevant point 'grain, rice and wheat are already stored, awaiting shipping to the wholesalers and then into the supply chain. You will arrange for your crops to be contaminated by spraying as they lay in warehouses awaiting distribution. The chemical lies dormant until activated by interaction with any liquid. Examples are milk with cereal, tea, coffee and washing fresh fruit and vegetables. Even wearing damp clothes will set off a reaction. The possibilities are endless. We need you to quietly trigger your down-lines right through to the farmers without any fuss to ensure maximum effect and minimum questions. Obviously once the news gets out regarding the crops, your prices on the exchanges will collapse, creating a wild panic and allowing the General' he again nodded at the military man 'to take control with a coup d'Etat until the effects wear off. By the time that the targeted incumbent governments realise what is going on it will be too late and we in Tentacle will have control and that, gentleman, is that and there is nothing they can do about it!'

The distinguished gentleman representing the Chicago Board of Trade immaculately attired in a pin stripe suit and sprouting a large waxed handle-bar moustache leaned forward towards Joe. 'Are you suggesting that it is not *just* overseas governments that are being targeted?' The implementation of his question was not lost on all those listening. Before Joe could answer him, he rammed home the point. 'Are we really going to topple our own Administration? I, as you can see, am a black man' smiled the Kansas representative, his shining negro skin contrasting sharply with his pearl white teeth, red tongue and pink, but perfectly crafted, fingernails. 'What I am truly trying to come to terms with is me being responsible for millions of my black brethren suddenly and frighteningly mutating into their worst nightmare. How do I reconcile my feelings? After all, and with due respect,' he looked around him, 'I have to be absolutely sure that the panic among my creed is more than outweighed by the social and political gains that will be made at the end of this. Can you therefore be absolutely sure that the blacks of this nation will really benefit?' His dark eyes swung around the group stopping on Joe as Chairman.

'Yes' he said 'you *can* be assured that the advantages more than outweigh all the negatives, but let me make this very clear' he stood up to make a point 'this will benefit every skin shade. The colour is irrelevant, only the end result. If'

he emphasised, 'it was necessary for my whole family to

suffer the effects, I would do it without hesitation. Does that

satisfy you?'

For a moment the Kansas man looked up at Joe, the whites

of his eyes topped by brilliant red pupils. He looked deeply

into Joe's eyes trying to see his soul, like a poker player

holding a flush across the table from a convincing

cardsharp. Joe's eyes did not waver and continued the

game of 'chicken' giving nothing away behind his cold, firm

stare. After a minute, during which both men could have

been mistaken for Roman statues, the Board of Trade man

blinked first, his right eye giving way under intense

psychological pressure. He smiled and gently nodded his

head acknowledging defeat.

'You know' he continued, smiling at Joe 'it would be

interesting if we both become white brothers and were able

to bury our prejudices.' His smile now became a grin and

finally a laugh as he stood up and affectionately reached

forward and pulled Joe to him, wrapping him in a giant bear hug that almost squeezed the life out of the entrepreneur's body. As the Negro held him in a vice like grip, he covertly whispered in Joe's ear 'Don't let me down, because like Arnold Schwarzenegger said, I'll be back!' and pushed him away laughing.

For a moment there was silence among the others, until seeing the two warmly embrace, they all murmured their approval. Only the General sat unmoved and stony faced at the backslapping in front of him, his years of military training and rigid discipline rejecting any thoughts or actions clouded by sentimental emotions. His attitude to everything was immediate and uncompromising. All decisions were framed in black and white, right and wrong. He could not afford to deal with people who had liberal ideas and were woolly minded. 'These' he thought, 'were responsible for a sloppy society where the rule of law meant nothing and *do-gooders* prevailed upholding the 'human rights' of rapists and killers above those of their victims and families.' So, when he saw the Kansas man express his 'feelings', the General slowly and unobtrusively reached for his service sidearm knowing that if the official decided to back out and cry off the operation, he, the upholder of freedom would shoot the son of a bitch there and then without a second thought and certainly without any emotion. Now, with the crisis over, he quietly clicked the 'safety' back on and slid the weapon into the concealed holster beneath his pressed uniform jacket, while keeping a very suspicious eye on the man he certainly did not trust and nearly shot without any compunction at all.

As they settled again Joe called the meeting to order and for a fleeting second, and imperceptible to the others, he locked onto the General's eyes. Joe watched the fury and rage within the man and it disturbed him, especially as he showed no visible signs of emotion. It was like watching a dormant volcano writhe within itself, seeking a vent to release all it's pent up energy over the long silent, but precariously placed foothills around the peak. When they had all settled again, Joe stood up.

'Let me make this absolutely clear. We in Tentacle are not seeking the overthrow of anybody. What we are demanding is the immediate change in the way that certain governments treat their fellow human beings. Unfortunately our own administration, despite having a black liberal President, is not immune to some severe criticism. Promises made prior to elections are invariably watered down and that is no different here as in other democratic nations, while under tyrannical regimes, the poor have no chance of ever achieving a better life and will be dead before any real action takes place. So we are hoping that we do not have to implement anything and just the threat of positive action will spur those respective politicians on to *immediately* change or amend their policies. But let me underline our commitment. We will take action firstly against the leaders and if that does not work, then you gentlemen will be given the green light to infect the populous. When we first started planning Chameleon several years ago, we had in mind the opening ceremony of the Olympic Games as a perfect cover. London is already in chaos as millions arrive from all over the world totally jamming the road and rail networks. Racial tensions in strong ethnic areas that have been simmering for some time have now imploded and large gangs have taken to the streets.'

Joe paused as Donna entered and covertly whispered in Dick's ear while handing him a one sided typewritten sheet which he read, his lips the only movement on his face. 'Thanks' he looked up to her and nodded. Having spent many years with him she read his mind and without being asked promptly left the suite as quietly as she had entered. Everyone's eyes were now fixed on him and more importantly the document on his lap. Without a word he stood up and inserting the paper firmly into his inside breast pocket, paced over to a massive oak door and eased it open revealing a large round dining table set for seven beneath a glittering cut crystal chandelier. A centrepiece of exquisite oriental flowers and tropical fresh fruits rose from the table like a mini Tower of Babel.

'If you don't mind gentleman, lunch is served' he boldly announced. 'We can resume afterwards if necessary' and politely stood inside the brightly lit room by the entrance, as the men filed past him and sat where indicated on the place markers. Three large sash windows bordered one side of the room masked delicately by white full length net curtains, while along the opposite wall sat a giant Edwardian sideboard supporting a range of solid silver tureens containing a lavish range of culinary delights. At the opposite end to where the guests had filed into was another oak door in front of which stood a Head Waiter and three waiting staff, all attired in conventional black livery.

'Please begin' said Dick, waving his hand in the direction of the oysters, while the Head Waiter expertly poured either white or red wine to the preference of each respective diner.

To the background music of James Last, the lunch proceeded cordially, only personal small talk being engaged in, much to the General's chagrin and undisguised annoyance. Time passed and soon the invited guests found themselves alone again, the staff having diplomatically removed themselves.

'Now' said Joe walking across to both doors and checking to ensure they were locked. 'I am sure you were all wondering what Dick had received earlier?'

A low accord greeted his ears.

'This' he held up the sheet 'is a report from our operative and my good friend, Hardeep, in India. If you're all ready, I'll read out the bullet points.'

They all casually settled into their green leather chairs, the General balancing on the two back legs only, his long limbs pushing him precariously at an angle of almost sixty degrees to the table. From his top blouse pocket he removed a large Winston Churchill cigar and held it aloft, seeking everyone's approval before lighting it with one of the decorative tall candles on the table. He closed his eyes and exhaled a light blue plume towards the graceful, multi-armed chandelier straddling the ornate ceiling some ten feet above them all. With a nod of satisfaction, he indicated with his cigar hand that he was ready to receive whatever information Joe would like to throw at him.

'Ok then' said Joe, getting everyone's attention. 'Hardeep reports that some rouge Indian elements in Tentacle have not waited for a response from their own government and have started unilateral actions in the cities and countryside. Mass strikes and demonstrations have taken place against multi-nationals, particularly those from the soft drinks industries whose wholesale exploitation of the indigenous population has led to the water table dramatically declining in the villages where these people live. To date, thirty plants across India have been burnt down by the local populace with others damaged beyond use. Delhi and Mumbai are under marshal law with dawn to dusk curfews strictly enforced and all train, ship and air travel has been severely curtailed. Food prices, particularly wheat, are soaring due to a boom in demand coupled with severe droughts and flooding in the south and east of the country. These renegade individuals have infected some water supply systems triggering skin mutation and general panic in the populace before we gave them the go-ahead.' He paused. 'That's why' he looked hard at each one of them, 'you must act *only* when Dick here' he laid his hand on his friend's shoulder 'tells you. Are we all ok with that? No questions?' He looked around the group but there were no takers. 'Ok' he said smiling at them, while handing the paper back to Dick.

For a moment there was silence, then one after the other they stood, brushed themselves down and walked across to Joe hands outstretched. The Negro was first, followed by his two fellow board members.

'Remember' Joe said, still smiling 'get everything ready, but take no early action until Dick advises you. If Tentacle does not receive a satisfactory response by the time of the opening ceremony, only then do we start moving. Good luck to you all!'

As soon as they had departed and were on their way down to their waiting limousines, the General, who had held back, aggressively approached Joe and, lifting a stubby finger, pointed to the table accusingly. 'You haven't been totally straight with us have you?' he demanded, staring into the New Yorker's face.

'What do you mean? I've told you everything' he implored.

'That's right, General' said Dick striding over to support his friend. 'Joe doesn't tell lies!'

'I didn't say he did' turning on Dick. 'What I said was that he hadn't been totally straight.'

'Look General' said Joe, totally bemused 'just tell me what bit I wasn't clear with you about. I am honestly at a loss to know what your problem is.'

'You're my problem right now!' snapped the military man, starting to feel he was being set up. 'There were six of us for lunch and yet I noticed that the table was set for seven.

Who is the seventh person and why didn't you mention this to anyone at the time? What's going on? Who are you covering up for? I want to know *now* and no bullshit!' he spat the questions out a like a blazing overheated machine gun. His eyes bulged like a giant bullfrog, while his hand moved quickly to the holster beneath his jacket and pulled out the concealed gun. 'I will *not* be lied to and with the trouble that we are about to unleash upon the good people of this country, I want to know the truth right now!' And with that he expertly flicked the safety catch off the slim weapon and pointed it directly at Joe's head. 'You have five seconds to advise what the hell is going on before I shoot your fucking brains out. Don't think that I won't do it!'

Joe looked at Dick who stood inches away from the barrel, trembling and sweating, knowing that this General would execute his friend and then possibly him next. This, he thought quickly, was not a game of poker where you could walk away from the table if you lost. This high ranking officer held all the aces and bluffing wasn't one of them.

'One!' he shouted. 'Two!' and to make the point pressed the muzzle hard against Joe's head and looked deeply into his terrified eyes.

'Please!' whispered Joe 'I don't want to die!'

'Then tell me! Three!'

Joe heard the gun's mechanism pre-lock and squeezed his eyes shut, praying that he would die instantly and not have to be shot a second time or be supported by an array of tubes and pumps for the rest of his life. He felt the heat from the General's hand close to his face which was marginally cooled by the cold yet lethal steel of the Chicago made weapon pressing deeply into his forehead. Holding his breath for what he believed would be the last time in his life, he thought of his wife and kids and mentally prayed for them, knowing that they would miss their father so much and he them. Tears welled up in his eyes and he stupidly calculated if they would have time to roll down his cheeks before his head exploded over the carpet. Even more crazily, he wanted to apologize to Dick for the mess he would make over the floor.

'Four! Say your prayers Joe!' screamed the General.

The condemned man gritted his teeth and waited for what he believed would be a blinding flash and total oblivion.

'General! Put that weapon down, now!' boomed a far off but commanding voice. For a split second Joe's precarious grasp on life was held in limbo. Semi paralysed and daring not to move a muscle he tried hard to place the dour yet familiar tone of this newcomer into his still conscious being. Was he dreaming or had the process already started where he had entered the near transient state discussed avidly amongst all religious leaders when describing the gateway to heaven? Did he have a subconscious to dream within?

'General. Put it down. Now!' the voice commanded again, but this time with a cold clinical menace behind the oratory. For the second time Joe heard the confident and autocratic voice and annoyingly couldn't quite place it within his memory. For a man who was about to have his skull perforated by a high speed explosive shell ripping through the skin, bone and soft tissue that surrounded the cavity where the forebrain and neocortex gave life to the conscious cognitive mind, it was absurd that he pondered this miniscule identity problem. But this was Joe. A perfectionist to the end! Being in this state of mind also acutely sharpened his senses and he slowly became aware that the pressure on his skull was weakening by the second until it as if by magic it had suddenly gone. He stood still, not knowing if this was a game of Russian roulette played by the uniformed man at Joe's expense or did the voice he had now heard twice really give him a reprieve. Still, he dared not move, until the heat from his executioners hand had left his face and even then he cautiously opened one eye. The scene before him was almost out of a James Bond novel. Immediately in front of him stood the General, dejected, his gun lowered and hanging limply in his right hand. To his left was Dick, smiling, but breathing heavily and to his right, silhouetted in the doorway where the waiters had exited, stood a little man in a smart blue suit, flanked by two extremely tall and muscular federal marshals displaying on their belts the blue and white bald eagle of the United States. They carried and were pointing directly at the General four Magnums, probably the most powerful handguns in the world. Their stance, legs apart, short cropped hair and muscles the size of the Rocky Mountains left no one foolish enough choosing to take them on in any doubt at all what the outcome would be. These men were killers, short and simple and, like the General, they didn't bluff either. The little man between them however stood at just five feet four inches and weighed in at one hundred and forty pounds, but what he lacked in size he made up for in authority. In fact there was no-one in that room, building, street, city or state that had his power. Only one other person in the whole nation had more influence than him and that individual resided in the White House on Pennsylvania Avenue, Washington DC.

'General?' the small bespectacled man softly addressed the exhausted army man. 'Come and sit down and let me explain' he said to the now totally confused officer. With the slightest motion of his head, the Vice President of the United States of America gave permission for one of his 'aides' to step forward and remove the gun carefully from the General's loose grip and guide the exhausted man over to one of the dining chairs that only a short time ago was occupied by the head of the Chicago Exchange. The Federal men cautiously checked the suite and the dining room for any other threats and, only when they were satisfied that the area was secure, did they allow their 'boss' to sit next to the General in the vacant seat that was actually meant for him all along. Joe, who by this time had opened his other eye still stood like a statue, his heart racing faster than a nuclear reactor, his knees weak and trembling beneath him. The New Yorker ran his tongue around his dry mouth and softly moistened his lips while accepting the grateful shoulder of Dick to lean against. He had never been religious, but for maybe the first time in his life had silently prayed to his God for a second chance.

Over Dick's broad shoulder he saw the General conversing with the little man at the dining table and whispered in Dick's ear 'Is that who I think it is?'

'Yes, ol' buddy. It is. I'm sorry I couldn't let you in on the secret. I was sworn to secrecy' and pushed his good friend back so that he could look into his eyes and apologise.

'But I might have died! That bastard might have killed me!' he whispered incredulously while looking across towards the dining table and the seemingly convivial conversation taking place between two men near the top of their respective career trees. The Vice President adjusted his thin wire spectacles and, with a small hand gesture and out of earshot of Joe and Dick, explained some key point to his table guest who responded with 'Oh my God!'

This went on for some time until both men eventually stood up, the West Point Officer saluting, then enthusiastically accepting a handshake from the number two in the country.

Joe had now recovered enough now to be sitting semi-relaxed with Dick in the deep green armchairs of the adjoining suite, each having consumed between them four glasses of Ballantine's finest scotch whiskey, especially imported directly from the distillery in Dumbarton, Scotland. When the Vice President entered a quarter of an hour later followed by the man who nearly sent him to the next parallel universe, Joe still showed a nervous disposition to them both. He and Dick both rose, but the politician bade them stay seated and took a pew on one of the adjacent chairs, the General remaining standing but within striking distance of the two federal men. After introductions were made between the Capitol man and Joe, the Vice President again for the second time in the last half an hour repeated what he had just run past the General, to whom Joe cast a cautious but obvious warning glance. Stressing the sensitivity of his involvement with Tentacle, he apologised that only those who fell under the 'need to know' category could be aware of his connection.

'Dick here' he turned to his left 'knew all the time, but was sworn to secrecy as you will also do now. I assume you have no problems with that?' his small blue eyes peeping over the top of the thin, expensive, light tinted lenses, transfixing Joe with a vice like stare.

'No sir. I will honour your anonymity. Could I ask a question though?'

'Go ahead.'

'Well. How many others know of your involvement, including the three gentlemen who left just before you arrived?'

The Vice President leaned forward, head down in a conspiratorial fashion. 'Well, Joe let me answer it this way. You, I understand, are a very successful businessman. Is that right?'

Joe nodded.

'And your rise to the top and your business dealings were made by only disclosing that which you wanted to be known at a precise time and place. Am I right or am I right?' It was a rhetorical question and Joe, having been around long enough to keep his counsel and listen carefully when dealing with powerful men like this, nodded again. 'Like in politics. You keep all your cards to your chest but also use sleight of hand and discreet signals to throw your opponent off balance before administering the coup d'Etat. Therefore Joe, I will only tell you what you need for this operation. Your question asked how many others know of my involvement. The answer is not many and now that circle has been extended to you and the General. The three gentleman that you referred to earlier are on the outer circle and know nothing of my involvement, unlike you all' he motioned to everyone in the suite. 'You can imagine' he smiled 'how it would look if the deputy to the most powerful man on earth was seen to be one of the prime movers in a military putsch to overthrow the very same constitution that he had sworn to protect and uphold under God at all times.' He looked forlornly at both men, lowered his head and stared at the floor between his legs. 'God knows how much I love my country gentlemen.'He looked up and stared deeply into their eyes. 'I would be the last to cause any disruption and pain to the flag and its peoples that I swore an oath to. But, after much soul searching and countless debates and arguments lasting many months, I, with many others, sadly realised that the government of this country, of which I am a key player, is taking us down a road to ruin leading to the total disintegration of the United States of America and all that it represents. I could not stand by and allow that situation to develop without voicing my objections and, if necessary, using my power of veto to block such devastating policies. Unfortunately, even that wasn't enough to stop my colleagues introducing programmes that were against everything that we stood for and the country was demanding. Even when they did decide to move in our direction it was only done as a token measure with so many strings attached it became meaningless. These idiots really have lost touch with what the people want. The constitution says it all. *'For the people and by the people.*' When Lech Walesa, the first generally elected President of Poland since 1945, addressed both houses on the 'Hill', he couldn't speak a word of English, except for three words that he had picked up from our Bill of Rights. Do you know what they were?'

The little man swivelled his eyes across both men and before they had a chance to respond, said with tears in his eyes. 'He stood before the dais and with over a thousand of the most powerful and intelligent citizens in this country analysing his every move and breath, looked up from his prepared speech and uttered in a calm but quivering voice *'We the people.'* You would have to be there at that precise moment to feel the energy and the power of those three little words. The place erupted with cheers, clapping and massive applause. Every member of the joint houses spontaneously rose to their feet in a tidal wave of emotion that this humble electrician in an ill fitting suit from the deprived and cold shipyards of Gdansk delivered up to them. He touched a nerve. The soul of the nation. He reminded them all of their roots and of their struggle for independence two hundred years before. This man was able to see the wood for the trees. To him it was simple, something a lot of our leaders have failed to pick up on and deliver. This should be an inspiration to us all and it certainly has been to me. As a young lawyer, having just graduated from Yale Law School, I was lucky enough to have been posted by the State Dept to London in 1962 as the Cuban missile crisis swung into uncharted waters. It was during that period that I had the privilege to meet Churchill and although in his eighties and out of politics, his vision of disaster if we did not stand firm was awe inspiring. I have never forgotten that moment. It has given me the belief that all with us share as we move forward in this second United States Revolution.'

For over a minute there was silence as the impact of the rhetoric delivered with such heartfelt passion and sensitivity enveloped the small select gathering. For a brief moment Joe even thought he saw a glimmer of emotion in the eyes of the two granite monoliths flanking the General, but if there was any it was fleeting, their mammoth frames and cold grey eyes keeping their secrets within.

'Does that answer your question?' asked the country's top conspirator.

'Yes sir. It does' he smiled back.

'Very well' he continued. 'We need to get this plan executed and fast! I am holding a high level meeting for the entire inner circle tomorrow at which I will give the go ahead for immediate action assuming we have all the pieces in position. If we do go then this plant will be the place it all starts. Dick has the details. I cannot again stress the importance of tight security. Nobody, nobody, must know what you are doing or where you are going. This includes your wives, children, girlfriends and mistresses.' He smiled and cynically added. 'That is of course if you have any of these!' He looked at his watch. 'Time to go! It's been a pleasure' he looked sternly but forgivingly at the General 'and God willing we will meet soon and set our country straight again.' With that he rose, turned and dwarfed by his two 'aides' stepped out through the suite doors, riding the private lift down to the unmarked black limousine sitting three floors below. With a deep growl the giant Chrysler V12 engine producing 600 brake horse- power, topped by a bullet proof chassis and blackened glass windows, slowly moved out past the large security complex gates and headed for the heart of Chicago and its teeming multi-ethnic masses.

HARLEM

As twin brothers growing up in 'Black Harlem' in the 1990's, Blanco and Negro Hamilton had what can only be described as a very fast upbringing. Twins of the same sex are rare but these domino coloured boys had something so unusual it would test to the bone whether their friends would be supportive to each of them separately, as the boys were to each other. The 'Bradhurst Section', where they gained their 'street cred', was the roughest district in this gang related 'turf war' neighbourhood, long known as the capital of black America and being situated between Adam Clayton Powell Jr Boulevard and Edgecombe, from 139th Street through to 155th. The entire area of this original Dutch settlement dating back to 1637 named Nieuw Haarlem stretches from the East River to the Hudson River between 155th Street (where it meets Washington Heights) to an undefined border close to where 110th Street sits now.

This densely populated narrow prominence of land sitting to the north of Central Park and it's affluent neighbour of Manhattan to the south, was already simmering with the seeds of racial unrest, when into this desperate society of dingy slum tenements, falling plaster, cold rooms, rabid rats and unsanitary plumbing Martha gave birth to her twins on that storm-filled June night in 1990. Being from the 'poor side of the tracks' she had no medi-care provision and had to make do with a home birth attended by Dr Royston Emmanuel, the only black Professor of Gynaecology and Genetics in New York State. Also present at the delivery was her husband of ten years, Jethro, together with Pastor Jimmy Ignuma, both men of deeply held religious convictions who followed in the teachings of the African Methodist Episcopalian sect or 'AME', as had their respective fathers and grandfathers. The local place of prayer was actually like so many others in Black Harlem, a 'storefront church' operating out of the empty cocoon of Kolinsky's, closed since the mid-nineties following the

'Freddy's Fashion Mart' riot by black activists against Jewish shop owners on 125th street. Adjoining this poor excuse for a building stands the sad, burned out and boarded up shell of the Church of Nazareth on 144th Street and Hamilton Terrace.

With both parents being aged thirty five and certainly not expressing any outward signals that they planned or wanted any issue from their seemingly barren marriage, all of their friends and relatives had totally discounted that the sound of tiny feet would ever emanate from the third floor, one-bedroom apartment on 125th street between Park and Madison Avenue. In fact, in private, Martha and Jethro had also resigned themselves to as the Pastor had put it 'Let God's will be done' and had even considered the possibility of adoption within their faith of a black child. Then, a year earlier than this blessed day, with the Pastor's guidance, they had approached the local adoption agencies via the social services only to be met with a wall of bureaucracy not the least was of the need to have their blood checked for the second time, the first being prior to getting married.

'It was' explained the little fat lady at social services sweating below the lazy fan that turned slower than the large flies that landed on it 'to be sure that you do not have or could pass on via any bodily fluid transfer, cuts or abrasions a virus or other strain that could be of detrimental health to the child.' Mechanically, she handed over a pack of forms to be completed in quintuplicate, certified and supported by a battery of utility bills, driving licences and, if held, passports. Parting her bright red thick lips she continued, her rough nasal Bronx accent accompanying a strong garlic breath, which wafted across to them every time she exhaled. 'Failure to complete everything properly will mean everything will be rejected and you will have to re-apply again no sooner than one year. Even if you do get approved, the normal process is at least two years.'

They noted that she had stressed *everything* twice and wondered which of the two repeated words was of more importance. Taking the package, they thanked her and quickly moved away from the battered, Formica clad, sticky counter through the multiple lines of shuffling claimants. Outside in the full glare of the summer sun, only partly shielded by the scrawny excuses for trees in this part of the borough, Martha emotionally laid her head on Jethro's shoulder and sobbed.

'It's so unfair. What have we done to deserve this? It's not' she whispered in his ear 'as if we haven't been trying. It's so unfair.'

He gently lifted her chin and smiled at her. 'Listen to me. I thought that this might happen and I have had a word with Dr Emmanuel. He tells me that looking at our blood samples it is possible to have a child through IVF. He also has connections.'

Wiping the tears away she looked deeply into his eyes. 'Jethro. When did you discuss all this?' She stood in front of him, mouth open expecting him to answer her then and there, but he was having none of it.

Firmly guiding her away from the busy doorway from where they had just exited he said 'This is not the place to talk. Come with me' and arm in arm they carefully crossed the busy street, she never taking her eyes off him once until they had entered and sat down by the large plate glass window of Starbucks, financed in part by Magic Johnson, the iconic black sportsman. Outside on the grey weed encroached flagstones that gave the pretence of being a pavement, two black portly women argued intently, their voices silenced by the thick glass. One held a bible which she proffered to the sky after delivering what appeared to be abuse at the other who stood by a large bag of shopping brimming over with milk, cereals and fresh fruit. Suddenly, and without warning, the bible owner reached into the shopping bag, removed a cream carton and violently opened it, pouring the contents evenly over the shopper's head. Even through the glass Martha and Jethro heard the muffled scream as the white liquid slowly eased itself over the shopper's short cropped hair, down her face, soaking her black dress into a sodden white mess. Suddenly, for a split second, both women froze as if time-warped in a modern day tableau of a slapstick comedy. Then, seeming quite oblivious of the sticky mess between them, they both reached out and hugged each other as if they had been parted for years and suddenly miraculously re-united, strolled off chatting as if nothing had just happened.

'My God!' exclaimed Jethro. 'For a moment you couldn't tell white from black!' and religiously crossed himself without realising how devastatingly these words would come back to haunt him. Martha laughed and fleetingly he saw her as he always had. Happy, bubbly and full of confidence. 'Stay here' and kissed her lovingly on the forehead. 'I'll just be a mo!' Crossing the floor he ordered two large coffees sprinkled with a dusting of fine chocolate and carefully returned to her, manoeuvring his large supple frame delicately between two black college students intensely pre-occupied on adjacent tables layered with text books from Einstein to Plato.

She smiled as he sat down opposite her next to the window. 'That was funny!' she smirked peering through the toughened glass for the now long departed squabbling women.

'Yes' he smiled back. 'You see everything has a way of righting itself. Nothing is impossible' and leaning forward cupped her head in the palms of his hands and gently kissed her on the forehead. 'Let me tell you what the Doctor said' and proceeded to impart all that he had only been aware of in the last 24 hours. Her face brightened at every revelation as her inner soul shone through, happy at being granted her wish for a child, her child.

'But' she suddenly frowned 'how can we afford this? It costs thousands and thousands of dollars. We don't have that kind of money!' The gloom of despair hit her again and for the second time in the last half hour she lapsed into a downward spiral of wretchedness.

'Hold on, my Vandella!' referring to the endearing nickname he had given her when they had first met based on their joint love of the American pop trio of the 1960's, Martha and the Vandellas. 'That's all taken care of! You can relax. It's all fixed!' He gently lifted her chin. 'Honestly darling. We can have our baby!'

She furrowed her brow and looked quizzically at him. 'How? Where is the money coming from? Be honest with me. I won't be lied to!'

He paused and then looked up, whispering very low so she had to lean forward to hear him. 'There is an organisation that helps people in our situation. Dr Emmanuel and Pastor Ignuma both are members and put our names forward some time ago. They are funding everything, even the baby's education.' He smiled broadly at her looking for understanding.

'But why would they do that?' she said incredulously. 'We don't belong to their group or club or whatever you want to call it. And you say they help people in *our situation*. What is *our situation* and what does that mean and more importantly what do they expect from us? After all we will never be able to pay them back, so what do they want?'

'They have a plan, far in the future to truly free the black people and give them the equality that Abraham Lincoln and Martin Luther King gave their lives for. Our child will be one of the leaders of that movement. There are others also selected whose parents have our background. God fearing, poor and childless. They, like us, have been given the gift of children and in return the organisation will watch and help us nurture our child into a world where he and his brethren will want for nothing.'

'It sounds too good to be true!' she whispered back focussing on every word he said.

'I know. When I was first approached, I said the same. But after I talked to the Pastor and the Doctor, I was convinced. I didn't tell you at the time as there was still a hope for the adoption and I felt it better that we run this course first and see what happens. As you have just seen it's a non starter. So what do you think?'

'I don't know. This is all coming at me very fast. I need time to think.'

'But why? This is what we planned for. Hoped for. Prayed for. Don't tell me that you've changed your mind?' he said frustrated at her ostensible lack of enthusiasm.

'Of course not Jethro! I want the baby as much as you, probably more. But give me time to sleep on it. This is our and our baby's future. How do we know it's not something sinister or even some type of terrorist organisation?' She looked adoringly into his eyes and he melted. He knew he couldn't force her and as strong as he was mentally, he realised that at the end of the day it was as much her choice as his, probably more so and therefore acquiesced for her decision the next day.

That night was the longest in his life. He tossed and turned, running all the possibilities of her objections through his mind until as dawn broke, he could stand it no longer and gently nudged her.

'Martha?' he whispered close to her ear. 'Are you awake?'

Her slim, well formed body turned lazily under the patchwork duvet, with her head the only visible sign of life.

'Martha?' he asked again. 'Are you awake?'

Slowly, like a heavy stage curtain lowering itself softly onto the boards for the last act, did the duvet slowly descend, her pretty hands with perfectly manicured pink nails easing the puffed sheeting down below her chin. She stretched her arms skyward and smiled easily at him. 'Yes. I'm awake. I've been awake nearly all night turning over all our options and do you know, I've come back to where I started!'

Cuddling up to her, he carefully asked 'So does that mean you agree?'

She smiled back and putting both her hands around his neck, pulled him gently to her. 'Yes' she whispered. 'Mr Hamilton, we're going to have a baby.'

'Yes!' he shouted, punching the air in delight. I must tell the Pastor and the Doctor before you, young lady' he looked lovingly at her 'change your mind!'

'There's no chance of that!' she teased him, happily pulling herself away and disappearing under the warm folds of the covers, while he made the calls even at this God awful time of the morning.

Within the hour and unknown to the happy and prospective parents, two non-descript men quietly parked up in a Chrysler saloon diametrically across the road from their flat and maintained a watching brief. For Martha and Jethro, everything that they now did for the rest of their lives would be controlled and monitored by this shadowy ephemeral group called Tentacle, whom they had just sold their soul and that of their offspring to.

For Martha to bear one child after all the disappointments that society threw in her path was blessing enough, but when two months after the successful IVF implants a scan detected a slight shadow behind the foetus, she naturally expressed some concern.

'You're not to worry' smiled Dr Emmanuel patting her hand gently, 'unless of course you don't want twins!' teasing her.

'What did you say? Twins? Are you sure?' she mumbled back amazed and stunned.

'Yes, Martha. I'm sure. In fact it's what I was expecting. When IVF is used the body can react in different ways and in a quite a number of cases this can lead to multiple pregnancies. It would seem that in your case this is also true. Look at this.' He guided her over to a small screen atop a three tiered stand and ushered her down onto a low, soft bed. Exposing her stomach he gently applied some fluid across her navel followed by a hand scanner and finally depressed a luminous red button to the right of the unit. Slowly an image appeared, blurred at first but by the second the clarity improved until within a minute a small, but perfectly formed foetal shape came into view. As it lay floating within a warm, safe environment, an involuntarily spasm triggered a second image to roll into view. Martha held one hand to her mouth, the other reaching out to touch her babies, still unborn, but all the same hers.

'Are they for real?' she blurted out.

'Yes, Martha. Absolutely' he smiled back.

She reached out again and gently touched the small images knowing that all her prayers had at last been answered. For ten minutes she watched fascinated as the twins manoeuvred past each other like a tag wrestling match, each vying for the maximum amount of space they could gain in the confines of her ever expanding womb. 'Are they alright?' she suddenly asked sitting up and adjusting her clothes after wiping off the liquid residue from her stomach.

'If you mean do they appear to be healthy, the answer is yes, at this stage. All their features seem to be in place, but as they are still developing it is a little early to be absolutely sure. We can't be sure of sex yet, but in another month we will be able to make a more accurate assessment.'

She left his practice happy with a spring in her step and headed off home to tell Jethro the good news.

When she was half way down the street and virtually out of sight from his second floor practice window, Dr Emmanuel picked up his phone, dialled a Midtown number and waited for the connection. 'It's Royston. We may have a problem.' The listener said nothing, during which time the Doctor imparted the information regarding the possibility of one of the twins having an abnormality.

'When will you know?' said the listener.

'I can't be one hundred per cent until birth. Then we'll know. Will it make any difference?'

For a moment there was a hushed silence.

'Just keep me posted.'

After a soft click the Doctor held the receiver, the dialling tone humming back at him.

At ten pm on that rainy June night, Martha's water's finally broke after a fifteen hour painful and back-breaking period of labour. Within minutes the first of the boys was delivered into the firm, but competent hands of Dr Emmanuel and, after a cursory health check, Jethro gently held the next generation of the Afro-American dream in his arms. On the sodden blood-infused bed, Martha screamed, almost crushing the Pastor's hands in a vice like grip as she exhaustedly attempted one last push while trying to follow the doctor's advice of blowing with her lips pursed.

'Nearly there' he said as he saw the head emerge between her straddled legs and carefully eased the baby out as she managed one last thrust. She collapsed backwards onto the sheets, totally spent from her birth throes and lay, eyes shut and sweating under the glare of the bedroom ceiling light. No sooner had the doctor delivered the younger twin and had him in his arms than the power failed. Outside in the street a torrent of rain lashed the windows, while in the apartment the wind howled menacingly like a banshee through every nook and cranny. For a brief moment the lights powered up, flickered and died. In that millisecond the doctor's eyes looked down into the bright blue eyes and onto the pale epidermis of the new born in his arms. The contrast between the boys was astonishing and undeniable. He held his breath as Jethro and the Pastor watched him from across the bed.

'Everything alright doc?' the former asked, assessing the medical man's body language to be out of tune with the delivery of the elder boy. In the gloom of the bedroom Royston lifted his head and babe in arms turned and faced the mother, father and holy man. Martha, although totally shattered detected a problem and sat up staring at Royston.

'What's wrong? Is he' she paused 'alive?' knowing that anything better than that she could deal with. The baby cried as if in response to her question. Her anxiety allayed she looked at the Doctor's face. 'Give him to me!' she demanded and held her arms out while Jethro cradled their first born and stood by her side as he pulled her youngest to her. Instinctively she immediately cradled him to her breasts kissing his soft warm skin and gently rocked him. And in return he suckled her as if the eight months in her womb had prepared him for this moment. She watched him feed from her, the only lights in the room radiating through the window from the pulsating blue and red emergency beacons of a passing FDNY ambulance wailing through the darkened streets and avenues to a 911 call. Although tired she looked up and bid Jethro pass across their first born while like his brother he hungrily fed, her tired body rejuvenated enough for this once in a lifetime experience. Suddenly the power returned bringing the lights on and the rotating fan back to life. For a split second everyone blinked through the brightness; the twins unaffected by the sudden glare. The Pastor was the first.

'Oh my God!' he uttered unable to control his feelings.

'What? Oh my!' stammered Jethro.

'What is it?' shouted Martha scared by their reaction and not knowing what they were referring to, until she followed their eyes and looked at her babies. 'Oh! What?' she exclaimed with a sharp intake of breath.

'There's no need to worry' interspersed the Doctor quickly. 'They are both fine and healthy. Sometimes nature has a way with her and as long as they both have their health and all good bodily functions then you have no need to concern yourselves.' He looked from Jethro to Martha to the Pastor.

'How is this possible?' asked Jethro. 'I mean how can one be white and the other black, unless' he quizzically looked at Martha leaving an unasked question in the air.

'Don't you even think that Jethro! I have been with no other man but you. Don't you dare suggest otherwise!' she shouted indignantly at him. 'I married you and my vows mean something to me, even if you have doubts!'

He hung his head in shame, knowing that what he had even inferred she could never have done. 'I'm sorry. Forgive me! This is such a shock!' and leant across to hug her and both of the tiny boys. 'I don't care' he said proudly to all around. 'These are both my boys individually and collectively' he said passionately. 'I have always believed that the soul comes before the colour and the Almighty has today given us' he looked lovingly at Martha '*a gift*. Yes. It will be hard to explain. This is our family and I will remind anybody and everyone of the fact for the rest of my life if necessary that we are all one race... the human race!' He looked into Martha's eyes which were full of tears at his impassioned speech and, leaning forward, he kissed both boys on their heads. She in turn held him and the boys tightly, while Pastor Jimmy Ignuma delivered an impromptu prayer of thanks for the safe delivery of God's special twins that storm-ravaged night.

The following years, as the boys grew, were testing times for them all. Growing up in a predominantly black neighbourhood did not at first create many problems, just a lot of initial gossip among the neighbours as they at first pointed at the twins as possible freaks then later gradually accepted the notion that they were both black. It was like the three monkeys. See no evil. Hear no evil. Say no evil.

Martha took a pride as most multiple birth parents do in dressing them identically, so the obvious difference was not at first as noticeable as it might have been. The media, of course, had a different agenda and although Martha and Jethro tried to keep the boys out of the limelight as much as possible, the press interest at local and national level ensured that their every move was acutely watched and commented on by both sides of the racial divide. This notoriety, however intrusive, did have one advantage. Money and lots of it. The family and, more importantly from a headline point of view, the twins, helped sell papers. Not since the days of the Beatle's had there been such media attention. At first Jethro advised everyone that they would handle all the media themselves, but after a while with cameras still in their faces at every turn, the initial excitement of being continuous front page news started to become tiresome and one evening they called the Doctor and asked if Tentacle could help out. Within minutes of their call to him, he had spoken to his contact who rang them directly back requesting that they all meet in his office at ten am the next day in Lower Manhattan.

'Please bring the boys. I would love to meet them. We have a fully qualified au pair and nursery nurse to look after all their needs. The Doctor will accompany you and arrange all the transport. Please be ready to leave by nine. The traffic, although bad, will have thinned a bit by then' he laughed sarcastically. 'We'll have lunch and I'll show you around. We can talk formally later. Have a good night's sleep. I'll see you tomorrow.' Jethro put the phone down and sat on the bed next to Martha who had listened in on the extension.

'Sounds a nice man' she said.

'Yes. I agree. How are the boys?'

'Sleeping soundly. It's going to be a very busy and interesting day tomorrow, Mr Hamilton' she teased, tickling him in the ribs. 'I suggest we follow what the man proposed and have a good night's sleep.'

'Yes Maam!' he quipped back cheekily saluting her, knowing at times like this she not only wore the pants, but the tie and jacket too.

They fell asleep quickly in each others arms, the twins not waking until seven am.

The black limousine arrived at nine and parked unobtrusively at the north east entrance to Marcus Garvey Park adjacent to the North General Hospital, one block from where they lived. Jethro had received a call earlier that morning from the Doctor, requesting that they leave by the rear alley at nine thirty and exit at Park Avenue where a yellow cab would be waiting for them to connect with him in the limo. They must, he insisted open their apartment windows slightly, leaving the TV and lights on so as to give a semblance of occupancy to the paparazzi camped outside. At precisely nine thirty the Hamilton's quietly left the rear of the building entering the alley and ran to the open door of a cab from the famous Yellow Cab Company which moved off sharply making an illegal one hundred and eighty degree turn down Park Avenue.

'Geez! You people must be important!' said Carlos the driver looking in his rear view mirror at them. 'I mean, I've been given one hundred bucks to get you out of here and drive just two blocks.'

Silently they sat in the back, babies in arms, Jethro checking the rear window for any obvious signs of a tail. Within seconds Carlos had swung right into East 124th Street by the hospital and then first left into Madison Avenue gently pulling up behind the black limo.

'Have a nice day!' he beamed, leaning out of his driver's window in his best Spanish Harlem accent.

The limo's large rear and centre pavement-side doors with cobalt reflective windows swung open allowing them to step from the cab and quickly disappear into the dark, luxurious seating of the preferred vehicle of New York's glitterati. Inside the Doctor leaned across and greeted them, making sure they all buckled up, including harnesses for the twins.

The chauffeur had already closed the doors and looked back for permission to move off. Royston nodded his approval and almost silently the two ton vehicle eased forward to engage and waltz with the near gridlock traffic of Lower Manhattan. Sitting opposite them and with his back to the driver's sealed soundproof divide, the Doctor asked them how they felt.

'To be honest' Jethro whispered lest the driver hear 'I am amazed, shocked and anything else that you can throw at me.'

'Same here' echoed Martha.

'You don't have to whisper' smiled the Doctor 'the glass is soundproofed.'

'Thought of everything, haven't you?' cheekily quipped Martha.

'Well, we do our best!' he drilled back, smiling at them both. 'Sit back and take in the view' nodding emphatically at the windows. 'It'll take another thirty minutes or so in this traffic.'

The sleek vehicle with its 'boomerang' TV aerial rigidly secured to the boot, moved past the park on the left, emerging on East 125th Street and swung left towards Martin Luther King, Jr Boulevard and Broadway.

'Look!' gesticulated Martha, pointing to the army of press and media outside their apartment block. The scrum had become so intense with reporters and camera crews lobbying for the best positions, that New York's finest in their blue and white squad cars were in attendance supported by four mounted police officers plus two more dismounted from their bikes.

Jethro involuntarily ducked below the window as they passed just feet away from the melee, forgetting that he was invisible to anyone outside.

'It's ok!' said the Doctor smiling. 'They can't see you.'

Even with all this noise and activity Blanco and Negro, the principals in this high drama of cat and mouse, content with their bellies full, slept the sleep of the innocent. The boys lay side by side, comfortably ensconced in a dual baby carrier topped by a large blue blanket and sporting two soft toys supplied by the Doctor. As they passed the world famous Apollo Theatre, opened in 1913 as a whites-only opera house and subsequently changed to all races in 1934, Martha looked lovingly at her two sons and silently prayed that they would not have to face the burdens of racial stigma and social segregation that she had in her youth.

Outside on the pavement and beyond the comfort of the plush interior of the car, an ebony skinned vendor of an iced tea and cold soft drinks tricycle called out for business. His rough, unshaven, white, stubbly beard and tatty shirt, trousers and shoes provided enough evidence that business was not good. Even at this time in the morning he was sweating under the growing heat of the rising morning sun glued to a clear blue motionless sky. He certainly couldn't see or know the occupants as they sped by, but twenty years hence his two year old grandson would encounter the twins in a decisive moment that would reshape all their lives forever. As they entered Broadway, the in-car phone rang softly.

'Royston' the voice asked 'are they with you?'

'Yes. The Hamilton family are all here' he announced so Jethro and Martha could hear his side of the conversation.

'Excellent! Give them my best. I'll see you all soon!' The line went dead and the Doctor replaced the handset.

'The gentleman you are going to meet wishes you well. You'll be seeing him soon.'

'What's his name?' asked Jethro curiously.

'All in good time. All in good time' the Doctor repeated, sitting back and taking in the views that he had seen many times on his 'business trips' downtown.

For Martha and Jethro though, this was another world entirely. Even living only a few miles from the heart of the 'Big Apple' they had never wandered this far from home and gawped through the darkened windows at buildings and monuments that they had read about but never seen. They felt like tourists in their own country especially when traversing Columbus Circle, the last signs indicating an entrance to a partly familiar Central Park flashed by in an instant. As Broadway hit Seventh Avenue bearing down on it from the left, the Doctor pointed forward.

'Look' he pointed. 'That's Time Square coming up' and Martha and Jethro stared, open-mouthed, at the vibrance and glamour of the spectacular lightshows on display even at this hour of the day. Within minutes with the traffic amazingly still flowing freely, they passed the Empire State Building on their left and bearing right along West Houston Street they entered what New Yorkers call 'the Village' but what to the rest of the world is affectionately known as Greenwich Village. This narrow crazy-mosaic pattern of streets, historically created by the boundaries of early farms or streams now housed the bohemian, yet eccentric, recluse who resided at 75 ½ Bedford Street, the City's narrowest home at just 9 ½ feet wide. Peering through the half closed wooden slats of his first floor window in this famous three storey building, formerly the residence of

Cary Grant, he closely observed the occupants emerge from the car. The chimed doorbell rang in the claustrophobic hallway, where his trusted and faithful housekeeper slowly opened the solid wooden door to the expected guests and showed them into the bright ground floor reception room.

'Mr Luuz will join you soon. Could I get you any tea, coffee?' she enquired of them and suddenly seeing the carrycot, 'warm milk perhaps?' addressing this to Martha.

'Thank you. I'm fine' she replied.

'Same here' Jethro and the Doctor answered almost in unison.

The housekeeper stepped out of the small room and Martha turned to the Doctor 'Is this for real? I mean it's so small. Our apartment is bigger than this!'

Jethro twirled himself around. 'What type of person lives here?'

'A very important one as far as you guys are concerned' the Doctor replied. 'He is *very* rich and incredibly generous in his desire to help other people less fortunate than himself.

Some misinformed people call him 'a freak of nature', so please don't judge him on his physical appearance. It's what in his heart that counts.'

Martha and Jethro looked at each other. 'We are just getting used to the hand that nature dealt us' she said 'so whatever appearance he has, I'm sure we can deal with it.'

Jethro nodded in total agreement.

'Just warning you. That's all' said the Doctor.

Suddenly the door opened and one of the tallest men they had ever seen entered. He stood at just over seven feet and had long flowing white hair that cascaded over his broad shoulders. His mode of dress was unusual in that he wore a black cloak, over a bright green silk shirt, connected at the collar by a gold chain from which a strange medallion hung. A pair of black leather boots completed the look, except for some ultra thin blue-tinted Benjamin Franklin spectacles that perched upon the bridge of his nose.

'Good to meet you' he smiled stepping forward, arm outstretched. Jethro stood agog as he leant upwards to shake the tall man's hand. Like Martha he found the grip was firm but friendly and he immediately warmed to him. 'I hope your journey and your travelling companion' he looked at the Doctor 'was to your satisfaction. I gather you've been offered some refreshments, but declined. Still, at any time you want something, please don't be afraid to ask. After all, we're on the same team now.'

A low murmur from the crib distracted his attention from them and he walked over to where the twins lay, snuggled up against each other. 'Oh my!' he exclaimed, bending down over them. 'It's a miracle! Isn't it Royston?' addressing the Doctor. 'Just look at them. You two are truly blessed! These boys have been chosen by the almighty' he looked up to heaven 'you both should be so proud.'

'We are' Martha countered back.

For the next minute nobody moved except Mr Luuz. The room was so quiet you could hear a pin drop. Pulling himself up to his maximum standing height, he looked directly at them. 'You are probably wondering what you are doing here?' He held his hand up. 'Please let me explain first, but not here. We are going upstairs. It's more comfortable. Leave the boys with Mrs Jones, my housekeeper. She can be trusted to look after them. After all' he added 'she has had five children to bring up, including one set of triplets, so I think you have no worries there.' As if on cue Mrs Jones entered and picked the crib up, disappearing almost as quickly and silently as she had appeared.

'Let me lead the way' he said and in file, all three followed him up the narrow, steep, well lit stairwell turning to the right at the next level and entering a small but very sumptuous dining room. 'Please.' He motioned to them standing to one side as they filed in. 'Are you sure you don't want any refreshments?'

For the second time they declined. 'Please take a seat' he indicated the gold braided Georgian dining chairs. 'First let me tell you about myself and then you will get to understand my involvement with the organisation known as Tentacle and how your lives and that of the boys will be the richer for it. Royston here' he indicated to the Doctor 'has heard this story a hundred times before, so forgive me, old friend, if I repeat myself.' He looked across to the window seat where the eminent medical man sat in the shade of the retreating shadow cast by the ever rising golden disc in the sky. The Doctor bowed, acknowledging his friend and sat comfortably listening as if this was the first time of telling. 'When I was a child, I suffered with a multitude of ailments, some of which nearly killed me and others that have caused me immense pain and suffering to this day. My parents were very poor and had no access to medical care that could have greatly improved my lot in life. As you see, my growth was accelerated and I had to endure the humiliation of endless name calling that could have had a traumatic effect on me if I had let it. Coming from a God fearing stock, I became mentally strong and was determined not to let the bullies and thugs of the world be my betters. Through grit and determination I got to the top and was determined nothing and no-one would stop me. I worked in hot kitchens, cleaned toilets and swept roads. All the menial jobs. But at the same time, I studied. Not books, but people. Very quickly I realised that this world worked on who you knew, not just what you know and I made a point to get to know everyone I could, from the lavatory man to the Chief Executive. When I wanted to get a job as a dealer in a bank, I did not have any qualifications and was consequently turned down by all the agencies I approached. In fact I later learned that as soon as I walked away from the interview with the agencies, they ditched my CV and sniggered under their breath at the freak who had dared show his face through their doors. I was so annoyed at having seen class friends of mine who were stupid as hell get these positions, that I researched where the Chairman of one large bank lived and travelled by bus forty miles to his private residence. I scaled his high walls and trudged up the gravel driveway to the front door and rang the bell. His wife opened the door and asked who I was. I told her I was here for the appointment with her husband. She asked me to wait and the great man appeared in the doorway totally confused and also a bit anxious about how I got into his grounds. I explained that I wanted a dealer's job with his bank and that I was being blocked at every avenue to get in. He asked me how I got to his premises. I told him I borrowed some money from a friend for the long bus journey and scaled his wall to gain access. For a moment he stood looking up at me threatening to call the police, but then recanted and said that if I had the balls to take this cheeky approach, then he would like to see me on the following Monday morning in his office. He gave me a card and fifty dollars to help me get back home while opening the electronic gates for me to pass out through. I saw him on the Monday and got the job. Many years later when I had made my fortune, I went to see him and returned his fifty with a cheque of my own to his selected charity of one hundred thousand dollars. What I learnt from that was one should never give up if they believe in their cause deeply enough. The other thing I learnt was that bullies should never succeed and I have given my life to promoting both of these principles. That brings me to where we are today. My friend here' he motioned to the Doctor 'introduced me some time ago to a Professor Lang, a Scottish world class genetic scientist who was researching the possibility of isolating a unique gene in the top layer of skin, leading to the total destruction of all Cancer impurities and skin blemishes for millions around the globe. His research is just in the early stages and although there are many hurdles to cross, sometimes taking years to gain approval by the respective government regulatory boards, early results are promising.' Pausing, he looked up at the Hamilton's whose total attention he had seized. 'Anyway' he continued 'because this research will take many years and millions of dollars to fund, this government and many others decided that weapon development and sales should come first in deference to any other projects as they could generate vast and immediate profits. To many people, this approach is totally abhorrent and no amount of lobbying has got any of the leaders to change their minds. Therefore, a lot of influential people decided that we would form an organisation. We planed to change the world, by doing what the governments should have. However, several board members thought that we were not going far enough and wanted all the rotten governments worldwide overturned. The majority disagreed with them and voted to continue with the original plans only. These few discontents, however, met in secret and slowly developed a master plan code-named Chameleon to be implemented by our organisation, Tentacle. I, with Royston and many global community leaders, both here and abroad, are members. We hope that when the time is right we will be able to call on you and, especially the twins, to help lead this country back to its great principles. The advantage that the boys have is their unique distinction to unite the masses. We will arrange for their education to be second to none and you will want for nothing. All you have to do is say yes and we will put everything in place. One day we will ask for a small favour from you and we would hope that you will agree without question.' Mr Luuz stood up and without waiting for an answer left the room, leaving Martha and Jethro gobsmacked.

'Did I just hear all that correctly?' Martha addressed the Doctor.

'You did. Every word correctly' he responded.

'Jethro? What do you think?' she blurted out.

'Me? I'm as shocked as you.'

'Doctor?' he said.

Royston looked up, knowing what was coming.

'What should we do? Is it in the boy's interests as well as ours? What would you do?'

'Well' said the Doctor 'speaking professionally and, not as a member of Tentacle, I would recommend that you accept, purely from the point of having a better life for the boys and yourselves. That is my opinion. Incidentally, regardless of your choice, you cannot reveal what went on here today to anybody. It would be denied in any event. You have no proof.' Royston got up and walked to the door. 'Mr Luuz and I will return in five minutes. Please let us know your decision.'

During the following twenty years, since Jethro and Martha had given an undertaking to support Mr Luuz and Tentacle in that little strange house in Greenwich Village, their lives had evolved into nothing short of a turbulent roller-coaster ride. Outwardly, there appeared to be no discernable change, except that all their bills were paid automatically as they became due and the whole family had access to the best private health packages in the nation. Their bank account, historically in deficit and levied with crippling overdraft fees, now showed a healthy balance financed in the main by the media, ever desperate for their continuing true life stories. For the first time since they had been married, Jethro and Martha could afford to buy decent food and clothes, while the Pastor and his fellow clergymen fielded the media, constantly keeping them all at a safe distance from the family. Two burly security guards were hired to accompany any of them whenever they left the safety of the apartment and a yellow cab would also magically appear to whisk them away from the press attention. Several times as their cab moved off, paparazzi photographers on fast bikes had attempted to roar off after them, zoom cameras in hand but had always been cut off by one or more of the cars that had attended the family from the day that they agreed that Tentacle should look after them. Annoyed by these deliberate attempts to thwart their activities, the journalists tried to track down the registered owners of the cars via the number plates but found that they all had been 'blocked' and were therefore 'unknowns'.

Growing fast, as all healthy children do, it soon became clear that space was becoming an issue and if they were to have the quality of life guaranteed to them by the organisation then a move to a larger home was becoming a necessity.

A Mr Goldstein of City Real Estates contacted them. 'Is that Mr Hamilton?' he queried on the phone one morning.

'Who wants to know?' Jethro cautiously replied, knowing that only Tentacle connected people would be given this number.

'My name is Goldstein. Harry Goldstein. I have been asked to contact you by Dr Emmanuel. I believe you know him?'

'Yes. That's right' said Jethro.

'He suggested I make contact with you and your wife regarding a more suitable property for your needs. I hope you don't mind, but I've taken the liberty to source a few that may be to your liking and I was wondering if I can arrange to come and meet you to discuss this further?'

'Please hold on Mr Goldstein. I just want to check this out with my wife.'

'Of course. Please take your time.'

A minute passed. Then another.

'Hello? Are you still there?' asked the real estate agent, believing that the line had accidently been cut or Jethro had taken an instant dislike to him and had pulled the plug deliberately.

'Yes. Mr Goldstein. Sorry about that. I was just discussing this with my other half. You know what women are like! Yes we would like to see you, but not here. I would suggest somewhere in this vicinity.'

There was a mutual silence from both parties until Jethro announced. 'I think Sylvia's restaurant at 328 Lenox Avenue would be good for us. Can you manage that? How about midday tomorrow?'

'Perfect. I'll see you there. Incidentally, are you bringing the boys with you? I would love to see them.'

'Unfortunately no' Jethro responded. 'They'll be in the middle of their sleep. Sorry.'

'That's ok. No problem. It's just that the Doctor has said how sweet they both look. But I understand. I have kids. Now all grown up, so I can empathise with your circumstances.' Almost as an afterthought he quickly added 'Oh! I nearly forgot. I will arrange for a courier to bring round to you today the pictures and details of the properties that we'll discuss tomorrow. Until then. Have a nice day!' and he clicked off before Jethro could reply.

'Wow! That was fast!' he remarked to Martha who sat on the bed trying to conceal her amusement. 'I really drove him hard' he said trying to convince himself that he had been in control of the telephone conversation.

'What's funny?' he asked looking at her.

'Nothing' she sniggered.

'Martha. Please tell me what you are smiling at?' he said, totally bemused.

'Jethro. I know you think of yourself as sharp and businesslike, but that was Mr Harry Goldstein. He is Jewish and the Jews are expert at business, having been around for thousands of years making deals. I bet he has already got the property for us and is at this moment trying to match-make the boys to two nice Jewish girls.' She couldn't stop herself bursting into laughter at the sight of Jethro's innocent but sweet face before her.

He sat down next to her and suddenly, like an exploding supernova, burst out laughing uncontrollably, realising that Harry had indeed outsmarted him without batting an eyelid.

The next morning, the Doctor called round with a trained nursery nurse. 'Martha. This is Mary. She will help out today with the twins while you're out and at any other time that you need her. She is a fully-qualified nurse, but has one other qualification that I am sure you'll find interesting. She is a mother to twins as well. Not' he quickly added 'as unique as yours, but' he cast his eyes quickly across both women's faces 'twins all the same. Isn't that right, Mary?'

Mary smiled and with a broad Irish American accent said 'What the Doctor says is true. It will be me pleasure to help you bring up the boys. To be sure it would!' and smiled back with such a soft and warm motherly glow that Martha fell in love with her immediately. Quietly easing open the bedroom door, they both crept in to see the boys in their respective cribs. Negro rolled over blowing bubbles from his lips whilst Blanco lay on his back gently snoring. Both women smiled at the adorable scene before them.

'Come' said Martha pulling Mary away and gently closed the door. 'I'll show you their food and milk. I'm not breast feeding them' she added apologetically.

'That's alright m'dear' responded Mary. 'Neither did I. The bottle is fine. Believe me, they will still grow strong and healthy. You have nothing to concern yourself over.' She put her hand in Martha's and gave her a squeeze of reassurance. 'I'll treat them as if they were my own.'

Martha turned her rich charcoal face towards this new woman in her life and knew that apart from Jethro who was irreplaceable, she had at last found the soul mate that she had secretly been searching for since the tragic death of her sister and best friend five years previously.

'Time to go' announced the Doctor, watching the sweep hand hit eleven thirty on his Omega. Through the heavy net curtains he saw the regular pack of hungry newshound cameras at the ready, interspersed with a generous sprinkling of arrogant paparazzi riders sitting astride their fast Yamaha V Max machines. 'We're doing something different today' he smiled. 'Just watch'.

From a distance wailing sirens and honking horns of the New York City Fire Department drew nearer. With screeching tyres and flashing lights several engines in gleaming red and white livery pulled up by a building fifty feet away on the opposite side of the street. Under the direction of the Fire Chief, the various crews split into two teams. One went into the grey stone tenement entrance while the second cleared the street of pedestrians which included all the media teams. Blue and white striped tapes were strung across the roads while the reported building was fire checked. Down the street a large red command vehicle complete with flashing lights ponderously made its way to the scene and pulled up on the pavement next to their steps. The Doctor unzipped a large sports bag he had brought in with him and pulled out three bright yellow fire capes complete with hoods. 'Put these on' he directed to Martha and Jethro. 'Be quick. We haven't got long!' Within seconds they were attired and with the Velcro gripping the hoods tightly over their heads, they made their way down the street stairs and into the vehicle. As the darkened doors of the truck closed electronically, it trundled off through the lines of the unsuspecting press corps and transported them two blocks and fifty feet away from the blue canopied eatery, lest they attract any more unwanted attention.

Being a very successful business man, Harry was there before them at a table set for four and underneath photographs of earlier diners such as Nelson Mandela and Magic Johnson. 'Welcome' he beamed standing, having recognised their pictures from the wild TV coverage in the past few weeks. 'And you must be the Doctor?'

Royston bowed slightly and they all sat down.

'Now. What would you like to drink?' Harry enquired.

'An apple juice for me' said Martha.

'Same here' said Jethro.

'I'll take a root beer' smiled the Doctor.

'Wow!' said Harry. 'The last of the big spenders!' he laughed.

The waitress came across with a pad, Harry ordering a Martini, shaken not stirred.

'Just like James Bond!' he quipped.

While they waited for the drinks to arrive, he handed around extra details of the properties that they had viewed the previous day matching their requirements. 'You will notice that they all have excellent security features and several exits in order to evade the media spotlight. All come with underground parking, a twenty four hour concierge and banks of security cameras linked directly to the Police or' he looked at the Doctor 'your own security team.'

The drinks came, followed by a selection of Southern-Fried chicken adorned with spicy ribs, black-eyed peas, collard greens and sweet potato pie. Because it was Sunday, the diners were entertained by a once weekly performance of a quintet of Gospel singers who literary brought the house down with renditions of old Negro ballads. Several times during their meal, Jethro thought he felt penetrating eyes on him from one or two of the four hundred and fifty diners who quickly filled this famous food emporium. At one point he whispered his concerns to the Doctor who immediately allayed any worries he had.

'A lot of people in here' he whispered back 'are already part of our team.'

When they had finished eating, Harry asked if they had any preferences of the properties seen.

'Actually' said Martha, 'we do like this one' and she passed the details via the Doctor to Harry.

'A good choice and if I was in your position that is the one I would have chosen as well. If you want I can take you there after our lunch. It's not far and no-one will know that you are viewing. It's vacant now, save all the furniture that it comes with. The previous owners are big into music and needed this place as a bolt hole to escape the press and publicity that followed them everywhere.'

'I know the feeling' empathised Martha.

'They've now bought a small island off Bermuda' Harry added 'and don't need this anymore. It suited their requirements while they were here and I believe it will do for you too. A very important feature is that it has enough space to accommodate both of you and the boys as they grow. Remember, penthouse apartments have great views and like this one are split over two entire floors. Do you want to go and view it now?'

'Can we?' asked Martha excitedly, addressing Jethro and the Doctor.

'No problem here my Vandella' replied Jethro smiling at his wife's positive and bubbly attitude.

'Royston? Please!' she begged the Doctor softly.

'Well. I've got nothing else to do this afternoon, so I think we should take a look.'

'Thank you! I owe you big time!' she beamed at him.

'Don't thank me yet. We've got a way to go' he countered.

'I know. But I feel that everything is starting to fall into place and I have never felt as positive as I am right now!'

'Well okay then!' whispered Harry, leaning forward and smiling. 'I'll get the bill and then drive us there. Waiter! Can I have the tab?'

The drive did not take long. In fact, under fifteen minutes door to door and that was allowing for the heavy afternoon traffic that started building up after the Churches finished and families headed off to lunch or for an afternoon stroll in the nearby parks.   Pulling into the leafy and quiet Morningside Drive, Harry drove down to the concealed entrance of a private underground car park under the stately eight floor apartment block and swiped his pass through the scanner. The formidable electronic gates swung open and he pulled up into one of three spaces marked 'PENTHOUSE ONLY'. He stood aside as they all entered the lift, pressed P and entered a security code into the touchpad by the emergency phone. The elevator silently rose and within seconds they had arrived at the top.

Stepping out first Harry led them to the front door and using the combination of key and swipe-card entered the apartment. Martha was right behind him with the Doctor and Jethro bringing up the rear.

'Oh my!' she exclaimed whirling around the large central area graced by a massive crystal chandelier above her and the biggest tropical fish tank she had ever seen set directly at the bottom of the stairs. Like a child given her first bar of chocolate she ran excitedly everywhere.

'Oh my!' she called again and repeated this every time a new vista broke in front of her. After almost twenty minutes Jethro found her curled up in the arms of a massive armchair overlooking Columbia University, Riverside Park and the Hudson beyond that. He touched her neck gently.

She looked up at him looking radiantly happy and bit her lower lip mischievously. 'We've got to have this Jeth!' she half pleaded. 'It's what we always wanted. Just look at it!'

Although he normally was a man of few words, this sumptuous palace made him totally speechless and like

Martha he knew they could be secure and happy with the boys here. 'Yes, I agree' he whispered back.

'What do you think? Is it great or what?' said Harry walking across the mosaic marble floor.

'We love it!' said Martha, now looking appealingly at Royston. 'Can we have this? Can we? Pleeease?'

If he had not known her better, he could have been mistaken into thinking that he was dealing with a child at Christmas begging to open all her presents the night beforehand. 'Give me a moment' he smiled at her. 'Harry. Can you step over here for a second or two?'

The two men conversed for what Martha thought was forever, during which Royston made a call. Again they talked in whispered tones, their heads nodding and then shaking as calculations and notes were made by both men. Finally, after what seemed hours but in actual fact was five minutes, they shook hands firmly and hugged each other.

'Yes!' Martha jumped for joy, recognising the signs of a done deal and kissed first Jethro, then Royston and finally a very bemused Harry.

'The place is yours' smiled Royston, handing over the keys and swipe-card to Martha that Harry had just given him. 'All the furniture is included in the sale price, so you don't have to buy anything. You can move in today. I would suggest that we get all your personal belongings over here this afternoon. I will arrange that. You don't need to go back. Mary will bring the boys later this evening. Nobody knows her so the media will not be surprised when Mrs Green from the floor above you takes her baby for a walk with her friend Mary. What they don't know is that Mr Green will actually baby sit their son while she and Martha walk out with the boys covered up in a single pram. We will have a car waiting nearby for the transfer. Please don't worry about the Green's. As I mentioned to Jethro earlier many people want to help you. The Green's are part of that group and have been watching your backs for some time. I am going to leave you now. Harry can run you past all the details.' He looked across at the realtor who nodded in agreement.

'If you have any problems' Harry said 'call this number' and he handed Jethro a card. 'There is a new car, complete with darkened windows, in the underground car park fully tanked, taxed and serviced. Here are the keys. Again Harry will guide you. There is one thing though and I can't stress this enough. You must not make any contact with anyone, including friends and family until we give the go ahead. The media are very savvy and will latch onto anything you do. So absolutely *no* contact with the outside world. You will be able to use the car when we say and not before. In the meantime any journeys outside must be arranged via me. Is that clear?' Now, for the first time since they had agreed to Mr Luuz's terms and that of Tentacle, did they realise that their lives and that of the boys would forever be in the hands of other people.

By the time the boys had attended kindergarten at age two, they had once again become the talk of the neighbourhood.

The press had found out by this time where they lived, but the security that now surrounded the entire family was almost watertight. When, however, they had to step out, the flash cameras of the jostling press did feel intrusive, but as time went on they accepted that this was the price they had to pay for the notoriety that the twins created. Martha and Jethro tried as best they could to give the boys an element of privacy, but as they grew and mixed within their peer groups it was not always possible to keep the media at bay. Other parents were approached by unscrupulous journalists with a view to gain an insight into the Hamilton's way of life, but to the chagrin of these few sorry hacks, the community closed ranks and shielded the family. It wasn't until their eighth birthday that the boys had their first personal exposure to any form of media attention and racism. During a Christmas shopping trip to Macy's, a black youth of fourteen was caught in the act of stealing some leather goods by a sharp eyed security guard. As he was marched away to the holding room in the store, he struggled free and ran past the boys, tripping over Blanco's outstretched legs as he sat on the floor playing with a model car that Jethro had just bought him. The chasing guards pinned him to the floor and applied handcuffs. As he was being hauled to his feet he looked directly at Blanco and screamed 'Tanks for nuttin', you white honky!'

Blanco just stared at the youth as he was marched off trying to understand the meaning of the venom that had suddenly and unjustly come his way.

Negro had also seen and heard this verbal assault on his brother and automatically shouted after the perpetrator. 'Don't you talk like that to my brother you piece of black shit!'

The youth, although now in two arm locks, turned his head and together with many others who had witnessed the event, stared at the little black boy who cradled protectively his sobbing white brother in his small arms. Jethro and their security team from Tentacle immediately picked the boys up and made a hasty retreat to the safety of their car in the underground car park two floors beneath street level. Unfortunately the news burst on to the pages of the press in various modes causing a mini debate regarding race and children. A picture taken by a member of the public showed a sobbing blonde boy hugged and comforted by his twin black brother both surrounded by a multitude of brightly coloured toy cars. When they arrived back in the safety of their penthouse apartment, Martha knelt down and hugged them lovingly before carefully chastising Negro on the language he used to the youth.

'But Mom, he was black and he called Blanco a white honky and I only went to help him. Did I do something wrong? Shouldn't I help Blanco? I don't understand!'

With that Blanco grasped his brother's hand while ruffling the same's coconut matting of black curly hair. 'Thank you for being my friend today' he said lovingly. 'You are not just my brother, but my *best* friend. I will always love you.'

Martha put her hand over her mouth, gulping deeply on seeing the love these two little boys had for each other. She silently prayed that the rest of their lives would be rich in love to each other and others. Purposefully ignoring Negro's questions about morality, she cooked a hearty dinner then put them early to bed.

The years passed and soon they were in their teens, mixing with girls, music and bikes. Because they were brought up in a predominantly black neighbourhood with street gangs fighting turf wars against other immigrant groups that abutted their territory, the boys were always treated as equalisers without a colour tag and as one of the gang. This especially applied to Blanco, who in any other scenario would be the outcast, but here was the undisputed leader of the 'black pack' as they liked to call themselves. The respect that he commanded as an ash-blonde, white, rich kid was in no small way due to Negro, who always protected him against the hard core elements within the black community. This also cut both ways as one evening during the Manhattan rush hour the twins were strolling across Central Park with their minder in close proximity when a white youth pointed at Negro and started taunting him with the words 'Nigger'. To the consternation of the security man, Blanco now fuming, ran screaming after the boy, pursuing him all the way back to his house. Shouting, ranting and raving, he rang the doorbell and kicked at the door until the father of the boy appeared and asked him what he wanted. When Blanco told him that his son had hurled racial insults at Negro, the father told him to 'fuck off' and he would allow him to do it again if he wanted. He couldn't see what the problem was and called him a liar especially when Blanco told him that it was his twin brother that had been insulted. By the time the father had slammed the front door in Blanco's face and threatened to call the Police, Negro and the minder had arrived and pulled him away into one of Tentacles 'unmarked' cars.

As Martha and Jethro approached fifty, they received a call from Royston who requested a meeting with them the next day.

'There's no need to worry' he reassured them hearing a slight panic down the line. 'It's just something we need to discuss relating to the boys education.'

Putting the phone down, Martha still felt apprehensive regardless of what the Doctor had said.

'They've never asked for a meeting in all these years' she motioned to Jethro. 'What can they want?'

'Be calm Mama' he assured her. 'If it's for the boys' good then we should listen. After all, they've kept their word all this time and provided for us all without question. Am I right or am I right?'

'You're right, Jethro' she agreed stroking his thinning white hair, still not entirely convinced and wondering what the ulterior motive was behind this unexpected call.

The next morning at ten, while the boys were at school, they sat again for the second time in fifteen years at 75 ½ Bedford Street. Mr Luuz, seeming incredibly not to have aged in all these years, suddenly appeared in the doorway gripping a short, brightly decorated spear in his right hand which he casually leaned against the door frame. He asked after them and as before was the perfect host offering tea with scones, topped with fresh cream and English jam. The general talk was of the weather and travel. After complimenting Martha on how well she looked for a woman of just 'thirty six' he looked up at her and smiled knowingly. She smiled back and seriously blushed not expecting the compliment.

'And now' he said. 'I want to explain why you are both here again.'

Martha looked concerned and Mr Luuz picking up on that immediately set out to put her mind at rest.

'Please don't worry, Martha' he said, reaching out to touch her on the shoulder. 'What I have to say is for the boys' benefit, but it is important that you both know which direction their education is now going. As you know Tentacle has paid to date for all their fees to the best schools that money can buy. And rest assured that will continue. But we now need to really raise their standards and feel that in order to fully equip them for the world that we have planned for them they need to experience life outside of the community that they now live in.'

Martha ears zoomed in on the words 'experience life outside of the community that they now live in' and momentarily panicked. They were going to take 'her boys' away. From the arms that had raised, cared and protected them. From the loving home that she and Jethro had built for them. She thought she must be mishearing and tried desperately to listen to what Mr Luuz was saying in detail. 'Does this mean' she cut in on him 'that the boys will be leaving home and attending a school away from the borough?'

'Actually' he replied 'it will be out of the State' and passed across a pack containing brochures and a DVD. 'I can assure you that the standards as good as they are now, will rocket and set them far above their peer groups. Please note that they will board for the week and come home at weekends unless there is a need for them to stay over. This means that you will   be giving them the opportunity to mature and show you what they are made of as young men coming into their own.'

He leaned forward to them both. 'I want you to both agree with me that this is in the boys' best interests. If you remember the meeting we had here many years ago when I mentioned that I would probably be calling on you for a favour. Well here it is. I hope you both agree. We have spent a lot of time, effort and, certainly not least, money, on the boys and yourselves. We do not regret it for one moment, but would hope that you can now honour your side of the agreement. Just so it's crystal clear, you will still have the penthouse and all the funding to maintain your lifestyle and that of the boys.'

Unlike the meeting from fifteen years ago, Mr Luuz made no effort to leave the room, sitting comfortably back into a large leather-backed armchair and sipping tea. Martha also noticed that his stature and complexion had not changed in all that time. 'If anything' she thought 'he actually looks younger' but realising how ridiculous that seemed, she thought better of it and said nothing. For a brief moment she and Jethro exchanged a knowing glance.

'When is this due to start?' she enquired.

'Not until the beginning of the new school year starting in September. That's another nine months' Mr Luuz confidently replied. 'Do we have a deal?' he asked, holding his hand out.

For the second time Martha and Jethro exchanged knowing glances.

'Yes, Mr Luuz. We do.' Martha said. 'It will break my heart and that of Jethro to have them out of our sight and touch every day except the weekends. But it was going to happen one day and we both know that it will be in their interests. So reluctantly, yes.' The Hamilton's leaned forward, extending their hands to meet the outstretched palm of Mr Luuz.

'We will make all the arrangements. The Doctor here will see to that.' He looked at his friend who amiably nodded. 'It was a pleasure meeting you again after all this time. I wish you well for the future and that of the boys. We might never meet again, but do not worry. Everything has been planned for the boy's future happiness. I will retire in *my* homeland safe in the knowledge that the world will be a better place after I'm gone and when your boys are in charge.' Rising, he bowed gracefully to them, picked up the spear and left the room.

'Time to go, I think' said Royston, looking from one to another.

They both followed him out and into the waiting car. It wasn't until they had just passed the Flatiron building on Fifth Avenue and Broadway that Martha posed a question to the Doctor that had been on her lips since the meeting had finished. 'Royston. I want you to level with me.'

'Certainly. Anything you want' he said frankly. He smiled at her. 'What's the problem?' he enquired.

'Well' she paused not knowing how to put it and upset or annoy anyone. 'A couple of things have been bugging me and I just have to get it clear so I can move forward.'

'Go ahead. Ask away.'

She took a deep breath. 'Mr Luuz. How old is he and where does he actually come from? It's just that since the time that we first met fifteen years ago, he doesn't appear to have grown any older.'

'And the second point?'

'Well. He mentioned that he would be spending his last days in *his* homeland as if this was not his country.'

'Martha. Good questions' responded the Doctor. 'I'll give you the answers as best I can, but be prepared. It may not be what you are expecting. I have known Mr Luuz for forty years and in all that time he hasn't appeared to have aged at all. I believe that he may be over seventy years old, but I honestly can't be sure. As to your second point. All I can say is that he is going back to his homeland where he was born and raised. He also wishes to be buried there amongst *his* people.'

'Which country are you referring to?' Martha enquired.

'South Africa of course' said the Doctor.

'Ah! South Africa' she repeated. 'Yes' she said. 'I did detect a slight South African accent. Is he to be buried with his white Colonial family?'

'Why do you say that?' he asked her.

'Well that would be *his* family. The British, Dutch, Belgian, German, Portuguese or French. They were the predominant white's in Colonial times.'

'Martha. You are correct in all your assumptions, but one. There is one more family that you failed to mention.'

She scratched her head and eyed him quizzically. 'What other family, Doctor? There are no other white family's out there. Isn't that right, Jethro?' She looked deeply into her husband's sun-wrinkled face and realised that she had missed something. Something enormous. He knew it. Royston knew it. She'd missed it.

'Shall I tell her or will you?' Jethro asked the Doctor, teasing her.

'You tell her.'

'Tell me what?' she said.

'It's very simple Martha' Jethro began. 'Mr Luuz is returning to his homeland. One that has been in his family's blood for thousands of years. He is returning to the great African nation of his forefathers. The land of the proud Zulus. Martha. Mr Luuz is actually from the Royal Zulu bloodline. Just research his name, Luuz Goodwill. Luuz is an anagram of Zulu and Goodwill is the Christian name of the current King of the Zulus. And one more thing. Mr Luuz may appear to be white. By blood he is black, very black!'

When Martha and Jethro broke the news to the twins about leaving home and boarding on a weekly basis, they both presumed the boys would be shocked and possibly emotionally upset. In fact, to their surprise and sadness, the boys were ecstatic about the possibility of stepping out into the wider world, although both did display a concern about how their doting parents would handle the daily loss of contact.

The months came and went. Suddenly it was September. For Martha and Jethro the time for departure had come too soon, but for the boys the opposite was true. On that Monday morning, Martha had been running around like a headless chicken fussing over 'her boys' and ensuring that they had packed everything down to their toothbrushes. She hoped that the man-to- man talk that Jethro had had with them the previous night would keep them on the straight and narrow, while also explaining to them about Tentacle and their involvement with the boy's lives. He made them swear on the Bible that they would not reveal any information to anybody, unless the Doctor or they gave permission. To say they were shocked was an understatement. They had genuinely believed that Jethro had inherited a fortune from a deceased aunt and that was why he did not need to work. Being honest and true, they gave their word which was good enough for their parents.

'Just watch each other's backs' was the only deep advice they both gave the boys. And then too quickly for Martha and Jethro they were gone, leaving the bereft couple all alone again with only fond memories to comfort their lonely evenings together.

As the seasons washed the Earth, the twins matured physically and mentally. Handsome, tall, muscular and each weighing in at over fifteen stone, Blanco and Negro epitomised the stereo-typical American Olympian. Having already shone in all the major debating and sporting activities that the elite private college could provide, they entered Harvard with some of the highest scores ever recorded since the founding of that prestige institution in 1636. Indeed, only a young relatively unknown student by the name of Obama scored slightly higher. It was here that their paths parted for the first time in their lives. Blanco, even as a Freshman, had his eye on the medical faculty while Negro was drawn like a magnet to the legal campus and the political trail beyond. They still saw each other outside of classes, but were now slowly developing their own circles of friends and peers. Even at this level there still existed a sprinkling of unspoken racial bias, but it was so slight to as be almost invisible. Harvard itself is spread liberally over ten principal academic units comprising of nine faculties which in their turn oversee eleven schools and colleges. The University has its own President backed up by twenty Professors and a faculty of over thirteen thousand staff responsible for over twenty thousand students. The oldest institution of higher learning in the United States was effectively a mini city of the intelligentsia and, for the twins, it was the perfect arena in which to network and build up their contacts for the day that they would be called on to repay their benefactors in spades.

Because of Blanco's unique talent to quickly absorb and fearlessly challenge the status quo on any research and development project, he had attracted some of the brightest minds of his day into an inner circle of unofficial boffins. His aggressive approach to undergraduate life also brought him into constant conflict with the University elders, who, while recognising a brilliant ability to challenge current conceptual ideas, felt he frequently overstepped the mark in his relations with his peers. On the occasions that he had been summoned to the Dean's office for a 'dressing down', leading to suspension or possible expulsion, an incoming phone call always ended the proceedings, allowing Blanco to leave with a 'flea in his ear' as the only action taken against him. The calls always came from Professor Michaels, head of the Dermatology Department and a distinguished Nobel Laureate in the field of Genetics and Pathogen research. Ever since he had received a message from his old friend Royston, he had taken a more than a passing interest in the progress of the twins, as the time would soon approach when their days of grooming would be over and the last chapter in the development of Chameleon and that of Tentacle would be ready to be enacted. On the same campus, less than a mile away from the classically styled buildings in which Blanco studied and resided, was the Octagon Medical Research Centre. Standing six floors tall and set within grounds of five acres, it gently rose from the lush manicured lawns and shrubbery that bordered a small tranquil mirrored lake at its rear. The shady tree-lined paths that criss-crossed each other within the shadow of the gold windows exuded a feint jasmine fragrance that lingered lightly on the passer-by in the afternoon breeze. To the casual observer, the building looked like so many others designed for the twenty first century; clean cut lines and able to adapt itself to multiple uses. A closer inspection would reveal large air ventilation shafts concealed by deep bushes, located at nearby strategic points and on the island in the centre of the lake. A private service road complete with a guardhouse, cameras and electric gates ran from the main highway two miles away, disappearing into the dark bowels of the building's massive underground storage facilities. To all intents and purposes the structure was a research faculty within the establishment to which students attended their daily classes totally unaware of the secret production facilities several floors beneath their feet. To reinforce the subterfuge, students checked in daily at the reception desk under the floral Harvard seal embossed with the six letters of the University's motto; '*VERITAS*', meaning 'truth'. Of the occasional scholars that used the external glass lifts, no-one had ever asked what lay at the subterranean level indicated by 'B' and only accessible by a special override key. A double locked wooden vestibule marked 'storeroom' led down from the end of the bright entrance foyer to a set of hidden stairs that descended three gloomy levels and halted at a large, steel door flanked by a luminous green bio-card reader.

At the end of their second year, Professor Michaels and Professor Wilson, (the Chair of Law and Politics), asked the twins to attend one evening for an informal meeting at the Octagon. Professor Michaels stressed to both of them. 'Please do not tell anyone about this meeting. You will see first hand how Tentacle is developing Chameleon.'

The weather for that July evening in 2011 was warm and clear. The boys arrived, as agreed, by separate routes lest they draw undue attention to themselves. Not that they could avoid the still curious, but nowadays less frantic, attention of the media. Time and other people had made the front pages in the years that they had moved from Harlem to Cambridge, Massachusetts, but they still attracted the odd looks and consequently kept a low profile especially when together. Blanco arrived at seven, ten minutes before Negro and a full half hour before the agreed meeting time. His dress code reflected his attitude. Rolling Stone tee-shirt, stone-washed blue jeans, supported by a pair of black leather Chelsea boots gave him an air of complete arrogance and indifference. Negro, by contrast, was the typical undergraduate. His face was the one that would appear in all the collegiate magazines, generating a mixture of admiration and jealousy. Sporting a Harvard crimson blazer, white pressed slacks, crisp linen shirt and white boating shoes with socks to match, he epitomised the

Harvard man through and through. Separately one could envisage different parents and dissimilar cultures for each boy, but that is where the differences stopped and the deep bonding of self-protection for one another and their family began. Anyone who studied maths would know that one and one equals two, except in binary code where one and one equals nought. The same was true for the twins. They cancelled out their weaknesses and became stronger than two separate people when challenged together. This was visibly evident when they met in the shade of the blossoming Weeping Willow by the lake on that cool summer evening. They hugged each other cautiously now as men, yet embraced firmly with the passion of brothers. The tone of their skin did not divide them. On the contrary it made them as one. Whole.

At seven thirty they stepped through the large glass revolving door and into the chilled, lifeless reception area. The black and white mosaic floor gleamed back at them through the thin layer of watery suds drying quickly from the janitor's mop. The vestibule was vacant except for a cleaner, her head almost level with the grey marble coffee table she was enthusiastically polishing. She heard them move behind her, looked up and nonchalantly continued her back-breaking task. Seating themselves comfortably on a leather couch well away from her polishes and soft yellow dusters, they each picked up a glossy magazine from the fan shaped piles carefully displayed before them on an ultra low glass coffee table. Blanco flicked aimlessly through a hundred pages of glossy pictures of supercars stopping now and then at a vehicle that briefly caught his eye. He smiled at his brother's choice of Newsweek and watched him carefully as he absorbed every detail of the article as if his life depended on it. Blanco reflected deeply and smiled to himself.

'Just like Negro. The more detail, the better.'

'Good evening Blanco and Negro' came the soft voice of Professor Michaels. 'It was good of you to come' he smiled standing a pace ahead of them. His tall, bean-pole frame, dressed immaculately in a classically hand-made tailored suit gave him an air of superiority and breeding that would be expected from one of Boston's oldest families. Behind him stood a highly nervous Professor Wilson, attempting to fill the bowl of his old, yet large colonial clay pipe with brown Virginia tobacco. Strands of the 'backy' fell onto the floor, a point not missed by the cleaner. She tutted her disapproval and with hands on hips, threw him a contemptuous look. Timidly, he bent down and scooped up the offending weed, placing it carefully into the large poacher's pocket of his Scottish Harris Tweed sports jacket complete with matching 'plus fours' and hiking boots. Unlike his counterpart he epitomised the nihilistic side of the campus; untidy, disorganised and radical. Yet he was no fool having gained a First at Oxford at age thirteen and a Professorship on his sixteenth birthday. More plaudits followed with the highest Mensa score since Einstein and a special Nobel Prize for Peace and humanity following the Pan African Wars of 2010.

'Let's go quickly' Professor Michaels said smiling at his peer 'before the redoubtable Mrs Jensen has my friend washing the dishes!'

Leading the way, they followed him into the lift where he inserted a red necked key into the illuminated slot, turned it and pressed the large green 'B' on the panel. Then silently and almost imperceptibility the transparent wraparound doors gently closed, dimming the internal lighting by fifty per cent and transporting them on a slow, silent descent through the illuminated lift shaft. Within a matter of seconds the air-conditioned capsule tardily came to a halt. The doors silently opened and Professor Michaels stepped out, followed by his party into a white, brightly lit cube-shaped room with an area of some thirty feet. There was no sound or furniture, save for a bubbling tropical fish tank filled with a myriad of exotic sea life in one corner and two unblinking CCTV cameras watching them from above a secure doorway to their left. Again Professor Michaels stepped forward and ran a swipe card through a concealed wall reader near the door. With a hiss, the double doors opened and the party entered into what appeared to be a laboratory filled with long, waist-high test benches supporting a mass of physics equipment. Along one wall, ten one-metre diameter spinning dishes mixed a cocktail of chemicals together while a mini-computer absorbed the digital information and transmitted it via an encrypted link to an orbiting satellite two hundred miles above the Earth. A tall man with ginger hair and a freckled face greeted the quartet, requesting they all follow him down a long brightly lit corridor to a doorway on the left, marked 'Theatre'.

'Gentlemen. My name is Doctor David Snowball' he said, standing aside to allow the four men to pass him. 'Please take a seat. The other guests are already here' he said indicating the open doorway.

They entered the compact auditorium from the rear, under a raised projection booth and proceeded down a short, inclined gangway with plush, red velvet executive chairs on both sides of the aisle. Negro counted twenty seats of which only four were occupied by a group, one of whom he believed he had seen somewhere before. They sat alongside the current incumbents, with Blanco adjacent to a beefy looking General, his chest smothered in a sea of campaign medals.

Addressing the General's group, the Doctor introduced the newcomers while moving behind them and placing his hand on their respective shoulders as he announced their names.

'This is Professor Michaels, Professor Wilson, Negro Hamilton and his twin brother, Blanco.'

A silent, but convivial greeting came from the General and his small team.

'If I may, General?' the Doctor asked, requesting permission to return the compliments.

'Go ahead, Doc. Let's get on with it' he aggressively replied. 'We haven't got all day!'

'Calm yourself, General' extorted the little bespectacled man sitting three seats away. 'All good things come to those who wait.'

The General pulled his tunic top sharply down and huffed loudly in a stifled annoyance.

The Doctor had now moved along to the General's team and stood behind the uniformed man before moving to his right along the wide row of upturned seats.

'This is General Weaver, Mr Joe Williams, Mr Dick James and last but not least, a man I am sure you all know from his outspoken political reputation, Senator Eagle, the Vice President of the United States of America.'

Negro leaned forward past his brother and cast an eye along the aisle at the man he had recognised but could not place when they walked in.

'My God!' he whispered in Blanco's ear. 'Did you see who that is?' he exclaimed in total surprise.

'Yes Negro. I saw him. Now calm down and keep quiet!' he whispered back.

'Can I have your attention and then we can move swiftly on' the Doctor said, now standing facing them beneath a large screen at the front of the cinema.

The disgruntled military man impatiently twisted and turned in his seat.

The host looked down thoughtfully, coughed into his open palm and lifting his head a smidgen, ran his eyes across the eight men before him. 'Now that the introductions have been made' he continued 'I intend to bring you all up to speed on where Chameleon and Tentacle are in the greater scheme of things. As you know some years ago, Professor Lang, a brilliant genetic scientist with his team developed a formula that at a stroke would eliminate all forms of Cancer from this world, in addition to clearing up all types of skin blemishes and scars whether created by accident or natural causes. He had also experimented with a second formula, but when the results were not as he anticipated, he closed that area down and concentrated on the first. The research into this had taken him many years and although the United

Kingdom government had granted him a budget, it was not nearly enough to cover all his needs. Luckily a group of successful entrepreneurs had heard about this project and feeling that it had merits that could benefit the underprivileged of the world, decided to fund all further development from their own deep pockets. As the trials continued and targets were met and exceeded, the group, those who called themselves Chameleon, requested certain governments to take the capsules and distribute them to their populations for free. Unfortunately, the response in all cases was that the costs of distribution would be too high and since there would be no immediate return, it was not commercially acceptable. To make matters worse, these same leaders expanded their arms deals and while creating vast trappings of wealth for themselves, left the majority of their peoples' economically impoverished. In many countries, tens of thousands have been killed by government sanctioned militias or have just starved to death. The West and the East have all rung their hands in pretentious despair while making heart-wrenching speeches layered with platitudes. In short, gentlemen, nobody cares about the downtrodden masses and certainly no-one is willing to bring down these despot leaders. That is everyone except Tentacle. We were formed out of the ashes of the Chameleon project. I mentioned that Professor Lang had shelved a second version of Chameleon because he felt that the research was not progressing as he had anticipated. We managed to obtain the research notes into this formula and have now re-engineered it into two formats. The blue version has a limited mutation life of seven days and then the tissue, after healing, would revert back to its original condition. Our black version also heals in the same way, but the reversal process does not take place, leaving the infected person with a permanent aberration. It is our intention to infect the leaders of these troubled countries and overthrow the respective governments with the help of the local military as the chaos sets in. General Weaver has his connections and will utilize all means at his disposal to effect the changes. Correct General?'

'You bet. Just let me at them. Let's rip their throats out!' he said clenching his fists tightly and punching the air.

The Doctor continued, not fazed by the General's rhetoric. He knew him too well. 'We will be in possession of both types globally and, depending on what influence our political friends have in getting these leaders to acquiesce to our demands, will we know what action to take. Our main targets are the leaders and their cohorts. By isolating them we can infect them with type 'black', making it much easier to effect a revolution on a top down basis than the other way round. But if needs be, we will infect the populous with type 'blue' and shake the system from the bottom up. Either way, we will be able to radically improve the lives of millions. Our friend here,' he motioned to the Senator 'will assist in all matters political and legal.'

The politician took the statement to be rhetorical and looking around at the other seven, briefly nodded his concurrence.

'And now Blanco and Negro' he addressed the two undergraduates. 'You are probably wondering where you fit into all of this? We at Tentacle wish you to be our eyes and ears in the respective Headquarters of the United Nations and the Olympic Games. As freshman graduates, it is very easy to position you within those establishments considered the norm for students that wish to advance their careers. Further, for you two particularly, it will be a natural move to have you placed within these bodies, if only for the fact that you both excel in politics and sport and have developed your own high-profile connections. You will find that both of these organisations are composed of gregarious extroverts who will leak information willingly without you even having to prod. We need to know the location of our 'targets' at any given moment and therefore we have provided mentors in both organisations who will assist you at all times. Although your academic finals don't take place officially until May 2012, we want you in position well before that. The Olympic Games in London opens on 27th July and we must be in a position to act before then. Therefore, we have arranged for you both to sit a special final in three weeks time. In order for you to pass first time, both of the esteemed Professors here tonight will personally coach you. If there are any questions, I would ask you to hold them until you have viewed the following film originally made by Professor Lang.'

Doctor Snowball raised his hand to the hidden projectionists and sat alone as the film started. It was the same one to be viewed many months later by Chekhov in The Radisson SA Slavyanskaya Hotel in Moscow.

After ten minutes, the film finished and the lights slowly came up. Apart from the Doctor who had seen the film before, the rest all squirmed uncomfortably in their seats trying to regain whatever composure they had left after viewing appalling scenes of disease-ridden, unsanitary conditions.

'Sir' the General addressed the Doctor. 'I am a military man and have over thirty years of battle hardened experience behind me. I have served in many conflicts and also in humanitarian relief zones. I honestly thought that I was aware of most of the global problems that the human race faced until now, but I was wrong. After viewing this' he pointed at the now blank screen 'I am even more convinced that what we propose is morally right. It's about time that someone took affirmative action. We can't leave it any longer to the UN and wishy-washy talking shops. People are suffering now and we must take the bull by the horns and kick some ass as soon as possible.' He looked across the aisle at the others and was offered no objections.

Standing in front of the group for the second time, the Doctor addressed them again.

'Thanks General. I know that was very difficult to express your emotions, but you could only have done that if the film showed in absolute detail the wretched conditions that others are having to endure every minute of their waking day.' The Doctor paused then walked slowly up the incline between the two sets of seats. 'Gentlemen. If there are no questions then I propose that you all join me in some light refreshments.'

A silence of acceptance followed. On route he covertly listened to their chatter regarding the upcoming operation, as the final pieces of this long-planned jigsaw started to fall into place. A small muscle located just to the left of his mouth began to twitch nervously. Its effect was cumulative and within seconds a nervous smile began to spread across his lips.

The weeks rolled by and the twins, as expected, sailed through their finals, both achieving Firsts. Because of the extra curricular nature of their studies, it was not possible for them to receive the customary scrolls dressed in gowns and mortar boards from the Dean in front of their peers. Martha and Jethro however were invited to a small informal presentation in the Dean's office where pleasantries were exchanged regarding their education to date and the upcoming placements. Though they were sworn to secrecy, it was decided not to give out any further detailed information to the two boys, lest they accidently let slip what the real nature of the operation was. Only time would reveal to them the true effect of what Tentacle threatened and would carry out. It was as Professor Michaels said later 'a strictly need to know basis only.'

UN

September found Blanco on neutral soil. To be precise, even though he was standing in the open grounds of the Headquarters of the United Nations between East 42nd and 48th Streets, overlooking Franklin D Roosevelt Drive and the cold, but fast flowing, East River, the skyscrapers of New York City dominated his peripheral vision. Ahead of him there stood the thin, glass-curtained slab of the Secretariat, the sweeping curve of the General Assembly Building, whose chambers can accommodate more than 191 national delegations and the low rise Conference Wing, which connects the other two structures. The vast Library sitting alone and adjacent to the main conurbation, attempted to mirror it's namesake in ancient Alexandria, and formed the last piece of this gigantic Lego kit. Since he wasn't due to meet his mentor, Senator McGarvey, until the next day, he decided that he would take the one hour guided tour to familiarise himself with this leviathan of an organisation. As the guide led the group of flag-waving and camera-carrying visitors which he had attached himself to through the dull, lifeless corridors, he very quickly came to the conclusion that the organisation, like the tour, shuffled at a snail's pace; weighed down with asphyxiating regulations and a massive lack of funds. When they entered the General Assembly, where over many years, too many sanctimonious leaders had stood at the dais pledging peace and harmony while simultaneously carrying out mass slaughter and discord to their own peoples and those of their neighbours, did it suddenly bring home to him how important his mission was. No sooner had it begun than the tour finished, leaving him with the other brain-dead tourists in the basement of the General Assembly Building, littered with a few soulless shops selling nick-knacks from around the world, a post office and an irritating excuse of a restaurant serving overpriced, bland and so-called 'international' food. The only saving grace to the eighteen acre East River site was in its beautiful, flower rich gardens, complete with contemporary and oversized pieces of art including, he noticed, a twelve foot high 1880's revolver with its muzzle twisted into a tight knot, symbolizing the organisation's declared aim of peace and unity.

Just after one, he was feeling a bit peckish and remembered reading about lunch being available in the Delegates dining room. Although it was necessary to reserve a place at least one day beforehand in order to secure a seat, he felt that he could try on the off-chance that he might get in anyway. As he approached the security control in the queue behind a mixed grouping of officials from Nigeria and Malaysia, a uniformed police officer wearing the distinctive logo of the United Nations Police Force asked him to leave the line where he stood and escorted him past the surprised diplomats into the dining area, where Senator McGarvey stood waiting for him.

'Hello Blanco' he beamed, holding out his hand in greeting. 'I bet you didn't think that we would be meeting until tomorrow?'

Taking the Senator's hand the young graduate from Harlem smiled back.

'You're right Senator. You've got me there. How did you know I was here? After all I didn't let you know I was coming here today.'

The Statesman, ignoring the question, withdrew his hand and without a word led the way to a secluded window seat overlooking the river and bid Blanco to sit opposite him.

'Good day Senator' smiled Russell the head waiter, arriving out of nowhere and now hovering over the party of two. 'The usual for you? Your guest?' he turned to Blanco.

'Actually Russell this is by way of a small celebration. Mr Hamilton here is joining our team in the Assembly and will be dining here from time to time. Today though, I think a bottle of your best Rothschild by way of a celebration would be in order.' He winked at his newest protégé.

Blanco nodded his acquiescence and smiled back, waiting for Russell to leave them.

'Senator' Blanco leaned forward whispering to his mentor 'how did you know I was here?' he asked for a second time. Sitting comfortably back into the crushed leather chair, the elder man stared out over the grey river towards U Thant Island and the west bank of Queens.

'You know, Mr Hamilton. I didn't know, but I anticipated and I was right, wasn't I?' he smiled back.

'Amazing' declared Blanco 'I don't know what to say, but what made you predict my attendance?'

'Patterns. Mr Hamilton. Patterns. Grand Masters in Chess evaluate their opponent's move even before it's made. Everyone reacts in the same way to certain triggers. You are no different. All I had to do was set the bait and wait until you nibbled, which you did, didn't you?' he smirked.

'Alright. You've got me there. It seems I've got a lot to learn.'

'And not a lot of time to do it all in' responded the Senator conspiratorially.

'Touché' Blanco added.

The wine came, followed by a main course of Lamb Shank with all the trimmings. Only after the coffee, did they briefly and quietly discuss Blanco's schedule for the next day with no mention of Tentacle or Chameleon.

'Just be in my office by eight. We start early here' the Senator quietly added 'but please remember, this place has more multi-lingual eavesdropping facilities than a watering-can has holes.'

That evening Blanco relaxed in his up market apartment with a Chinese take-away and a bottle of Jacob's Creek 'Three Vines' for company. He watched an on-demand movie and climbed into bed by nine, setting his alarm for six the next morning. The night was uneventful and he slept well, rising before the alarm at five thirty for a jog around the neighbourhood. By six he was shaved and re-energized by the multiple shower jets strategically placed around the large, blue, wet-room. Breakfast consisted of a banana washed down with a tall glass of ice-cold Tropicana Pure Orange. Wearing a simple, but elegant, grey mohair two-piece suit and matching silk tie, he stepped into the lift and descended to the basement car park where, after dropping the roof of his Porsche 911, he sped out, tyres squealing into the early morning sun of the 'Big Apple'. The journey from the 'Village', where he now lived, would in rush hour take almost an hour, but leaving at this time meant that he could cut across Manhattan and be with the Senator in less than thirty minutes flat. In actual fact, because he had hit the road just ahead of the 'early' morning traffic he was standing outside the Senator's office at seven thirty. The big security guard greeted him with a courteous smile and opened the ante room for him to repose together with a spread of that morning's newspapers. When the Senator arrived at quarter to eight, he was impressed to see this young, gifted man at ease and calmly waiting for him. 'Come in' he requested to Blanco and led the way into his plush, air-conditioned office overlooking the luxuriant green lawns one floor beneath his bay windows. 'Breakfast?' asked the Senator, sitting facing Blanco, across a magnificent oak desk.

'No. Thank you Sir. I've already had mine earlier. Fresh orange and a banana.'

'Good choice, but I need my coffee. Black, decaffeinated and strong.'

Almost as he finished, his secretary knocked and entered holding a fine china cup and saucer, the aroma of hot steaming coffee wafting into the air ahead of her.

'Wonderful, Michelle.' He looked at Blanco. 'Are you sure you won't partake?' he asked in his broad Texas accent.

'No. Thank you Sir' he repeated again, sitting opposite from the politician.

The Senator sipped the black brew and shut his eyes inhaling the aroma.

After Michelle left, closing the door behind her, the older man leant forward. 'I understand you wish to know the movements of these people?' He passed a thick envelope containing several sheets of paper across the desk to the Harvard man who picked it up, withdrew the contents and ran his eyes over the typewritten details and accompanying photos. Blanco looked up and deferentially smiled at his host who leaned even closer and strongly emphasised his next words. 'You have just over ten months until the start of the Games. Get to know *everything* about these characters well before then. Take heed. All of them are meticulously careful and will know if someone's tailing them in any way. That means every type of communication including physical contact. If they scratch their asses, I want you to know which side and how hard. I'll be checking in with you from time to time. Your cover here is my aide which means you'll have clearance at the highest level, making it natural for you to be circulating around them all. If you have *any* problems call me on this number day or night. It's a secure line. Liaise with your brother. You're both going to London.'

With that, the Senator rose and walked his new aide over to the door.

'Till we meet again' he whispered before opening the double doors to the outer office and letting his protégé go.

INTERNATIONAL OLYMPIC HQ

At six thirty Sandra nudged Negro awake in his bed. He stirred and gradually opened his eyes, conscious of the background drone and dimmed lighting around him. After stretching his limbs and stifling a yawn with his hand, he smiled at her and electronically raised his bed upright to the seating position.

'Good morning, Sir. Can I get you some tea or coffee? Breakfast will be served at seven and we are due to land in Geneva at eight thirty.'

'Tea please' he replied, looking around at the Business section, completely full with all thirty seats occupied. Around him other travellers were also waking and starting to re-align their seats to an upright position following the uneventful and placid ten hour flight aboard this BA 747 en-route from JFK the night before. Leaning down, he picked up his complimentary personal refreshment kit from the bedside pocket and waited till Sandra returned.

'Could you show me where my suit bag is hanging?' he asked amiably.

'Please wait here Sir. I'll get it for you' and she was back with the zipped carrier before he had time to realize she was even gone.

'Thank you' he smiled, his mixed Harlem and Harvard accent causing her to tilt her head slightly, trying to pin the dialect down.

'Boston?' she enquired, her soft English West Country accent just faintly discernable against the hum of the four large jet engines.

'Close' he countered. 'Massachusetts actually.'

She shot him an admiring glance.

'Clever as well as good looking' she coyly whispered, knowing that he was referring to the USA's oldest seat of learning.

'Yes Maam. If you say so' he smiled, taking the bag and heading to one of the four washrooms.

Within fifteen minutes he had freshened up and changed into a blue fitted shirt, sand coloured two piece suit with no tie and matching shoes. He had no sooner returned the suit bag to the locker and resumed his seat, than breakfast arrived, accompanied by an immigration card for completion before they landed. In the space 'purpose of visit', he entered 'US Olympic Committee' and for 'period of stay' he wrote 'one month'. He was sure that his low profile and confidential manner would not prove a problem, since Tentacle via the US Olympic Secretariat had cleared all barriers for his entry into the country. As far as he was concerned he was invisible to any enquiring mind and could therefore pass through the eye of a needle unnoticed. That was except for the nondescript black man sitting two seats behind him who had surreptitiously noted his every move since arriving at JFK in a yellow cab behind Negro's chauffeur driven limousine the evening before. Had Negro been aware of the man the chances of recognising him would have been one in a million, even though the two of them had initially grown up in the same area some twenty years earlier, their paths momentarily crossing and then dividing as the years rolled on with Leroy eventually holding a highly classified post within the US Secret Service. In any case there would be no reason for Negro, or for that matter Blanco, to remember him, except for the fact that they had purchased three iced teas from his grandfather's cold delivery tricycle one hot summer's day when they were still innocent and unassuming kids.

As the plane banked easily to starboard above the French border and entered Swiss airspace, lining up for the glide path into Geneva airport some three miles to the north of the city, the cold but formidable mountains of the Jura and Alps rose up menacingly on either side to greet the Jumbo, being the fifteenth inbound flight of the day. To Negro it was his first time in Europe and, although this was essentially a business trip, he was determined to absorb as much of the culture as he could during his stay. From the comfort of his window seat, he watched the aerofoil adjust its dynamic positioning as the aircraft gently slowed and descended past the south-western tip of Lake Geneva landing ten minutes early at eight twenty.

'Good morning ladies and gentlemen. This is the Captain. We hope you all had a good flight and on behalf of the entire crew welcome you to Geneva. The time is eight twenty local time and the weather is bright, dry and cloudless with a forecast of eighty by midday. We look forward to you flying with us again.'

As the plane came to a halt and the doors opened Negro rose from his seat, collected his holdall and accessed the airport's moving walkways. Although glitzy and strategically straddling the French and Swiss frontiers the terminals were small, messy and disorganised, with multiple and lengthy checks from the two countries immigration and security services. For the visiting tourists flooding in to experience sailing on Lake Geneva known as the 'blue lung' of the city, the queues and rugby scrums for their baggage was chaotic. Even the regular travellers who were visiting this, the grandest of Switzerland's most famous cities for other reasons, especially watch-making and exclusive banking, had to wait irritatingly in line for their luggage as the carousel hiccupped and ground to a dead stop. Negro, however, was met at Swiss immigration by a UN official who had had his bags cleared under the diplomatic seal and without any challenge, was waved through the exit channel to the official Mercedes saloon waiting for him outside the arrivals hall. A few steps behind him strode Leroy, who with no baggage except his large shoulder holdall, took the first available cab on the rank, requesting the driver with a crisp one hundred dollar note and in his best French to closely follow the Mercedes. The two vehicles quickly gained the A1 motorway and keeping the Swiss side of Lake Geneva to their right, headed north-east towards Lausanne some forty five miles distant along the shoreline. Because the heavy tourist traffic was the normal feature of this fast moving road, it gave Leroy the opportunity to instruct the driver to drop a couple of cars back and mingle with the other taxis and commercial traffic moving at high speed around them. In the back seat of each respective car both Harlem men sat back, seat belts on and relaxed, Negro opting to doze while Leroy scanned the landscape keeping his eyes firmly fixed on the black Mercedes ahead. After fifteen minutes he picked out the signs for the coastal city of Nyon, which was only accessed via the Nationalstrasse highway running to his right, sandwiched between the blue, but rugged shoreline and the Autostrada that was even now taking him mile by mile closer to Lausanne.

'We'll be in the city in the next few minutes, Mr Hamilton' announced the beefy Swiss chauffeur, easing the two ton car gently across three lanes of slowing traffic and onto the exit slip lane that led into the outskirts of this vibrant yet cosmopolitan city.

As the car entered the corkscrew streets, Negro became acutely aware of the steep inclines on which the city is built and the precarious way that it's buildings overlooked the shores of the lake below.

'I'll take you to your hotel first and then collect you later, at three, for a brief meeting at the HQ of the International Olympic Committee' added the driver, looking at Negro in his rear view mirror.

'Thanks. I could do with some sleep' he replied, looking up at the cold blue eyes staring back at him.

After a few hair-raising turns down the narrow, twisting, lanes of the lakeside village of Ouchy, the car pulled up smoothly outside the elegant belle époque buildings of the Beau-Rivage Palace, having a reputation for being one of Europe's favourite hotel's since it's inauguration in 1861. An elegantly uniformed head porter and two accompanying concierge staff greeted Negro as he stepped out of the rear door being held open by his chauffeur. Within a minute, he had been whisked inside, his bags already on their way to his executive suite in the neo-baroque styled Palace Wing commanding breathtaking views across the lake to the magnificent French Alps beyond. Before resting, he stepped outside onto his lakeside balcony and watched a slow moving, single funnelled, white paddle steamer elegantly dock at the quay to his right, its triumphant siren announcing to the assembled travellers the end of a two hour trip from Geneva. Six floors below and still seated in the taxi, Leroy watched the Harvard man turn and disappear from sight, the curtains being drawn behind him. He noted the metered clock and paid the driver with an additional tip, while waiting patiently for a receipt.

'Even the State Department needs to keep its expenses in order' he remembered his boss stressing, 'otherwise it will come out of your pocket' and that, even on his well paid salary, he didn't want.   Entering the hotel lobby, he requested a room on the sixth floor overlooking the lake, but was advised that they had all been taken, except for one that faced inland overlooking the manicured lawns and vast floral parklands of this regal hotel.

'American Express?' he asked producing the rarely seen black card.

'No problem Sir. How long do you intend to stay?'

'Unknown at this time. Just keep it open for me.' With that, he took back the swiped card, accessed his room and made a call from his secure mobile to the President's personal line at the White House before setting his alarm for two that afternoon.

The gentle knock on Negro's door at first went unanswered, but a second and more urgent rat-a-tat-tat had him up and peering through the convex eyepiece in the door, the stretched and distended image of a man's nose and face filling the frame.

'Yes?' he asked, his face pressing up against the dark, heavy, panelled wood surface.

'It's Jonathan. Your chauffeur. I know I'm a bit early, but I did try calling you on the internal phone. It appears to be off the hook.'

Negro turned and viewed the bedside table, where as stated, the receiver was disengaged, it's trailing handset spread out on the floor by the flex, like a hot, coiled rattlesnake about to strike. He rubbed his eyes and focussed onto his watch. Two thirty.

'I'll be out shortly. Just wait for me downstairs.'

He cursed deeply at being woken so abruptly, but accepted that he would have had to been awake within another fifteen minutes anyway. Stretching as he walked over to the bathroom, he scratched at a small irritation on his arm, washed and then changed into formal clothes. By ten to three he was in the rear seat of the Mercedes heading west along the Avenue de Rhodanie. The traffic at this hour was still light and Jonathan was able to turn off early onto the Route de Vidy which led to the IOC Headquarters well before the large Rond Point de la Maladiere round-about less than a mile up the highway. A couple of minutes later he slowed the car to a halt outside the stunning Chateau de Vidy, flying the symbolic five ring Olympic flag on a tall white mast on the front lawn ahead of the main entrance. For a moment Negro held his breath in total awe, originally believing that he would be visiting some glass monstrosity, but instead was presented with this beautiful chocolate-box of a mansion. He emerged from the car and looked around at this icon of sporting elitism and still wondered how he could help effect the global revolution that Tentacle was planning. Everything here seemed so perfect, so good. Wherever the problems of the world were, they certainly were not here.

'Mr Hamilton?' came the voice from behind him.

Negro spun round and was confronted by a small chubby man dressed in a two-piece Prince of Wales check suit, brown shiny leather shoes, shirt and cravatte to match. He carried a gold-topped walking stick and stood, legs apart, in a semi-defiant manner on the top step of a set of four, looking downwards at the American.

'I am' the Harvard man replied stepping upwards and extending his hand.

'Claude Bell' the smaller man said diplomatically shaking Negro's palm. 'I was told to expect you by our mutual friends. Please follow me. We don't have much time and for God's sake keep your voice down.' The two men strode across the black and white chequered marble lobby and into a small, lavishly furnished Prussian parlour room. At the far end of this narrow room, religious shafts of light streamed in via an ornate set of tall windows set within a pair of Napoleonic double doors leading out to a blooming rose garden. Claude quietly closed the door behind him and walked across to an antique bureau.

'Drink?' he said, lowering the front of the cabinet, revealing a classic dispensary of vintage drinks in ornate crystal decanters.

'I'll have a Southern Comfort thanks' the Harvard man said, seating himself in one of the four wooden carver chairs loosely spaced around a tiny ball and claw footed table.

Claude poured himself a brandy and carried both glasses across, placing them firmly on drink mats in front of each man. Sitting down opposite his guest, he raised his glass.

'Salute!' he exclaimed loudly. 'To our success!'

'Cheers' retorted Negro, closing his eyes and relishing the potent liqueur as it ran easily across his tongue, hitting the back of his throat in almost one divine movement. By the time his eyelids had re-opened, Claude had poured another brandy.

'Chaser?' the small man asked, his cheeks now turning a rosy red.

'Thanks, but no thanks. One is enough for me' he politely answered. 'If we can get down to business, I would be obliged.'

'Of course' Claude confided quietly, his lips savouring the Martell.

'Let me first tell you that in order to hit our targets, we must have them all in one place, so it is crucial that you make sure that everyone that we have listed is in London for the Olympics.' He leaned forward and lowered his voice to almost a whisper. 'We tried to get the heads of all the Olympic committees to join us, but we were not successful. It doesn't mean that they are against what we are planning, but they cannot and will not get involved at any level into political activity in any way, even though they all unofficially sympathise with our aims. There are, however, several members who *are* with us and will actively do whatever it takes to achieve the overthrows in their respective countries. Let me also say that no details have been passed to *any* of these Olympic people, save just getting their views on global corruption. This, therefore, will keep our plans limited to people like you and me, our other field operatives globally and our London agents in particular. This capsule' he held up a black plastic pellet, 'is our primary weapon.' He flicked open the cap of his walking stick and inserted it into a narrow tube running its entire length. 'Just in case' he smiled wistfully, gently closing the gold top. 'When we have these bastards in our sights we will infect them. You will not need to actively get involved. Our London team will do the work. Your job specifically will be to arrange that all persons on the list inside are travelling.' The IOC man handed over a sealed envelope, similar, but not exact, to the one that Blanco was given by the Senator at the UN. 'Just make sure they're all on their flights. Some of the *targets* will be travelling with their respective Olympic teams, but most will arrive only a day or so in advance of the opening ceremony. We've made sure, through our London contacts, that they will all be staying in the same hotel in the Docklands. When you arrive you will be contacted. All you do then is update them and get the hell out of there. Your travel and accommodation details are also included with an unlimited Visa card and five thousand dollars cash for incidentals that you may need. You'll meet the rest of the team when you arrive. That's it. Have you any questions?'

Negro sat back heavily into his chair and exhaled deeply. He put his hand to his mouth and thought intensely. 'What's the timetable? How much time do I have?'

'The Olympics begin in just less than eight weeks, but remember that the teams will be travelling well before then, anything up to two weeks in advance. So that means you have effectively just under six weeks to get to know all the details of every one on the list, although your *research* over the last few months should have brought you up to speed. We have it on good authority that various governments have got wind of what we are planning and are putting their best operatives in to try and thwart us. So be on your guard and trust no one except those that you've already had contact with.'

Negro looked across at this little portly man, who increasingly looked like a comic caricature of Dickens's Mr

Pickwick. He wondered why he was involved and what he hoped to get out of this increasingly dangerous operation.

As if able to read his mind, Claude opened his little round mouth and gave Negro his answer. 'Brain tumour. I'm dying of this little bastard in here' he banged his head angrily, 'but my Government won't help me. I've been on the waiting list for years, but they'd rather spend my taxes on themselves and their fat corrupt cronies. By the time I get the treatment, I'll be dead. So you see, I've got nothing to lose and therefore I can go down knowing that I will take these shits with me as the people will finish them off. I've got nothing to live for. Most of my friends are dead or badly injured from the violence meted out by the so-called 'security police' back home and more importantly to me, my wife and close companion of thirty years, also passed on recently due to lack of medicine that could have saved her from a contagious infection. I put the blame firmly on my Government and its leaders and I'll do everything I can to bring them down.'

Negro looked bomb-shelled by this revelation and sat back trying to absorb what Claude had just imparted to him. 'Can I ask' he asked sympathetically, 'what country do you come from?'

'That's for me to know and I'm not telling you or anyone else, lest any of my friends who are still living there are put at risk. Let's just say' he chose his words carefully, 'it's on the South American Continent.' His body language reflected his words and he briefly looked drained and exhausted. But that was fleeting and with a swift movement of his hand he recovered his composure again and brightened up. 'Just make sure you get them all' he implored Negro. 'Just get them all' he echoed again, this time stressing each word with an unrestrained passion, his lips forming every consonant. He looked out through the garden doors and momentarily appeared mesmerised by the calm and beauty outside. 'Before you go, I'll show you around' he said rising from his seat, gulping the last drops of the five star liquid down his throat.

Negro rose and followed him out to the lobby area where, after forty five minutes, he had experienced what only the most privileged and selected international politicians were ever to have knowledge of. His tour over, he exited the building closely followed by Claude, shaking hands on the steps before disappearing into the dark and cocoon-like security of the waiting car. With the drink now starting to soften his resolve, he decided that he had had enough stimulation for one day and asked Jonathan to drop him back at the hotel, where, after securing the envelope in the room safe, he slept easily until eight. It was still light when he rose, the ambient air temperature just tipping seventy when he strolled out alone for dinner to a nearby local restaurant, returning to his suite at ten thirty for a deep, but meaningful sleep.

Again unknown by the pro-tem Olympic man, all his movements had been watched and monitored by Leroy who had trailed him at a distance from the safety of a mundane Ford Mondeo that he had hired for an unspecified period from the local Hertz dealership. With the aid of a specially equipped zoom camera, he was able to film and record Negro's initial meeting with the small man known as Claude and track his movements via the invisible gossamer micro-transponder brushed under the American's skin by Sandra when she gently poked him awake earlier that morning on the plane. Knowing the value of this intelligence, he sent an encrypted flash message direct to the White House that evening after dining in an adjacent restaurant to where his 'target' sat alone enjoying a traditional French meal of Onion soup, Lobster and Apple Pie.

The next day broke bright and fresh and found Negro out jogging early at six thirty along the tree-lined waterside promenades of Quai de Belgique and Quai d'Ouchy. The only traffic he encountered that morning, apart from the council cleansing vehicles, were a smattering of dedicated hip inline skaters, practising their wheeling and fanciful turns on the deserted pavements next to the city's stunning lakeside Olympic Museum. Above him the early morning gulls shrieked and dived around the paddle steamers, raising smoke since their trips the night before. On the shore the near silent electric milk floats stopped by the early opened restaurants and café's along the medieval heart of the city with it's twisting lanes, quaint squares and cobbled roads located around the Place de la Palud, Switzerland's greatest Gothic monument. By seven thirty he was in the shower, his clothes strewn across the floor like a man in a hurry. He dressed casually for breakfast in a cotton shirt, trousers and a pair of white casual shoes, then left his room with the sign 'DO NOT DISTURB' prominently displayed for the attending staff. At the far end of the quiet corridor, the lift doors opened and he stepped alone inside the mirror-walled vehicle, leaning casually against one of the cushioned support rails that ran around the interior. As he pressed 'G' and the doors started to close accompanied by the sound of The Electric Light orchestra, an arm followed by a shoulder jammed themselves between the rubber door stops with the cry of 'hold that lift'.

Negro instinctively reached across to the controls depressing an illuminated green arrow, allowing the trapped man to enter the opening doorway, his clothes and persona slightly ruffled, but otherwise intact. For the second time he hit 'G' and the doors silently slid shut, followed by a gentle vertical movement downwards.

'Are you ok?' he asked of the now freed man.

'Yes thanks. I nearly lost my wallet' the intruder joked, tapping his inside jacket pocket, while noting a slight, but almost invisible blemish on Negro's lower arm in the reflection of one of the surrounding mirrors. 'Thanks again' he repeated as the lift slowly came to a halt on the ground floor. 'No problem' replied the Harvard man as he smartly exited the lift, heading to the dining room and a traditionally served full English breakfast.

Brushing himself down, Leroy stepped gingerly out between two waiting passengers and with just a cursory glance watched his recent lift companion take his seat on a single table by a large bay window overlooking the lawns.

For the next three weeks, Negro kept his own counsel, having most of his meals except his breakfasts in his room and utilising the laptop that came as standard with the suite. When he did go out, it was for short periods and at varying times to visit the Cathedral and its tower from where the traditional evening call of the hour was made by the night-watchman whenever dusk fell. To any bystander observing him, he was just a tourist with a camera, climbing up the dark and narrow lanes, pausing quietly by the squat medieval chateau at the peak of the old town. Casually, he leaned against the old, cold stonework and gently eased his hand into a crevice behind it. His every move was closely monitored by Leroy and Sandra *on extended leave* from the airline. They both knew this was a regular 'dead letter drop' and she made sure that his every move was captured through her telephoto night-lens and relayed within minutes back to their respective handlers in London and Washington. Although they could not see the documentation that he had collected, they were pretty sure of the gist of the material and its significance to the overall operation that they had been tasked to identify and stop. It had occurred to Leroy to call in a specialist safe-breaking team but his handlers overruled him on the grounds that they needed to kill the entire global operation in one move and the risk of a counter-surveillance bug being activated and alerting Tentacle was too dangerous to contemplate. They did, however, arrange for a 'Tiger in the Tank' or linear amplifier to be delivered the next day in order to improve their listening facilities, although, with hindsight, this piece of hardware would not be utilised as this latest pick up was to be Negro's last since he had identified all of his 'targets' and their planned movements.

His instructions were to depart for London the next day and make contact with the other operatives already there and flying in from across the globe. The brisk walk back to his suite that evening took him ten minutes from where he booked the midday Swissair flight from Geneva to London City Airport for the next day. He sent a brief text to Jonathan requesting that he collect him at nine am and then proceeded to shred any incriminating documents that he could not safely take with him. By seven the next morning he was packed, leaving his cases and a fifty dollar tip with the bell captain while he read a copy of Newsweek over a continental breakfast at the same table he had used for the past twenty one days.

His movements had not gone unnoticed to Langley and their British *cousins* in London, of which Leroy and Sandra respectively were an integral and very important part. On learning of his imminent departure and his flight details, Sandra contacted her London team and arranged for a British agent to 'watch' him when he arrived, while they followed an hour later on the next available aircraft.

Again, the same as three weeks earlier, Negro was ushered past the queues, but this time escorted directly to the well hidden VIP suite on the upper floor and then onto the plane where he took a window seat in the Business

Class section.

NANDI

The name Nandi in Zulu translates into 'sweet' and at six feet tall, weighing just over ten stone, this strikingly pretty Zulu girl epitomised that name in every aspect. At just twenty eight she was one of the most intelligent girls in South Africa, with an IQ that put her in the top 1% of the population. She breezed past the Kwa-Zulu Natal M.E.N.S.A. test with flying colours at age eight and was declared by the national press as a genius, only second to that of Einstein. Her uncanny ability to predict and react quickly to any given threat opened the door for an attachment to the South African Army Intelligence at an incredibly early age of eighteen, followed by one of the few coveted security positions within the Parliament of the African Union located in Midrand, South Africa. This body, founded in 2002 from the now discredited and dying embers of the Organisation of African Unity, consists of 265 members representing 53 African states with a combined population of over one billion. It has a remit to promote pan-African democracy that would act as a salvation for millions of it's long suffering citizens from starvation, diseases and genocide brought about in no short measure by a number of portly, be-medalled and ageing dictators.

Sitting strategically on the banks of the Jukskei River and midway between Johannesburg and Pretoria, Midrand is the Rainbow Nation's most rapidly developing city and Africa's fastest developing financial centre with a booming population expected to reach twenty million by 2015. Despite the rapid commercial growth since it's humble beginning in the 1880's as a halfway point and resting stop for horse drawn traffic between these two cities, Midrand has never lost touch with it's farming roots, and horse power here literally means just that. Coming herself from the fertile peaks and deep valleys of the traditional Zulu heartland of KwaZulu-Natal, Nandi lived and breathed the politics of her traditional community, topped with a generous sprinkling of ANC politics formulated by Nelson Mandela. Her parents, both of whom came from the royal line of Zulu Kings, recognised in her an inherent ability to absorb, digest and relate ideas and concepts far in advance of her peers. She won prize after prize at school, which led to other parents complaining to the governors' that she was somehow cheating, although after many investigations all the charges were unceremoniously dropped as no irregularities could be found. All the same, she and her parents had a bitter taste in their mouths and it was felt better, especially for Nandi, that she moved to another school. This was easier said than done, as places for top schools needed large amounts of cash raised and then to be constantly maintained. Her father, always with his eye on the future, had already decided to back his only child and called a tribal meeting in uMgungundlovu, the capital of the Zulu King Dingane. Within the boundaries of this recreated Zulu city and flanked by the dark mass of the Drakensburg Mountains that loomed menacingly on the horizon, forty elders gave their word to back Nandi financially until she attained her twenty first birthday. Their combined hopes were that she could be the Moses of their time and lead them out of the yoke of economic and political enslavement into a brighter and more hopeful twenty first century. There were no arguments and no dissention among them. Such was the Zulu code. Unfortunately, the ever spiralling costs of private education regardless of the 'honour payments' made by the tribal leaders were not enough to cover the fees. Her parents, desperate to solve the approaching crisis, retired sullenly to their rondavel shaped homestead to discuss the problem. At thirty feet in circumference and fifteen feet at its apex, the large semi-circular entrance to their thatched beehive hut ceremoniously displayed the mounted heads of three large Wildebeest. On the broad approach flanking this ingress, stood two ten foot piles of hewn rocks, held together in a corset of twine and rough raffia matting, each topped off with a massively heavy boulder. The craftsmen who constructed this, the largest of the tribal homes, would not be out of place with their skill-sets in the deep countryside of Olde England with its own rustic cottages, thatched roofs and fast running babbling streams. Inside, in the shade of the pitched roof and shielded against the hot rays of the midday sun, her proud but concerned parents, both wearing matching blue faded denim shirts and shorts, leaned against the cool straw walls while stretching their tired and sun-kissed limbs out on the bleached wooden seating that ran around the inside of the tribal homestead. 'It's becoming a nightmare' said Vusi looking at his wife. 'How are we going to continue her education? The fees keep going up and we cannot keep turning to the elders. It doesn't seem fair. She's sixteen now and to maintain this level of expenditure would bankrupt everyone. I don't know what to do' he looked and sounded desperate at Nomsa, his wife of twenty years.

Having fought the white racists in the streets of Soweto and cheated death many times, nothing scared him normally, but this was a conflict that he was genuinely afraid of. Understanding strategy was second nature to him, but only if you knew your enemy and could identify it. How do you challenge economics? Who is the enemy? The deep furrowed lines on his weather-beaten face seemed more pronounced and his head ached with the increasing stress that this was causing. His spine tingled and he momentarily shuddered. A thin film of sweat formed on his temples, dripping down and across his broad, but bushy white sideburns that sharply contrasted with his large mane of matted black hair. Using his palm, he wiped away the residue and looked downwards, feeling ashamed at his inability to support his daughter in this, her hour of need.

'Think of *my* name' she smiled at him. 'Think what it *really* means' she pulled him to her and held him, rocking his entire body like a baby. It soothed him and comforted his being.

'I don't understand' he mumbled, his face pressing gently onto her generous breasts.

'Think' she repeated again. 'What does my name translate to?'

'Well' he looked up at her 'your name means the caring one, with faith' he whispered tenderly in her ear.

'Yes' she smiled, pushing him gently backwards and looking downwards into his dark brown eyes. 'Faith! Have faith Vusi! Something good will happen. You must believe!'

He looked up at this wonderful woman who had been his partner, his friend, his rock for longer than he could remember and smiled. Easing himself off the seating he pulled her down with him onto the raffia matting that covered the base of the hut. For a few minutes they lay silently, on their backs, side by side, hand in hand staring at the concave roofing above them. Slowly their eyes succumbed to the lazy warmth of the day and this, combined with the distant bleating of a goat tethered near a gurgling stream down a nearby valley, mechanically pulled down their eyelids and put them into a state of bliss. Outside in the full glare of the noon sun, a group of chickens ran squawking from a tall teenager, axe in hand seeking the family dinner. With feathers flying in all directions he managed to grab a large bird by its legs and casually walked away, the bird complaining vociferously as it viewed for the last time from an inverted position the Kraal with its many tethered oxen and snorting horses. From above the eye line of a small upright fence he menacingly raised his arm and propelled the razor sharp axe downwards upon the poll-axed bird, cleaving its head from its still decapitated, but post-life trembling body. A few blood stained feathers wafted into the hut on the light breeze that emanated from the upper mountain slopes some five hundred feet above the village. As if in synchronised diving, the blood-splattered, multicoloured plumage twisted gently through the air, silently settling next to Vusi's relaxed, but inert body. Then, out of nowhere, a green Two Horned Chameleon scampered in across the dusty floor from the bright daylight and settled into the cool and shade of the rotunda shaped hut. For a brief moment it disappeared under the circular seating, leaving a tongs-like claw impression on the sandy floor of its fusing of five toes into one group of two and another of three. Within seconds it reappeared high on the sloping wall, its two 360 degree eyes rotating and focussing simultaneously in stereoscopic vision on a large locust less than its own body distance away. Suddenly, with a speed of thirty thousandths of a second, a sticky, bulbous tongue flew out, sucking the unsuspecting prey back into its crushing jaws, to be consumed almost in one action. Satisfied that this large 'kill' had set it up for the day, the Chameleon relaxed and this, with the reduction in light exposure and ambient temperature, triggered a cell change in the melanin of its pigmentation. Within seconds its entire body had mutated from the original grass green to a softer brown allowing it to blend into the background of the flaxen walls and virtually disappear.

The same could not be said of the next visitor. Standing tall and sharply silhouetted with the sun at his back against the frame of the open archway, this giant of a man looked inwards and downwards at the two sleeping forms ahead and before him. He smiled as Nomsa's right arm snaked itself tenderly across Vusi's flat belly and gently eased her head onto him, sighing deeply. He in turn responded with his left leg snaking itself over her narrow waist, softly coming to rest on her right buttock. High above them the Chameleon suddenly moved, startled by a pin point beam of reflected light from a large medallion that hung from an ornate gold chain around the visitor's neck. The rapid scampering of the lizard down the walls and across the sandy floor caused both sleepers to stir from their slumber, slowly becoming aware of a stranger's presence within the hut. Easing themselves from the floor, they gently rubbed their eyes attempting to focus on the intruder.

'Who's there? Identify yourself' said Vusi, holding his arm up to shield off the glowing halo that surrounded the visitor, giving him an ethereal presence.

With a bit more imagination, one could almost believe that a heavenly angel was staring in on them. The visitor though, was very mortal and had no obvious celestial features, as Nomsa discovered when rising to her feet and squinting her eyes, she approached the figure and held her hand out in greeting.

'Nomsa' she stated her name in a positive and friendly way. Because of her cautious nature her statement had just a hint of menace in it, so minute to be almost imperceptible, but it was there all the same.

Vusi now stood erect and slightly ahead of his wife. His large Zulu body rippling with bulging biceps and weather beaten skin made Nomsa look disproportionately small in the sullen shadows. The black iris of his large round eyes surrounded by tired bloodshot corneas looked steadfastly across at the stranger.   'Greetings!' he said, stepping forward, hand outstretched to join that of his wife awaiting a response.

For a split second no-one moved. Then the stranger smiled, his ultra-white teeth radiating brightly against his contrasted darkened face. He leaned forward and with both hands took hold of the offered palms and gripped them firmly.

'My name is Luuz. Emmanuel Luuz and I come in peace. What I have to say is for your ears only.' He leaned towards them cautiously, while lowering his voice to a whisper. Still holding their hands in his powerful grip he turned and suspiciously peered over his broad shoulder into the bright sundrenched farmyard beyond the hut's shaded entrance. Satisfied that they could not be overheard, he turned to them and released their hands. 'Can we talk?' he asked gently.

Intrigued, but suspicious, they stood aside and offered a place to him on the dry timber seating that ran around the inner skin. As he made himself comfortable, they saw that he was shaved bald and dressed in a flowing white cotton robe similar to that worn by traditional Arab traders. On his feet he wore soft open-toed leather sandals, mounted with a large ornate metal clasp to one side. Although his dress was simple, it made a powerful statement about his personality. He struck them immediately as a man among men, a man after one's own heart. In short he came across as reliable and more important, trustworthy. It would seem strange to an outsider that Vusi and Nomsa could have summed up this stranger so quickly and be so comfortable with him so soon. However, they had an advantage that no other outsider could have. It was the medallion. They had both seen it almost immediately and understood its significance and no-one, unless they were totally stupid or very tired of life, would have been brazen enough to wear that fabulous trinket without being aware of the consequences of doing so. They sat either side of him, Nomsa dwarfed by him to his left, while Vusi matching Emmanuel pound for pound sat upright and proud to his right.

'Is Nandi nearby?' Emmanuel asked, peering into the shadows of the deepest recesses of the large hut.

'No' Nomsa quickly responded. 'She's staying later in school today. Her final exams are approaching and she wants to finish top.' She blushed with pride, knowing that unless one of the other students who were also very bright suddenly had an 'Einstein moment' her daughter would automatically gain the top spot regardless of competition. Yet, Nomsa was also humble and had been taught and passed on to Nandi the principles of humility coupled with a deep compassion for others less fortunate than herself. This, while admirable in its intent, also brought additional problems for the M.E.N.S.A. girl, as further awards created more jealousy. In essence she was making a rod for her own back and try as she may, she was digging herself deeper day by day into an unenviable position.

Hearing in her voice this uncomfortable pride, and sensing her exasperation with the curt hypocritical comments from certain quarters, Emmanuel sensitively broached the subject he had come to discuss.

'It's about Nandi' he said, looking from side to side at each of them. 'Don't worry. Nothing's happened to her. She's fine. This visit. This talk with you both is about her future and also ours.''As you are both fully aware' Emmanuel added 'Nandi is an exceptional student. Her grasp of almost any subject matter is far beyond the attainment of any of her peers. But it is just not academically that she excels. She is a natural sportswoman. I could envisage her at the Olympics. Her sporting and outdoor activities and survival skills are so good that experienced military personnel with several years' know-how are hard pushed to keep up with her. This, added to her ability to pick up any foreign language in a very short amount of time, is one of the reasons that I am here today.' He turned his head from side to side, trying to gauge their reactions to his opening remarks, but they gave nothing away. Their body language and facial expressions revealed nothing. He continued. 'We in the Zulu nation and *all* the peoples of South Africa are *very* proud of your daughter's achievements to date and would like to see her excel beyond even your wildest dreams. Some amongst the people I represent have suggested that she may have the ability in the future to lead politically here and possibly on the world stage. We have been monitoring her progress to date and are well aware of the financial hardships that you find yourselves under.'

At this point, he discerned an embarrassed movement from Nomsa, but diplomatically ignored it.

'We want to help Nandi get to the top and we realise that your finances can only stretch so far. So, we are willing to step in and help to give her every chance to succeed. We will take over the necessary finances and you will owe us nothing. Just think' he pressed the point 'you will be giving her the chance of a lifetime. Isn't that what you want? A great opportunity for your only daughter and for her to be happy in something she can excel at?'

Again he turned to both of them, but this time their composure had changed. Their faces now seemed to sparkle and seemed vibrant, alert.

Vusi, taking advantage of this natural break, rose and stretched his limbs. He had a habit of clicking his fingers and toes and he wasn't going to stop the habit of a lifetime even for this man who seemed to amazingly have delivered all the family's Christmas presents several month's early.

'What's the catch?' asked Vusi towering over his guest. 'I mean, you walk in here and make all our dreams come true. You make it appear that we have won the lottery. Why? What's in it for you? You keep mentioning 'we'. Who is 'we'? And another thing. If you know our financial circumstances, you will also know that the Zulu Chiefs who you appear to represent are not made of money. Their finances, although promised, are not finite.'

Nomsa, sitting quietly next to Emmanuel, perceptibly nodded her head in concurrence. Emmanuel looked up at Vusi and to his right at Nomsa.

'You're right and you're also wrong. If you give me a minute I will lay to rest all your concerns.'

He waited for Vusi to sit again.

'First of all I am not here representing the Chiefs that you mentioned, but a global organisation called Tentacle. It is true that the Chiefs are with us, but only because we also wish to see the Zulus great again within a vibrant South Africa. Tentacle are sponsoring gifted individuals around the world, more often than not from poor and impoverished backgrounds to be nurtured and consummate in an array of sophisticated skills that would one day put them in a position to take power in their own countries and if necessary overthrow the sitting incumbents. Finally, if I was in your shoes I would be very suspicious of accepting everything that I have just imparted to you, except for two things.' He paused. 'One. Please ask the opinions of all the tribal leaders. If they reject my proposal then you will have nothing further to do except inform the authorities, who I am sure will not treat me too well. Planning to legitimately or otherwise usurp a sitting Government is not an action to be taken lightly. If, however, you find that I have been honest with you and then call me, I will explain in detail what to do next.' He paused. 'Two. I noticed that you both saw the medallion. It conveys great responsibility on the individual to be morally upright and unpretentious at all times. Your families and mine are linked. I would not lie to you or give you false hope. I would rather wish you well and send you on your way. For your further information, the development of selected individuals will continue regardless of what your decision is. I would rather you are with us than not. If you do decide to come on board, then I promise you, it will be the best decision that you have ever made for yourself and your daughter.' Emmanuel lowered his head, took a breath and stood up.

He extended his hand first to Vusi and then to Nomsa, gripping their palms both warmly and firmly. 'Call me!' Emmanuel said. 'Make it soon!' Lowering his large frame, he silently ducked down under the archway from where he had appeared some fifteen minutes before and was gone.

For a moment they both stood quietly, staring at the empty space that he had just occupied and that was now devoid of his presence. Nomsa stepped forward into the bright archway of the early afternoon sun and after a few seconds regained her focus, sharply distorted by the dark shadows of their hut.

'You see' he said, now standing close behind her, 'you told me your name meant something wonderful. Well here it is. If this is not divine providence, I don't know what is.'

'I agree' she said turning to him and smiling. 'But you know there is one other strange thing that I have just noticed. Can you see it?'

He looked around, trying to focus on what her eyes had picked up.

'I can't see anything' he questioned, trying to pinpoint what she could obviously see. 'No, Nomsa. I don't see anything. What is it?'

'Exactly' she empathised. 'You can't see it. It's not there!'

'What woman? What's not there?' he said, now slightly irritated.

'His footprints!' she stressed. 'He has left no footprints!'

They both stared at the dusty ground which Emmanuel had just occupied and as Nomsa had said, there was not an indentation nor any pressure mark to indicate that the big man had ever stood before them. In his place, however, she saw a card and bent down to pick it up. It was unusual in that it bore a picture of a Tentacle on it and a phone number.

That evening, after consulting Nandi and the Chiefs, they called the number.

Situated within the most exclusive private nature reserve in the Cape and nestling high on the magnificent cliffs overlooking the Indian Ocean, sits the exclusive sun-swathed residence of Plettenberg Park, it's breathtakingly beautiful and rugged coastline, displaying jaw-dropping panoramic vistas of Blue Whales frolicking against the background of an oversized sun, slowly dipping its bulbous mass into the all embracing sea. It was here in his private suite that the big man waited. It had been three weeks since Vusi's call. The get-together was arranged for midday, leaving enough time for the family to travel in the early morning, crossing the low veld in their old Toyota 4x4 to Ulundi airport and then onwards, catching the two hour flight to the coastal city of Port Elizabeth. Their tickets had been prearranged, as was the chauffeur, standing, sign in hand by the arrivals gate. He recognised them at once, not by sight, but by grouping. Theirs was the only family off the plane. In addition, they were the only black travellers, the rest being a mixture of Afrikaner's, Indians and Germans.

'Have a good flight?' the coloured chauffeur asked, touching his grey flat cap which matched the liveried double breasted suit complimented by a traditional blue shirt and tie. It was a rhetorical question. He led them outside to a small, modern car park, filled with an assortment of rental cars covertly disguised as everyday residential vehicles, in order to pre-empt any car-jack attempts that were the norm on any unsuspecting tourists. From his pocket he aimed a black key fob at a large grey Mercedes, complete with all-round darkened windows. The car 'cheeped' back at him using a high pitched whistle and then flaunted itself to the other stationary cars with a dazzling visual light display. Opening one of the rear doors he stood aside allowing the family to enter. He proficiently shut it behind them and strolled round to the front, settling comfortably in his own seat. Depressing a switch on the dash, a glass divider between him and his passengers silently descended, disappearing into a thin leather crevice. He looked round over his shoulder at them. 'The journey's going to take about an hour. If you need to call me, just pick up the phone on the wall. Help yourselves to anything you want. There's a bar ahead of you with soft drinks and sandwiches. To operate the TV, just press the green button. Oh, by the way, my name is Fabrice.' Flicking the switch again he raised the soundproof panel, slipped the automatic gear into drive and effortlessly moved past the vertical security barrier onto the slip road leading to the N2 coastal highway.

In the back, Nandi was in her element. Although she had never been in a plane or chauffeur-driven car before, it felt right. In fact, she was so excited by the experience that she could not wait to tell her classmates, especially Tabatha, her best friend and closest ally. The two of them had first met at the M.E.N.S.A. tests when eight and had kept in touch ever since, meeting when they could, the last time being in March when Nandi stayed the weekend at Tabatha's parent's luxurious mansion in Christmas Rock, ten miles south-west of East London on the Eastern Cape. Their way of life was in stark contrast to Nandi's lifestyle of living off the land, but Tabatha's parents did not treat her any differently to their own daughter. She had her own room with bathroom en-suite, a television and the full use of anything in the house she wanted including the cool, blue, lined pool which she had to be levered from when they all went out to dinner in town. Years before apartheid was abolished, it would have been impossible for the girls to sit together at a restaurant, never mind attend the same school. But times had brought changes and although racial groups still tended to band together, it was not unusual for younger South Africans of the 'Rainbow Nation' to mix more than their parents had done. In this regard, Tabatha's parents shared these views and tried to implement them at a family level. Nandi had become over the years not just a friend of their daughter's, but a true family member, unconditionally accepted and never judged by the colour of her skin. In any event, she could now brag to her best friend of the day's adventure and feel that for once she could go 'one up' in the lifestyle stakes. A sudden braking brought her back to the present as Fabrice applied the brakes to avoid running into a bright yellow Jeep Wrangler that had come to a sudden stop in the inside lane ahead of them.

'Sorry about that folks' he announced via the intercom. 'Just sit tight while I see what's going on.' He stepped out of his door and stood behind it, always suspicious of any unusual traffic incident that could so easily turn into an armed robbery or worse. Satisfied that it was only a tyre burst, he carefully manoeuvred the Mercedes into the outside lane and accelerated past the four-wheeler, leaving the three white teenage youths to curse their luck as they sought the jack and spare tyre. 'They'll be alright' he laughed. 'Nothing that a bit of elbow grease won't fix!'

In the back, Vusi's head was now drooping onto Nomsa's shoulder, his eyes fighting to keep awake.

'It's the flight' she whispered to Nandi. 'He was so scared, he almost broke my hand in two when we took off. Once we were up, he was ok, but on descending he joined 'the white knuckle brigade' and is now trying to relax again.' She looked lovingly at him and confided in her daughter.

'This is the man who scaled a vertical cliff as a dare just to get me to agree to marry him. He is totally fearless, but on a plane ride. Well. He was petrified.' She smiled and thought 'What a baby!' She pulled his head down gently to her and stroked his curly locks. He sighed and visibly relaxed.

Nandi looked lovingly at this perfect couple and secretly hoped that her future partner would have the same attributes. Solid, loving, but she hoped, like a bottle of fine wine, able to travel well. The gentle swaying of the car on the wide highway also had the same hypnotic effect on Nandi and very soon, despite her best efforts to stay awake and absorb as much of this day as possible, she too succumbed to the power of sleep, her head lolling forward onto her chest, the seat belt being the only restraint holding her upright. Time seems to drift when you are asleep and, as the sun climbed majestically towards it's zenith at twelve, Fabrice softly announced via the intercom they were about fifteen minutes away from their destination.

'In about ten minutes though, if you folks look to your left, you will see the perimeter of Tsitsikamma National Park, with its dense forest full of 800 year old Yellowwood trees towering to over 150 feet. But before we even get there, we are about to cross the Bloukrans Bridge, claimed to be the world's highest bungee jump. If you look this time to your right you will see some of the stupid idiots who climb over the wall and walk along the maintenance support arm underneath the road. There's a spot on the other side where you can film the morons who choose to leave mother Earth and pitch down to the rock strewn gorge on an elastic band. You wouldn't catch my black arse anywhere near that son of a bitch. No, Sir. Not me! I've got no intention of going to the big savannah in the sky just yet!'

Nandi looked on in awe as brightly clad individuals, some with mini-backpacks on and carrying nylon ropes clambered over the parapet and disappeared from view.

Nomsa caught her attention. 'If you think that we would ever let you do something that crazy' she nodded to the bridge 'then young lady, you have sorely misjudged us.

Never in a million years would your father or I agree for you to risk your life on something that stupid.'

'Yes, Mum. I know. I was only looking.'

'Alright then, look only, but don't let me catch you anywhere near that type of thing. Risking your life for a reason I can understand. But on a whim, Nandi, please don't disappoint us.'

But it was too late. The seed had been sown, and Nandi had already made her mind up. With or without her parents consent, she was going off that bridge soon.

'Hold on folks' Fabrice announced. 'It's going to get a bit rough for a few minutes.'

They left the coast road peeling down a rocky track littered with small boulders and patchy scrubland on either side. The vehicle unceremoniously trundled along, dodging potholes and discharging fine particles of dusty stones that layered the roof and doors like an explosive shrapnel burst. With a thunderous crunching of tyres against earth, Fabrice brought them to a halt outside a pair of green metal, six foot high gates, lethally spiked with sharp stainless steel barbs.

'You all stay here' he announced, although from his tone it was taken as a direct order and they heeded his advice.

They watched him approach the intercom, while a lonely CCTV camera stared menacingly downwards from its lofty perch on one of the large white topped pillars that supported the gates. The walls that formed the perimeter of the grounds were also white and, like the pillars, were over six feet tall. But unlike the gates, these walls were glistening with lines of razor wire, enough to make the hardiest of intruders think twice before attempting a break-in.

'Yes?' inquired the clipped, but metallic sounding accent.

'Fabrice. I've brought Mr Luuz's guests, Vusi, Nomsa and their daughter, Nandi.'

'Please wait' he was ordered.

Pirouetting on his right heel, Fabrice paced towards the car, the camera swivelling and tracking his every move.

'Won't be long' he assured them. 'Their security is very tight. Nelson Mandela, Richard Branson and the King and Queen of Norway have been guests here in the past' he added.

Suddenly, the metallic staccato voice announced 'proceed' followed in quick succession by a deep buzz and then a gentle 'click' of the automatic gate locking system. Fabrice stepped back into the driver's seat, closed the door and slowly rolled the car through the ever-widening gap as the huge gates opened their arms inwards in a half-hearted welcoming gesture. Inside the grounds the same dusty road appeared, but this time at a slight gradient, revealing what seemed from a distance to be a collection of small white caravans abutting each other. As they drew nearer, the caravans evolved into a collection of single storey and split level buildings, overlooking a calm lake shore of an inland wild duck sanctuary. Fabrice expertly brought the car to a serene halt outside the main reception area where uniformed staff were already unloading the cases from the boot before the family had even exited. A smiling manager stepped out to greet them, cold soft drinks in hand.

'Welcome. I hope you had a good journey. If you will follow me, I will show you to your rooms.'

The sudden contrast from the shade of the limousine to the relentless glare of the sun and then finally the shade again of the luxurious reception area with full air-conditioning was a bit too much for Nomsa to take and she stumbled, almost fainting by a large tropical fish tank. Vusi caught her before she fell and eased her with the staff's assistance onto a large green sofa. The concerned manager stepped away and within a minute was back with a glass of iced water and some hot tea.

'Which would you prefer?' he worriedly asked, leaning over Vusi's shoulder.

'Tea please' she whispered.

'I think you should sit up' said the manager.

'He's right' reinforced Vusi.

She sat up slowly, Vusi easing the tea to her lips. She sipped the liquid and closed her eyes.

'I'm sorry to cause you all this trouble' she apologised to the manager.

'Please madam. Think nothing of it. Would you require a doctor?'

'No, thank you. Just give me some time sitting here and I'll be alright.'

Within minutes the colour started returning to her cheeks and shortly after that she was well enough to be escorted by Vusi and the manager to their suite. The heavy curtains were drawn shut and in the gloom, without undressing, she slipped her shoes off and climbed into the King-sized Sleigh bed, pulling the soft duck-down quilt close around her neck.

'Go. Let me sleep' she insisted, closing her eyes and pulling her legs upwards into a foetal position.

Vusi leaned over and softly placed a gentle kiss on her forehead.

Quietly stepping backwards, he silently opened his suitcase deposited on a low table in the corner by the window, withdrawing a fresh linen shirt, trousers and soft leather shoes. He changed after freshening up in the en-suite bathroom and emerged some five minutes later, tip-toeing out of the suite, gritting his teeth in the corridor as the locking mechanism appeared to amplify the sound of the door shutting. Noting the time on his chunky Elephant watch, he turned left towards the reception area looking for Nandi. The deep velvet carpet underfoot was like walking on air to this man whose natural flooring was either the dusty base of a cave or rough reed matting within the traditional Kraal huts.

He had not gone more than ten paces, when from his left Nandi appeared from an open doorway.

'How's Mum?' she anxiously asked, stepping back inside, Vusi following.

'Fine. She's suffering from an acute change of temperature. We're not used that. It's something her body has to acclimatise to. She needs sleep. In a few hours she'll be alright. In the meantime, show me your room.'

Looking around he saw she had the same size bed that they had, with matching side tables complete with elegant table-lamps and four enormous pillows bulging from a traditional wooden bed head. A large wicker chair sat sedately on the cool marble floor by the full length open veranda door, while a soft backed chequered recliner casually faced a simple table by a wall complete with a selection of some light refreshments and a large overbearing plant in a simple pot. On the ceiling in the centre of the room hung a large motionless fan, it's outsized white blades unnecessary at this time of day due to the air-conditioning.

'Isn't it nice Dad?' she squealed with delight. 'Just look at this!' and she opened a sliding door revealing a massive built-in wardrobe in which her clothes were already hanging. He looked at her beaming, happy face and knew that even if he wanted to, he could not take all this away from her. He was her Daddy and all Daddies look after their little girls and God help anyone that stood in his way in giving her what she deserved.

'Dad. Come outside.'

She pulled him over to the patio doors where they stepped out to a lazy blue pool, surrounded by immaculate lawns, gracious wooden sun loungers and large colourful umbrellas.

'I want to swim now!' she begged him, her large, pleading eyes almost melting his heart.

He bit his lip and considered.

'Nandi. We are here to meet this man who, with his organisation, will change your life forever. Do this for me. Let us see him first and after you can swim. Hopefully your Mother will be better by the time we finish and she can join us later.'

She looked down and forlorn, but knowing that her parents were going out of their way for her, she relented.

'Alright Dad. I agree. Let's see the man first. I'll do whatever you think best.'

Arm in arm they stepped back into her suite and, after she shut the patio door, the two of them headed off to the reception to meet Emmanuel Luuz. They sat relaxed in the refreshingly simple, high ceilinged architecture of the exclusive entrance area with an elongated natural skylight running above them. The airy, understated, Afro-Colonial décor of natural materials in neutral earthy tones and crisp whites gave an unrushed, timeless feel and Vusi in particular felt unexpectedly at ease.

'Mr Vusi?' the receptionist asked, standing in front of him.

For a moment he didn't respond, the name not triggering any meaning. He looked up quizzically at this pretty slip of a white girl, her short pure blonde hair bobbing slightly at every movement of her head.

'My name *is* Vusi' he replied looking up at her. 'That's my first name. The family name is Nongoma.'

'I see' she said, checking her list and confirming that she was addressing the right person. 'Do you have an appointment with Mr Luuz?' she enquired politely.

'Yes. That's right. Is anything wrong?' he sounded concerned.

'Oh no sir. He heard that your wife was not well and thought that it would be better that you all stayed overnight and he will meet you in his suite tomorrow after breakfast. I hope that will be alright? You don't have to worry about costs. Everything is paid for. He asked that if you need anything, please charge it to him via the desk.' She stood, awaiting his answer and raised her eyebrows expectantly.

'Yes, of course. That would be fine. Will we see him for dinner?'

'Unfortunately not sir. Mr Luuz is a, what can I say, a very private man and has all his meals in his suite. The dining room is over there.' She pointed to a small dining area with what appeared to be ten, at most, circular tables seating a maximum of four apiece. 'Breakfast is also served there.

Dinner tonight is at eight with breakfast from seven. Would your wife require her dinner later? We can keep it hot for her?'

'Thank you. I'll let you know later, if that's alright?'

'No problem, sir. Just pick up the phone. We're here for you.'

'She's nice' said Nandi. 'A bit like Tabatha, but older. I think she's about twenty five. Wouldn't you agree Dad?'

'Yes' he replied, suddenly realising that he had never met Tabatha, his only judgement being on the receptionist.

'Let's go!' he said, suddenly standing up.

'Where are we going?' she asked, getting up to join him.

'Well, since your mother is sleeping and we are not now due to meet Mr Luuz till tomorrow, I think that we should both take advantage of this opportunity and go for a swim.'

'Oh. Dad!' she smiled and reached up to him, pulling his head down while affectionately kissing him on the cheek.

They spent the next few hours in and out of the water, frolicking like children who have discovered a secret pool that might suddenly disappear and were therefore going to make the most of their good fortune.

At around four, while Vusi dozed by the pool, Nandi, attired in a slinky black one piece swimsuit that enhanced all her growing curves, pulled on a large white towelling robe and strolled off to the outside wooden stairway leading to the wide veranda and sea facing Jacuzzi. The bubbling tub, surrounded on three sides by soft glowing candles and large enough to accommodate six comfortably, was vacant. She gingerly dipped her large right toe into the water and, finding the temperature agreeable, lowered herself from the decking, through the open sliding glass partition, into the foaming liquid. Closing her eyes, she stretched out, letting her legs float ahead of her and gently leant back onto a sculptured neck headrest, enjoying the pulsating jets against her young, firm muscles. It seemed that she was drifting on a cloud such was the tranquil state of mind that now caressed and enveloped her body. So when she heard a strange voice calling her, she quickly tensed and unintentionally slipped under the water taking down a mouthful of liquid.

'Do you mind if I step in?' the voice asked, but by this time she was submerged and completely disoriented.

She surfaced to find a well built, handsome, white man looking down at her in a very concerned way.

'I hope you're all right. I thought you were in deep trouble and I was just about to jump in and save you.'

'Thank you, but I'm alright' she said standing up, the water cascading off her. 'I was just slightly startled by your voice. I lost control of my flotation technique.'

'Your what?' he laughed, kneeling down on the decking so that his head was nearly at the same height as her erect stance in the water.

'My flotation technique' she stressed indignantly, all the time thinking who the hell this man was. '*Everyone* knows about flotation' she stated, teasingly. 'Don't *you*?' she taunted him.

'Sorry, but the only flotation that I know about is to do with my boats and I let the crews deal with that.'

She looked at him and for a minute couldn't work out if he was serious or a complete bull-shitter. She plumped for the latter and hauled herself out, lest she say something that she might regret.

'You're not going already?' he goaded her, as she slipped her towelling robe on and sauntered away back to the pool.

'Loser!' she thought. 'What a pretentious lying bastard! I hope I never have to meet him again. Even so' she reflected, 'for a white guy, he wasn't bad looking' and casually turned to see him slipping into the tub in his trim, blue shorts.

When she got back her father had gone, leaving a note on his sun lounger that her mother was awake and feeling better. They'd both see her for dinner at eight. It was now six thirty and with the heat of the day rapidly making way for the cool of the evening, the light started to fade fast and very soon a blanket of darkness that pervaded this part of the world fell upon the hotel, revealing its own charm, soft lights and calming music. Like most women, Nandi wanted to make an 'entrance' that would have others turning their heads. It followed, therefore, that after stepping back into her suite, she closed the blinds, turned the lights down low and undressed to a soft jazz CD supplied as part of a musical collection by the hotel. She ran a bath, pouring a soft coconut herbal essence into the oversized tub and lit the half dozen chunky candles in their deep holders, strategically placed for maximum effect. Away from the bathroom, she twirled in front of a full length, wall mounted mirror, admiring her sleek curves and pert, firm breasts.

'Not bad' she uttered, turning this way and that to try and establish her better side. 'No difference' she thought. 'I'm good all over!'

With that, she meandered over to the soft, warm, therapeutic water and gently sank her lithe sun-kissed body into the perfumed bath. After emerging, she thoroughly washed her hair and when fully dried, sat in front of the large dressing room mirror to add the make-up and perfumes that came by way as a compliment of the hotel. When the phone rang, it was her mother, advising her to dress correctly for dinner and not wishing to offend, Nandi chose a simple, blue, knee length silk dress that Tabatha had bought for her a few months previously as a birthday present. With matching shoes, also down to her friend, she radiated poise and style.

At five to eight, she stepped out of her suite into the cool, but softly lit corridor and made her way to the dining room. Her parents were already there, talking to the maître d', who showed them all to an exclusive table for three, situated by a tall white lattice frame, complimented by a view of the blue floodlit pool that she had spent much of the afternoon in with her father. The silence in the dining area was accentuated by the fact that only three other tables were occupied and this, combined with the almost noiseless approach of the waiting staff, appeared to make every sound amplify ten fold. The food, wine and company was excellent and it would have stayed that way, but for the unwanted approach to the table of the man Nandi had dismissed earlier as a charlatan.

'Excuse me' he stood over them addressing her parents. 'I heard that you' he addressed Nomsa, 'were taken poorly this afternoon. I was sorry that you went under the weather and presume that you are better now? I had the privilege earlier today of bumping into your daughter' he looked at Nandi 'and I just wanted to wish you well and hope the rest of your time here goes smoothly.'

'Well, thank you, sir' said Vusi rising from his seat 'for enquiring about my wife. She, as you can see, is better now. It was probably a combination of sun and travel. Won't you join us?' He indicated a spare seat next to him.

Nandi prayed that he would say no and for once her prayers were answered.

'I'm sorry' he responded 'but I have to take an urgent phone call from the States. Business you know. I try to get away, but somehow they find me. You know how it is.'

'Of course' said Vusi shaking hands. 'We'll see you tomorrow then' he added, as the man turned and disappeared out to the corridor.

'You can count on it!' he called back.

'What a pleasant man' said Nomsa. 'Fancy just coming over to wish me well. A complete stranger at that!'

'Amen' said Vusi, 'except that he's not a stranger to you, Nandi. You didn't mention him to us. Where did you meet him?'

She shook her head in boredom. 'Oh. When you were sleeping by the pool, I went to the sea view Jacuzzi and he happened by. That's all. Nothing else' hoping to kill the conversation dead in the water by showing total disinterest in the subject.

'Still. It *was* nice of him to go out of his way' Nomsa repeated again.

They rose and exited the dining area wondering what else they could do at this hour, as there was no communal lounge and certainly no entertainment supplied by the hotel. This was certainly isolation in the extreme.

'I think we'll turn in now' Vusi said to Nomsa, suddenly feeling the strain of the day catching up on him. 'Are you coming too?' he asked of Nandi.

'I'll be a few minutes Dad. I just want to sit and read a newspaper, first.' She indicated to a low table in the reception area piled high with national and international publications.

'No problem' he replied. 'But don't be too long. We've got this meeting tomorrow and I want you bright and fresh.' He leaned across and kissed her gently on the cheek.

'Daaad!' she said slightly embarrassed at his open adoration of her.

He smiled. 'Not too long' and turned, with Nomsa at his side, slowly moving out of sight down the corridor.

Making sure they had gone, she walked over to the reception desk and addressed the blonde receptionist from earlier in the day.

'Excuse me' Nandi asked. 'Could you tell me the name of the tall, blonde, blue-eyed man that had to take an urgent call earlier?'

'Oh. You must mean Mr Williams?' she asked.

'Yes. I must. Please forgive me,' she stumbled awkwardly over her words 'but what does he do. I mean. Who is he?'

Raising her eyebrows in astonishment, the receptionist stepped back in surprise. 'Well' she said, searching for the right words. 'Mr Joe Williams is one of the World's top entrepreneurs. He has an interest in almost every country on the planet. Is that sufficient?'

'Oh yes' said Nandi totally amazed. 'When he told me earlier today that he had his crews running his boats for him, I frankly didn't believe him. What an idiot I've been.'

'I wouldn't worry' said the receptionist 'he almost told you the truth.'

'What do you mean, almost?' Nandi replied suspiciously.

'Well. He doesn't just have one or two boats, but entire

fleets of ships around the globe. He probably didn't want to brag. He's a very humble man.'

'Yes. Now I see' said Nandi, totally taken aback.

Totally embarrassed and realising her complete misjudgement of the man, she started making plans to effect an apology.

The next morning, dawn broke at four thirty over the Plettenberg Peninsular. At first the light was soft and grey, but as the sun's rays pierced the gloom of the night and transformed the ocean beneath the cliffs from a frightening pitch black to a calm turquoise blue, Nandi stirred in her bed. She had eventually succumbed to sleep at one am, after concocting a way to apologise for her arrogance, but still retain her dignity in front of the man she had appallingly slighted the afternoon before. Still, she couldn't put any of that into effect until after the family meeting with Mr Luuz. It still intrigued her though, how she, a teenager with little worldly knowledge, could be of use to his organisation and also benefit South Africa as a whole, the Zulu nation in particular. 'Strange' she also thought, 'how within hours of leaving the secure family enclave, her exposure to one of the world's most influential business leaders was affecting her judgement.' Right now though, her priority had temporarily changed and was now focussed on gaining access to the private, snow-white and sun-drenched beach nestling at the base of the rugged cliff, sixty feet below the wooden veranda. Changing into a tee-shirt, shorts and trainers she quietly accessed the external wooden stairway that descended sharply down the cliff face and stepped out onto the small, wind shielded sandy shoreline. Towering protectively over this cove stood a primeval, twisted rock stratum, its multicoloured layers gradually being warmed by the slowly rising sun. Nandi looked around as she slowly trudged across the small beach, leaving her imprints in the soft sand behind her. Ahead of her stood a white square sunshade and beyond that a large natural rock pool and a discarded, yet good quality, snorkel and mask. Picking the items up, she looked around, amazed that someone could have forgotten to take them back.

'Anyone here?' she called softly, afraid her voice would carry and wake the other guests still sleeping way above her.

There was no response. She smiled and slipped the mask over her face, adjusting the straps to form a tight seal and placed the snorkel in her mouth after clipping it to the side of the glass frame. She stepped into the pool and gently lowered herself beneath the tranquil waters. For a second, she couldn't distinguish anything as the sand rose from her feet and obscured her vision. Then, quite suddenly, it was clear, displaying a magical world of exotic tropical fish and sand crabs, the like of which she had never seen before. Stunned by the experience, she gasped in admiration and inadvertently opened her mouth, breaking the seal and sending a lung full of sea water down her throat. Panicking, she ascended quickly and broke the surface gasping for air. For a brief moment she was totally disorientated, not knowing which way was up and was even more confused when she felt herself being hoisted from the water by two very strong hands and slung unceremoniously onto her back against the warm soft sand. Then, without realising what was happening, her mask was ripped off and she felt the pressure of a pair of lips pressing against her salt laden mouth. With her eyes still smarting from the irritation of the stinging saltwater, she was unable to see her assailant, but somehow knew that there was only one adversary. She struggled against the downwards pressure on her face, smashing with wild fury against this large framed enemy hovering above her. With a mammoth effort, she swung her right leg sharply upwards and slammed it into the antagonist pinning her down. Moaning loudly, the attacker rolled off her and Nandi sprang up and away from any further contact. She spat out a mouthful of salt water and stood her ground, as the aggressor writhed painfully to his feet. As he turned, she was shocked to see that she knew him. He put his hand up in mock surrender.

'Second time to save your life, wouldn't you agree?' Joe smiled, holding his hand out in a conciliatory way.

'Excuse *me*' she said indignantly while getting her breath back. 'Are you telling me that you thought I was drowning and you took it upon yourself to hoist me out? I suppose you thought that you were giving me the kiss of life?'

He smiled. 'Yes. As a matter of fact I did think you were in trouble. As for kissing you, I think you're flattering yourself. I *am* a qualified lifeguard and I *was* applying the official technique in the recovery situation. Please check it out. Unfortunately, you seem to have a bad habit of almost drowning in front of me.'

'Well alright then!' she said defiantly, now humiliated for the second time in twenty-four hours. 'But what the hell are you doing here? I never saw you when I arrived. Where are your footprints?' she said suspiciously. Inclining her head slightly, she took stock of him standing ahead of her at over six feet in his khaki shorts and fashionable short sleeved shirt. They hung simply, but elegantly on him and although she wouldn't admit it, there was a certain attraction that he had for her.

'I climbed down the rocks' he pointed above him. 'I always do it when I come here. It's my early morning challenge!'

'Well alright then!' she repeated again, knowing he had her beaten on every answer she posed.

'Are you alright?' he asked as she turned and stomped defiantly over to a couple of fresh water showers mounted against a rock behind a semi circle of large stones.

'I'm fine' she replied angrily, closing her eyes, tossing her head backwards and letting the cold fresh water cascade over her face, clothes and through her long dark hair.

By the time she had stepped out of the shower and turned the tap off, the light had improved, raising the ambient air temperature to an acceptable sixty degrees. But for all that, she was still wet and uncomfortable from her second run in with this arrogant man and needed to get back to her suite and out of his proximity as fast as possible. Cautiously, she looked around but couldn't see him. His absence unnerved her, as he had a habit of arriving out of nowhere unannounced. 'Where the hell is he?' she thought, scanning every rock, expecting a surprise at any moment. 'Where *is* he?' she thought again. Suddenly, her attention was drawn to the rock face soaring above her and the shower of cascading stones shattering on impact from a sudden movement above. She stood back and gazed upwards at the solitary climber in bare feet just clearing the cliff top. Standing proudly with his hands on his hips, he turned and teasingly waved at her, before quickly disappearing from her vision. Now, very annoyed and feeling extremely slighted, she accessed the bottom step and made her way up the winding staircase to the hotel and her suite.

Breakfast with her parents was difficult. She was glad that they dined at seven. It hopefully meant that the chance of running into Joe would be diminished, as she understood that the majority of residents arrived for eight and she fervently hoped that he would be among that group. Vusi and Nomsa both noticed her nervous and fidgety manner, especially when a waiter passed.

'Is there something wrong?' Vusi asked. 'You seem very much on edge.'

'No Dad' she lied, trying to put on a smile. 'It's just that I'm a bit nervous about this meeting after breakfast.'

'Don't worry my daughter' he put his hand on hers. 'We're all going together, so nothing will go ahead without all of us being in total agreement. Alright?'

'Alright Dad' she smiled back at him, afraid of his reaction if she revealed her secluded, but innocent, encounters with Joe.

Finishing her breakfast of cereal, two eggs on toast and all washed down with a glass of freshly squeezed orange juice, she politely left her parents and headed back to her suite.

'Phew' she thought, looking at herself in the bathroom mirror. 'Thank God I didn't run into Joe. I wouldn't know what to say.' Guiltily, she bit her lip and cheekily smiled at her reflection. 'Still', she had to admit 'he did kiss well, even it was a life saver's.'

By nine she was formally dressed in a smart, black business suit that her mother had made in preparation for this meeting. With black court shoes to match and a simple white blouse, she epitomised the up and coming new breed of 'black diamonds' that this emerging country was producing. Looking carefully at herself in the long mirror, she closed her eyes and applied an essence of 'Eternity' by Calvin Klein, left as a compliment by the hotel management. Pleased at her appearance, she then stepped out to join her parents. When she arrived in the airy, cool reception, they were already there conversing with the manager, who had been briefed to accompany them along to Mr Luuz's suite.

'Please follow me' he requested and quietly led the way along the shadowed, white tiled floors, adorned with compact but expensive contemporary art pieces.

They followed closely, with a serious looking Vusi. Because of the compact nature of the buildings, it was only a matter of minutes before they arrived outside Mr Luuz's suite, still trying to fully organize their thoughts. To the sound of the manager's soft, but firm, knock, the door swung inwards and they were greeted by a large white man who appeared to fill the entire frame of the doorway.

'Ah!' he said, broadly smiling. 'This must be the Nongoma's? Nomsa, Vusi and your charming daughter, Nandi, who I've heard so much about?'

Before they could respond, he had shaken the manager's hand, passed a fifty dollar note into his palm and wished him a good day.

'If you need anything, Mr Luuz, please call' he added as a passing comment and with that he turned on his heels and swiftly, but silently disappeared down the corridor.

For a brief moment, Nomsa and Vusi were totally bewildered. Expecting to see again *the* Mr Luuz that they had originally met some weeks before, this surprise encounter totally confounded them. Apart from the fact that he was white, the other strange issue was that his name was also Luuz. Nomsa and Vusi stood stock still, staring at him, their mouths agog like gulping trout, while Nandi, unaware of any misgivings and standing at the rear, beamed innocently at her host.

'Please?' he stood to one side, beckoning them in ahead of him.

The suite into which they entered was not like any of theirs. It was enormous. The bed and en-suite bathroom looked the same, but there the similarity ended, as a wooden lattice frame shielded off and divided the bedroom from the living area. Ahead of them stood a curved white leather lounger, with matching armchairs set around an ornate wooden table. Beyond that, to the right of a low contemporary coffee table, stood a tripod mounted telescope pointing out to sea, while two large patio doors led out to a private decking area into which an external sunken bath proudly spread its girth. Two bookcases exhibiting the works of Dickens, Byron, Nostradamus, Darwin and Churchill sat alongside an imposing drinks cabinet by a far wall. With two long candles mounted into floor based wrought iron frames and a large log fire set into the wall, this executive suite oozed tranquillity par excellence. Mr Luuz ushered them towards the table and waited till they were all seated before lowering himself into a chair by the window.

'Thank you for coming' he looked around at his guests. 'Let me introduce myself. My name is Luuz. You may be surprised to meet me,' he addressed this particularly at Nomsa and Vusi, 'because I imagine you were expecting to meet for the second time Emmanuel Luuz who you both met some weeks ago. Before we go any further, let me please apologise for his absence. He has been called away on business and sends his regards. I agreed to fly in and meet you on his and Tentacle's behalf. I have total confidence in what he may have said to you, not just from the organisation's point of view, but also from a personal standpoint. After all he is my brother and as they say', he smiled 'blood is thicker than water.'

At this statement, Nomsa gasped and held a hand to her mouth, astonished at this revelation. Vusi didn't react, but was clearly taken aback.

All this time, Nandi had been watching Mr Luuz and was fascinated by several things about him. One of course was his height. She had never seen anyone of that stature before and certainly not in a white man of whom her exposure, it had to be said, was minimal. Secondly, he wore an unusual pair of glasses, had long white hair and beautiful white flowing robes. Finally, but certainly not least, he had hanging from his broad neck a brilliant gold chain, from which dangled a medallion similar to the one that her parents had seen when the 'black' Luuz first introduced them to Tentacle. She thought briefly and then recalled that Joe was of similar build and colour. How strange it was that two people could be so similar and be residing at the same place. It must be a million to one. Her parents were also thinking the same, but not about Joe. They were dumbfounded regarding the revelation that these two Luuz's were brothers; especially because of their being of diametrically opposite colours. To both their minds, odds of that occurring were also more than a million to one. Still, Nandi had no knowledge of that and just accepted this giant of a man on his own merits. All of them did notice, however, that his South African accent was tainted with an American dialect, although his mannerisms were typically Zulu.

'Before I begin to explain how we as Tentacle can help Nandi develop her education and her future life' he motioned to her and smiled, 'I will first of all tell you why she fits perfectly within our organisational framework. The Tentacle group is multi-ethnic, pan-global and financed by individuals who are in their own rights multi-billionaires. But' and here he paused for effect 'they all wish to be magnanimous with regards to assisting the poor and needy of the world. Coincidentally, just about the time that these individuals had reached their zeniths, a brilliant Scottish research scientist was starting to crack a genetic code which would lead to the total eradication of all forms of Cancer and skin diseases. This, as you can imagine, is the modern day 'Eureka!' moment. He had pursued this research up till that time, while being employed and funded by the British Government. Upon realising what was not just theoretically possible, but if all the trials proved positive, actually deliverable, he requested better facilities and more funds. The response, as with all governments when faced with a demand for more funding, was typically cautious and bureaucratic. The result was that the research stalled for over one year while various committees looked at feasibility studies and more importantly, from their point of view, what the bottom line in costs to complete the project would be. They just could not see further than the end of their political noses at the benefits that would accrue to mankind and therefore a monumental long-term cost saving in hospitalisation for millions around the world.

Eventually, though, some funds were delivered with restrictive covenants attached. The Professor continued his research, but was deeply exasperated at the time lost and the limitations this put him under. He at one stage had stated that his world was *existing within a moral anarchy in a scientific age*. By chance his research and what he was trying to achieve came to the ears of some of these philanthropists and they offered to assist him in whatever way they could. This, as you can see, would down the road put them on a collision course with the UK Government.' Mr Luuz stopped talking and took stock of his audience's reaction to his remit so far. All three were sitting mouth's agog and hanging on his every word. He continued. 'We in Tentacle are helping Professor Lang develop this formula financially, but on a parallel course, we are also putting in place dynamic leaders, who, when the time comes, will be able to lead the world out of poverty and oppression.' He looked at Nandi. 'You, young lady, have all the attributes that we are looking for. You're intelligent and passionate about other people. In addition, you are ambitious and want to experience new vistas, different ways of doing things. We would take care of all your educational needs and guide you in the right direction as your career blossoms. Eventually, you will be in a position to enhance the prospects not only of the Zulu nation, but the whole of South Africa. Just think of the possibilities. As for your parents, we would make sure that they never have to want for anything again. How does that sound?'

Nandi sat speechless. No one, let alone a complete stranger, had ever made offers to her of this nature. It was a lot take in and she turned to her parents for advice and guidance. 'Dad? Mum?' she looked at them imploringly. 'What should I do?'

'Mr Luuz' Vusi leaned forward, his elbows on the table 'we are a simple people as well you know, though not stupid and what you have proposed is, to say the least, an incredible chance for Nandi. In this world no one gets something for nothing. The phrase 'there's no such thing as a free lunch' springs to mind and therefore I want to know just two things and I need direct, honest, answers. My daughter's life is on the line.'

Mr Luuz sat slightly sideways, impossible for him to get his long legs under the table. He gently removed the strange, wire rimmed glasses off his nose and placed them on the table to his right.

'Mr Nongoma. I have a principle in life, never to hide from anything and anyone, while always telling the truth. If my answers are too frank and offend people then so be it. I would rather do that than lie. So please, ask away. I will not flinch from your questions.' Vusi turned and looked at Nomsa, who nodded. He turned back to make eye contact with this giant, white-haired man.

'What are the downsides for Nandi? I mean, is her life going to be at risk if she joins Tentacle? What would come of her if she didn't?'

Mr Luuz rose from his seat and with one great stride, stood by the large telescope on its tripod. He beckoned Vusi over.

'Please' he said, standing to one side, allowing Vusi to gain the eyepiece. 'What do you see?' he pointed to a misty horizon ten miles to the west.

Vusi bent down and closing one eye, focussed in the direction that Mr Luuz was pointing. For a second or two he scanned the horizon, seeing nothing but a vast sea of blue water, crested now and then by a white breaking wave.

'I can't see anything except water. What am I looking for?' he replied.

'Just look' Mr Luuz said again pointing in the same direction as before.

Vusi rubbed his right eye, readjusted his stance and peered out at the powerful churning ocean before him.

'Nothing. Nothing. Noth…Wait. I see it. It's a whale. My God! It's big and oh, so beautiful! Oh look at it jump! What a sight!' He remained transfixed at this wonderful spectacle of nature for at least another minute and then slowly stood up and smiled. 'That was wonderful. I've never seen anything like that before.' He turned to Nomsa and Nandi. 'You should have seen that. It was incredible!'

He turned away to go back to the table, when Mr Luuz held him back by his arm.

'Great wasn't it?' his American accent suddenly strongly discernable in the question.

'Yes, it was' Vusi replied looking down at his arm and the large white hand firmly holding him.

Letting go of Vusi, Mr Luuz said 'Does that answer your question?'

'I don't know what you mean' replied Vusi totally confused.

'Let me explain' said the white haired man. 'You saw that whale out there. Well, I gave you an opportunity and you took it. If you had decided not to look, you would have missed that great spectacle and then could not have told Nomsa and Nandi about it. The downside is that you would have missed it totally and possibly never forgiven yourself. In the same way I can't say that Nandi will be more or less at risk whether she joins Tentacle or not, but she will definitely miss the experience. If you want to talk it over and stay on here while you do it, there's no problem.'

Vusi turned and faced his wife and daughter. 'I'm convinced' he said to them. 'I think Nandi should have this opportunity. It may never come again' he stressed. He looked back at his host and smiled. 'I see what you mean.' Vusi walked over to Nandi, who stood up as he approached.

'Dad. If you think that this is a good opportunity then as long as you and Mum agree, I'll do what you want.'

Nomsa smiled and nodded her agreement.

'Then it's all agreed?' asked Mr Luuz, looking from one to the other, seeking definite confirmation.

'We agree. Tell us what happens next?' smiled Vusi sitting down again at the table.

'I think you've forgotten something?' asked the Greenwich Village man of Vusi.

'I don't think so' Vusi responded perplexed.

'You're right' said Nomsa. 'Don't you remember, Vusi, you had two questions? Mr Luuz has answered one.'

'Yes, of course' Vusi said, embarrassed that he had been put in this invidious position, especially by Nomsa, to whom he shot a fleeting, but annoyed glance.

'Your question please?' said Mr Luuz still standing by the telescope.

'Well. I really don't know where to begin' said Vusi, feeling embarrassed and very uncomfortable.

'Try asking me directly Vusi. I'm not an ogre. I'm not going to bite your head off. At least not today.'

He smiled knowingly at Nomsa. Almost imperceptibly she nodded her head and smiled back.

Vusi looked up from where he sat and tripped over his own words. 'I. Umm. Err. Well. If....'

'Mr Luuz' said Nomsa robustly, stepping quickly into the breach to save her husband from further embarrassment. 'I think I know what Vusi wants to ask. Many years of marriage have afforded me this second sense to almost read his mind. So, if it's alright with you, dear' she looked across the table at her partner, 'I will ask the question?'

Vusi looked back at her and humbly, but thankfully, nodded his agreement.

'Alright. Mr Luuz. Here it is. A few weeks ago when we first met Mr *Emmanuel* Luuz within our Kraal, we were taken aback by what he said, but needed this meeting to fully understand the implications and the detail in so far that it affected Nandi. But when you introduced yourself as Mr Luuz and stated that he was your brother, we were both shocked to our black skin's souls. I am sure you know where this is leading and we would like you to enlighten us as to how you can be brothers to each other since you are white and he is most definitely black?'

Suddenly and briefly the world stood still for Nandi, as the full implications of what she was hearing hit home, like an arrow piercing her vulnerable young heart. Her mouth opened wide like a dark train tunnel expelling a hurtling locomotive from its cavernous mouth. She looked across from her mother to her father, settling finally on Mr Luuz and like her parents waited for his explanation. The American smiled affably and purposefully strode over to the bookcase, picking up a copy of Darwin's *The Origin of Species by Means of Natural Selection*.

'This' he said, holding it above his head, his hand touching the ceiling 'is to understand where we all come from. Darwin did not claim to know everything, but he did show us the way. Some academics still dispute his conclusions and have pointed at people like my brother and I as proof that he was wrong.' He paused then continued. 'Maybe those academics are right and people like my brother and I *are* freaks from a skin colour point of view. But beauty is skin deep and as Martin Luther King said in the last century, *Judge not a man by the colour of his skin, rather by the way he treats others.* Our parents are Zulus, black and proud. Through a genetic twist, I was born white and was at first hidden from the outside world as the country was split under the unacceptable apartheid regime. The tribe kept me close to them and I wanted for nothing. My skin colour was not an issue inside the kraal and I was treated like everyone else, a Zulu of Royal Blood. As I grew up, I became aware of others outside the tribe looking at me, and by the time I started school at five, my parents had received demands that I should attend a white's only school, as racial integration of black and white in education was not allowed. Our parents, fearful of the psychological effect that this could have upon me, arranged, via our white friends in the United States, to adopt me as an unwanted child. That is exactly what happened. I have spent all my life in the U.S., but as I prospered and grew financially successful, I set up a trust fund with my brother so that he could assist in the enhancement of our people and that of the entire African continent. When apartheid finally ended, I was determined to accelerate this development at an even faster rate and that is where Nandi' he looked admiringly at her 'and other selected individuals will take the helm and change our and other nation's lives for the better.

Sometimes I am asked what race I belong to, since my birthright is African Zulu yet my adopted land is America. The answer of course is the human race and I will do all in my power to achieve a just and harmonious world for all mankind equally! I hope that answers your question, and I sincerely hope that unless you have changed your mind after hearing me out, you still allow Nandi to join Tentacle.' Weary by his homily, he sat down opposite the family and waited for their reactions.

Nandi was the first to react. 'Dad' she turned to Vusi excitedly. 'I wanted this before and after that' she smiled at Mr Luuz 'I want it even more. Please say yes and let me be a part of this incredible experience?'

Vusi leaned back into his chair and closed his eyes. 'Mother. What do you say?' he whispered to his right.

She reached out and placed her gnarled weather beaten hand gently over his on the table and slowly caressed his fingers. 'Vusi. I've always trusted your judgement, especially when it comes to our daughter's future and it's no different now.'

He opened his eyes and saw her gentle face nodding slowly in agreement. Then, turning to his left, he watched his daughter, his only child, eyes closed, her palms placed together in a silent prayer. She suddenly realised that he was watching her and slowly opened her eyes to catch his loving gaze.

'Nandi' he said softly 'I give you the world and all that is good in it.'

She jumped up and threw her arms around her parents. 'Thank you Dad. Thank you Mum. I'll be forever in your debt!'

Turning to Mr Luuz, she said 'I have one question for you. I can't keep calling you Mr Luuz. Please tell me your first name?'

'No problem' he said. 'Prepare yourselves folks' he said in an unmistakeable American way. 'It's Moses. Moses Luuz.'

'Well, what happens now?' asked Vusi, not comfortable in being able to address the host by his newly discovered first name.

The American stood up and strolled over to the open veranda door. 'Because I was fairly confident that you would both agree for Nandi to join' he looked at Vusi and Nomsa 'I took the opportunity to invite here today a very close colleague who will be the link in her education and career moves for the next few years. You, of course, will be able see Nandi whenever she is free outside of her studies. My friend will also arrange to cover all your expenses, in addition to paying you both a very generous allowance every month, directly into your bank accounts, for your 'work' within one of our companies. We must be seen to do this legitimately, so as to avoid attracting any unwarranted interest. Please do not tell *anyone* about our plans, no matter who they are.' He looked at Nandi. 'This also means Tabatha and her family, I'm afraid.'

'You know about Tabatha?' she responded, amazed.

'Nandi. We know about everyone! In this business, information is power. If you don't know what to say to people, say nothing. I can't stress enough what the consequences would be, if even the smallest smidgeon of information got out. It would be disaster for us all! So again' he addressed them all 'tell no one anything! Right now,' he changed his tone, 'I want to introduce to you my trustworthy and long time confidant, who will be the link in guiding Nandi forward from this day onwards.'

From the sweeping outside terrace, partly obscured by the white lattice screens that stood by the open doorway, stepped a man in an elegant white cotton two piece suit complete with matching white canvas shoes and a pink linen shirt. At first his image wasn't clear as the morning sun backlit his silhouette creating a golden aura around his frame. But as he moved further into the suite, away from the light, Nandi had a sudden, sharp intake of breath. She knew this man all too well, as did her parents. Joe Williams was as polite and charming as Nandi's parents had remembered him the evening before and seeing him again gave them no qualms about his motives. He sat down with them and formally introduced himself, telling them about his wife in the U.S.A. and his rise to global economic power. He gave them a card and he noted their details on a small blackberry communicator that he withdrew from his inside pocket.

'I believe you've met Nandi?' said Vusi, explaining to him and Mr Luuz about the brief encounter that she had had with him.

'Yes, I have. She appears to be a very determined person and knows exactly what she wants' he replied, while almost ignoring her in the conversation as if she wasn't there. He turned to face her. 'Nandi. Is there anything that you would like to do while you are here that I can show you?'

She thought that he was baiting her, but knowing that her parents were hanging on her every word, she bit her lip and answered as convincingly as possible, knowing that because of her father being present, there was no possibility of her suggestion being implemented.

'Yes, Mr Williams there is. I would like you to' she paused 'take me on the bungee jump from the Bloukrans Bridge. You know the one that we passed on the way here.'

'Nandi!' exclaimed Vusi in surprise. 'You can't expect Mr Williams to take you on something as dangerous as that!' He looked earnestly to Joe for backing his objection.

'I have no problem with that Vusi' said the entrepreneur, overruling the father's concerns. 'It's not dangerous. I've done it many times before. In fact, I'm quite an expert!'

Vusi sat back, amazed at Joe's response. Here he was, undermined by the man who was meant to be his daughter's safety net and who casually laughed in the face of death.

Mr Luuz bent down and whispered in Vusi's ear 'Remember the whale and that opportunity?'

Seeing that he was outmanoeuvred, he acquiesced to his daughter's request and reluctantly gave her permission to go with Joe later that morning. Vusi looked across at Joe and wagged his finger. 'Take very good care of her Joe' he warned. 'She is my precious little girl! Don't let a hair on her head become at risk!'

'No problem sir. I'll have her safely back here in time for lunch!'

Joe rose and addressed an astounded Nandi, still trying to work out how her suggestion had backfired so badly. 'Come on Nandi. We can be among the first to jump.'

She stood and demurely followed him outside to his car and the bridge some five miles distant to the east. True to his word, Joe brought Nandi back before lunch, her attitude to him now mellowed since their brief time together. She no longer saw him as a predatory male, but as a kind, caring and compassionate man, who had only her interest at heart and no hidden agenda. When they arrived back, she met her parents, with Mr Luuz, in the reception area.

'Are you alright? You're not hurt?' her mother asked, relieved to see her back unharmed.

Vusi stayed quiet, still smarting from being overruled earlier.

'Yes, Mum. It was fantastic! Joe is a *very* skilled jumper and looked after me at all times. It was' she sought the correct words '*out of this world!*'

By this time, Joe had joined them, after locking the vehicle up outside on the gravel car park.

'It looks like you have had a *very* positive effect on our daughter, Joe' said Nomsa, smiling at Nandi, who even within her black skin, showed signs of adolescent blushing.

'Just to bring you all up to speed,' Moses said addressing Joe and Nandi. 'All the details have been sorted and Nandi will be attending our technical college next week. Joe here,' he nodded in the entrepreneur's direction, 'will meet Nandi at Cape Town Airport and drive her to the campus, where she will meet the other students. If there are no further questions, then I will take my leave of you all. I have a plane to catch and won't be forgiven if I'm late. If you wish to stay on to the end of the week, please be my guest. Everything is paid for. When you are ready to depart, just advise the reception and Fabrice will take you back to the airport, where your tickets will be waiting for collection. We may not meet again, but you have a number on the card my brother handed you if you need to talk. In the meantime, Joe will be your link. Good luck and may your God go with you.'

The next few days back at home were manic for Nandi and her parents. Joe had communicated with her school and made the necessary arrangements for her withdrawal. In the normal course of events there would be a plethora of forms to be completed, but because of his contacts in the political and education systems, everything was settled quickly, with calls placed to several high profile figures in authority. True to form, Joe met Nandi in the arrivals hall of Cape Town International Airport and before travelling to the college, he gave her a personal tour of Cape Town, checking her in at just after nine that night.

For the next three years, Nandi's academic brilliance really started to show great potential, while her natural leadership skills in orienteering and weapons training put her in a class of her own. Awards and trophies followed, eventually leading to her being elected college captain and President of the debating society in her final year. All this time, Joe had kept in touch, even sometimes dropping by unexpectedly to see her between studies. Rumours spread quickly about them around the campus, but as they appeared not to have had any concrete foundations, the tittle-tattle disappeared fast. Her appointment to the South African Army Officer Training Course, followed by a long spell with military intelligence, was not altogether surprising, as her commanding officer at the college, Colonel Regis, had recommended her directly to his opposite number at the Selection Board. One year later, after passing out with the highest marks in the country's history, she was sent on attachment to assist in the security of the Parliament of the African Union in Midrand, allowing her unfettered access to all the heads of the African Union, which she took full advantage of in social and business networking circles. To say she was trusted by everyone was an understatement. With her good looks, intelligence and personal charm, she quickly allayed any doubts they may have had about her when first introduced. This applied particularly to the cynical dictators, who as a rule trusted no one, especially military officers. After all, this was how, with calculated brute force and fifth column activists, they created and maintained a climate of tyrannical fear leading to a total stranglehold on their long suffering peoples. These 'leaders' were Tentacle's primary targets, with Nandi being the hustling sheepdog capable of outsmarting and outmanoeuvring them all into oblivion and out of power. The downside of partially overthrowing these unscrupulous megalomaniacs was that given half a chance they would attempt a counter-coup, putting her and all the other members of Tentacle at risk, never mind the downtrodden masses that wanted them gone. Therefore, their removal had to be total and uncompromising. It could be that the International Criminal Court in The Hague would be convened to try those responsible for crimes against humanity, but only if Tentacle's plan succeeded. That was for others to concern themselves with. She had her task to fulfil and if her military training had taught her one thing, it was to stay focussed on the target at all times and never let it out of your sight.

Nandi, having been well briefed by Joe over the years that they had closely spent together, believed fully in the Tentacle raison d'être and if the truth was really known, was their most dangerous weapon. In her time with the military and especially the secondment to the intelligence arm, she had acquired unique contacts with other foreign agencies and their personnel. However, there were times when running joint covert operations with some of these groups, that she had to be extremely careful in displaying any emotions that may arouse suspicions and compromise her own security and that of Tentacle. It followed then that she was walking a very thin tightrope and could not afford to expose her position to anyone until the upcoming Olympic operation started in just two weeks time. With a bit of subterfuge and pressing of palms, she now had the majority of her target's travel plans for the 'Games'. These she passed back to Joe by an encrypted email link, who in turn advised Moses.

'Excellent!' the Zulu exclaimed, standing in the cabin of the family's private yacht, moored off a deserted coral reef near Mauritius, in the Indian Ocean.

'It's looking good Joe' he said, talking on his VHF set.

'When does she leave for London?' Moses asked.

'We are trying to get the last few targets' details, but it's proving difficult. I don't think it's because they know we're on to them. It's just their secretive ways. But to answer your question, I believe that if we can't obtain the movements of these last few within seven days of the games starting, then she should be on her way. We can always get them later. That won't be a problem.'

'I agree' said the white twin. 'Have you arranged her flights, hotels etc?'

'Yep. It's all taken care of. I've arranged her cash, contacts and credit cards for when she arrives. I'm leaving nothing to chance.'

'Be careful, Joe. You know what the Brits are like regarding security. Remember nothing was reported in Beijing in 2008, so they're *really* geared up for any trouble now. They'll be on full alert for terrorists, the proof being that unfortunate shooting of the innocent Brazilian guy at Tooting in 2005. Don't even think that these guys are pussycats. Just don't underestimate them.'

'I know. Take my word. She won't be compromised in any way at all. I'll put my life on it. She's a very valuable asset.'

'But not just to *us*?' Moses subtly asked teasingly.

For a second there was a silence between them as Joe contemplated his reply. 'You're right. To me as well' he replied thoughtfully.

'I know' responded the Zulu. 'Therefore, even more reason for keeping a low profile until the last minute. We don't want to be associated with any terrorist's groupings. Keep your emotions out of this. Our success depends on hitting all our targets at the same time and getting out fast.'

'I agree,' said Joe, 'but what we are planning is *so* different that while the Yard's SO15 will be targeting al-Qaida and its lunatic activists, we will not appear on their radar until our London team starts the ball rolling.'

'Moses. There's someone coming. I've got to go now. We'll speak soon. Cheers!' With that, Joe cut the line.

Moses flicked the receiver off and stepped out on deck, a glass of cold orange in his hand, topped with a sprinkling of the local speciality, Goodwill rum. Raising his glass in a salute, he leaned against the rigging and watched the sky turn crimson red, as the sun disappeared below the horizon. 'Cheers' he said to himself smiling at this, God's view of heaven.

KAREN

In Karen's bedroom, the Sun flickered through the half closed blinds, tracing a long finger of light over her foot and up her bronzed leg, resting just below her crotch. The girl who had delved into every scandal in Whitehall was now being investigated for the umpteenth time that morning by Alex's roving hands, as he traced a line between her breasts and began to pull her to him. The clock radio suddenly snapped on, jolting her automatically away from his groping hands and causing a snigger at him lying there, slightly put out at not having his nuptials.

'Karen!' he called.

But beneath the pulsonic shower she could not hear him. When finally she emerged into the lounge wearing only a kimono it occurred to her that he had gone.

'Oh well!' shrugging her shoulders, as if to say 'many more fish where he came from!' She dressed in denims and listened to the news and weather.

'Hot sun. Blue skies, 30c. Forecast 33 by Friday.'

'Another heat wave' she muttered, heading downstairs to her racing green MGB convertible and the short drive to the Wapping editorial offices.

The desks on her floor looked lonely, quiet. It was the same when she worked late at night or weekends. Her desk overlooked the old Royal Docks, long since devoid of the ships, barges and cranes that once made London the shipping capital of the world.

'Anything?' throwing her bag at the Picture Editor.

'Quiet night, except for the usual rumblings of the upcoming Olympics. Costs, security and transport' he mumbled.

'Oh and this. Couldn't understand it really. Some crap about genetics.' He showed her his scribbled pad with names, numbers and dates on it. 'Anonymous of course.'

'Can I have this?' she asked of him.

'Be my guest. If you can work out what it means let me know. I've got a meeting with the team shortly.' He indicated upstairs and left her to ponder his notes.

She smiled and, taking an early edition from the proof pile, grabbed her bag and headed to the canteen for breakfast. While consuming copious amounts of coffee followed by lashings of bacon and egg, she looked at his notes, trying to work out what it all meant. Her brain was tired and she put them down and read the early edition trying to take in the main points. Skimming through the pages, she was suddenly drawn to a small piece on the science page about something called The Chameleon Effect. She quickly glanced at the short piece by Colin the Weather Man and after reading a bit more, she saw that the original information had emanated from a Professor Lang, a leading genetic scientist. She moved the notes that the picture man had left her and compared them with the piece. 'Strange' she thought and tapped her pencil against her lower lip. 'I wonder?' She took her communicator out and dialled the numbers in quick succession. Every one was a dead line, except the last where a woman requested her pass code.

'I'm sorry' Karen said. 'I must have the wrong number. I'm trying to return a call to Professor Lang. Do you know where I can reach him?'

'Hold on' the woman said.

There was silence then a click. Then a man with a distinctive Indian accent came on the line. 'Sorry to keep you' he said apologetically. I understand you are returning a call from someone called Lang. Is that right? Can I please ask who you are?'

'Karen. I am a journalist with the Mail.'

'Ah' he said. 'Would that be the Daily Mail?'

'Yes' she said confidently. 'Do you know where I can find him?'

'I am sorry to advise you, but we have no knowledge of such an individual at this number. I believe that you have been misinformed.'

'But I have his name associated to some other numbers as well, which all seem to be dead lines!' she said exasperated.

'Again young lady, I cannot help you. As I have already said, he is not known to us. I think someone is, what do you English say, winding you up. In my opinion you should forget all about trying to contact him. Goodbye.' The line went dead, except for another light click just before the end of the call.

'Strange' she thought. 'Very odd.' She made some other calls and every one came back with the same response. Untraceable, disappeared. Finally she called Colin. He was just going into the meeting upstairs. She relayed her conversations and left him with some niggling questions regarding the Chameleon Effect. Sitting at a window table she sipped her now cold coffee and watched with interest as the Docklands gradually came alive.

CRANFIELD

'Jump higher!' Cranfield shouted at the tanned youth bouncing on the trampoline.

'Higher, higher, keep going.'

The sweat glistened on the athlete's body, soaking the white tee shirt as he drove himself well beyond his personal best. With his bulging muscles glistening in the late afternoon heat, he resembled the classically handsome Greek youth, Adonis. He bounced to a dead stop, as only professionals can do and eyed the trainer.

'You ok boss?'

His words fell on deaf ears. Cranfield was studying some photos. His dark, bottomless eyes and hardened face gave nothing away.

'Boss? Ok if I wind up now?'

'Eh?' grunted Cranfield, still transfixed by the multiple sets of snaps in front of him.

'Something wrong boss? You look worried.'

Cranfield sighed like a steam train letting out air. He spun on the boy, fixing him with a stare that is usually only seen by poker players in a bluff situation.

'Jeff. I gotta ask you something. You can call me crazy if you like, but where do you come from. You know your family?' He tapped the photos.

'Oh! I know where *you're* coming from.' Jeff picked a family group taken several years ago when he, via his Dad, had first come training. 'That's me.' He stubbed his finger at a boy standing shyly between his parents. 'Small wasn't I? Now look at me! We used to live over there' he pointed towards Bow about two miles away. 'Dad had his own business but lost it when the Olympic training ground was planned. The last Mayor, Ken Livingstone and that cow Tessa Jowell, the Olympic Minister, are both responsible for his loss. Compulsory purchase I think. He got paid a lot because he was the last one in the street to refuse to move. Seven days later his whole world and that of thousands of other East Enders came tumbling down to make way for all of this.' He motioned at everything around them. 'Progress I think they call it. Dad was torn apart. You could tell. Mum wasn't happy. She now had him on top of her every day. Jamaican women don't like that.' His gaze went over the Olympic stadium and seemed to drift, transfixed, into a time of innocence and cobbled streets, where kids wearing hoodies and baggy jeans would cycle like mad holding their MP3's around the council blocks and dive into Mc Donald's under the Bow flyover.

Cranfield saw a tear well up in the boy's eyes. 'Hey!' he said. 'Go home, have a rest and get ready for that Gold Medal!' He slapped the boy on the shoulders and watched him jog towards the changing block. 'Nice kid. Lot of promise.' He furrowed his forehead and scratched his bald head. 'Enough already!' and walked across the all weather track towards the afternoon Sun.

It had taken Cranfield just twenty five minutes to shower and eat a light supper. Although he felt refreshed physically, his mind could not settle. Donning a British Olympic shirt, with a pair of matching slacks, socks and shoes, he caught himself glancing into the floor to ceiling mirror in his suite. His athletic prowess, coupled with his bull frame and dominant personality, stared back at him. As a slight shudder ran down his spine, he slumped into an easy chair and closed his eyes. The more he tried to stay awake, the closer the swirling mists of his mind closed in, until finally after mindlessly drifting through a void, he fell into a slumber and for the first time in many weeks, was overtaken by a deep need for sleep.

The Sun peered into Cranfield's bedroom and not finding him there, spread its rays like long fingers around the apartment, until one shaft climbed lazily across the sofa, easing its way up his body, finally resting gently across his eyelids like a feather landing on a still pond. Across the park two dogs barked, their calls echoing in the distance. Silence followed, broken only by the far off sirens of ships manouevering their way past each other in the morning mist, some miles away. Yet this was only a respite. The radio activated, the announcer having verbal diarrhoea.

'And now we bring a special report from our correspondents in Washington and India. With global food prices soaring due to the combination of the longest drought in human history and governments responding with unpopular and counterproductive controls on prices and exports, the world faces a food crisis of epidemic proportions. In short we have entered a period in which there is not enough food and water for the World population of seven billion. The worst hit of course will be the developing countries. The days of cheap food are long gone, as waves of discontent have started to be felt, particularly in the poorest nations. Angry and violent protestors have taken to the streets and local media have already reported deaths not from violence, but from starvation. More details after the break.'

A series of commercials backed by contemporary music followed. He blinked twice, tried to focus and felt stiffness in his neck that he didn't like. Rolling like a gymnast, he fell onto the floor in a heap trying to work out where he was and how long he had been there. Seeing the blue jacket in front of his nose, suddenly jerked him into a kneeling position. He was annoyed that he had no recollection of the previous night, even though his clothes told another story. Standing and stretching, he eased himself over to the fridge where he poured a large glass of fresh orange from the external chiller and tossed it down his dry throat. It felt as though his tongue was at the bottom of a dead parrot's cage and quickly shot a chaser down, licking the residue that he had spilled over his lips. Opening his window onto the park, he drank deeply of the sweet innocence which was the morning air. His eyes watched the sparrows nip in and out between the fat male pigeons that were parading up and down in front of their intended mates, while nodding their heads and cooing like demented butlers bowing to their masters' every whim.

With the adverts over, the presenter's voice cut back in. *'And now, as promised here is that full report that we promised you earlier.'*

The banal voice was cut off by Cranfield's large finger striking the off button. 'Not interested' he muttered, disrobing for the second time in twelve hours before heading for the shower. He came out dripping, refreshed and sat quietly sipping black coffee. The phone rang. It was a reporter angling for a story. 'Piss off!' he snapped. Now the real fun would start.

CHEKHOV

Over in the training area of the sports stadium, most of the athletes were limbering up for the practice events against the Russians, which had been arranged some time ago. Even though it was a 'friendly', every competitor treated the match as if gold medals were at stake. Cranfield felt the same, but did not show it outwardly. Instead, he chewed gum and sweated from every pore in his chunky body. He keenly eyed the Russians, mentally noting their great numbers and massive physical prowess. Only the USA had larger numbers and stronger bodies. Still, his Great Britain team, although the 5th biggest in numbers, did have proportionally more world champions and record holders than anyone else. You only had to look at the medal table from Beijing to back that up. He smiled, but only for a moment, as an IOC drug team randomly tested a group of athletes by the side of the track.

'Bloody hell!' he snarled under his breath. 'Haven't we got enough pressures without this?' he said, looking to heaven and cursing.

'I agree comrade. Why don't these bastards leave us alone?' It was Chekhov. His opposite number on the Russian team. He slapped Cranfield on the back, kissed him Soviet style on both cheeks, stood back and smiled at his old adversary and friend for over 20 years. 'How are you Mr Cranfield?' he chuckled. 'Cat got your tongue?' added the Russian, indicating his pink muscle protruding from his mouth.

'Well, I'll be Karl Marx!' Cranfield replied, grinning from ear to ear. 'What are you doing here this early? The games don't officially start for another two weeks.'

'I know. But I wanted to be here early and see the east end of London as a tourist, before kicking your English arse in battle. Some of my ancestors settled here 100 years ago. I think I might have some relatives nearby.' He smiled the smile of a long lost brother and Cranfield warmed to him as he always did when they met.

They walked and talked around the arena, stopping occasionally to express a point or two and enjoy each other's company in the summer's sun. Now and again Chekhov would cover his mouth with his hand and confide in Cranfield, the latter showing no emotion since he knew that Russian intelligence was watching his friend and was therefore practised in the art of deception himself. The training held no surprises for the two men, as their respective teams warmed up in the late afternoon heat.

'Let's eat later' said Cranfield suddenly.

'Smolenskies in the Strand or Blooms Whitechapel?'

'I don't care' smiled Chekhov. 'I'm starving, as you capitalist's say. I've got my own apartment outside the 'village'. 'Here's the address' and he passed across a handwritten card with his personal details scrawled in badly written, but decipherable English.

'I'll pick you up at seven. Bring your wallet! You owe me from last time' the Brit said.

Parting under the Royal Box, Chekhov strolled after his athletes towards the locker rooms. He did not see the two large men rise from the shadows of the stands and follow him. Cranfield would be dining alone tonight.

The 3 litre engine of the Jensen Interceptor purred like a ravenous lion about to devour its prey. Cranfield loved this car. It was his baby. He adored it more than he would have his own children, if he had ever got around to having any. The giant wire wheels embodied into the gun metal body sparkled like diamonds and with the roof open and the speakers blasting out the Best of the Beach Boys, Cranfield felt invincible. At exactly six fifty five he parked 'the beast' as he called the Jensen, outside Chekhov's four storey private apartment in Carpenter's Road, Stratford. A uniformed traffic officer discreetly displaying the butt of a black revolver beneath his stab vest, approached his car.

'Sorry sir. Can't stop here' he shouted, above the bass tones and harmony of the west coast group. His partner also armed, stood back observing the encounter by the open door of their brightly emblazoned yet incredibly powerful Jaguar Interceptor.

Cranfield nodded, turned down the sound and proffered a high level security pass issued from the Assistant Commissioner's Olympic Command Office at Scotland Yard. While the officer went over to his car to confirm the details that Cranfield had handed across, the British coach raised the volume slightly and closed his eyes, reminiscing about the golden beaches of California and his squandered youth in Santa Barbara and Malibu.

'Very good sir! Just checking!' the solidly built Constable nodded his approval at the clearance, while handing the pass back. 'I still would be careful about where you park, for all that anyway sir. With the amount of 'unknowns' in this area for the Games, we would *still* prefer if you could to choose to park in one of the official zones. But for the moment you're ok. Please make sure though that you lock your vehicle up. This monster' he looked admiringly at the classic car 'is a very valued steal and I would hate it if some low-life deprived you of your pride and joy.' With that he strolled off to another 'sus' car parked nearby on triple red lines.

The Police of the Met's Olympic Command were on high alert after the DLR siege at Mudchute the previous month, where 5 illegal immigrants seized a commuter train for 6 hours, finally releasing all the passengers safely in return for asylum. Cranfield looked at his watch. Ten past seven. He looked in his mirrors. Couldn't see his friend. Strange. He's always punctual! Twenty past. Nothing. Picking up his Olympic communicator he ran Chekhov's card through the swipe. It rang and went into message mode.

'Sorry. Can't make it. FSR!'

Cranfield was confused. He rubbed his chin with his hand. 'FSR. What's he talking about?' He revved the engine sending 2 kilos of carbon into the atmosphere. 'Something's up!' he thought.

His dash-board communicator buzzed urgently like an angry bee and Jenny's face appeared on screen. 'There you are' she said scoldingly. 'I take it you're waiting for Chekhov?' she added.

'Yes' he responded clinically, irritated by her questioning. He stared back.

'You guys going to dinner?' she teased.

'Maybe. Maybe not' he replied.

'Oh! Sorry. Bad timing?' she said, slightly embarrassed.

'Could be' he said looking at her.

'We'll leave it then' she apologised.

'No' he said.

'You free?' he asked.

'What, now?' she responded, surprised by his volte-face.

'Yes. Now!' he insisted.

'Are you standing him up?' she mocked.

'I'll pick you up at eight' he forcefully told her, ignoring her question and abruptly killing the call.

At her end she held the handset and smiled, knowing him well enough not to get offended by his brusque and forthright manner. Checking his watch for the umpteenth time, he got out of 'the beast', locked the car and called over the Police officer that had attended him before. He asked him to keep any eye on the car, explaining that he was just going to his friend's apartment. The officer said he would watch it as long as possible, but his job was not to 'baby sit' the car. Thanking him, Cranfield stepped across the pavement and into the lobby of the building. He used the stairs to reach the second floor as he did not trust lifts, being stuck in one for six hours once many years previously. On the enclosed landing four flats positioned themselves at the corners of the building. A quick look told him that flat eight was Chekhov's overlooking the Olympic Park. The door was suspiciously ajar and that combined with a deafening silence coming from within the quarters put him on his guard.

'Hello? Chekhov? It's me Cranfield' he called out. Cautiously edging forward into the darkened interior, he snapped on the nearest light switch. A large 150 watt bulb hanging naked in the deserted hallway and suspended by three thin power wires radiated a glow as bright as a Toc H lamp. The place appeared to be empty! His voice echoed around the walls and softly reverberated back to him. What the hell was going on? Where was his friend? Stepping over to the flat's audio wall communicator he requested the latest replay. The last inbound call was almost useless except for the repeated and garbled name of someone called Lang hurriedly disseminated during the final few hissing seconds of the digitised recording. Realising that this recording may be of some significance, he quickly patched it through to Jenny's inbox. Even though he now also presumed that the place was stripped 'clean as a whistle', a further careful check for his own peace of mind confirmed his worst suspicions. All traces of his friend's stay had been thoroughly and professionally sanitized. Scratching his head and furrowing his brow, he killed the bright light pitching the lonely flat back into its former state of gloom, while stepping out and firmly closing the door behind him. Still trying to make 'head from tails' he descended the stairs and nonchalantly strolled over to the 'beast'.

Seeing the officer and his partner still there he thanked them and brought the Beach Boys back to life as he headed off to dine with Jenny. She had been his P.A. for two years now and felt she knew him very well. His mood swings particularly were a problem when the press and politicos started hounding him, but other than that he was a good boss. Now and again he would pay compliments to her hour glass figure, long blonde hair and stunning model looks, but that was where it stopped. He was the epitome of a gentleman and would never step across the line and mix business with pleasure. All the more surprising then, when he proposed dinner tonight, she thought. 'Something's up! Be careful girl.' Her mother's words floated down the years to her. Something about mid life crises for men. She smiled to herself. Wouldn't be so bad though. He may not be a trim athlete, but he's all man! Again she smiled, inadvertently seeing him step out the shower one Saturday morning several months ago, while delivering some DVD's for the Olympic training team to his penthouse flat in the 'village'. He didn't know she saw him, but her memory was just as vivid today as it was then. Yep! He had it all. She trembled nervously, waiting for him to come, like a virgin teenager on her first date. 'This was crazy! Stop girl. It will only be business. Get a life!' she thought.

The buzzer hummed like a bee on heat. She flew down the stairs, bypassing the lift and almost ran into him waiting in the lobby.

'Whoa!' he said catching hold of her. 'Where's the fire?'

'Sorry. Nerves!' she mumbled inadequately.

'With me? Never! Come on. Let's go. I want to ask you something.'

They sat in Blooms by the window, watching the traffic move in a circuit from the Whitechapel Art Gallery to the Aldgate pump. Buses vied with cabs for positioning, as the Commercial Road poured its Asian textile vans into the traffic soup, that was starting to pile up towards the Tower and the City. He ordered two set meals and a couple of drinks, the latter arriving within seconds of the order.

'Very impressive!' she said raising her glass to him and smiling. 'Here's to what? Britain and our team?'

'No!' he said. 'To life!' devouring his beer in one swig. 'Waiter! Another please' holding his glass up like the Statue of Liberty. 'How about you?' he motioned to her.

'I'm fine. Still got this one.' She tipped her head slightly and narrowed her eyes. 'Something's wrong. What is it?' furrowing her brow.

He quickly tipped the second down his throat and closed his eyes. 'Chekhov!' he muttered.

'Who?' she said leaning forward across the table.

'Chekhov. My opposite number in the Russian team. He's gone. Disappeared.'

'What do you mean disappeared? Have you called him? Gone to see him?'

'Yep. Did all that. His place is all cleaned out, like he's never been there. I met him today. We were to have dinner tonight. I went to call for him and nobody's seen him.'

'Ok' she said trying to think logically. 'He may have had to leave suddenly. Personal perhaps. Did you speak to his assistant?'

'Yeah! That's the real puzzle. They say he never arrived. In fact he wasn't even part of their team. Suspended some months ago. Some drug fixing allegation. I don't get it. Why would they lie?'

She shook her head and bit her lip in thought. 'Is he...' she trailed off not wanting to antagonise him.

'Is he what?' he demanded.

'Look. I'm only trying to help you' she said defensively.

'I know Jenny! Just tell me what you think.'

They exchanged confidences during which he told her of the file transfer and the FSR comment, while she suggested he *could* be a drug courier and an embarrassment to the Russians. The food arrived, during which he visibly relaxed and for the first time since she had known him, seemed to unwind. It was past midnight when they pulled up outside her converted warehouse apartment in the old cobbled streets of Wapping. They sat with the windows down, breathing in the warm night air and watching the early morning milk float head towards them with a light whine of its electric engine. A black cab chugged to a stop about twenty yards ahead, disgorging a young couple covered in streamers and confetti. The man opened the street door and they both fell in giggling and laughing while the cab did a one eighty turn and swished past the Jensen. Cranfield sat behind the wheel deep in thought.

'Jenny. I need your help. I know that what I am asking you is outside your job description, but I am concerned for my friend and I would appreciate it if you could see your way to assist. I will give you whatever you want. Money, travel, anything. Just help me find Chekhov. It'll mean a lot to me. I owe him.'

'Listen' she said turning in her seat to face him. 'I'm not an investigator. Call the police. Surely they can do more than me.'

'No Jenny. I can't go official. There's a history of bad blood spilt in the wrong quarters.'

For a moment they both sat deep in thought.

'Got it!' she suddenly said. 'I know this guy. He comes across on all counts except one.'

'What's that?' quizzed Cranfield.

'He can be as pig headed and single minded as you!' she blurted out without thought.

'That's the one I want' he snapped, ignoring her half insult. 'What's his name?' he demanded.

'Alex Mason.'

'Can you get hold of him? Will he do it?'

'I don't know' she shook her head.

'Please try. I'll be forever grateful!' She had never seen him beg before. It was disturbing, but sensual to see this powerhouse of a man almost whimpering next to her. She smiled coquettishly.

'If I do this, **how** grateful will **you** be to me?' she opened her mouth and ran her tongue slowly across her open lips close to his face, looking deeply into his eyes.

He froze for a second as the implication of her question sank in. But only for a second as her hand graced his upper leg.

MOSCOW

Chekhov stood, cold and frightened in his small sparse office and gazed outside across Red Square. The last twenty four hours had been a nightmare, following his abduction from London. Blindfolded, gagged and drugged, his captors had roughly and efficiently forced him, at gunpoint, from his Stratford Village apartment down the emergency stairs and into the back seat of the blackened window Mercedes. Within two hours he was flying back to Russia in a private jet. His fellow travellers sat either side of him filling the seats with their ample bodies. He asked no questions, as he had always believed was the best policy if you wanted to stay alive, or at least avoid a heavy punch. At his office, he was frogmarched up the stairs and unceremoniously thrown to the floor, the door being slammed behind him. Red Square was bustling with people and traffic as the final preparations proceeded for the visit of the UN Secretary General at the weekend. Banners and flags fluttered in the Summer sunshine, supported by various displays of youth groups, marching to marshal music booming into the square from hundreds of speakers. Pigeons flapped their wings in unison and lifted off in droves as the music grew to a crescendo. The tourists stood and marvelled at the structures and Imperial buildings that looked down on them, their guides carefully pointing out the salient features that their digital cameras could easily capture. One man, temporarily lost from his group, innocently aimed his zoom in Chekhov's direction and was quickly encircled by several large men until finally his official tour guide came along, freeing the terrified tourist with a stern warning. The Olympic coach jumped as his phone rang.

'Yes?'

'Chekhov?' came a familiar voice.

'Of course. Who's that?'

'Mahlkoff, from the Olympic Press Bureau. We must talk. Can we meet?'

'What for?' the kidnapped man replied suspiciously.

'Something to your benefit' Mahlkoff insisted.

'When and where?' Chekhov asked cautiously.

'Four this afternoon, you know where' the Bureau man whispered.

'I'll try' sighed Chekhov, still unconvinced.

'Just be there!' ordered the caller.

The line went dead, but not before a soft click resounded as he went to hang up. He frowned, worried that it was a trap. You couldn't trust anyone. Even your best friend. Still, he hadn't done anything to his knowledge. Nobody had told him why he had been forcibly returned. In fact no one had even spoken to him.

It was noon. He decided to force the lock, get to the meeting and disappear, all the time hoping he wouldn't be stopped. Rolling up the threadbare carpet that desperately tried to cover the flooring; he focussed all his attention on a loose board in the corner by the window. Kneeling down, he jammed his fingers into the small space between the board and the wooden skirting board. Pushing downwards and sideways at the same time he gradually levered the board out, revealing a dark void beneath, into which he pushed his right hand while probing with his fingers. Suddenly he felt it! Concentrating with all his being, he eased the tool out and crossed silently to the door frame. With a quick movement, he slipped the catch and eased the door open while realising that it had not been locked after all. He peered outside and to his total surprise found that there was no one there. 'What the hell is going on?' he thought, as he stepped onto the deserted landing, quietly closing the door and descending downstairs from his first floor flat to the street below. Lowering his head and looking downwards away from any CCTV cameras that are a part of Moscow and its environs, he sauntered across the busy road and headed for the local street market. It was very vibrant, with stall holders hollering to the crowds and the omnipresent smell of fresh fruit and fish pervading the warm sunshine. Someone proffered a MP4, while a burly grocer tried to tempt him with the latest food from the USA. As he pushed through the throng of the crowd, he caught sight of a man trying to keep up with him. He had to be sure. Straining with all his might, he moved through the jostling melee into a narrow alley away from the market and then ducked into a shop doorway, disappearing into its shadows. He waited for what seemed forever, but was actually only about a minute. The sweat poured from his forehead as he took a deep breath and considered his next move. He was about to step out when a strong hand on his shoulder pinned him to where he stood and a soft, but firm voice whispered in his right ear.

'Not yet! Come this way' and tugged him further into the shop. 'Quickly!' said the voice, now moving further into the rear of the shop. 'Hurry! This way!' it insisted. Blindly he followed the voice, until he stood motionless in pitch darkness on a damp floor.

'Where are you?' he said. Silence. 'Hello?' he asked, now slightly worried. Nothing. He stretched out his hands into the void like a blind man clutching at air. Where was he? Who was this voice? Was this about to be a violent robbery? Something brushed across his face. He stepped back. 'What do you want? Show yourself!' Again he felt the soft material brush his face, but this time he also detected a perfume. He knew the scent, but could not place it. 'Come on!' he challenged. 'I've got a weapon!' he said bluffing.

'No, you haven't' said the voice that he thought he recognised. 'Take two steps back with your hands in the air!'

Feeling totally vulnerable and exposed, he complied and stepped back. If he had had a pacemaker he would have been dead by now, as his heart was pounding furiously below his chest in abject fear. A sudden explosion of light burst in his face as a powerful bulb ignited in the ceiling above him. For a second he tried to focus, as the incandescent flash gradually settled down, leaving a bright but fading starburst of colours floating in front of his pupils. Then, slowly, a familiar silhouette settled in front of him as his eyes became more accustomed to the light.

'Morag! What are you doing here?' kissing his wife.

'No questions now. I'll explain later. You must get to your meeting. Alexi will drive you.' She motioned to the small framed, bespectacled teenager standing behind him. Alexi smiled, displaying a perfect set of white teeth, looking as though he had just left the set of a toothpaste commercial.

'Go!' she said urgently, waving him away with her hands, while blowing him a kiss as she disappeared through a back door.

For a moment his emotions roller-coasted from joy to fear.

'Come. We must move now!' said Alexi insistently; pulling Chekhov through the same door that Morag had just departed from and into an old Lada.

Moscow Central Station stood at the hub of an axis of roads that daily disgorged an estimated ten million workers though its barriers and onto the capital's streets. It was down one of those broad, lifeless avenues that Mahlkoff came, limping on his twisted right leg, carrying a document case for the rendezvous. It was because he was so noticeable for his war shattered ankle and the precarious assignments that he often had, that he had made it his business to be as indistinguishable as possible and have any meetings in crowded, bustling areas. To the nondescript men who had followed Mahlkoff to the station, they saw and learnt nothing. Chekhov had been waiting in advance in the men's toilet on the third carriage of the Trans Siberian train pulled up at platform twenty. Their meeting was over before the agents even boarded, leaving Chekhov with the documents and Mahlkoff pushing through the crowds towards the street. Only after one hour did Chekhov exit the train and the station, walking in a zig zag route, while checking behind him for any unusual movement. After all, two surprises in one day were too much to take, even for him.

The Radisson SA Slavyanskaya Hotel is centrally located on the banks of the Moscow River with good views of the Russian White House and Europe Square. The US and British Embassies stood on the opposite side of the river, separated by the Parliament of Russia. From his dressing table Chekhov could see all three buildings as well as the riverboats from the Kievskaya pier, chugging slowly downstream towards Gorky Park and Red Square. At any other time he would stand and stare for hours, but now his time was precious as Max, his close friend on the desk, let him have the first floor room for the night without registering.

'Don't be too long. You know that I officially have to inform the Police of every guest. You've got it only because an American left early and the room is still in his name and unmade.'

Chekhov spread out the documents and for a moment couldn't understand what he was looking at. He picked up a catalogue of photos, all numbered and dated, obviously taken in hospitals or research clinics. The enormity of the photos meant nothing until he played the accompanying DVD. Hosting the video was a Professor Lang, who claimed that extensive global 'human trials' had taken place covertly over the past few years. His conclusions accompanied scenes from what can only be described as a 'B' horror movie. Stunned by what he had just seen, Chekhov sat perplexed and tried to evaluate its meaning. 'I don't believe it!' he rationalised, before running the video again to get a better understanding. As he sat on the edge of the bed, the facts, as expressed by the Professor, suddenly dawned on him. He picked up the documents and reviewed them for the second time. 'My God!' he mumbled, as the possibilities of events far removed from his world of sport began to fall into place. He pored over the cuttings from the western press as well as Pravda, including a two liner in the May Day edition under the weather page. The sweat glistened on his forehead as he started to understand the implications of what was now the biggest political bombshell the world had ever known since the Russian Revolution and he, Chekhov, was sitting on the slow burning fuse. He lowered the summary document and stared into the distance. It was five in the afternoon when he received a knock at the door. At first he sat there not moving, not making any sound, fearing the secret police. But the knocking continued with Max calling his name. Carefully he opened the door and saw his friend standing there.

'Sorry Chekhov. This is all the time I can let you have. I am about to hand over to the night team and I won't be able to explain you're being here. You must leave now!' He looked down the corridor nervously.

'No problem. I'll just pack up. Be with you in two minutes.' He closed the door, put all the material into a hotel complimentary bag, left the room and exited the hotel without acknowledging Max. Within half an hour he was back in his office, knowing what he soon had to do.

JENNY

Jenny could not locate Alex at any of his known locations and many avenues of enquiry were being uncommunicative and openly hostile. She squinted her eyes and concentrated. Try as she might, she could not find him. After numerous leads, all finishing in dead ends, she slumped backwards onto the sofa and searched her mind. He was known as a data miner and she tried to think where she would be in his shoes. She flicked her communicator open and hit the speed dial.

'Yes?' he questioned. He never used name or number.

'Alex. This is Jenny White. You did something for me some time ago and I want to use your services again. Can you help me? Are you available?'

He shut his eyes and remembered her alright. It was a frustrating memory as he wanted to *do* something *to* her the last time they met, but it had not taken place and he had left her apartment not knowing why she had rejected him. He visualised their last meeting. She was blonde, lightly tanned and had a provocative way of moving her supple body like a cobra swaying before it strikes.

'Yes Jenny. I remember. How have you been? A year I believe.'

'Two years actually' she countered quickly. The words hung in the air uneasily and uncomfortably for both of them, but more for her.

'Sorry Alex. I should have called you. Please forgive me?' She begged on the phone, a tear running down her cheek, knowing that this was the best guy she had ever come across and lost. She bit her lip. 'Alex? Are you there? Please talk to me?'

There was silence.

'Ok Jenny. Let's put it behind us. Water under the bridge and all that. How can I help?'

Jenny briefly explained, as Alex listened on the hands free while dressing. He looked out over the Thames from his

Chelsea penthouse, as the freewheeling gulls swooped and dived around the pleasure craft below him.

'Just a tick Jenny' he put her on hold. He checked his e diary, took a swig of Jack Daniels and reconnected. 'Ok. I'll do it on two conditions.'

'Well. What are they?'

'One. Five hundred a day, plus unlimited expenses. One thousand up front, plus another one thousand when I locate Chekhov. All in cash.'

She choked on the figures. 'Alex. Please hold while I check this out.'

After what to her seemed an eternity, Cranfield pondered, then gave his reluctant consent.

'It's agreed' Jenny confirmed to Alex. 'When do you start?'

'I don't, unless the second condition is met fully and without reservation. Do you agree?'

'Go on' she said cautiously. 'What do you want?' she asked.

His answer was fast and uncompromising. 'You. I want you!'

NEWSPAPER

The morning meeting at the paper held no surprises for anyone. A few scandals, tooing and froing of politicians, a defeat for the England Test Team in Karachi and a Government/ Union dispute. This, though, was the normal boring midweek pattern, as was etched on the faces of the subeditors attending the seven a.m. breakfast meeting with the Editor. The Columbian coffee percolating away in the corner of Jim Wilson's office, together with the bacon sandwiches, provided a pleasant start to the day. All the team were there. Six heads of departments and the Picture Editor. They sat around the oval table with a speaker phone in the centre and a pad and pencil at each seat. Small talk ensued until Jim came in, compressing his sweating fifteen stone frame into the Editor's Chair at the head of the table and below a picture of Robert Redford and Dustin Hoffman in a scene from 'All the President's Men.'

'Morning. What's news?' his eyes ran around the table while twisting his chair back and forth, his muscular arms resting just inside the arm rests. 'Anyone? Come on guys, what's happening?' He swung his mass towards the sportily dressed Picture Editor. 'Come on Fred!' he bawled across the table. 'Royals and Sex. You must have something we can use?'

'Fraid not Jim. It's this bloody heat. No one is doing anything. Even the paparazzi aren't calling with much. We do have a snap (he passed it around) of one of the Iraqi Olympic runners in bed with some D celebrity starlet.'

They all looked intently, some turning the image through three hundred and sixty degrees, trying to work out who was who.

'This is shit!' screamed Wilson. 'Don't you have anything else?' eyeballing the picture man.

Silence.

'Then I suggest you go and get something and fast! Who's next?'

Before anyone else dared answer, the large fan brought in to counter the air conditioning failure whirred vindictively to a halt.

'Fuck me! Doesn't anything work round here?' he screamed.

The meeting continued with the jammed window behind Jim's chair being forced open by Colin and ended ten minutes later with an agreement to print the headline IRAQ'S SECRET WMD FUSED WITH USA STAR! over the picture. As the meeting finished and the others all filed out, Colin had managed to isolate Jim and have a few words with him. Through the soundproofed glass wall, all the hacks could see was Jim leaning across to Colin and scratching his stubbled chin. His eyes narrowed as he poked a finger at the Science man and turned in his chair, indicating the Watergate picture above him. Suddenly the Venetian blinds snapped shut and the private talk continued unobserved for another five minutes. When eventually the door did open, Colin flew like a bat out of hell, leaping two stairs at a time down the internal stairway to Karen's desk, where they talked furtively for ten minutes.

'He's given us a go!' Colin said excitedly, like a small boy opening his Christmas presents. 'An open budget until we find him and get all the answers. It could be nothing. But there again'.... his voice trailed off. 'The best place to track him down is.......'

'The Science Museum!' burst in Karen. 'I've a friend in a good position there. I'll arrange a meeting and see what I can dig up' she said.

Colin was about to suggest a name, when he suddenly realised that he was talking to himself. Karen had already left.

Karen swung her MGB across the Sun drenched gravel car park of the Museum and into one of the shady 'reserved' spaces adjacent to the line of tall marching conifers. Rummaging in her glove box between the tissues, mints and de-icer spray, the 'PRESS' card fell out onto the floor of the car. She picked it up and placed it on the dashboard, its tired condition a reflection of the numerous places visited in her many years as a journalist. A few minutes later, she was talking with Anne in the cool of her air conditioned office. They had not seen each other for over two years, but had remained in touch. The cordial small talk went on for five minutes until Karen asked about the Professor. Anne nervously looked across the desk at her childhood friend and glancing around her as if someone could be listening, suddenly stood up.

'I am sorry Karen. I can't help you' she said coldly and loudly. 'You'll have to leave. I have a meeting to go to. I am sure you can see yourself out.' With that, she marched out leaving Karen rooted to her chair and completely dumbfounded.

'Wow!' she mumbled to herself. 'What was *that* all about?'

Anne was already half way down the corridor, when Karen realised that she had dropped a folder on the floor in her haste to leave. Picking it up and about to replace it on the desk she noticed a tab protruding. 'LANG-

CONFIDENTIAL-EYES ONLY'. Looking inside, she stared wide-eyed like a rabbit caught in the full glare of oncoming headlamps, as she absorbed the information. Realising that her time was limited, she quickly took copies on Anne's laser and replaced everything as it was, before heading for her car and a meeting with Colin at his flat. They both agreed that what she had was headline grabbing, but also dangerous. After several hours and a phone call to Jim, they had decided on a plan.

The shadowy figure across the road took the call, walked along the pavement and quickly but expertly attached a small plastic box under the MGB's boot. He returned to his car and made a call. 'It's done!' he announced. He turned on his radio and tapped his fingers to the song 'We have all the time in the World.' 'Some of us do!' he smiled cruelly as he drove past Jenny's car and then began to laugh.

ESCAPE

Chekhov had been dreaming of hot Summer days and long balmy nights when he had been a youth, having had a superb sporting future in addition to many amorous affairs for one so young. Then the atmosphere darkened, with his recollections of War and the blitzkrieg inflicted by the Germans, followed by his patriotic defence of Moscow together with his fellow soldiers of the Red Army. Although his mind was visualising past scenes, a part of his subconscious awoke when the door handle began to turn slowly. His eyes focussed on the locked door and then the clock on the shelf....5am. He knew that the FSR or even their powerful and secret allies of Zasion or Shield often raided at dawn and reactionary groups had always had the motto 'be prepared', Chekhov being no exception. Stealthily he crossed his office to a knapsack standing in the corner, slid the documents into a pouch and hoisting the strap onto his shoulder, climbed out of the side window onto a fire escape and had disappeared into the dawn, just as the first of the two men crept furtively up to his door. He had prepared well in advance for this, even though he had hoped it would never come. Moving down selected side streets and ducking into doorways, brought him to a bleak car park near Kievskaya Metro and Rail Station. Praying, as he hadn't done for forty years and keeping as low a profile as possible, he scurried across the lot to a near respectable Lada that stood in a corner, away from the bulk of the other cars. After carefully looking around, he opened the front door, got in and sat behind the wheel. A quick check of his sack told him everything was there. Money, food, documents, passport. His watch read 6am. 'Must not move before 7.30' he told himself, thereby merging with the rest of the traffic chaos in and around Moscow Centre. Gradually the traffic flow increased, until at approximately 8.15 it was in full flow and the Lada ambled out to be submerged in the crawling dioxide mass. After leaving the main highway, the road north diverged into three tracks. It was on one of these that Chekhov was now heading, bouncing along the tortuous and twisting route until it abruptly ended in a vast field that appeared to stretch for miles. In one corner of this expanse stood a large derelict barn, which from all appearances had not been attended to for years. Wood had dried and peeled under the Summer Sun, while the vicious snows and winds had cracked the corrugated roofing, leaving it tattered and rusty. All this pleased Chekhov, for it meant that no one knew his secret. Opening the front and rear barn doors with his key, he felt the butterflies in his stomach rising. After a quick glance around, he was inside and ripping the tarpaulin off the jet plane kept for just this purpose. As the engine coughed and roared into life, emitting a whine followed by choking blue fumes, Chekhov eased the joystick forward, the plane trundling out to the first light of day it had seen for some years. Within minutes he was airborne, amazed at how simple it had been to remember the controls. Most important were his planned tactics of hedge hopping below radar levels and listening in to Soviet Air Traffic. After less than an hour, radio chatter increased as he approached the Soviet/ Norwegian air border. His heart rate climbed as he now was going to attempt to shadow a foreign airliner out of Soviet airspace and fool the ground radar into thinking that there was only one plane on their screens. He heard a British Airways call for clearance amongst the signals and knowing it was now or never, positioned himself within its flight path. As the old style Jumbo thundered down the runway, tipping its bulbous nose skyward whilst clawing at the air, Chekhov rapidly increased his knots until he matched its speed and angle finally latching close behind its mass and rising with it until the altimeter read 30,000 feet.

In the air traffic tower, now five miles below and ten downrange, Petrov, one of the outgoing controllers, watched the four digit code representing the Jumbo momentarily flicker, stretch and resume its constant bleep.

For a moment he considered calling his supervisor across, but remembering the last time he did that and the sharp rebuke he received when it was discovered that it was a system error, he bit his lip and said nothing. Far above, even allowing for the fact that he was sweating profusely and breathing through his oxygen mask, Chekhov was happy and becoming more confident by the minute. It seemed unbelievable, but his plan seemed to be succeeding! In fact, as he checked his position, he saw that it had succeeded. He hopefully would avoid any military involvement, as long as he kept to the same altitude and bearing. After some time he suddenly realised that he had no idea where the Jumbo was headed. On this current bearing it could be England or beyond......possibly the USA! A terrible thought then occurred to him. He had not intended a long flight and would soon have to leave the cover of the Jumbo as his fuel depleted, exposing him to RAF fighters on constant vigil against intruders. No sooner had this thought crossed his mind than he noticed the

Jumbo start to descend with radio traffic confirming Glasgow as its destination. He dipped with it through the clouds but on emerging found that he was now totally alone and very exposed. Hurriedly scanning the skies, he knew it was only a matter of minutes before RAF interceptors would be closing in. He pushed the joystick forward, thrusting the jet into a suicidal steep dive, the altimeter crazily spinning anticlockwise towards zero. As the vibrations rapidly increased, Chekhov prayed he hadn't left it too late. His clammy palms grasped the joystick at 10,000 feet and eased it back. At first nothing happened, but then slowly the nose came up, the G force decreased and gradually the plane levelled off at about 3000 feet to reveal a wild and inhospitable terrain, comprising windswept escarpments, raging rivers and vast forests. Having gained a few minutes from possible detection by hostile fighters, Chekhov banked through the clouds until suddenly he saw what appeared to be a clearing amongst the trees. He overshot and established its suitability. 'Seems ok' he thought and prepared for a short and maybe violent landing.

ALEX

Jenny arranged to meet Alex in St James's Park by the bridge. It was, she thought, a neutral piece of ground, especially after last time when she found herself trapped in his apartment and almost tanked out of her mind with the booze he was plying her with. She had to admit that she quite liked his company, but was very wary of his motives, especially towards women and particularly towards her. After all, she was the first, as far as she knew, to avoid his bed and it was quite possible that she would be the jewel in the crown to be acquired and conquered, at all costs, by him. He arrived in impeccable style; Italian light blue striped suit, with Gucci shoes to match, and a crisp white shirt sporting a Windsor-knotted crimson tie.

'My! Aren't you the one?' admired Jenny, giving him the once over. 'Bet you don't do this for *all* your girls' she said cynically.

'You're right' he countered 'and because you're someone special, I've got you this.'

She hadn't noticed that he was carrying anything, so when he produced a single red rose, it took her aback.

'Oh!' she gasped. 'Thank you Alex. It's beautiful!'

'It's my pleasure!' he smiled, bowing in mock salute.

After a second or two admiring the rose, Jenny snapped back into gear. 'This is lovely Alex, but we must remember that this is a business assignment. I am paying you to find Chekhov.'

He held up his hands in mock surrender. 'Ok. Ok. If this is business, let's get to it! First let me tell you what I've discovered since you called.'

They strolled along past the idyllic lake and lazing ducks, exchanging facts, ideas and views, until at last they sat down on a bench and recapped.

'Well, if he's disappeared, surely the UK and Russian authorities will be concerned?' she said.

'That's true' said Alex. 'But remember. His wife, who is Scottish, was also Lang's Associate Professor! If he's gone missing, you can bet your bottom dollar she's mixed up in this as well!'

'Yes, it's possible. But that's not why I'm hiring you. Your job will be to locate Chekhov and that's all!' she snapped. Her eyes were full of fury and he felt he had touched an exposed nerve and best leave it well alone, lest she release the full force of her venom on him.

'Ok. Ok. Point taken. I'll contact you when I can, or when I've got Chekhov' and started to stroll off.

'Just a minute!' she shouted at him. 'Where do you think you're going?' she added emphatically.

'I've just told you. To find Chekhov.'

'Not without me you don't.'

'That's not part of the deal and besides, I always work alone.'

'It's the *only* way you'll do this job. You take me with you. After all, I'm no novice. I've been where the action is as part of my job before.'

He scratched his chin, gave a slight mumble of displeasure, adding 'Well come on if you are coming!'

'Where are we going?'

'Bonnie Scotland my girl' striding off towards Horse guards, with Jenny in hot pursuit.

MOTORWAY

As Karen motored up the M1, all of her instincts told her that this investigation could be the biggest story to break since sliced bread was invented. Her stomach called to her with a deep rumble and her eyes drifted to the clock. Eight pm. Tired and hungry, she felt the need for rest, so when she spotted the motel sign, she drove the quarter mile distance and pulled up in front of the brightly lit reception. After checking in and having a satisfying meal followed by a brandy, she returned to her room, showered and flopped into bed like a sack of potatoes. Had she not been so tired, her journalistic instincts might have put her on her guard against possible repercussions in the wake of her visit to the Science Museum. She might also have noticed the black van that drew up beside her car and the shadowy figures crouching between the two vehicles.

Karen slept like a log and so was amazed to see the time at 9am on waking. She pulled the blinds and stood looking out across the car park, to rolling green fields enhanced by blue skies and a blazing sun. Everything seemed bright and rosy, even when a coach load of football supporters passed by slowly waving and gesticulating wildly, she thought of only the day ahead and not of the current moment. She was therefore brought sharply down to earth, when minutes later an aggressive knocking came from her front door. She quickly pulled a sweater and jeans on and half tripped to the door.

'Yes?' she said, tossing her hair to one side.

A middle-aged heavily built man in a dark suit and tie stood glaring at her in the doorway.

'Well! How can I help you?' she said impatiently.

'Help Me? Help Me?' he growled. 'I think that you've done enough already, don't you?'

'Look' she said 'I don't know what you are talking about and if you don't go away I'll call the Manager!'

'I am the Manager!' he snapped. 'I want you out in 5 minutes. Understood? Gone up the motorway to flaunt yourself elsewhere. This is a respectable business and your sort we don't want.'

'Just a moment! What the hell are you blathering about? Just what am I supposed to have done?' she said indignantly.

'Little miss innocent are we now? Protesting your virtue while enticing every pervert in the district here! A slut is a slut in any language! Out in 5 minutes!'

'Just a damned minute!' she screamed. 'How dare you accuse me of something indecent? What am I supposed to have done? Where are your witnesses?'

The Manager turned to his right and spoke to someone just out of sight.

A middle aged couple stepped into view.

'That's her! That's the harlot!' said a greying elderly woman pointing with an accusing finger.

'Mr Archer. Do you agree with your wife?' the Manager asked.

Mr Archer peered through his glasses, eying Karen from head to toe. 'I think it is, only has more clothes on now!' A wicked smile came onto his face as Karen felt his eyes undressing her slowly and methodically. For a moment she felt vulnerable, hurt. But only for a moment.

'I'll be a lot quicker than five minutes!' she yelled and slamming the door in their faces shouted 'and I don't like dirty old peeping toms!'

She stood gasping for air, distraught and shaken. 'What the hell are they all talking about?' She eyed the room; and then it clicked. The bed and window. Quickly she ran to the blinds and closed them. Then it flooded back to her. She had waved to the youngsters on the coach! No wonder they were whistling at her! She had been stark naked and in full public view! She blushed at the thought of the embarrassment.

Carrying a hot coffee, it took her a couple of minutes to check out and join the mainstream traffic heading north. As she eased the car into the fast lane and hit eighty the black van also moved out, but this time with a purpose. A glance through her rear view mirror showed the van moving up very fast on the outside lane, it's headlamps on full beam while closing the distance with her. At first she thought nothing of it and eased over to the centre lane, giving the van a clear run. To her worry it moved over close behind until its bumper touched. Other cars sounded their horns as she wildly weaved through them accelerating quickly only to see the van respond, tagging right behind her. All she could see & hear was dazzling light and a deafening horn. Then it happened. For almost a mile in any direction there were no other vehicles. The van swung out and drew alongside while opening its sliding door. A hooded figure tossed what seemed like an egg into her window and onto her lap. She screamed and holding the wheel with one hand grabbed the grenade and tossed it out with the other, while swerving drunkenly across 3 lanes. With a blast of hot air, a blinding explosion violently tossed red-hot shrapnel through the air. The MGB cart-wheeled through 360 degrees ending up on it's side, heavily pot marked by flying fragments. By now several other vehicles had screeched to a halt, their drivers sprinting across the carriageways to offer assistance.

Thirty minutes and several cars back, Alex and Jenny sat waiting for the traffic to clear, as the blaring sirens and blue lights of the emergency services raced by on the hard shoulder.

'Very exciting isn't it?' said Jenny.

'Very. Makes the day pass, don't you think?' replied Alex whimsically.

She poked her tongue out like a schoolgirl and he smiled. Same old Jenny. Young at heart yet cool and sophisticated when necessary. After about an hour, the traffic started moving slowly up the incline, passing the scene of carnage on full view to all the rubberneckers. Suddenly Alex swung the car violently in the direction of the blue lights and pulled up. He jumped out and ran over to a brightly marked police Traffic Car and yanked the rear door open, revealing Karen sitting forlornly and alone in the back seat. Two nearby police officers instantly rugby tackled him to the floor, one whipping out his handcuffs, the other writhing on the dusty floor under Alex's powerful frame.

'Let him go' shouted another officer, holding a warrant card which had fallen from Alex's trouser pocket. Extracting himself from their grip, he stood up, brushed himself down and faced the officer who had called his colleagues off.

'I believe this is yours?' said the Inspector, handing over an open wallet displaying Alex's official identification.

Karen clambered out and throwing her bruised and cut arms around him, burst into tears in his arms. 'Oh Alex!' she sobbed.

'Do you know this lady?' said the Inspector.

'Yes, I do. What's happened?'

'Well sir, it would appear that the young lady's car has been involved in a near fatal incident! We need her to come with us to give a statement. You can come if you want.'

Alex carefully brushed her hair back, revealing a few bruises and a couple of light scratches.

'You're alright' he said sympathetically. 'Nothing that a hot bath and a double scotch won't fix' he added.

She smiled up at him. 'Thanks.'

'Inspector. Is it ok that she travels with me?'

'No problem. Just follow us.' He took the 'governor's' traditional front seat in the Mitsubishi Police Interceptor and moved off slowly, allowing Alex enough time to escort Karen to his car, where she sat in the back, wrapped in a police blanket.

LANG

The plane had somersaulted on landing after hitting several tall trees and had ground to a halt upside down in a hollow. Although he was cut with shards of flying glass, Chekhov's most immediate concern was the fear of explosion due to leaking aviation fuel. It was extremely difficult to manoeuvre whilst suspended upside down and bleeding, but after several attempts, he released his buckle and kicked open the jammed cockpit hatch. He dropped to the ground and still dazed, painfully hobbled well away from the debris towards a mass of large boulders nearby. No sooner had he gained cover, then a deafening explosion followed by an orange ball of fire and dense black smoke engulfed the fuselage. The shock wave tossed him backwards like a rag doll, causing him to violently strike his head and lose consciousness. He awoke feeling cold, hurt, bruised and disorientated. At first he couldn't see anything. Panic gripped him as he terrifyingly believed he was blind. Then, gradually, he saw lights flickering and shimmering in a misty vision. Rubbing his eyes hard he suddenly realised that he was observing the Milky Way and visibly relaxed as he observed with relief it's many outlines. Still he couldn't comprehend the gloom. It then occurred to him that it was night and this, together with a creeping mountain mist, explained his poor vision. Feeling exhausted, his eyelids heavily lowered themselves and he quickly dropped off to sleep as the night temperature quickly plummeted.

The morning found Chekhov gone, after he thought he heard noises in the pre-dawn period. Not wildlife, but human. He peered into the gloom seeking the source, but seeing only shadows he cautiously left the area and melted into the landscape. He avoided roads, knowing his present appearance and accent would raise more than one or two questions. It was important that he blended as far as possible into the local environment, but since this would require guile and a change of clothes, his task would be much harder. By noon he had covered about ten miles and was heading north across lush fields and trickling brooks. Only twice did he venture onto the roads; once to cross an unmanned level crossing and the other when unable to go further due to a six foot barbed wire fence that confronted him, disappearing into the distance with the notice 'MINISTRY OF DEFENCE-NO UNAUTHORISED PERSONNEL'. This, together with a metal plate bearing the insignia of a skull and crossbones attached to the fence, persuaded him to cross an adjacent stile with caution and continue along a stony track.

Around four that afternoon, a whining sound from the south caused him to stop and listen intently. The noise grew louder and soon changed to a steady chopping sound. He dived for cover as the dust flew about him, while a massive helicopter hovered nearby, its green clad occupants scanning the area with binoculars. It was twenty minutes before they left, twisting through the air like a demented whirlwind and disappearing over the rugged hills with no trace of their visit, bar tufts of grass caught in the downdraft from the blades, strewn over a small area. He watched them go from a small cave he had found and dusting himself down, couldn't help wonder how they knew which way he was heading.

As dusk approached and the sky painted itself a golden halo, Chekhov found himself near an old log cabin on the banks of a Loch. It was eighteen hours since the crash-landing and he was now cold and starting to dehydrate badly. Any fear that he held now was suppressed by a longing for food and sleep. Even so, he could not relax. Furtively scanning the trees and the area around the cabin, he gingerly crept to its only window. Wisps of smoke drifted from the wooden chimney into the trees, curling into the darkening sky. The flickering light and warm glow from the log fire that he saw through the grimy window bewitchingly enticed him. He peered through the panes in vain for the occupant and seeing no one, checked once more before easing open the creaking heavy door.

'Hello? Any one there?' in his best English.

Apart from the door, the only other sound was the crackling of the logs on the open hearth and a fresh pot of coffee bubbling away by the fireplace. He looked around. The cabin seemed well stocked with food and books on fly fishing. A table with old chairs stood silent with a photo of a man holding a fish on a wall, surrounded by various cups and medals. At one end of the cabin, standing proudly on four stout legs, was a single bed with a large Norwegian duvet billowing over the edges like puffy cumulus clouds playing in the sun. A lavatory and sink made up the rest of the cabin, save for a large rocking chair which stood in front of the fire and to the left of the coffee pot. Chekhov slumped in the chair. He watched the flames perform their hypnotic dance, as his eyes grew heavier, tipping him into a deep black void.

He awoke with a start. He didn't know why. It was still dark but as he attempted to rise from the rocking chair, he was catapulted forward onto the bare floor. He tried to rise, but was rewarded with a swift kick in the back sending him sprawling into the fire grate.

'Don't move or it'll be last thing you do! Lie on your stomach with your hands behind your back!' a gruff man's voice barked.

Chekhov wasn't into the hero stakes and quickly complied. His legs were spread apart by the man's foot, who then frisked him with one hand, the other pressing the wooden stock of an axe into his neck.

'Who are you?' growled the axe man.

Chekhov thought quickly. 'If he was FSR or MI6 he would know me. If not............' 'My name is Chekhov. I am trying to find a Professor Lang' he said uncomfortably with his face pressing into the floorboards.

'Why?' growled the axe man.

'I can't tell you, but I must get to him quickly!'

'Is that so!' the axe man snidely said, with menacing undertones. 'Get up! Quickly!'

Chekhov warily got up and was thrown forcefully against a wooden wall.

'What identification do you have?'

'None. All my documents burnt in my plane that exploded after I crashed.' Chekhov felt a sharp painful jab into his ribs. In blind panic he shouted. 'Wait. I've got proof. Let me take my shoe off!'

'Why?' the axe man asked suspiciously.

'I have a paper in my right heel!' the Russian pleaded.

'Alright, but with your left hand and do it *very* slowly.'

Carefully Chekhov dropped to his knees and slowly removed his right shoe.

'Take out the paper!' barked the axe man. 'Slowly. No tricks! Left hand only.' Twisting the heel on a pivot, a hollow appeared containing a piece of folded paper enclosed in a plastic wrapper, which he carefully passed behind him.

The axe man took the paper and while Chekhov silently prayed his assailant read. It was the longest minute of his life.

'Put your shoe on. I had to be sure' the axe man barked. The axe was lowered and Chekhov slumped relieved into an old wooden chair. 'You like Whiskey?' said the axe man, producing a bottle of scotch and two tumblers.

'Vodka, Whiskey, Rum. We Russians drink it all!' Chekhov grimaced, rubbing his bruised rib.

They raised their glasses, toasted each other and downed the measures as if Highland Whiskey was as cheap as water.

'To you Chekhov!' he raised his glass in salute. 'You're a very brave man. I hope I can be as strong when my moment comes.' He looked forlorn, subdued.

'What do you mean your moment? You look content. Why should you be in fear?'

'Chekhov, my boy. Before you came today, I had hoped that I was safe and out of peril. But now you have opened up a Pandora's Box. We are both in mortal danger even more than before.'

'What are you talking about? How can we both be in danger? I am the one who is on the run not you, unless your problem is bigger than mine.'

The axe man filled both glasses to the top. 'Chekhov. I like you for your honesty and guts. By the time you've heard me out, you will realise that your problem is my problem. Let me first apologise for the axe and the bad welcome. I will make amends immediately.'

They shook hands across the table, but when Chekhov eventually eased his hand away from the iron grip of the axe man, he held a tattered paper in his palm. He stared long and hard at it and then swivelled his eyes incredulously at the tall man.

'Oh my God! You, you ………'

'Yes. Let me introduce myself. I am the man you came to find. I am Professor Lang. Let's have another drink and you can tell me why you have risked your life to find this old man.' He tapped himself on the chest, sat back and watched Chekhov's face drain of its entire colour, while spluttering most of his mouthful across the cabin in shock.

The Professor raised a hand and refilled Chekhov's glass. Furtively the Professor leaned across the table to his new drinking companion. Even though there were only two of them, they quietly exchanged confidences in the fear that even the walls had ears. It was past two in the morning when both men had finished their stories, together with three bottles of the finest to match. They lay like children, sprawled out, heads on hands across the table, oblivious and uncaring about anything around them. For them the night was uneventful.

GILES

July 2nd the Post Office Tower, top floor. The lonely printer standing in the corner chugged out reams of data, whilst the rain lashed down on the surrounding windows, almost drowning the small talk of the invited specialists. The Government had enacted emergency measures in the search for the Professor; such was the potential danger of the situation getting out of hand. Advice and demands from Civil Servants and junior ministers, all hoping to bolster and further their careers, were the order of the day. No one was left out of this question and answer circus, save one minister, conspicuous by his absence. Charles Tullett was absent by design. He was a minister without portfolio and any visible interest by him would raise more questions than it answered. His brief was to keep a low profile and not alarm the public. High in his office at the top of the Post Office Tower, Tullett convened the executive meeting. He looked up over his half rimmed glasses, smiled and, with a gracious wave of his hand to the four men at the table, lowered his 6ft agile frame into the Chairman's seat.

'Gentlemen, you all know each other'. He looked at each one in turn. 'None of you, however, know me except for the gentleman on my right and for security reasons I will be known as Chairman. This is a classified meeting and you will all be bound by the Official Secrets Act, a copy of which is in front of you now. Please sign before we start and pass it back.' He watched them all carefully read the agenda and sign where indicated, collecting the papers across the highly polished walnut conference table. 'Excellent! It will be obvious to you that your *invitation*' he smiled at them 'came from the *highest* level and therefore my authority is absolute? Any questions?'

The silence that followed was contrasted only by the howling wind and rain that battered and swayed this iconic 1960's building. Beyond the 360 degree ceiling to floor windows, streaks of lightening ignited and illuminated the highly charged atmosphere, followed a few seconds later by a deep rumbling, as the storm moved eastwards from Windsor to Stratford.

'Then I will take it as understood that what I say carries the utmost urgency and secrecy in every aspect.'

A whispered murmur went around the room.

The chairman leaned forward. 'Gentlemen' he repeated. 'Before I begin, let me introduce you to my colleague, Giles' (he indicated the sharp featured, clean shaven man of military bearing to his right) 'who will be your link to me. Everything goes through him without question.'

Even though they had never met him, the assembled men immediately felt that they had to be very cautious of Giles. As he focussed carefully on each man, they noticed that his eyes were cold and without depth, almost like a shark.

'In a nutshell, Gentleman, we have a rogue scientist who has gone missing with a highly contentious research project that we in the UK cannot afford to lose. Not only that, but he has threatened to release his research papers to anybody who wants them. To make matters worse, his assistant is also missing and she also has the knowledge to develop the project if need be. We must find them both before these details are leaked. If this gets out and in the wrong hands it will be extremely damaging to the country. We also believe that this information may have already fallen into the wrong hands and there could even be a threat of some type to the upcoming Olympics.' Tullett looked across at them all.

'Well! What do you propose?' asked the fat man. 'Surely if he's that dangerous' he added 'you would already have activated MI5 and the other agencies?'

'Those are my feelings exactly. Why would you need us?' said the immaculately dressed distinguished man.

'We, as you know, are scientists, not spies or detectives. I really can't see how we can help' said the third man. 'Surely you have this under control? In any case, who is this scientist?' he added.

Giles now stood up and for effect slowly paced over to a window, the light storm behind him heightening the atmosphere in the suite. 'It is true' he said 'that we have this almost buttoned up, but we have to make sure. You gentlemen, as you say, are not detectives but notable academics in your own fields. We need you to advise us of any contacts and any details of his research that he may have that we are not aware of. We can then track him down.'

'Of course we can assist' they all volunteered in unison.

'But it *would* help if you could let us know who he is and what he was working on' said the fat man huffily.

Giles looked across at Tullett and saw him nod slightly. Outside the storm was reaching a crescendo with forked lightening jabbing the clouds at intervals of no more than two seconds. Suddenly a violent gust caused the building to sway dramatically, followed by torrents of heavy rain pummelling down on the triple glazed panes. All three scientists held onto the conference table in terror as the storm abated almost as quickly as it started.

'The scientist in question is Professor Lang' Giles informed them. 'His latest project was developing an anti-Cancer drug.'

'You don't mean that Darwin genetic scientist with madcap predictions who believes in that Nostradamus crap?' said the fat man dumbfounded.

'Precisely' said Tullett.

'But' started the fat man 'he's crazy....'

'But brilliant!' interjected Giles.

'Gentleman! Gentleman!' ordered Tullett. 'We are here to evaluate and if possible execute the best plan for the immediate crisis in hand. We are not here to discuss the merits or otherwise of Professor Lang.' His icy stare swung across the group. 'Are we clear?' he said stressing each word robustly.

The scientists all nodded in agreement.

Tullett stood up, pushed back his chair and walked round to the three academics, shaking their hands briskly. 'I have another meeting to attend and will leave you now in the capable hands of my colleague Giles. I know you will all do everything you can to help your country!'

Giles followed Tullett across to the penthouse lift and looked over to the three assembled men.

'I didn't want to mention anything about the genetic research' whispered Giles, his voice masked by another loud but declining storm-burst. 'You do know what else Lang has predicted aside from this don't you?' added Giles quietly.

'Whatever do you mean?' said Tullett. 'Everything he is working on is in this report' he emphasised.

'You mean everything he has told you?' whispered Giles again. Tullett suddenly pulled Giles sharply aside by the sleeve and stared into his lifeless eyes without blinking. 'Giles. I don't want you to mention that subject *ever* again' he said in a calm, but menacing voice.

Giles nodded nervously and stepped backwards as the lift arrived, taking Tullett to his waiting chauffeur in the private car park at the base of the building.

At the top of the building Giles regained his composure and strode over to the conference table, taking the vacant Chairman's seat.

'Now gentleman. I want *everything* you have on Lang within twenty four hours. Locations, contacts and as important, any research details you can get your hands on.'

As his car swung out of the massively tall electrically operated gates, Tullett picked up a red phone in the car and made a brief call to New York, after which he poured himself a double scotch, smiled and said softly to himself 'Poor black bastards!'

TRUCKERS

Karen was sleeping when Jenny crept out of her hotel room, where Alex had booked them all for the night just outside Manchester. They had all made statements, after Karen was released from casualty with only slight bruising and mild concussion to show for her ordeal. The Police had been very sympathetic but also extremely curious. Since she was not considered to be a political journalist or one who frequented with criminals and terrorists, they could not understand what motive there could be for an attempt on her life, save mistaken identity or the assignment she was on now.

Alex sat down on his hotel bed and closed his eyes tightly, trying to concentrate. He grunted a couple of times, took a deep breath and slowly smiled.

'What's so funny?' demanded Jenny.

'I've just had a crazy thought about our Karen in there' he pointed at her scantily clad inert form on the bed in the adjoining room.

Jenny followed his eyes and cut him dead with a jealous glare.

'Not that!' he said knowing her quick imagination and lethal temper.

'What then?' she demanded, narrowing her eyes suspiciously.

'Later. It's not important now', eying two undone top buttons on Jenny's blouse. 'I think we'd better be on our guard' he said quietly, looking again at the bedroom door. 'If this was an attempt on her life, whoever it was will try again, but this time could include us as well.'

'Terrific! That makes me feel very secure. What would you do if they came bursting in through that door now?' she demanded, standing up and pacing across the room, straightening her skirt and blouse as she walked. Before he replied, her face had turned bright red in embarrassment as she knew he had glimpsed her bra and she hastily re-buttoned the blouse. Then, as if to silently answer her last question, she watched him do something that really scared her.

Alex sat by his overnight bag, screwing different tubes together, until within a few seconds he had assembled a thin, lethal pistol, fronted by a matching cobalt silencer, which he placed under his pillow. She did not ask any questions for the rest of the night, but now saw Alex in a different light than she had known before.

The following morning the three of them drove north, but this time Alex kept the weapon in a shoulder holster under his left arm, while the girls sat and nervously chatted about their collective problem. When Jenny told Karen about the gun, there was no reaction, except a shrug of the shoulders in resignation. By the time they had cleared the Scottish border, Alex was sure they had not been tailed, as he had stopped several times quickly to see the reaction from other drivers. Alex was right about the tail. There was none, except a GPS transmitter in the nearside front wheel arch, placed there by a smartly dressed black woman during the night at the hotel car park.

It was past two in the afternoon when they drew up alongside a large articulated truck, outside a transport café. Alex did a visual check before they left the vehicle and took a table by a window, opposite the 1950's jukebox, from where he could see the entire lot. It was crowded with big beefy truckers who slapped each other playfully, while the air wafted ravenously of eggs, bacon, baked beans and sausages. Alex ordered three 'travellers' meals and looked around. A few salesmen with their Mondeo's and Astra's were also present, but other than that all seemed normal. Nothing was out of place and that was what worried Alex. It was too normal. He spread a map out on the table to plot their position.

'Looks like a few more hours girls' he said. 'We'll be there about six, if we don't get lost. These highland roads can be treacherous!'

'Is that your car over there?' asked a burly, unshaven lorry driver, pointing at Alex's car.

'Yes. Why?' said Alex cautiously.

'Just thought I'd let you know, that someone was taking pictures of it a few minutes ago and asked if I knew you. Of course, I didn't say anything. Smelt like filth to me.'

'Thanks. Do you know where he is now?'

'Oh. No! Took off right after!'

'Right after what?'

'After I was given this'- he held up a £50 note.

'What's that for?' said Jenny.

'Don't know. I think it was to get me to distract you from seeing the photos being taken. You want some help? The boys will cover for you.' He waved his arms around the diner. 'We don't like filth!'

'Thanks, but we'll be ok' Alex assured him.

The trucker walked out to his truck, climbed in and then came back over again.

'I think you might need this' he said and gave them a print from a Polaroid camera located in his glove box.

'Who's this?' said Jenny, pointing at the figure in the snap.

'It's the one who took the picture. Now we've got theirs! And I also got the car number plate in the shot!'

'But this is a woman! A black woman! Who is she?' said Jenny.

'Let me see!' said Karen. 'I've seen her before. Where?' She racked her brains. Suddenly, she sat back, shocked. 'I know. The Science Museum. She was near my car. Oh God! What's going on?'

'How stupid!' said Alex. He slapped his forehead. 'Could you help us?' he asked the burly trucker. 'We have to get here' he said jabbing his finger at a marked spot.

'But they're tracking us' said Karen.

'No problem! Leave your car in the woods up the road and have a lift all the way. I live only 5 miles away from your destination.'

After dumping the car and carefully concealing it, they were on route to the cottage and hopefully the Professor.

Several hours later they alighted, stiff and tired from the truck journey and only a short distance away from the cottage. They carefully trekked through the woods until a wisp of smoke could be seen rising silently in the distance through the trees and then lay down and rested until the stars came out in the crisp night sky.

Now, with his body and mind recharged and a few hours sleep under his belt, Alex woke the girls who had huddled together for maximum body warmth.

'Here we go!' he said, as they headed in single file, quietly through the trees to the cottage door.

ASSASSIN

Lang sat bolt upright, with all five senses on high alert. Even after three bottles of Highland Scotch shared with his new found friend Chekhov, he still retained his primitive survival instincts. They were especially needed now as deep down in his psyche, alarm bells were ringing that something was very wrong. He gingerly climbed over his drinking partner who lay on the wooden floor in the middle of the cabin, oblivious to the world and the real danger that was only yards away and getting closer by the second. He clamped his large hand firmly over Chekhov's open mouth while urgently kneeing him in the groin. The Russian's eyes opened while trying to move away from the sharp, continuous pressure on his lower body. Lang brought his other hand to his own mouth signalling silence and the cut throat sign which Chekhov, even in his semi-drunken state, immediately understood. Hoisting Chekhov up, Lang carefully tiptoed over to a cupboard and withdrew a large baseball bat with THE DODGERS embossed and signed by the whole team on it. Nodding to the Russian to take the bat, he then grabbed the large red handled axe which he swung through the air with a violent whooshing sound just missing the chimney breast and the table. Lang dowsed all the lights and signalled that they should both take up a position behind the door with him at the opening edge and the Olympic man behind him. This done, they stood with baited breath not daring to move, lest the floorboards groaned and gave them away. Sweat now trickled down Chekhov's brow and for the second time in as many days, he realised his life was on the line again. A shadow passed across the window, followed by a crunching sound, as a foot impacted upon the gravel outside the door. Silently lifting the axe over his head, Lang stood motionless as the door was slowly pushed inwardly towards them, revealing a black leather shoe and the long muzzle of a silencer. The intruder crept slowly into the cabin, stopping by the empty bottles while viewing one of the wall photos. Lang kicked the door back shut and swung the axe with all his force. The intruder pirouetted bringing the barrel up to meet the challenge. But it was too late. The axe had already found its mark, with the blade carving its way into the forehead and slicing off the right ear as Lang's grasp relaxed, allowing the axe to fall heavily onto the floor near the gun. Crimson blood from the right eye socket sprayed around the cabin and onto Lang. The assassin fell screaming face downwards as Chekhov ran over with the baseball bat in a raised striking position, but stopped mouth gaping as he saw the pole-axed and inert body lying at Lang's feet.

'Is he dead?' murmured Chekhov.

'Absolutely' said Lang, his chiselled face showing no sign of emotion.

'Who is he?' asked Chekhov, looking at the bloodied corpse on the floor.

'Let's see, shall we?' and with that Lang pushed the body, with his foot, onto its back. The head lolled backwards and sideways, exposing a black mass of blood soaked hair, with the one remaining eye staring madly at the ceiling. For a moment Lang looked intensely at the face, but couldn't see the overall features because of the gloom. The lights came up after Chekhov had re-lit the gas burners and joined his companion over the body.

'Your man is a lady or to be precise was a lady and a black one at that!' spluttered Lang in surprise.

'My God!' said Chekhov mortified. 'A woman! Who is she? Was she after you or me?'

'Let's find out' Lang said kneeling over the corpse and rummaging the pockets. 'What's this?' he said pulling out a digital camera and a note book. He put the camera down and flicked the notebook. Most of it was gibberish and undecipherable, but one page had a cryptic notation added.

'GAMES, AFRICA, INDIA, USA, TULLETT'

'What does that mean?' said Chekhov, turning his face enquiringly to Lang.

'Hell if I know!' retorted Lang tossing the notebook on the floor. 'The only games that I know about are the Olympics and they start in about two weeks, as you well know.'

Chekhov nodded sullenly, his mind drifting back to all the events leading up to today, while feeling very confused and frightened. He peered over Lang's broad shoulder and stared for a brief moment into the assassins face. What could she want with him? Ok. He had been bundled out to Russia by their operatives and held incommunicado, but they could have killed him at any time. Why now. Why here?

'Let's have a look at the camera' Lang said picking up the Panasonic Lumix. He moved from the body and sat down awkwardly on one of the chairs while fiddling with the buttons. 'Bloody thing!' he snorted angrily. 'Bugger! What's wrong with this?' he fumed, now getting really annoyed and impatient.

'Let me have a go' demanded Chekhov, easing the camera away from the Professor's large unwieldy hands. 'My wife is better than me at this' he mumbled revealing the first image. 'Let's see....look here! That's you!' He spun round to show Lang a picture taken some time ago, in what looked like a research laboratory.

'Yes! That was in the States last year at the Centre for Disease Control. I was giving a speech to a mixed group of genetic scientists at the time, on my research on genes and antibodies. Why.....?'

Before he could finish his sentence Chekhov had clicked forward to pictures of three people, two women and a man travelling in a car and then parked in a transport car park. The previous few images were of one of the women getting in to a sports car outside what appeared to be the Science Museum in London.

'Who are they and how do they fit into all this?' said Chekhov, his hands now covering his face in despair. 'What are we going to do? We can't go to the Police' his voice trailed away while looking at the Professor for enlightenment.

'That's it. What did you say about your wife being better than you?' exclaimed Lang.

'I meant with a camera! What are you getting at? What's my wife to do with this?'

'Everything and nothing!' replied Lang.

'I don't understand. What are you talking about?' the Russian replied.

'Did your wife ever tell you what she did for a living? I mean really did?'

'Yes of course. She is a doctor working with RSK on animal research. She travels abroad a lot. So what?'

'Is that what she told you?' asked Lang, his face almost touching Chekhov's.

'I think so. Yes of course. What are you suggesting?'

'I am not suggesting anything. I'm telling you that your wife is central to all this. Her name is Morag, is it not? She is not a research scientist employed by RSK, but my personal research assistant. How stupid I am!' He banged his forehead with a palm.

'Why didn't you say anything when we met?' quizzed the Russian.

'I wasn't really in the mood for talking especially when I found you, a complete stranger, in my cabin.'

'My God! But what on earth can she have to do with us and *this*?' Chekhov asked, pointing at the twisted blood soaked body at their feet.

'Let me explain. Sit down please' the Professor asked. He motioned to one of the old rickety chairs and dragged another over, plonking his body heavily onto it.

'Morag has been, for several years, on secondment from RSK to my department, which in turn is controlled by the Department of Health. We are engaged in genetic research, which as you know has various moral and ethical considerations behind it. I cannot emphasise enough how delicate our work is and any mention of what we do could be disastrous for everyone.'

'But what has all that got to do with me? After all, I'm not a scientist. What do I know?'

'You miss the point' said Lang. 'Someone or some group are trying to get to her via you and ultimately me. If she knows that you are held hostage, then she may be forced to work for them. That's why you were not killed, but held and that's also why I believe that this one here', he tapped the body with his foot 'probably did not come to kill you or I, but hold us until we could be spirited away.'

'Oh God! What have I done?' choked Chekhov. 'Morag helped me get away in Moscow the other day. She must be in great danger. What can I do?'

'Hold on!' said Lang leaning forward. 'You can't do anything here. We must get away from here fast. Obviously something is planned for the start of the Olympics and whatever it is it can't be pleasant. If Morag is now being held, it is possible that the secret trials that she was testing on my behalf are now complete and ready for release. We must find her, or at the very least stop whoever is controlling the operation.'

'Alright my friend' muttered Chekhov. 'Where do we go and how do we get there without being seen?'

The Professor closed his eyes and leaned backwards. For a moment there was total silence. When he opened them, a plan had begun to formulate in his mind. He smiled.

'Well. What do we do? And why are you smiling?' said the Moscow man.

'I am smiling my Russian friend because we are going on a long trip to clear our names and save ourselves.' With this, Lang stepped over the body, reached under his bed and grabbed a small holdall containing, among other things, a large hunting knife that he always carried with him. 'I hope you don't mind walking?' he asked Chekhov. 'You better put this on' tossing a spare hunting jacket at the Russian. 'It may be morning, but it's still cold! I also think you should pick that up' he suggested to Chekhov pointing at the gun on the floor 'as well as the camera. We may need them!' he stressed.

'But you still haven't said where we are going' blurted Chekhov.

'Didn't I? Sorry. It slipped my mind. We are going to London to meet a very good friend of mine, who owes me big time. He will be able to sort this out and fast.'

'How can you be so sure that he won't give us up?'

'Because he and I are like that.' Lang symbolically crossed his fingers.

'What does that mean? Who is he?' asked Chekhov curiously.

'I'll show you' said Lang rolling his left sleeve up. 'You see this?' He indicated to Chekhov a small scar near his wrist. 'Blood brother! You don't get closer than that!' Lang insisted.

'I see. But who is he?' insisted the Russian coach.

Lang took out his communicator, pressed a button and the screen was filled with a photo of a large black man with his details beneath it. Chekhov stared at the photo but what really caught his eye was the man's title. CRE

COMMISSIONER. He held his breath as the pieces started to fall into place. This was crazy. Why would this man's organisation be involved? After all the Commission for Racial Equality was supposed to be active in smoothing the edges between racial groups, not stirring them. What the hell was going on?

COTTAGE

From their vantage point, high above the cottage and hidden between the trees, Alex, Jenny and Karen watched transfixed as the lone figure circled the darkened cottage, gun drawn. The sudden slamming of the door and the piercing scream, followed by total silence, froze them in their tracks.

'Nobody moves!' whispered Alex, his hand now firmly clutching his revolver, safety catch off.

'Keep down and don't say anything!'

He took out a pair of night field glasses from his hunting jacket and focussed in on the door and then the window, as the internal light came back on. Two shadows passed the window and stopped. He couldn't make them out, except that one was very tall and the other more heavily built. They appeared to sit down and then after what seemed forever, got up and turned the light off. He saw the door open and the taller of the two stepped out, followed by the other, both scanning the surrounding area before moving off along the loch shore. The early dawn of a midsummer day in the Highlands, with melodic birdsong and trickling brooks, came softly to the three watchers, as they cautiously approached the cottage with great trepidation. Telling the girls to stay behind a large scotch pine, Alex kicked the door in and dived head first and gun drawn into the gloomy interior. At first he could not focus too well as shafts of sunlight pierced through the open door, brightly illuminating the interior of the cabin. He placed his hand on the floor to balance himself, but withdrew it sharply as he felt a sticky substance under his palm. Rolling carefully to his left side he collided with what appeared to be a large matted football. Being partly blinded by the streaming light, his instincts told him that this football was a skull and as his eyes regained the balance between light and dark, he also saw that a good part of the cranium was split apart by a large bloodied axe laying by the body. A sudden noise caused him to wheel his gun round on the two figures silhouetted in the doorway. They stood frozen, eyes staring, mouths open at the violent orgy of destruction before them.

'Oh God!' mumbled Jenny, her hand covering her mouth.

Karen took one look and ran to the nearest tree throwing up. All her years as a reporter had not prepared her for this. Jenny watched her rush past, but although feeling the same, she was transfixed by the horror of it all.

'Get out!' ordered Alex. 'Jenny. Get out!' he barked a second time.

She turned and slowly stepped out the doorway as if in a daze. By this time, Alex's eyes had accustomed to the lighting conditions and took stock of the situation. His eyes swept the cabin quickly, but efficiently, noting the body and the smashed furniture around him. He put the safety on the gun, slipping it into an under arm holster and stood up. Satisfied that they were alone, he started searching for anything that could tell him what had happened and who the dead person was. Rummaging around he quickly discovered that this cottage did belong to Lang and judging from the pictures still hanging on the walls, he also surmised that the tall man that he had seen hurrying out earlier was indeed the Professor. Of more immediate concern was the corpse laying in a pool of blood by their feet. He looked round and found Karen by the fireplace, staring at the body.

'It's her! The one in the photo! The same one at the Science Museum! Look Alex! Just look at her face!'

Alex was looking. But his attention was also drawn by her right hand and the fresh impression of a gun still firmly in the clenched position. He noticed her expensive hunting clothes and realised that this woman was a professional and very highly paid at that. Why did she want to kill Lang and why did she follow Karen? It was raising more questions than it answered. He searched his mind and tried to make sense of it all.

'Alex? What's this?' said Karen, holding the notebook dropped on the floor by the two fleeing men.

He reached out and gently took it from her shaking hand. 'Karen. Go. Just go.' He pointed to the door. 'It will be alright. I promise' squeezing her hand tightly and putting the other round her shoulder, while walking her outside to the pine scented morning air. They joined Jenny who was sitting on a felled log facing the loch.

'You ok?' he asked of her, while gently holding Karen.

'No' she said 'But I'll get over it! Who was she? The black woman?'

'Don't know yet. But this might help us find out.' He held up the notebook that Karen had found. Slowly he turned the pages, skipping past the indecipherable jargon that the Professor and Chekhov had first come across and stopping as they had on the very same spot with 'GAMES, AFRICA, INDIA, USA, TULLETT' scrawled clearly for all to see. 'Any ideas?' he asked them both.

'Could be something to do with endangering the upcoming Games' offered Jenny.

'Same here. Can't work it out' chipped in Karen. 'Maybe those two who left have the answer' she added. 'We should get after them and fast. I don't know about you guys, but I don't intend to hang around here waiting for the Police while trying to explain a dead body away.'

'One thing's for sure' said Alex. 'Professor Lang *was* one of those who left in a rush. I saw his pictures on the walls in there.' He pointed over his shoulder towards the cabin. 'And since the idea is to find this Chekhov via Lang, we must get after them and pronto.'

'What are we going to do with the body?' said Jenny. 'I mean we can't just leave it there, can we?' she started to cry.

Alex bent down in front of Jenny and gently taking her head between his hands, whispered. 'Jenny. There's nothing we can do. She was already dead before we came. We'll get on our way and I'll put an anonymous call in when we are well clear and miles away. Alright?' Looking deeply into her eyes, he saw a small tear form and run down her cheek. He leaned forward and kissed it dry, helping her to her feet.

Karen watched him, surprised at this gentle side that she had never seen before. She was curious and envious at the same time. He caught her glance and probably for the first time in his life, he felt uncomfortable.

'Come on. Let's get out of here!' he said strongly, quickly regaining his confident, bullet proof composure. He zipped the notebook into his inner pocket and led them along the lapping water of the Loch, in the footsteps of the Professor and the Russian, some two miles up ahead.

TRAIN

Giles was a murdering bastard. Everyone in Tentacle knew that. He would not hesitate to kill someone if they stood in his way, while inflicting as much pain as possible on the victim. His flight to Scotland on the company's private jet was uneventful. One of the flight attendants gave him an Indian head massage to try and relax him. At the private airstrip he met Stewart, the local field operative, who had rented a black Range-Rover for him. They discussed their deceased agent and the possible whereabouts of the Professor. After a couple of lengthy calls, Giles sped out of the shingle car park and headed towards Balmoral. The sun shone through the puffy clouds, as the Scottish landscape, with its craggy rocks and trickling brooks, looked disdainfully at this intruder from the south. He hit the CD and inserted a disc. Jay and the Americans boomed out from the multiple speakers, as he swung the vehicle round bend after bend, the crash barriers to his left standing with their arms spread wide, ready to catch him from tumbling down a thousand foot sheer drop. Normally the only reason that he would stop, apart from petrol and lights, would be for the Police and he tried to stay out of their radar as much as possible. Therefore, as he dropped his speed to accommodate a sharp bend with a one in five descent stressing out the gear box, he was amazed to see two attractive girls sitting alone on one of the grey crash barriers ahead of him. Pulling up a few yards in front of them, he watched in his nearside wing mirror as they got up and walked towards him. He licked his lips and quickly brushed back his hair with his hand. As they approached he lowered the nearside window.

'Stuck out here alone girls?' he smiled innocently. 'Where's your car?'

'Actually' said Karen 'we do need a lift, but with our friend' she indicated Alex strolling up behind.

On seeing him, Giles's feelings turned from the loss of potential pleasure with the girls to jealousy towards Alex, while remaining as affable as ever.

'No problem! If you jump in, I'll give you all a lift. Where are you headed?'

'Aberdeen Station. We're trying to catch the next London train' said Jenny.

Alex thanked Giles and jumped up in front with him while the exhausted girls climbed in the back and almost immediately fell asleep against one another on the black leather seats.

'Seem shattered?' said Giles nodding in the mirror at the girls.

'Yes' Alex lied. 'We've been on a charity walk, got lost and need now to get back home.'

'What's the charity?' asked Giles, as they roared off down the road.

'Great Ormond Street' Alex said matter of factly.

'Good group. Won't they be looking for you?' Giles responded, not believing the story.

'No problem' said Alex trying to sound convincing. 'We have set times to call the sponsors and claim for the distance walked.'

'Long way to come for a walk. I mean, London, then walk around the Highlands?'

'Yeah, but we don't mind. It's for the kids at the end of it anyway.'

'I agree' said Giles, reaching down for a mint. 'Want one?' he asked Alex.

'Thanks' he took the pack and in doing so, noticed a small tattoo of a tentacle on Giles's wrist, which rang alarm bells in his subconscious.

Within the hour they were approaching the outskirts of Aberdeen, passing the harbour on their left with its brightly painted fishing boats moored against its wall. Flocks of gulls hovered above the boats, screaming for fish as the catches were unloaded, boxed and iced. The breeze caught the rigging and tossed it onto the masts, delivering a light chime sound in the morning sunshine. Out in the harbour, a cutter was heading out and beyond that, on the horizon, an oil tanker was ploughing the waves to rendezvous with one of the oil platforms that littered this part of the Scottish coast.

Giles pulled up in front of the updated Victorian station by one of the pay and display signs.

'We're here' Alex turned to the girls waking them from their slumber.

They rubbed their eyes and sensuously stretched. Giles saw this and grimaced, feeling cheated.

'Thanks for the lift. I'm sure we'll meet again' said Alex.

'You never know?' smiled Giles amiably. 'What's your name?' he asked.

'Alex'.

'And the girls?'

'Jenny and Karen.'

'Mine's Giles.'

The girls jumped out and walked to the station entrance.

'Thanks again' repeated Alex, stepping out and walking away.

'Excuse me?' shouted Giles leaning out of his passenger's window.

Alex turned and suspiciously came back.

'You forgot this!' Giles held out a bit of paper.

'I don't understand?' said Alex.

'It's for your charity. Great Ormond Street, wasn't it?' he said mockingly.

Alex unrolled the paper. It was a fifty pound note. He was astounded.

'Thanks! I'm sure the kids will appreciate it.' He pocketed the note and followed the girls into the station.

Giles drove off and, after stopping out of sight down the road, Googled the national rail timetable establishing that the next London train was leaving at midday.

He looked at his watch. Eleven am. He made a call. Within a couple of minutes his communicator had an image on it.

'Ah Ah!' he said looking at the petite face. 'The journalist.'

He made another call, keeping Karen's image on screen. 'Yes, it's her. She's not alone. Two others. A girl called Jenny and a bloke called Alex.'

He listened. 'Yes I can handle it. Yes. I'll sort them. What about Lang? Ok, let me get this right. I finish them all, but hold Lang. Consider it done. I'll call you when it's over.' Swinging the vehicle back to the station, he parked it by the pay and display in the forecourt and after removing a briefcase from the boot, headed to the entrance.

The station, although still having its original Victorian metal structure with glass in its roofing, had been upgraded internally and now held a modern curved concourse and bright red seats placed strategically around the interior. Platform one stood by one of the tall exterior walls of the station and it was here that the London Euston train stood waiting. A small goods train passed through the station on the bye line and headed with its trucks and containers into the dark tunnel that ran down under the City. Lang and

Chekhov proffered their tickets at the barrier and walked casually to the carriages at the rear of the train. They stepped into a corridor with fifteen numbered compartments and quickly found theirs.

'Thirteen. Lucky for some!' quipped Lang.

Using the electronic tag on their ticket, they opened the door and stepped in. The cabin was a sleeper for four so they had ample room, even a washroom which Chekhov immediately identified and entered. Lang meanwhile had slipped off his jacket and shoes and pulled one of the overhead beds down. When Chekhov eventually emerged, the Professor was sound asleep in the bunk snoring deeply. The Russian sat down on one of the bench seats, kicked his shoes off and stretched out. He was too tired to sleep and envied his companion the ability to crash out just like that. Also joining the train was Alex and the girls, but not before they had grabbed some food at the station buffet leaving him free to fax across the writing on the notepad and call Chelsea Barracks.

The trooper manning the switchboard was very bored. In all the training that he had received at Hereford, nothing had prepared him for this. He could take interrogation under stressful conditions, parachute into an enemy's backyard, kill someone with his hands, but this waiting. He had to have the patience of Joab. For him this was a test of the highest order. Colonel Tudor had designated him to man this station and he wouldn't let him down. So when the priority one call on a secure line came in, he was relieved to know that he had done his duty.

'Colonel! Colonel! It's Mr Mason!' he shouted to the next room, while extending a handset out to the Staff Officer.

Colonel Tudor stepped in to view, his six foot six and fifteen stone of pure muscle blocking the whole door frame.

'Alex. Old boy. Thought you had gone on holiday! What can you tell me?'

'Colonel. The Professor is on the Euston bound train leaving here at Aberdeen at twelve hundred hours. He has the Russian, Chekhov, with him. I and two of my girls are with me. The train's ETA at Euston is nineteen hundred hours. I will make contact soon with them and keep you posted.'

'Excellent. We can start the ball rolling at our end.'

'Colonel. Be aware that one of Tentacle's men is close. He will probably be on this train. I have a name of Giles. Height six foot, build muscular, weight twelve stone, age mid thirties, IC1, hair black, eyes dark, clean shaven and a tattoo of a tentacle on his left wrist. There were some cryptic notes on a black woman killed at Lang's cottage, with a name of Tullett mentioned. I've just faxed you the details. Can you get the *cleaners* in?'

'Alex. You know you are cleared for *any* affirmative action. Keep me posted. Your arse is covered. I've just received the fax and will arrange *cleaning* after this call. Out.'

The line went dead. Alex met the girls and they all boarded the train. Their cabin was by coincidence next to Lang and Chekhov's, at number fourteen. They settled in and locked the door.

Looking at the sleeping arrangements, Jenny said 'Who's sleeping with whom?' and winked at Karen, who returned the same.

Alex suddenly felt uncomfortable with them both. 'Look' he began to say.

'Alex. Don't worry, we'll not pressure you here. When this is all over you can choose one of us or, if you want, both!'

The girls sniggered at his embarrassment, while he struggled to see the funny side. The whistle blew on the platform and the train lurched slowly forward out of the station.

'Get some sleep' he instructed them.

The journey from Aberdeen to Edinburgh involved running beside the sea, cutting inland to cross the Forth Railway Bridge and heading into Edinburgh. Below the bridge, large ships looked like models and the submarines from the Royal Naval Base at Faslane were so small to be almost insignificant. A happy group of international passengers boarded at Edinburgh, heading for the Olympics in London, displaying a mix of multi coloured flags as the train headed south to the border. It was during this time that Chekhov needed a hard drink. He couldn't wait any longer and unfortunately there was none in the cabin. He slipped out and headed down to the buffet car taking a seat by himself.

A waiter approached him. 'Good afternoon sir. Can I get you anything?'

'Yes' he replied in his broken English accent. 'I'll have double Vodka, straight. No ice.'

'Yes sir. Be right back.'

Chekhov looked out of the window at the passing countryside. He sighed. 'Some of it looked like the Crimea' he thought dreamily.

'Sir?' the waiter announced.

He looked up.

'Your drink sir.'

'Thank you.' The waiter hovered. 'Yes?' said the Russian.

'The bill sir?'

'Oh. How much is that?'

'Two pounds twenty.'

'Wait a moment. I don't seem to have any cash.' He searched his pockets frantically while longingly looking at the drink.

'We take credit cards sir.' Chekhov looked glum and embarrassed. 'I.....'

'This will cover it' a voice beside him said.

To his left Chekhov turned and saw a well built, clean-shaven man holding out a five pound note to the steward, who took it and returned with the change in a saucer.

'Thank you. I am in your debt Mr?'

'Alex Mason.'

'Your good health! Mr Mason!' He raised his glass and tossed the contents down his throat in one go.

'Ahhhhhhhh' he said much more relaxed.

'Another?' said Alex.

'If you're buying I will.'

'No problem. Waiter? A chaser for my friend.' He passed another fiver across and this time told the waiter 'keep the change.'

'Thank you sir!' the young man replied happily.

'Mr Chekhov?' said Alex quietly. 'Could I have a word with you and your travelling companion, Professor Lang? I mean you no harm. I represent the good guys.'

Chekhov looked alarmed. 'What do you mean?' said Chekhov. He tried to sound confident and sure. 'How do you know my name?'

'Look. I know about your wife. Morag, isn't it? There's also a little matter of you leaving a crime scene earlier today.'

Chekhov, although grateful for the drink, was still very suspicious.

Alex detected that. 'Listen. If you talked to Mr Cranfield, would you then listen to me?'

'Perhaps' he said.

'Ok then' Alex said and dialled Cranfield's number on his handset.

The call lasted for about five minutes, during which time the two old friends exchanged personal views. Only when Cranfield had assured Chekhov about Alex via Jenny did the Russian visibly relax. Ending the call, he handed the unit back to Alex and, for the first time in many days, smiled.

'Good to meet you Mr Mason' he smiled, holding his hand out with confidence now.

Alex responded with a firm handshake and they both sat down well away from the other passengers, Chekhov having another chaser, while Alex still abstained. When Chekhov had downed this last of the three full measures, Alex raised the unspoken question between them.

'Where's the Professor? I must see him now!'

'Alright. Mr Mason. Follow me' he replied feeling more confident since his talk with Cranfield.

They walked out, the Russian leading and entered the corridor of compartments, stopping outside thirteen.

'Well blow me down!' said Alex. 'I thought that I would have to hunt you down door by door!'

'What do you mean?' replied the Olympian.

'This' he pointed to number fourteen 'is where we are!' smiling and shaking his head in amazement.

Chekhov smiled back and using the pass opened the door, revealing the Professor snoring away in one of the top bunks.

'So this is the great man?' Alex mocked.

'Don't laugh too much. He has saved my life in the last twenty four hours and I am very thankful to him for that.'

With the door closed, he shook his friend from his slumber.

'What is it? Eh?' he rubbed his eyes and stared at Alex then at Chekhov. 'Who's this?' he directed the question at his friend.

'Can I show you something?' said Alex reaching for his pocket. Lang immediately drew back. 'You are security cleared at the highest level, correct?' asked Alex.

Lang said nothing. 'Well. You should recognise this' and he pulled out a document and handed it over.

The Professor ran his eyes over it. 'Could be a fake?' said the scientist.

'Yes sir. It could. But if you call any number you want and ask about me, that should satisfy you. I think.'

Lang looked down from his bed at Alex.

'Ok I will, but if I find you are lying.........' he produced the assassin's gun from the cabin.

Chekhov sat and watched Lang make a call, while the pistol remained firmly trained on Alex. After the call, Lang lowered the gun and apologised.

'No problem' said Alex. 'Only the next time you point one of those at someone and mean it, take the safety catch off first' he said showing him the release mechanism.

They sat and talked for some time, Alex bringing them up to speed on everything he knew to date, with the Professor filling in the gaps with the help of Chekhov.

'I want to introduce you to the two girls with me. They are next door.'

'Please wait' the Professor said dropping down from the bed and refreshing himself in the toilet.

When he emerged, Alex said 'You two stay here. I'll get the girls. I can't have you exposed any more than you have to.'

He stepped out into the corridor and tapped softly on fourteen. 'It's Alex. Open up.' Slipping quickly inside, he updated Karen and Jenny and requested that they meet Lang and Chekhov next door. Karen in particular was enthused. She envisaged a world scoop on this story and was determined not to miss anything. Following Alex, they stepped into the corridor and disappeared again into number thirteen to meet the Professor and Chekhov. To Jenny, meeting Chekhov was a let down. She had anticipated a thinner man with long flowing hair and very muscular arms. Instead she was faced with an almost intellectual type with a strange grasp of English. Karen's preconception of the Professor was on the other hand spot on. She had imagined a tall eccentric and this is exactly how he came across.

They all sat and discussed the situation after which Alex summed up.

'Look' he said. 'There's a killer on the loose and it's more than possible he's on this train. In order to protect you all, I suggest you all move to number fourteen immediately, leaving me in here to deal with him if he shows.'

'But......' Karen started to say.

'There's no discussion. At Euston I have arranged protection, but until then you do it my way. Let's get all you guys safe.'

Within minutes they all moved into cabin fourteen leaving Alex alone. He locked the door, lowered the blind and turning off the lights, sat waiting quietly.

ABERDEEN

The Grampian Mountains are not the most hospitable region in Scotland, particularly if you are on the run and not sure who you can trust. This was very true for Lang and Chekhov, as they emerged from the prickly summer undergrowth almost tripping onto the road that led to Balmoral Castle and the Queen. They brushed themselves down by the wayside and headed to Ballater, a small nondescript village on the A93 that ultimately led to Aberdeen. It was 7am, too early for the tourists that would soon be descending on the locals; the farmers and crofters finishing their duties and heading to their traditional stonewalled cottages. As they walked single file, the Professor stopped and withdrew the communicator he had with him.

'Let's hope it works' he said and proceeded to tap a series of numbers onto the keyboard.

'Hello Brother. How are you?' the scientist said.

A short sharp conversation took place, during which questions were asked and rapid replies given. All Chekhov could hear was 'Yes, ahah, understand. Yes we'll be there' and ended with 'see you soon'.

'Well. Who was that and can he help us?' Chekhov enquired.

Lang stood ramrod stiff, towering over his new found companion.

'That was my Brother' tapping the scar on his wrist. 'Everything is being arranged as we speak. We're to catch a train from Aberdeen.'

'How far is it to Aberdeen?' said Chekhov, breathing heavily as they trudged along the road devoid of any traffic.

'About 30 miles' said Lang over his shoulder. 'Should take us about 6 hours walking' he added.

'Six hours! Are you mad?' Chekhov retorted. 'I can't walk that far. Even as the Olympic coach, I only managed a mini marathon of 5 miles and almost collapsed. No. I'm afraid I can't do that. Can't we get a lift?'

'Ok. But where from?' said the Professor. 'They'll be nothing around here for hours until they open up the Castle.'

They stopped while Chekhov gulped in volumes of air, as he sat slumped against a crash barrier.

Lang checked his watch and looked up and down the deserted tarmac highway.

'You're right. We must get a lift to Aberdeen.'

Together they looked in both directions at the open road. Suddenly the growl of a heavy vehicle was audible round the bend from where they had just come. Lang pulled Chekhov back away from the road into the deep cover of rocks and heather. The sound grew louder until the vehicle had turned the bend and was now in full view, its giant cab with multiple spotlights, bearing down on Lang, who stood tall and erect in the middle of the road, facing the thirty tonner with a large branch in his hand. The driver of the livery red supermarket truck saw the Professor almost at the last moment and slammed on his compressed air brakes with such force, that the cab bucked back and forward like a wild kicking bronco.

Screaming and gesticulating wildly, Chekhov sprang out onto the road as he saw his compatriot bravely but foolishly pretend to become the classic immovable object confronting a fast moving irresistible force.

'No. No' he mumbled to himself as the truck stopped just feet away from Lang's raised hand holding the branch aloft.

It could almost have been the scene from Moses and the parting of the Red Sea, except that this was Scotland and the nearest water was in the Loch, some five miles away.

Striding to the drivers door, Lang bellowed to him above the diesel engine. 'Can you give us a lift to Aberdeen? Our car broke down miles back there' pointing in the direction where the truck had come from.

'Get in to you both' the stocky Scotsman said warmly. 'I could do with the company.'

Lang waved Chekhov over and climbed up after him into the towering cab.

'Gregg. My name's Gregg' beamed the driver holding his hand out to them.

Chekhov being nearest shook first, followed by Lang stretching across him.

'Lang and Chekhov' the Professor replied indicating his friend.

Gregg engaged the gears, driving the monster engine beneath them forward, as it vociferously complained about the weight of its giant container behind.

'What are you boys doing out dressed like that?'

He indicated their dirty and unkempt clothes.

'Have you walked some way? I didn't see any car back there.'

'Birdwatchers' said Lang quickly.

'We are from the RSPB on an assignment and took a wrong turn down a track well off the road. We have called the AA and they will be here to recover the car while we get to our meeting in Aberdeen.'

'Don't fancy watching wee birdies for a living. I prefer this!' said the wheel-man, patting the driver's door as one would a dog. 'Still. Everyone to their own' he smiled affably. He turned and grinned at them, one hand on the large horizontal wheel, the other gripping the multiple gear sticks. 'Help yourselves to some tea or coffee' he pointed to a locker behind him.

'Me? I like a *real* drink. He winked, indicating a small bottle of Scotch Whiskey between them.

'Too early right now, but after this trip....' his eyes sparkled at the expectation.

They trundled along making good time, BBC Radio Scotland being interrupted by call signs on Gregg's CB radio.

'Roger that. Big boy signing off' giving his 'handle' to a fellow trucker somewhere
near Inverness.

Signs for Aberdeen were becoming more frequent and very soon they had entered the outskirts of this fishing and oil city, passing by the harbour and the large colourful seagoing boats, their catches twisting and writhing in the crisp morning sunshine.

Around each boat stood a bevy of big men, some wearing hats, but all with long fishing waders and gloves on. From the masts of each trawler flew a multitude of ensigns, fluttering and rattling in the breeze, enjoined by flocks of screeching and soaring gulls hovering just above the decks.

Chekhov watched fascinated, while several birds flapped their wings as in a ballet, attempting to catch the discarded fish tossed away by the sorters on the quay.

Gregg swung the juggernaut through several streets and pulled up outside the train station.

'Here we are my lads! Aberdeen Station. Safe and sound.'

'Thank you' Lang said. 'This is a real life saver for us. Is there anything we can do for you?'

'My pleasure. It was good having you boys on board even if you don't know anything about birds.'

He winked, smiled and nodded.

Lang returned the smile, climbed down after Chekhov and shut the large door. The truck swung sharply to its left and headed out, radio blaring down the road and out of sight.

'How did he know we were not from the RSPB?' said Chekhov.

'Simple, my Russian friend. He just watched you and your reaction to the gulls. To a bird man that wouldn't have raised an eyebrow.'

They strolled into the station and headed to the glass fronted ticket office.

'I believe you have a packet for me. My name is Lang.'

The clerk got off his stool and mumbling his annoyance at having his comfortable routine upset, poked around in the back office emerging a few seconds later with a small but neatly wrapped parcel.

'Have you any identification?' he smirked trying to assert his minor position of authority.

The Professor dug deep into his pockets and after fumbling around, took out a worn but official driving licence and passed it through the thin opening at the bottom edge of the bullet proof screen. The clerk cast his eyes over the well worn document, looked up at the tall man and dropping his shoulders in resignation, passed the parcel and driving licence through a lower one way hatch.

'Thanks' said Lang, bowing mockingly.

They headed to the gents where, making sure no one else was lurking, they undid the package, revealing money, tickets, two sets of clean clothes and a ready charged picture communicator.

'You *do* have good friends!' exclaimed Chekhov suitably impressed.

'Who you know!' replied Lang.

They quickly washed, changed and ate a good meal before boarding the train.

STEWARD

Giles boarded the train at Aberdeen and went directly to the dining car, asking the steward to bring him a tonic water. He sat and read a paper with all the hulla of the Olympics in it and the special colour magazine inserted as the supplement. His eyes scanned the news until he stopped on a small piece regarding a doctor being quoted regarding a few people of Afro/Asian skin tones being admitted because of some unknown rash doing the rounds. He cynically smiled. 'Rash? Wait until the opening then they'll really see a change!' He called the steward across again and asked him for another tonic. When he returned, Giles deposited a twenty pound note on the tray. 'Keep the change!' The young man was taken aback. 'Would you like to earn another twenty?' he asked.

'Yes sir!' he said enthusiastically.

'I don't want you to get into trouble, but a friend of mine is also on this train and I want to surprise him personally with an overdue gift. The problem is that I don't know his cabin number. You couldn't get it for me could you?' he smiled.

'Well. I don't know sir. If anyone catches me.......'

'Who's going to know? It will only be our secret. OK?' He produced another twenty. 'That's now forty pounds. What do you think?' Giles smiled at him encouragingly.

'What's his name?' asked the steward, the temptation too much for him to ignore. He disappeared and a few minutes later brought back a spare pass card with a number on it.

'Well done and thank you!' passing across the two crisp twenties to the youth.

'Thank *you* sir!' he beamed, clutching the notes and jamming them into his trouser pocket.

'I also want you to take care of this.' He handed over a double-locked combination case. 'I'll call for it later.'

'Yes sir!' said the steward, taking the case to the safe deposit area and then handing over a receipt.

The train was now in the Scottish Lowlands, heading to the border. Giles stood up, stretched and headed to the washroom, where he checked his pockets for his *tools*. He would have great pleasure in dealing with the girls, making them suffer before meeting their end. He licked his lips in anticipation. The sudden rush of a passing train and the suction that followed kept Alex alert. By his side was his silenced pistol and taped to his ankle a small throwing knife. Waiting, he knew, was always the worst part of any assignment and this was no different. It was tempting to let his eyelids drop with the motion of the train, but this could be fatal and therefore he massaged his brain with a series of IQ tests. Stepping into the washroom, he splashed his face with cold water and ruffled his hair. He looked in the mirror and then at his Omega on his left wrist. Two pm. Another four hours. When would Giles come? Might it be someone else? His answer was not long in coming. In the corridor he heard a footfall. It was not heavy, but it was there. He watched the light under the door throw a wide but menacing shadow as it stopped silently outside. Alex turned the bathroom light off and on tip toe climbed up into one of the bunk beds. Through the gloom he watched and heard the electronic pass key release the catch. He brought the gun up to bear on the doorway and coolly held his breath. Slowly, but surely the door opened, sending an ever widening shaft of light into the cabin. A figure stepped silently into the doorway, the light from the corridor creating a halo effect revealing a right arm holding a small handgun. Reaching out slowly with his left hand, Alex silently tossed a sealed pack of playing cards across the cabin. The intruder wheeled right.

Taking advantage of the distraction, Alex fired twice. Once to the heart and once to the head. 'Phut! Phut!' The outlined figure's knees crumpled and fell forward into the cabin. Alex jumped down and flicked the light on. Strange! He remembered Giles as stockier and older than the body appeared. As he rolled it over with his foot he froze. It was the bar steward, his mouth sealed with masking tape and eyes staring wildly upwards at the black hole in his forehead now poring with blood. By his limp, dead hand lay a blue pistol. It appeared to be transparent and leaking water!

'Good shooting Alex! You've now killed a defenceless boy armed only with a water pistol! You should be very proud! I bought it at the station shop before the train departed.' He twisted to see Giles aiming a silenced Magnum in his right hand straight at him.

With a cruel smile the Tentacle man stepped into the cabin motioning Alex to climb down, drop his gun and kick it slowly towards him. He closed the door behind him and looked fleetingly at the body. 'Such a pity!' he smirked. 'He certainly earned his tip though' and searching the body recovered the forty pounds adding 'Good as a human shield?'

Alex thought quickly, but showed no emotion. 'What do you want?'

'Alex. Alex. We are professionals. Let's not play games. The sooner you tell me where Lang, Chekhov and those two bitches are, the sooner I can finish my job. I promise that I will give you a head shot. Nice and clean. You won't even feel it. Just tell me, where are they?' He lowered the gun and aimed at Alex's groin. 'Now, Alex. I'll just give you to three and then I'll have to shoot you in the balls and continue upwards until I get the answer. So please co-operate. It will be easier on you, because I'll get the information anyway, so why suffer in your last moments?'

'Go fuck yourself! I won't tell you anything.' Alex glared down the barrel.

'Pity you took that line Alex' said Giles derisively. 'One. Two. Three! Sorry Alex, but you asked for it!'

Giles squeezed the trigger, but could not complete the action. He stood facing Alex, mouth open, eyes staring in surprise with a silent scream formed round his now blood drenched lips. Behind him, in the doorway, stood the Professor holding Giles close to him. In his right hand was the hilt of a large hunting knife, the blade embedded deeply into the neck, severing the jugular. Lang stepped back and pushed Giles forward, his body falling awkwardly onto the steward.

Alex looked across at Lang. 'Thanks.'

'My pleasure. I don't like *these* Tentacle people and one less is good for me.'

Alex kicked the Magnum away from Giles's blood soaked body and quickly frisked him. 'You look after this' he said to Lang pointing to the gun. Only a receipt for a deposited item held with the concierge and the communicator were of any interest. 'Professor. I think you should go next door and let me handle everything here.'

'But my knife. The bodies?' the Scotsman said slightly alarmed.

'Leave it to me. Just go. I'll be with you soon.'

Lang left, leaving Alex to sit on a seat and think things through. He stood up and cautiously opening the door, stepped into the corridor and headed to the Purser.

'Can I have a word?' he asked the smart, effeminate man, as he finished dealing with another passenger's problems.

'Of course sir. How can I help you?'

'Can we talk somewhere confidentially?' Alex showed his security service identification.

'Let's come in here' the concerned purser said. He led them into a small office reserved for his use.

Alex shut the door. 'Look Nigel.' Alex saw his name tag on his blue blazer. 'There has been an incident on the train. No one is at risk and there is no threat to other passengers or staff.'

Nigel visibly relaxed and exhaled deeply. 'What's the problem?' he asked.

'Sorry Nigel. I can't tell you. Security and all that. One of your staff though has been involved, a young steward. He is indisposed at the moment, so please don't call him. Also cabin thirteen is now off limits to everyone until we arrive in London, where the Police will take charge. Nobody must enter and it must now be sealed until then. One last thing.

Do you have the item that this ticket refers to?' Alex held out the paper receipt.

'No problem. Let me see. Number eight.' He ran down a computer list. 'Ah. Here we are. Yes. A briefcase deposited by a Mr Giles.'

'Can you get it for me?' Alex insisted.

'Right away.' He smiled, leaving Alex alone for a moment. 'Here we are!' he sang and handed the smart double locked case over.

'Thanks. Now don't forget. Seal number thirteen now!' They left the office and walked in file to the cabin. 'Seal it!' Alex ordered.

Nigel tapped a code into a portable hand unit with him and the door double locked itself from within.

'Excellent! Now please go about your normal duties until we arrive in London.'

'Of course sir.' He walked away wondering what the hell was going on and how his steward came to be involved. He made a mental note to talk to him later.

Alex watched him go and then tapped softly on number fourteen. 'It's Alex' he whispered.

The door opened slightly and the Professor stood in the frame, Giles's Magnum in hand.

'Its ok' said Alex. 'You can put that away.'

Lang stepped back and Alex eased his way in and sat down among them.

'No talking' he said to the others as he dialled Chelsea again.

'Alex here. Put me through to the Colonel.' Within seconds he had given a detailed situation report.

'Alex' said Tudor. 'We think Tullett refers to the government minister, Charles Tullett. I am going to see him now and find out how deep he is in this. Get over to the Tower with the others as soon as you get in. Transport is laid on. Don't move. We'll come to you. I've contacted the Deputy Assistant Commissioner and another clean up team will be at Euston also. Out.'

Alex lowered the communicator and looked up at the others. 'Don't ask' he said firmly. 'Let's all get some rest.' He looked at his watch. Three thirty. Another two and half hours to arrival. He closed his eyes and fell asleep, the briefcase by his side.

TUDOR

Colonel Tudor climbed into the back seat of the Range Rover, complete with blackened windows, and set off across London, Police motorcycle outriders clearing a path through the Olympic tourists. Beside him sat Captain Williams, also in uniform, the crests of the SAS and Parachute Regiments boldly displayed on his sleeve. Ahead of them the blue lights of the escort were now joined by two brightly marked police cars, assigned by the DAC Met Police. Even allowing for the heavy traffic, the convoy made it through to the Post Office Tower in forty five minutes, the Range Rover disappearing into the private underground car park. Tudor and Williams stepped into the foyer and walked over to the penthouse lift in the corner, indicating Tentacle as the only resident on that floor. At the top, they were greeted by Tullett and shown into the panoramic suite with incredible 360 degree views of

London spread out below them. Although it was still early and the sun was not due to set until nine thirty, the glistening Thames shimmering in the heat haze of the afternoon gave an ethereal vision of time and space.

'Great isn't it?' asked Tullett.

'Amazing' replied Williams, looking out to the East.

'You know' said Tullett 'from this height and on a clear day you can see Windsor Castle and Dartford Bridge.' He smiled. 'Your call to me said that this was important' addressing the Colonel. 'How can I be of assistance?' he asked amiably.

Tudor had already sat down on one of the large settees and asked Tullett to join him.

Captain Williams was still gazing to the East. 'Is that the Olympic Park?' he pointed past the tall blocks of Canary Wharf.

'Yes, Captain. Impressive when you get to see it close up.'

Tullett sat opposite the Colonel and unravelled a cigar, offering one to Tudor.

'Thanks. Don't indulge' he said quite emphatically.

Tullett lit the end and leaned back, relaxing.

'I want to know if you have any knowledge of this operation' the Army man asked. He placed a piece of paper in front of Tullett.

He picked it up, read it and laughed. 'Do you really think that I could have a hand in something as outrageous as this' he smiled. 'Whoever is arranging it should be congratulated though. Ridding the world of colour. That would put the cat among the pigeons, I must say!'

'If I told you that I have it on good information that you are one of the key figures in this plot, what would you say?' the Colonel asked, leaning towards Tullet.

'Are you crazy? What possible reason would I have for getting involved with this? I'm not a scientist, so how could I know how to do this? Come on. Please tell me that you have something more concrete than a bit of tatty paper purportedly implicating my involvement with this?'

'Ok' insisted the Colonel. 'Do you know a man called Giles? I gather he's your number two here?'

'Yes he is. So what? Is that a crime?' he answered defiantly.

'No. But conspiracy and murder is' Tudor pressed.

'What the hell are you talking about?' retorted Tullett, stubbing out his smouldering cigar in a giant glass ashtray and standing up.

The Colonel continued. 'Your friend Giles was good enough to leave his mobile communicator with us and following our de-crypt that you saw just now, is enough for us to hold you following further investigations. We retrieved the unit from him on a London bound train due at Euston in about' he looked at his watch 'half an hour.'

Tullett looked up. 'Stupid traitorous bastard!' he snarled.

'If you are referring to Giles' said the Colonel, he didn't give you away, the papers he carried with him and his communicator with all your calls recorded on it did that.'

'I hope he rots in hell!' Tullett shouted.

'Could be he's there already! He's had an accident on the train and won't be taking place at your trial in India.'

'What trial? What's this about India?' he stammered, feeling the noose slowly closing around his neck.

'It seems that you've favoured certain warlords out there and the others want revenge for what you've done or are planning to do without them' the Colonel added 'The UK Government, in order to avoid any racial tension and for political expediency, is going to extradite you. The Indian government have already submitted the papers. I don't fancy your chances!'

'You can't do this! I'm British and white! I was doing this for you! This way' he sounded panicked now 'we could have insurrection and get the blacks and Asians to riot and then we can get them thrown out. Don't you see? It's for you. I did this for you!' He looked at Tudor and Williams.

Tudor stood up. 'Are you coming quietly? We have other questions for you, like where is Chekhov's wife?'

Tullett smiled. 'You don't know, do you?' he said contemptuously. 'Lang's no good without her knowledge. I'll tell you nothing!' he uttered. He folded his arms in defiance and stared at the floor.

'Williams. Will you escort Mr Tullett to the car?' requested the Colonel.

The Captain moved round to seize Tullett, but the Tentacle man was faster, running over to a bureau, opening a drawer and pulling out a gun.

'Drop that!' ordered Williams closing the distance on him.

'If you come any closer, I'll shoot. I'm warning you!' shouted Tullett.

Undeterred, Williams advanced on him.

Tullett fired once just missing the officer and then sprinted across the suite just as two men wearing black assault suits burst in holding Uzi machine pistols.

'Wound only!' instructed Tudor.

One trooper fired at the full length glass window behind Tullett and the other at his legs. The glass shattered in an explosion of shards, blinding the Tentacle man who dropped the gun, overbalanced and tumbled silently, arms flailing down the side of the building.

Tudor and Williams rushed over to the window and saw Tullett embrace the pavement far below. A woman screamed while others looked up and pointed in their direction.

'Sorry about that' the lead trooper said, his mask still on.

Tudor held his hand up in acceptance.

'Just arrange for the *cleaners*. Link with the DAC Met Police' ordered Williams.

'It's done' said the second trooper, already in touch via his built in head set.

Within seconds they were gone, the 'clean up team' arriving and repairing everything in the Tower within the hour as if nothing had ever happened. Far below Special Branch were handling all aspects of the unfortunate 'accident', including the removal of Tullett's corpse. Tudor walked over to the bar, poured a whiskey and waited for Alex and the others to arrive.

Euston was very busy with Olympic fever everywhere. The train pulled in by the Royal Mail parcels entrance, as passengers poured out onto the platform, through the ticket barriers and onto the main concourse. In cabin fourteen they all sat and waited. Suddenly there was a knock on the door. Alex rose, gun in hand, and released the lock. The door slid back and a large black man stood grinning in at them.

'Put that away you silly white shit!' he said, smiling like Louis Armstrong. 'You remember last time, when I kicked your arse?' he added laughing.

'Peter! You black son of a bitch!' Alex happily responded, lowering the gun and flicking the safety on.

'Everyone' he turned to the others 'this is the cavalry!'

They all stared at the scene of this great big black man and Alex in a gentle friendly hug.

'Come on. Let's get you all out of here. The Colonel's waiting' Peter said.

As they stepped out of the carriage, a black mini-bus without any windows drew up on the platform. Within minutes they were out of the station, past the queuing red Royal Mail vans and en-route for the penthouse. It was six thirty. Meeting them was the Colonel, accompanied by several armed security men from MI6.

ROYAL LONDON HOSPITAL

The Royal London Hospital at Whitechapel, built in the nineteenth century, stood with its main frontage facing the Whitechapel market, that had flourished under the stewardship of nearly every immigrant group that had ever arrived in the east end of London. Over the years, the horse drawn traffic and slums of Stepney had made way for the car and large council estates. The Jews, who had been one of the first major immigrant groups principally from Eastern Europe in the late nineteenth century, had been replaced in the nineteen seventies by a cocktail of new immigrants from Cyprus, Turkey, India and Pakistan. This new wave inherited the garment making trade and towards the end of the twentieth century, imported various other religions including Islam and the Moslem faith. Churches and Synagogues, that had been in every street now started disappearing, as the Mosque started to make its mark. The hospital and its staff though, stuck to the same principles on which it was founded and the hand of Florence Nightingale was stretched out to all. Although the external façade had remained essentially the same during all this change, the advances in science and medical techniques left the hospital wanting for nothing. Over time, its Accident and Emergency division, supported by a fleet of ambulances, had to deal with everything from the Blitz in World War Two to terrorist bomb outrage casualties. All of these things made it the pre-eminent and main focal point for the Olympics, especially as it now sported a helicopter rescue team on its roof. During the months leading to the opening ceremony, medical teams from around the globe, under the Command of the Chief Medical Officer (CMO) were inducted into its wards as a necessary support to the extra five million additional visitors due in London for the games duration. His remit was to liaise with the NHS, Emergency Services and the Health Protection Agency in the event of a national disaster focussed around the Games. The five hundred acre Olympic Park, with the compact green site at its hub, held over seventeen thousand beds for the competing athletes and was only a few minutes walk from the massive stadium seating eighty thousand spectators. Nearby stood the Aquatics, Velopark, Indoor sports, training facilities and compact Media centre. Just outside the park, abutting the River Lee, was a giant filtration system which provided millions of gallons of fresh water to the stadium and it's supporting facilities.

In the days and weeks leading to the opening ceremony, the conspirators of Tentacle inconspicuously arrived, melting into the multi ethnic and teeming masses of athletes and their support teams. Among its leaders was the Deputy Head of The Council of Racial Equality, Morgan Ibotu. A giant amongst men, he stood six foot eight tall weighing in at two hundred pounds and contrary to his job title, treated all black people with disdain and contempt. Indeed, it was his contention that the African nations and their despot leaders should be taught a lesson that they would never forget, leaving him to evolve as the true African Continent President on a par with the EU, Chinese, Russian and USA Presidents. At the time of their arrival in London, the operational command HQ was based on the top of the Post Office Tower and the communiqués that flowed seamlessly between them all gave no indication of any potential disruption to their detailed plans. To the contrary, everything was working ahead of schedule, except for the inconvenience that Lang and his Scottish assistant was causing to Tullett and his team. They knew that if Lang made contact with her, their plans would have to be stepped up immediately, risking discovery and failure.

Dr. Steven Williams was worried. Actually, he was very concerned. In all his twenty three years as a clinical skin specialist, he had never seen as many acute conditions for colour blemishing and impurities, as were being admitted to the Royal London A & E in the last few days. The thing that really concerned him was the fact that all the admissions came from the Olympic Village and were either of Asiatic or

Black complexions. This in itself was worrying, but equally of concern was the fact that in all cases, the skin tone was bubbling and lightening by the minute. An example of this was Frederick Kowula, a sprinter from Sierra Leone, brought in with stomach pains yesterday and now showing distinct signs of turning from deep Negro black to a tanned Caucasian complexion. Strangely, only the skin was changing, not the eyes or bodily hair. Among some of the Chinese and Indian athletes, similar cases had been reported. Sitting in his office, he looked at the charts of the admitted patients. True, there were only about ten of them and this in itself normally would not be any reason for concern. Yet the more he looked at the symptoms, the less comfortable he felt. There was no logical pattern to this and certainly no valid explanation. There could only be one answer. He was sure of it and using his speed dial, he called directly to the Village Medical team.

'Harry? Steven here. Royal London A & E. How's it all going over there?'

'Normal athletic fare' Harry responded. 'Over stretching, heat stroke, remember its now thirty plus and getting hotter. The norm. You know?'

'Yeah. I know. Look. The reason that I'm calling you is because we've admitted your athletes for some type of stomach pain and I've got a nasty feeling that this is drug related. Did they all pass the IOC drug tests?'

'Should have. Give me a second. I'll check.'

In the background, Steven could hear the clickety click of a keyboard, followed by a brief phone call.

'Stomach pains. Yes. Ten I believe. No. I'll hold. Thanks.'

There was a silence down the line, only filled with Harry's fingers drumming on his table to the tune of 'WE ARE THE CHAMPIONS' to which he badly tried to sing.

'Yes. Still here. Are you sure? Thanks. Yes I will. Thanks again. Bye.' Steven overheard Harry's conversation.

'Steven? Are you there?' asked Harry.

'Yes. What's the answer?' asked the hospital specialist.

'Well the IOC drug and doping team have found no. Repeat. No trace of any legal or illegal levels of drugs in any saliva and urine. I have advised them of the stomach pains and they have alerted all the national teams' doctors. If you ask me Steven, it's either a case of localised food poisoning or something in the water and no more than that. The environmental health and safety team have already been advised and they will carefully monitor the situation with the food and drinks inspectorate. If there's any change I'll get back to you. Is that alright?'

'Mmm. I suppose it will have to be' Steven replied, still worried. 'Thanks anyway. Keep me posted. I'll do the same.'

He clicked off the mobile and slipped it back into his top pocket. Why didn't he mention to Harry about the skin discolouration? He knew that it could provoke more questions than it answered and at this particular moment when his wards were overflowing with heatstroke and heart patients, the last thing he needed was another layer of investigative medical teams, never mind the media. No. He was right to keep this local to the hospital and not volunteer for problems that could create a mountain out of a molehill, making his job and that of the hospital a million times worse. Yet, for all that, he was still bothered. What is this stomach pain and is it connected to the pigmentation change? He pondered for a moment, then took out his communicator again and sent a brief text to his old friend, another skin specialist, who also held the post as Chairman of the CRE in London.

NEED TO KNOW

With time running out before the commencement of the games, the Colonel and Alex, who by natural selection were both driving this operation, had hit a major stumbling block.

'The problem is people' the Colonel always quoted *people* to empower himself 'we must keep this to a need to know operation and apart from you all and my immediate staff' he nodded to the closed door, 'the only other people who we need to have contact with are the conspirators. Now since I know how these types work, we can assume that there is a hierarchy with a very flat structure beneath them, formed mainly of technical and military personnel. We cannot be sure on numbers, but if an attack is to be made at the Olympics, then numbers of twenty to thirty would be involved.'

'Is that all?' queried the Professor. 'I personally would have thought that there would be hundreds, if not thousands, involved' he added.

'If we were to count the numbers across the globe, then, Professor you would probably be right,' responded the Colonel, 'but groups like these operate in small cells, *so* small in fact, that quite often one unit doesn't know what the other is doing. This gives them the ability to operate unilaterally and without fear of giving the identity of the others away. The only good thing about this is that we only need concern ourselves about the top layer and the rest will fall. Once we have cut the head off the monster, the body will die immediately.'

'It was the Hydra's head' corrected Lang. 'From Jason's voyages' he quickly added.

'Quite!' replied the Colonel, classically chastised. 'Therefore people, we must find out who the other leaders are, before we move and that at the moment is one of our biggest headaches. I have called up a special intelligence gathering team who have been hard at work and will produce the answers soon, but I fear that unless any of you can give us a clue, we may miss the boat and I don't need to tell you what the consequences are for that happening?'

As he looked around the gathered group, they all hung their heads except Alex, who suddenly realising what the Colonel had suggested, and sprung rapidly from the arm of the chair that he shared with Chekhov and ran over to the brief case by the door, that he had acquired on the train. Everyone wheeled round and watched him march with it to a large glass table, where he proceeded to unpick the two combination locks. The Colonel was first at the table as Alex tripped the first code and by the time the second one had given its secret away, the other four were standing by his side, watching, curiosity mingled with anticipation.

'What's in there?' asked Karen.

Alex opened the lid, supported by two large cantilever hinges and lifted out a sealed manila envelope with what appeared to be the symbol of an Octopus stamped on the front cover.

'Tentacle!' said the Colonel, watching Alex carefully pull back the gummed tongue and remove the A4 document.

He put the envelope back in the case and silently read the page, his face expressionless. When he had finished he handed the paper across to the Colonel who also ran his eyes across the page, slowly absorbing the detailed material before him. He looked quizzically at Alex.

'It's your call Sir!' Alex said to him.

'Yes I know. Captain! Sergeant!' he commanded loudly.

The doors opened and the two uniformed men entered the room, flanked by two Royal Military Police corporals who then stepped outside, closing the doors behind them.

'Come in gentlemen!' and strode over to greet and guide them to another part of the large suite, out of earshot of the others.

A huddled meeting took place where the Colonel showed the paper to them both. Again, only a slight surprise from both men showed on their faces and within minutes they were heading out of the room, only stopping to salute as they left. The Military Police closed the doors securely behind them, leaving the Colonel and his guests alone again.

'Could someone tell me what the hell's going on? What was that about? What's in the paper?' demanded the Professor, turning to the Colonel.

'I think I can answer that. With your permission, Colonel?' said Alex.

Colonel Tudor waved him to continue, whereon Alex explained that the document held the details of the conspirators and that a plan was now in place to keep a watching brief until it was time to arrest them.

'The problem is' he turned to Chekhov 'we still do not know where your wife is being held, but as we move forward I am sure we will discover that.'

The Russian half smiled, but still looked worried. Lang put his large arm round his friend and squeezed him tight. 'Have faith. I'm sure all will be well.'

'Can I call my paper?' Karen looked at Alex.

'Sorry, my dear' interjected the Colonel. 'For security reasons, as I am sure you will be aware, I cannot permit any communication to anyone until this is all wrapped up.'

She looked stunned and fumed irritably. This could be the biggest scoop in history and she was being hog-tied because of protocol and red tape. Alex read her thoughts and walked across to the Colonel and had a brief word. Tudor stood toe to toe with Alex, at first shaking his head emphatically, but after a few furtive glances at Karen, his body language softened, followed by an almost apologetic nod and a stern wag of his finger.

Alex walked over to Karen. 'Listen. You cannot contact anyone while this is going on.' She looked deflated. 'But because you have been involved from almost day one and also, because of the attempt on your life, the Colonel will give you the sole media rights, subject to vetting, once this is settled.'

Beaming, she looked up into Alex's eyes and kissed him quickly on the lips. 'Thank you' she silently mouthed to him.

'No problem' he whispered back.

'People' the Colonel addressed the five before him. 'With just over thirty six hours to go to the games starting, I propose that you will all stay here until the crisis is over. This will be for your own sake and protection. I have already made arrangements for your personal possessions, clothes and so forth to be shipped here. Mr Chekhov, we have supplied a range of clothes for you, as we really couldn't ship them in from Russia! I would be obliged though if in return you could let me have the gun picked up in the cabin and still in your possession.'

Chekhov blushed. He had forgotten about it and now gently prodded the Professor who carefully removed the weapon from his jacket and handed it carefully to the Colonel.

'This may also help' said Chekhov, suddenly remembering the camera and handing it across.

'Thanks' said the Colonel. 'We have accommodation for you all and my staff outside will show you to your sleeping quarters after dinner. Questions?'

There was silence.

'Right' he continued. 'We have dining facilities on the next floor and dinner is being prepared as we speak. So if you will all follow me.'

The doors opened and they followed him past the MP's and down a flight of stairs to a sumptuous dining room centred by a long table laid out for six.

DAVID IWOKU

David Iwoku, MBE, had always prided himself on being honest and prompt in his duties as head of the Commission for Racial Equality. He had held the post since his predecessor had accepted the position of Deputy to the Secretary General of the United Nations in 2010. Although he had previously held a prominent position as the first black man to be Leader of Westminster Council from 2008, that was relatively mild to what this post was now throwing up. At Westminster he could take the moronic and feeble jokes regarding race and religion, even to the point that he almost believed sometimes that he was one of the 'boys'. The temptation to put down his own creed just to assimilate was tempting, but stuck in his craw and made him feel uneasy, especially when dining with members of the Afro/ Caribbean populace. In this post, he had to tread very carefully, as any position he might take could immediately be construed as a sign of weakness, causing civilian and industrial unrest. Therefore, when he received a missed call from his close friend and blood brother Professor Lang, he was excited and intrigued. They had not communicated for many years, but had watched each other climb the slippery ladders of their respective careers. When David received his MBE from the Queen in 2009, he had requested that the Professor be his guest as he had no other family that he wanted to invite. Unfortunately, the invitation was returned with the stamp of 'Unknown at this address. Return to sender' leaving David to invite along two of the 'boys' at Westminster, who savoured every moment of hobnobbing and sucking up to the society celebrities at the investiture. David was disappointed that his friend never made it, but felt there must have been a genuine reason and forgave him anyway. This call therefore provided the perfect opportunity for a reunion, since their bloods fused in Africa many eons ago when they were young and ambitious. Putting his feet up on his desk and sitting back into the studded brown leather executive chair, he dialled Lang's private mobile number. He looked at his desk clock. Ten pm. Yes Lang would still take the call. He was a night bird as well. They had that in common. Very little sleep, but bursts of intense burning energy.

'Hello?' asked the scientist.

'Professor? Is that you?' said David.

'David? How are you? Long time no speak' a smile passing across his rugged face.

'Same here. Is the family well?' asked the Commissioner.

'Fine. Yours?' asked Lang diplomatically, knowing that his friend had had marital problems.

'Better than it was' he stated matter of factly.

'How's the job?' the Professor enquired, trying to steer the conversation towards a subject less uncomfortable.

'Don't ask. It's very challenging and full of politics.'

'I know. We all have that!' the Professor looked around him.

'What are you doing at the moment?' asked David. 'I tried

to invite you to the Palace' he added, 'but you had disappeared. Is everything ok?'

'Yes fine. Sorry about that. I was working on something. You know how it is?'

'Yes, of course' David knew that 'something' was code for top secret and they left it at that.

Then suddenly, there was a deafening silence between them, broken quickly by the Professor, who now with the niceties out of the way, explained why he had tried to get hold of his old friend. 'David. I called you because I need your advice and help. I need to meet you tonight. It's *very* important. I can't take no for an answer. Please don't ask any questions. I wouldn't do this if I didn't think it absolutely necessary!'

'You know the time is ten now?' the Commissioner asked.

'I know. I'll give you the address. Just come yourself. Don't tell *anyone* where you're going. Ask for me or Colonel Tudor when you arrive, but please hurry!'

Within thirty minutes he had cut across Central London in his car and was heading up in the private lift to the top of the tower where the Professor and Tudor were waiting with Alex, the others having gone to bed.

'David!' Lang stepped forward smiling and hugged his old friend. 'Let me look at you? You've put on weight!' he smiled at the Commissioner.

'And you as well' David smiled back, patting Lang's stomach.

'Let me introduce Colonel Tudor and Alex Mason' the Professor said.

They shook hands and crossed the lobby, entering the private office still guarded by the MP's, the damage being repaired earlier. The doors closed and David walked over to the twinkling expanse of light spread out before him.

'Very impressive! I wish my humble office had this view!' He turned and faced them. 'Now what can I do for you gentlemen? My friend the Professor hinted this might be a matter of life and death!' He smiled at them waiting for a response.

'Would you like a drink Mr Commissioner?' asked Alex, pouring himself a glass of Teachers.

'Thank you. Scotch. Straight. And please call me David, especially with friends.'

'Same poison for me' said Lang.

'And again' added the Colonel.

They all sat with their drinks in hand.

'Cheers!' said Alex, raising his whiskey glass.

After their glasses kissed, they sat back comfortably into the deep armchairs surrounding them.

'Do you have a Deputy working for you called Morgan Ibotu?' asked the Colonel directly, not waiting to beat around the bush.

'Yes, of course. Good man. Very strong beliefs. Feels that everybody should be treated equally. Been here before I was appointed. Is something wrong?'

'Have you ever heard of an organisation called Tentacle?' the Colonel added.

'No. Never. Should I? What is it?'

'We have it on good authority that Mr Ibotu is one of the principals at the top of this group and that there are plans to, how can I put it, overthrow a few governments and take control.'

David sat there shocked. 'You must be joking! Morgan could never do that. He is dedicated.'

'Yes. He is dedicated. Dedicated to becoming the sole leader of the African continent!' stressed the Colonel.

'You're crazy! What proof do you have? I demand to see it!' said the Commissioner indignantly.

The Colonel passed across the paper, which David read carefully and then the developed pictures from the camera that Chekhov had handed across.

'Incredible! I don't know what to say?' the stunned diplomat said. He passed them back.

'My friend. Do you agree with this?' addressing the Professor.

'I'm afraid I do David!' Lang said.

David shook his head in disbelief. 'I think I'll have another drink!' he said, holding his empty glass up to Alex who filled it this time to the brim. 'Tell me everything and then ask what you need from me. I gather that's why you called me in?' he queried.

'Let me run it past you' said the Colonel and proceeded to fill in the salient points for his new guest. 'Morgan is in the strongest position at Tentacle. He probably doesn't know yet that his two top people in this country are dead and that's just the way we are keeping it until we get everything sewn up in one quick move. We must also establish the mode of delivery of the virus and therefore cannot afford to lift any of the activists early, as they could alert the others and trigger an advanced attack. This is why we need your help in giving us anything and everything about Morgan. Do you have any files on him?'

The Commissioner took a deep breath and pondered. 'Of course I have a file on him, since to take the position he was security vetted and cleared. If you have a network link here, I can access it.'

The Colonel stood up and with the Commissioner in tow, walked over to a desk with a laptop and printer. 'It's all yours' indicating the chair with his hand.

Mr Iwoku was not long in retrieving what he wanted and handed over the printed file to the Colonel, who quickly read it, taking in all the main points and gave it to Alex for his perusal. The information was as expected. All official with no mention of other conspirators or Tentacle.

'There's nothing here that we can use. No leads. No clues. Is this all there is? I mean could there be a hidden folder that you are not aware of?' said the Colonel.

'Could be, but that could take forever to find. I'm sorry gentleman. I would need a small army of IT experts to find any secret folders.'

They all sat silent for a moment with Alex still poring over the printout. A vibrating buzz suddenly came from the Commissioner's jacket. He took out the communicator and saw a message sent hours ago from Dr Steven Williams, indicating a call back was required on receipt of this text, no matter what the time was. It was very urgent.

'Gentlemen. Could you excuse me for one minute? I must take this.' He stood up, walked over to the window and gazed for a second at the Canary Wharf complex three miles distant, small enough at this size to mistake it for a child's Meccano building set. Lifting the display he hit redial and almost immediately Steven answered. 'Hello Steven. How are you? What seems to be the problem?'

'Oh. Thank God you've called back. I didn't know which way to turn. I need your advice.'

'Sure. It must be important. How can I be of help?'

'Listen' Steven said. 'Over the last few days we have been receiving a steadily growing stream of athletes from the Village. This would not be so unusual but for the fact that they all came in with stomach pains which then clear. But here's the thing. As the pains disappear their skin colour starts lightening. This is true of all Afro-Caribbean and Asian athletes. I thought at first that it could have been drugs, so I got the IOC drug team with environmental health to run checks. All clean. They think it could be food poisoning. I have my doubts. The reason I am calling you is for your expertise in skin problems. The wards will go critical if this continues. We have already had over twenty today. There could be panic if we do nothing and get accused of racial bias. I have spoken to the Deputy of the IOC and he has told me *not* to broadcast the situation. I personally feel it is building to a head and the next seventy two hours will be a decisive time. Can you give me any advice?'

'Where do you believe the source of the problem comes from? You said that food poisoning was ruled out. What's left?' the Commissioner asked.

'If you really want to know, then I believe that if this is not food poisoning then it could be water borne and crazily as it might sound and please don't repeat this, but I believe that it might be deliberate. There's no other logical explanation.'

The Commissioner stood frozen at what he had just heard. Steven was not a man to make sweeping assertions and would have checked out all the other natural avenues before coming to his conclusion.

'Why do you think it could be deliberate water poisoning at the Olympic Village?' he asked, raising his voice so that Alex, the Colonel and the Professor could hear him. He flicked the receiver to loudspeaker.

Steven's voice came strong and clear. 'I don't know, but something's going on and with all these skin changes and stomach pains preceding them, I am concerned.'

The Colonel scribbled a note for the Commissioner to read down the line.

'Look Steven. I agree with the IOC people. Don't panic and don't publicize this. I will get some of my people to be with you tonight. Do as they say and we'll get through this. One last thing. Where does the water get filtrated at the Village?'

'Oh. It's a giant filtering plant at the edge of the Village by the river.'

'Steven. Go back to work. I'll be in touch.' He clicked off the communicator and turned to the Professor.

'You're the expert. Is this possible? Could a waterborne virus get through a filtration plant?'

'The chances of that happening are about ten million to one' the Professor said emphatically. 'The controls and filters are stringently checked every hour and if any foreign body were to be detected, there are sufficient safeguards in place to protect the public.'

'What about a deliberate intrusion by *other* external factors?' asked the Colonel pointedly.

'If you mean terrorists' said the academic 'then I believe the authorities never planned for that eventuality. It's unthinkable that anyone could break in *and* have the expertise to sabotage the plant.'

'Well. You may have got it wrong!' snapped the Commissioner amazed. 'In all my years, I have never come across a facility, especially one that is critical to a major event like this, to be unprotected' he added. 'The quantum security failure between the Olympic Delivery Authority and the Government is staggering! It should have been, excuse the pun, watertight.'

'Well. We may have a serious health breach combined with a major threat now, so it's no good crying over spilt milk. We must stop this immediately!' said the Colonel. 'I also believe,' the Staff Officer glumly added, 'that although the filtration plant is to be the main target, rogue elements among the terrorists have been 'experimenting' with some of the athletes. With over one hundred and eighty thousand people in the village every day, it is not beyond the bounds of possibility that those athletes affected have had 'Mickey Finns' slipped into their drinks at any number of outlets. If we can stop the main attack, then it is more than possible that we will also be able to contain or eliminate any of the sideshows. I will arrange for my medical team to visit Dr Williams tonight and help him through this.' The Colonel lifted his phone and made three calls. The first was to The Assistant Commissioner Metropolitan Police 'Olympic Command' briefing him on the latest situation. The second was to the Cabinet Secretary at Downing Street requesting COBRA be assembled as there was a possible threat to the nations security, while the third call was to his own number two, the Commanding Officer of the Regiment's anti-terrorist standby team. 'That's that taken care of' he pronounced. 'Now for the water plant.'

'Colonel?' Alex said. 'We can't just blast our way in. They could get spooked and infect early. We must get Chekhov's wife free and then go in.'

'You're right, of course, Alex. But where is she?'

'Who is Chekhov?' asked the Commissioner, looking at Alex.

'It's a long story' Alex said 'but your deputy will probably know. We must bag him tonight or tomorrow at latest. Let's see that paper on him. Where does he live and where is he now?' he added urgently, 'bearing in mind that the Games start on the 27th. That's the day after tomorrow.'

'I can help you there' said the Commissioner. 'Morgan will have gone to Ronnie Scott's Jazz Club tonight. It's one of his haunts. He took his car. You have the details.'

The Colonel mentally reviewed the situation, flipped off his communicator and turned to the Commissioner. 'Thank you sir for your most invaluable help. I'm sorry that we've got you here so late, but we have a cooked dinner for you and a bed for the night.'

'That's alright Colonel. I have eaten and have my own warm bed at home to go to.'

'Sorry sir. Maybe I didn't make myself clear. I can't let you go tonight. The risk factor is too great.'

'But?' the Commissioner started to protest.

'Sorry sir. This is a major security situation, as I am sure you will understand. Although you may feel that you are not under any threat, I cannot take that chance and would ask you to bear with us. If you have your keys, I will arrange for one of my men to collect some clothes and personal possessions tonight for you.'

The Commissioner smiled. 'Can I call my wife and advise her? She'll be concerned.'

'Sorry sir. You are incommunicado. We will advise her that you are wanted on official business and will be home on the 27th. I am sure she will understand.'

'She'll probably think that I am having an affair. Chance would be a fine thing!' He smiled and handed his keys over to Alex, who stepped outside, instructing the duty Sergeant in the plan of action. As he re-entered, the Commissioner said that he would retire since the time was now close to midnight.

The Colonel buzzed the intercom and a trooper appeared, waiting to show the political man to his room. 'Good night gentlemen' he said to the other three, nodding at them all and quickly departing.

'Right' said the Colonel to the Professor and Alex. 'Wheels are now turning to obtain the plans of the water filtering plant. Find this Morgan Ibotu character and then Chekhov's wife. I suggest that we all get some sleep. The next forty eight hours are going to be manic. I've left instructions to wake me when anything positive arises. Goodnight gentlemen!'

'Goodnight Colonel' they both said in unison and headed for their respective rooms.

In Parliament Square, Big Ben chimed twelve, the deep bass tones resonating over the capital's roof-tops to the Olympic Village in the east, where it waited holding its breath.

MORGAN IBOTU

Dawn of the 26th July broke warm and sunny at four fifty am. The whine of the milk floats had been heard delivering their produce since eleven the night before, while the suburban bushy tail foxes were scurrying for cover across gardens and streets filled with decorative bunting last used to celebrate the England Rugby World Cup victory. Everywhere there were signs of festivities to come; streets were closed and tables erected across the pavements and roadways. Even the raucous early morning cawing of the crows was subdued, as if they also needed to take stock of the mounting excitement that was gathering in the east of the Capital. The Police of the Olympic Command had been on standby for months now and as the penultimate day arrived, their presence became even more visible. All transport systems were operating at full stretch, especially the Javelin express shuttle transporting twenty five thousand passengers per hour on the seven minute journey from central London to the 'Village'. But none of this bothered Morgan Ibotu, as he snuggled under the black silk sheet of the four-poster that he shared with Amanda Summers, in her apartment at Blackheath. Her waist length black hair lay tantalisingly across her plump breasts, stirring him deeply. He looked down at her, bit his bottom lip and smiled at this apparition of sensual beauty. How, amongst all those good looking white guys at the club, had he managed to leave with her? He pulled back the fabric and admired her hour glass figure, sensitively touching her most intimate part. She moaned, squirmed and opened her dark brown eyes while parting her lips slightly, in anticipation.

'Come' she said, pulling him down. He gently kissed her and patted her small, firm bottom.

'Not now. Later. I've got things to do. People to see.' He smiled at her. 'You go back to sleep. I'll call you later.'

She let him go, closed her eyes and rolled over, wrapping herself in a lush ball.

Morgan found the bathroom, showered and dried himself with the guest towel that she had laid out for him. Dressing in a fresh set of clothes, he left her apartment just after eight and walked to his Mustang parked a short distance along the pavement. In the glove box he withdrew his portable shaver and using the driving mirror's reflection, trimmed the overnight stubble off, applying a splash of Faberge Brute to freshen up. He made a call via his hands free mobile, buckled up and turned the ignition key. With a deep roar the engine fired up and he was off heading across the heath.

She waited till he left and watching the car go, picked up her communicator. 'He's on the move. Heading in the direction of the tunnel.'

'Is he alone? Have you set the bug?' said the voice from the Post Office Tower.

'Alex. How long have you known me? Of course I have. It's a micro chip in his collar.'

'Was he good?' goaded the ex-SAS Officer.

'Alex. What I do for the service is my business. Butt out! I'm not running a regular Honey Trap!'

'Sorry! I didn't mean.....'

'Yes, you did. You wanted to know if this black man was better than you. That's for me to know. Actually' she teased 'on a scale of one to ten he scored eleven. As the teacher says in your end term report. Must try harder. See you around Alex. Bye!'

He heard the click and shook his head in exasperation.'Women!'

Within seconds Morgan's car details and location had been flashed across all monitoring units. The decision had been made to let him run and hopefully lead them to Chekhov's wife. They didn't want to spook him and warn the others. Only unmarked vehicles would follow at a safe distance. He exited the heath and turned down the slip road towards the A102 (M) and the Old Blackwall Tunnel, finding the roads virtually clear. A few delivery vehicles and builders' lorries carrying Union Jacks passed him, risking a speeding ticket, followed by a couple of Porsches slowing to 30 mph just before the cameras and then crawling through the twists and turns of this masterpiece of Victorian engineering. Morgan kept to the inside lane, always amazed at how the weight of the Thames didn't come exploding in on him. He wondered if he would be able to accelerate out of the tunnel as twenty million tons of water cascaded in, drowning everyone. He worried about things like that, even though the odds of it happening were so remote, he had more chance of being hit by a slow moving bus. Even so, he was glad to be out of the other end and, breathing easier, took the second exit onto the A13 towards the east, pulling up by the traffic lights.

The Asian man and his wife in their old Audi drew up next to him. The woman was eating a piece of Nan bread and seemed totally oblivious of Morgan, while her husband sat ramrod straight waiting for the lights to change. On green, Morgan drew away from them and headed to the next set of lights a quarter of a mile ahead. As he accelerated away, the woman dropped the Nan and picked up a microphone.

The Mustang made good time and was soon taking the exit lane for the A406. Keeping within the speed limits, Morgan took the exit for Chingford and headed towards Chigwell and north Essex. The roads became narrower and every now and then he had to pull over to allow a tractor through. The only vehicles he now saw were horse transporters, 'Rollers' and a good sprinkling of Jaguars. This was, after all, footballer and celebrity country. After passing Abridge Golf Club on his right two miles on, he turned left onto a track and followed this for half a mile, before coming to a stop by a gate across the road. He hit his horn and a stocky man appeared, waving him through, then shutting the gate behind. After another minute, the hedges dropped away revealing a large farmhouse surrounded by open land. Turning onto the gravel, he stopped and got out. Two men, one black, one Asian, stepped out of the front door to greet him.

'Morgan. Good to see you man!' said the black man

smiling.

'Same sentiments' smiled the Asian man bowing slightly.

'Let's get in' said Morgan 'and you can bring me up to date'.

They filed in. Morgan, being last, shut the door.

TICKING CLOCK

London was buzzing. Everywhere bright, multicoloured, flags flapped in the early morning sunshine. The assembled armies of the World's media were everywhere. Hotels were jam packed, while the streets were heaving with the onslaught, visitors filing into the shops, restaurants and bars of Oxford and Regent Street. To enter the underground was folly, as the temperatures on the trains and platforms were now exceeding one hundred degrees. Cold soft drinks and ice cream were the order of the day, with even the Olympic Command Police touring in reflective yellow bibs and fast mountain bikes. Around Stratford and the Olympic Park, the organisation flowed like water. Literally tens of thousands of visitors were marvelling at the massive Olympic Stadium and its satellite venues. Live jazz bands played to the passing crowds, while electronic screens displayed details of the forthcoming opening ceremony the next day. Fast food and cold drink stands were everywhere, their tempting smells wafting across the bustling crowds. In the medical units spaced out over the entire park, The London Ambulance Service, supported by St John Ambulance Brigade and The Red Cross, were working to their limits, mainly dealing with crowd crush and heatstroke cases.

To the west of the park, adjacent to the River Lee, stood the giant Thames Water filtration plant, capable of supplying over twenty million litres per day to the gathered athletes, their teams and supporters. Bordered on one side by the river, the total area was the size of a football pitch, surrounded by a twelve foot high green metal fence, topped by layers of razor wire on its outside perimeter. A twelve foot wide perimeter road ran inside of this, supported by a sophisticated lighting and camera system. The electronic entry gates were of the highest biometric standards encompassing eye, DNA and fingerprint recognition. Once in the building, different levels of security were needed to pass from one area to another, the most sensitive needing a priority one code only issued to the top one per cent of management.

The men poring over the blueprints and model of the plant in the viewing gallery of the Post Office Tower crouched down beside the scaled building like Gulliver and stared into the dolls sized windows.

The field commander, a small squat man called Roger, looked up. 'Yes. It can be done' addressing the Colonel across the table 'but because we only have just over twenty four hours and a need for surprise, it will be really difficult to get in by road without being spotted. The best route will be by boat and for that we will need support from SBS, with two high speed Gemini's from the Thames. Can you appraise them and arrange it? Our back up team will be on Hackney Marshes with the choppers.'

'Anything else?' noting the first points, said the Colonel.

'Yes. Four things. One. If we are to have the element of surprise, I can't have any Police interference. Two.

Professor Lang must be with us in an advisory capacity. Three. Synchronization. We must be able to hit them at precisely the same time at the farmhouse. A minute either way and we could be compromised. Four. In order to minimize collateral damage and to arrange a cover, we need a fire evacuation at eleven thirty. H-Hour is set for one pm, one hour before the Olympic flame gets lit. That's it.' He looked around him for approval.

'There is one more thing' the Colonel added. 'The call sign for the operation is 'Jennie', named after one of our operatives working within ACRO at Fareham.'

Roger made a series of calls and set the ball rolling. His two troop commanders and their teams, being on immediate standby, moved off within the hour heading towards their respective start lines. The Colonel made his calls to the Met Police Olympic Commander, Head of SBS on the South Coast and the London Fire Brigade Chief. As a final move, he made a direct call to Downing Street on a scrambler phone, advising both the PM and his Cabinet Secretary.

The clock was ticking. Nothing more could be done except to watch and wait.

FARMHOUSE

It was late afternoon in the farmhouse and the ten men and two women were going over the plans again, for the third time that day.

Mohammed, more than the others, complained. 'Why do we keep going over all this? We know it backwards' he said in a stressed way.

'Do you now?' said Morgan sarcastically. 'Well. Let me tell you that in order for the plan to succeed perfectly, you must know it inside out and upside down. There can be no, repeat, no, slip ups. Do you really think that D-Day and Desert Storm were won on studying a plan once or twice? No, they planned for success and had a contingency in case anything went wrong. We must do the same.' He slapped Mohammed on the back and smiled. 'Just think that this time tomorrow, the world will be in chaos and only we will be in place to pick up the pieces and create a new global order.' He looked around the table. 'Are we all agreed?' They all nodded. 'Good. Let's run past it again then.'

The Honourable Fitzroy Barnes, leaning against a wooden upright in his blue sports jacket and cavalry twill trousers, began. 'I, with Caroline, Miyamoto, Abraham and Vladimar will hold the fort here, waiting for your success call and prepare the announcement for the media. We will simultaneously flash the other Government and NGO heads that are with us into action.'

Vladimar, although keeping his head down while checking his radio, suddenly sat up. 'What do we do with the Scottish bitch now that she has given us the codes to make more of the 'black' capsules? What use is she now, apart from being Lang's assistant and the wife of that traitor, Chekhov?'

'You hold her until you receive the success call' said Morgan 'and then you can finish her off. If anyone get's in our way, we can use her knowledge and connections as a bargaining tool. After that............' He shook his head.

'Who is going to do it?' Caroline asked.

'The pleasure can be all yours!' Morgan smirked.

Vladimar smiled at her. 'I'll help you if you want!'

'No. Leave her to me' Caroline muttered. 'I'll make her suffer before I finish her off. It's the least I can do since she took my research job, after all the work I put in working for Lang.'

'Good! That's settled then' said Morgan. 'What about you guys?' He looked at the other six.

'We' said Stuart 'will have changed into Thames Water uniforms and with the official van and passes obtained from our internal contact, get to the filtration unit by noon. After parking up, we will enter the service entrance, check in via security and make our way through to the main generator. Carl will cut the video feed, leaving the monitors blind and the rest of us will infuse the soluble capsules into the water, leave quietly and meet back here later.'

'Perfect' said Morgan, rubbing his hands together.

'What will you be doing?' Mohammed asked, looking at Morgan.

'Me? You obviously were not paying attention before. Remember, I said that a contingency plan must always be in place as a back up. Well I am taking care of that! I would suggest now that someone goes and checks on our *guest*.' He looked across at Caroline. 'We don't want any harm coming to her *yet*!' he sneered. She rose and headed to the cellar door, flicking the light switch on and descended into the shadows, where a gagged Morag was manacled by her wrists to an overhead beam, her toes just touching the floor, sweat rolling down her face. Her eyes stared in silent shock as her old work colleague smirked at her discomfort. 'Morag! So good to see you again' she smiled wickedly. 'The last time we met was when you stole *my* research job, you bitch! But don't worry. I am going to reward you tomorrow with an overdue going away present. One that you'll never forget! Until then….' She stepped forward and held a small sharp stiletto taken from her belt, just below Morag's right eye and slowly carved a thin, but perceptible incision down her cheek.

The scientist's muffled scream and wide panicked eyes was contrasted by a silent trickle of warm blood dripping down her chin and onto her clothes.

'I'll leave you now Morag', Caroline whispered maliciously in her ear, 'so you can imagine and look forward to what I will give you tomorrow! Sweet dreams, bitch.' She wiped the blood-stained knife over Morag's dishevelled shirt and replacing it back in her belt, walked calmly up the stairs killing the light, leaving Morag crying silently in the dark.

RIVER LEE

The balmy, clear night, with mean temperatures in the eighties, was a blessing for the organisers, who had prayed for perfect conditions as the Olympic Torch headed for London and the opening ceremony. In the streets of the capital, all emergency services were on high alert as millions of happy people from a myriad of nations poured onto the roads and pavements, many of them highly intoxicated from all night drinking. With the dawn came the gathering chorus of birds and this, coupled with the low tide on the Thames, saw the wading herons picking their way though the mud banks searching for food. By eight a.m. thousands of athletes had been up for hours, many at the training tracks, while others ate a leisurely breakfast and stayed in the shade of their rooms. All had been issued with the schedules for the day, especially the opening ceremony for two pm and their respective places within the march past. Above the park, a media blimp glided serenely between the early released, yet brightly coloured carnival balloons, while hosting live TV coverage to three quarters of the world's populace. Eurostar trains from France and Belgium were arriving every thirty minutes at Stratford International, disgorging thousands of excited passengers onto the pedestrian links leading to the park. The Olympic buses moved carefully down the four mile circular route from the station in a non stop convoy system, depositing noisy spectators at different venues including the Olympic Stadium, Aquatics Centre and Velodrome, before returning to begin the cycle again.

The tide had turned by eleven and at the mouth of Barking Creek, some four miles downriver from the park, the rushing waters of the Thames poured themselves into the breach which would eventually become the River Lee. Two black Gemini assault craft, concealed with camouflage netting, carried Alex, Lang and eight troopers into the creek line astern heading inland. The two patrols, dressed entirely in black, were armed with Heckler and Koch MP5K sub-machine guns, Remington 870 pump-action shotguns and the standard 9mm Browning High Power semi-automatic pistols. The trip was full of twists and turns, as the boats negotiated the narrowing channels of Canning Town and passed under the fast moving A13 with high steep walls on both sides. Minutes later they entered Bow Creek and, passing under the A11, powered their way through Waterworks River and into the Lee. As they approached the water plant, framed against the massive Olympic Stadium a quarter of a mile away to their right, the lead trooper noted that the entire area was cleared of civilians. The Fire Brigade, working with the Police, had ensured that the false fire alert had created a total exclusion zone around the plant, without raising any suspicions of the real operation. The patrol moored up in the shadow of the building, with the Commander calling a briefing on the bank behind a tall hedge. Instructing two troopers to stay with the boats and protect the main assault group's flanks, they checked their watches.

'Twelve hundred hours, check!' said the Commander. 'Alex. You go with red section. Professor. You're with me and green team. Both sections go!' he ordered.

Sprinting up the bank and entering the deserted area cleared by the evacuation, red and green cautiously entered the building, safety catches off. Using hand signals they split up, red taking the stairs to the upper floor, while green, with the Professor in tow, headed directly for the filtration room. Luckily, because of the evacuation, most of the doors were still accessible. Only a couple barred their way, leaving the specialist trooper with them to trip the locks. Red section was ordered to hold their position and put one man on the main door of the building, after they had advised of a 'clear area'. With only the inner security door to now pass, the trooper started to pick the lock, when he saw a Thames Water official through the glass peering at him.

'Can I help you?' the official asked, surprised to see this strangely dressed individual before him.

'Can you open the door? It's very important' replied the trooper.

'I'm sorry, but I can't do that unless you have clearance' he insisted politely.

'Please sir. This is official business at the very highest level' the trooper persisted.

'I'm sorry, but that doesn't impress me!' the man said.

Easing the trooper to one side, the Commander faced the man. 'Look sir. There has been an evacuation and you must leave the building now! Please let us in and you can return once we and the Fire Brigade have deemed it safe.'

Suddenly the man's eyes widened, as looking over the Commanders shoulder he saw Lang. He whispered to someone behind him and backed away from the door.

'Everyone back. Quickly!' ordered the Commander.

A hail of bullets ripped through the door at them, ricocheting off the plant and machinery nearby. Two troopers returned fire at point blank range, one using the Remington to blow a massive hole in the door and then the hinges top and bottom, the other giving close covering support with his Browning. The fire fight continued until the door fell inwards on top of a dead gunman sprawled out in the narrow corridor beyond.

'Green, green, give me a sit rep. Out!' came the urgent message from the red team.

'Red. Hold your positions. One bandit dead. Others unknown. Home team zero casualties. Out.'

'Wilco' crackled back the reply.

'Professor. I want you to stay here with the Corporal' the Commander ordered. He addressed the NCO. 'He does not come until its all clear. Understood?'

'Sir!' he barked and pushed the Professor unceremoniously down onto the concrete floor.

'Suppressing fire!' ordered the Commander, keeping himself down as the Heckler and Koch opened up into the corridor.

After a few seconds, a trooper tossed a stun grenade into the darkened and bullet ridden corridor.'Grenade!' he shouted.

The blast had not even settled before troopers stormed the cordite filled corridor firing high and low bursts into each room. The sound of 'Clear!' was heard as the lower part of the building was secured, leaving only the filtration room to take.

Gingerly, using a broom handle found nearby, a trooper eased open the room's door and rolled in another stun grenade while taking cover by an adjacent wall. 'Fire in the hole!' he screamed.

The building trembled with the shock waves, as two troopers assaulted the door, firing brilliant tracers in two arcs of fire into the void. Four terrorists holding Uzi machine carbines were caught in the cross fire, while a woman holding a pistol was ordered to drop her weapon and lie on the floor. The order was bawled a second time by another masked trooper and she lowered her gun, while dropping to her knees.

'Move away from the weapon and lie face down on the floor' he ordered again, his Heckler aiming directly at her, a red laser spot visible on her head.

She slowly complied and lay inert on the tiled floor breathing heavily, her eyes scanning the room. Next to her lay Kunti, his eyes vacant and mouth dribbling blood, but there was something wrong. Very wrong. His skin colour was perceptibly changing from African black to Caucasian white. Her eyes widened. It shouldn't happen unless he swallowed one of the capsules! 'Oh God!' she thought and rose, picking up the gun.

'Drop the weapon!' barked the trooper. 'Do it *now*!' he shouted with total menace.

But she wasn't listening. Instead, ignoring the order she inserted the barrel of her own gun between her teeth and blew her brains out.

SAS

As the sun rose above the farmhouse, only Abraham was awake, facing east towards Mecca and praying quietly. A cockerel called across the yard, answered by another some miles distant. One of the farmhands trudged down the private road, clanking two tin buckets full of feed for the hungry geese that saw him coming. They ran squawking and honking, their orange beaks pecking viciously as he scattered the seed over a wide area. While they flapped and ran in all directions, it gave him a chance to fill a large trough with feed from the other pail. 'Stupid birds' he thought and headed back to the barn.

'Bill!' someone called to him.

He looked over at the rented farmhouse and saw the man they called Fitzroy beckon him. He didn't like him. He talked down to him with his snooty upper class voice and attitude.

'Bill!' he called again.

'Yes sir. I'm coming' he mumbled and headed over to him.

Fitzroy was leaning out of an upstairs window. 'Morning Bill!' he beamed.

'Morning sir.' Involuntarily, he slightly nodded and lowered his head, avoiding eye contact.

'Could you rustle up an early breakfast? You know. Egg, bacon, fried bread, beans, tomatoes, toast and to start half a dozen fresh boiled eggs and a big pot of tea? Make it for five.' He shut the window and disappeared.

'Arrogant bastard. Who the hell does he think he his? Ordering me around like that. He might be the one that rented the place, but there's no need to treat me like that. I'll show him!' He dropped the buckets and headed to the farm kitchen, where Mrs Edwards had been up since before dawn preparing the farmhands food.

'Morning Bill' she smiled. 'How's life?' she added, brushing her apron down.

'Be a lot better without that' he pointed to the farmhouse 'shit of a snotty nosed git!'

'Don't fret and be too bothered Bill. They're leaving today and you can be done with them.' She smiled through her stained and chipped teeth.

He liked her. She reminded him of his Mum. Fat, warm and cuddly. You could talk to her and she would tell you straight. If you told a lie she would cuff you, but if you needed a shoulder to cry on, you could count on her.

'They want their breakfast, Mrs Edwards. Tea, toast, eggs, bacon, beans.' He started to forget. 'Beans, eggs, tomatoes um?'

'Don't you fret' she said again. 'I'll sort it out. They'll get what I give them and like it!' She patted his hand and smiled again. 'Get along with you. I'll have yours at seven.' He went to leave and she ran after him, pushing a hot sausage into his pocket. 'Enjoy!' she said and went back to her chores.

Caroline came down from her room in blue jeans and a pink, tight fitting top, her long brown hair tied in a bun behind her head. Vladimir and Miyamoto were watching the BBC morning broadcast.

'Morning' she said.

'Morning' they said in unison, not stirring from their positions.

She sat at the table and poured out a mug of tea from the large tureen on the table and topped it off with some fresh milk from the ornamental jug on the sideboard. Fitzroy descended the stairs and stretched, almost banging his hands on the low beams above him and joined Caroline at the table. Abraham stepped in from the yard.

'Good weather today' said Miyamoto.

'Yes indeed' replied Vladimir smiling.

Keeping the TV on, they all ate with confidence, especially Caroline, who walked over and sat in front of the screen. The news was only about the Olympics and the BBC was running a special report touring the park and its facilities. Suddenly the camera stopped at the River Lee, before swinging in on the Velodrome.

'There!' she said stabbing the screen. 'There it is!' she said excitedly, pointing quickly to the water plant in the background, before the camera concentrated on a shot of the main stadium. She swung round and faced them beaming. 'Just think. In a few hours we will change the world forever! Can you imagine?' She was like a child who had seen all her Christmas presents under the tree the night before and wanted to open them now.

'Patience. Patience, boys and girls. You will all have your rewards very soon' smiled Fitzroy. 'Let's finish breakfast and get started!'

By eight the TV link to all the news stations via the giant dish on top of the rented broadcast wagon in the farmyard had been tested. Miyamoto had timetabled calls to all their political and military conspirators globally. Allowing for time zone differences, the communiqué and call to arms would take place at two pm. The farmyard had quietened since the early morning and the original rush to feed the animals had crawled to a stop. As the heat grew, the shadows became shorter and suddenly it was ten.

'I think you should go and see our guest' Fitzroy looked at Caroline. 'Remember, we want her alive until we get the call.'

'Oh. Don't worry. She'll be alright in my hands!' Her eyes narrowed and darkened. She picked up a left over piece of toast and a tub of butter. 'Breakfast for her Majesty!' she snidely said, a cruel twisted smile spreading across her face.

Opening the cellar door, Caroline stepped down the stairs and flicked the light on. Morag hung by her swollen hands, her dark brown hair cascading over her fallen face and blood caked clothes.

'You look a mess' Caroline said, running her hand roughly over the slash on the Scottish woman's face, causing her to wince sharply. 'Did you have a nice dream last night about your Russian husband?' she sneered contemptuously, ripping off the masking tape.

'Why are you doing this? What have I done to you?' Morag gasped.

'You bitch!' Caroline screamed in her face. 'You took *my* job. **My** job! Not yours. I worked hard for that while you flaunted yourself at the men getting promotion over me! Well bitch, your time has come and I have been chosen to finish you off. But we'll have some fun first! A condemned prisoner always has a last meal. Let's see if you like this?'

Taking the toast, she smothered it in butter and forced it deep into Morag's mouth making her choke. She tried to spit it out, but Caroline pushed it back in, sealing her lips again with the masking tape.

'This' she said 'is your final meal. Make the most of it!' Looking around the dingy cellar, Caroline found a short handled horse whip leaning against a wall. She violently grabbed Morag's hair and pulled her head backwards while holding the whip over her tear stained face. 'When I next come back it will be your last moments. Until then, enjoy!' Smiling to herself, Caroline walked slowly up the creaking wooden stairs, flicking the light off and leaving Morag helpless in pitch blackness again.

Ten miles from the farmhouse and travelling at eighty miles per hour, the two assault helicopters threw their black shadows over the countryside beneath them. On board, the two groups from the SAS Special Project Team ran their final checks. The marksmen had been detailed to maintain the perimeter security, while the assault team would execute the actual rescue. Sweeping in with the sun behind them and in line astern to avoid detection, the two choppers disgorged their troops fifty yards to the east of the outbuildings and behind a small hillock. Two minutes prior to their touchdown, another troop in three unmarked cars swung into the lane and quietly opened the farmyard gate. Spreading out into the barn and outhouses they lay and waited for the 'go' signal. The time was eleven thirty.

'This is Zulu. Section One go!' came the message across their headsets.

Two men rushed forward and placed a set of 'earthquake' diversionary charges in the field next to them and withdrew. Within seconds of their return a loud, deep 'crump' shook the field and outhouses around them. Several farm-workers rushed out to see what had happened, but they were bound and gagged face down on the ground.

In the farmhouse, there was panic. Fitzroy and Vladimir rushed out in the direction of the blast, revolvers in hand. They looked around and saw a large hole in the ground, smoke still rising. Turning carefully, they looked for the cause.

'What is it?' Vladimir said.

'Don't know. I'm not sure' replied Fitzroy, looking around suspiciously.

Keeping their weapons drawn they backed down the track, stopped and dropped their guns as several black clad arms reached out and dragged them into an adjoining drainage ditch, gagging and binding them.

'Section One to Zulu. We have two. Repeat two xrays.'

'Zulu to Section One. Copy that.'

'Zulu to sections two and three. Go! Go!'

The airborne troops crossed the field and entered the farmyard. Two black clad troopers sidled up to the main door, MP5's carried in their left hands, enabling the widest possible arc of fire. One man placed a blast charge on the door and they both stood back guns vertical. With an almighty bang the door blew in and before the dust settled they lobbed a stun grenade in through the opening. Within seconds both men had rolled low into the room, followed by a third coming up into a crouch position, weapons trained ahead of them. Through the dust a figure was seen holding a weapon in their direction. The leader fired two directed bursts and the figure dropped.

'Section Two to Zulu. One xray dead. In lobby.'

'Zulu to Section Two. Copy that!'

Running down the stairwell, eyes wide, screaming and firing madly, came Abraham. 'I'll kill you all!' he screamed.

Two troopers caught him in a burst of cross fire, sending his body tumbling down the stairs in a bloody mess.

'Section Two to Zulu. One xray dead. Repeat one xray dead.'

'Zulu to Section Two. Understood.'

'Zulu to all stations. Look for one more xray. Be on lookout for hostage'

In the basement, Morag heard the explosion and the gunfire. Suddenly she heard the cellar door open and saw the light come on. Her eyes swivelled to the stairs and to her horror she saw Caroline stepping down.

'Hello bitch!' she spat out with venom. 'As you can hear, there's a rescue team for you upstairs. Pity that they won't get to you in time. No seventh cavalry riding over the hill to save you! There's just me and I've brought something with me that will make you blow hot and cold! Look bitch!' Caroline forced Morag's head down to see what she had in her hand. 'Yes, bitch. I'll put this' she showed her a clear plastic bag 'over your pretty face. We'll see how long you can hold your breath.'

Morag knew she would have only one chance to save herself. As the tape came off she screamed and swung her legs into Caroline's body knocking her heavily to the concrete. For a few seconds she lay on the floor dazed and disoriented, but quickly regained her composure closing in on the now screaming Scottish scientist.

'Now we'll see who laughs last!' she said pulling the bag over Morag's head from behind her. With a wicked smile she tugged the bag down firmly and tightened the draw strings. For a moment nothing appeared to be happening, but within seconds the air flow stopped and the scientist's eyes widened in horror as the bag stuck to her face with every inward breath she took. Her panicked screams and the violent death throes of her thrashing legs seemed to last forever. 'Die you bitch!' Caroline laughed into Morag's eyes through the bag. She was fascinated how it was that Morag was lasting so long and looked closely to check the seal. As she tightened the noose further, her eye caught a reflection on the bag, the slight difference between shade and shadow. She spun round and faced a man in black, with giant bee shaped goggles, earphones and a machine pistol in his left hand. Moving backwards away from him, she suddenly darted to the stairs and bounded two at a time, outpacing the trooper. As she opened the door at the top, another man dressed identically looked down and shot her twice in the head. Meanwhile the first trooper ripped the bag off Morag's head, cut the shackles and lowered her gently from the beam onto the floor. Still in shock, she gasped 'thank you', breathed a sigh of relief and fainted in his arms.

WATER PURIFICATION PLANT

The flash messages pouring into Roger at the Post Office Tower and filtered by his communications team looked good. Both the SBS raid upstream on the water plant and the SAS operation at the farmhouse had achieved their respective objectives. Eleven terrorists had been killed or captured and Chekhov's wife had been safely rescued, although needing medical care.

The Colonel slapped his operational commander on the back. 'Good one Roger! Send my best to the boys.'

'Yes sir! Attention all stations. This is Zulu. Repeat this is Zulu. Jennie achieved. Jennie achieved. Stand down. Stand down. Hand over to civil authorities as soon as possible. The boss says well done!'

On the face of it, Operation Jennie appeared to be a total success. All the targets had been either neutralised or captured and Tentacle's plans were totally scuppered. The only downside to the operation was a terse message received from Morag. It was brief and apologetic. Under torture from her captors, she had disclosed the genetic coding of the most virulent of the Professor's creations. When the scientist received the information at the filtration plant, his first reaction was relief at her safety, though tempered with a sense of ominous foreboding. He immediately called Alex across and explained the repercussions. Alex lowered his head and frowned deeply. Something was missing. What was it? He racked his brains, scratched his head and ruffled his hair. Nothing!

'What's the matter Alex?' said Lang, crouching down next to him by the river. 'Although the code is 'out', I can't see any problems as all the terrorists have been killed or captured.'

It was obvious to Alex that the Professor still felt nervous and didn't quite believe his own words.

'Should I worry Alex? Can we be sure we haven't missed something?'

'I don't know' the investigator replied 'but there's something not quite right here and I can't put my finger on it.'

The Professor looked at him closely. 'Well I always use logic to solve a problem. Can I help?'

'Ok' replied Alex. 'Go ahead.'

The Professor counted off his fingers.

'One. Morag is safe. Two. All the conspirators have been captured or killed. Three. Their entire plan has been brought to a stop. Four. The opening ceremony, due to take place in less than two hours, will go ahead without a hitch. You agree?'

'Yes, Professor. I agree. But there's still something dreadfully wrong. What the hell is it?' He rubbed his hair briskly and slapped his cheeks, sharpening his senses.

A trooper strode briskly over to the Professor. 'Call for you, sir!' and handed him the secure link to the Post Office Tower.

'Lang here. Who's that?'

'Ah. Professor. David Iwoku.'

'David. How is it with you? It's been' he searched for the right word 'interesting'.

Alex and the trooper both nodded at the Academic's understanding of security jargon.

'Same here' said the CRE Commissioner. 'It looks like though, I will have to get another deputy since Morgan Ibotu is now unavailable.'

'What do you mean unavailable?' asked Lang cautiously.

'Well. He is either dead or captured. I need to know whether any of my files have been compromised. Is he with you?'

'Hold on. I'll ask'.

The Professor had a word with Alex, who called the field commander over and requested a body check from his men around him.

Within a minute, a heavily armed sergeant ran back, saluted and reported to the Commanding Officer. 'He's not among any here, Sir. He could be at the farm. I'll check.'

Lang, Alex and the Officer watched the sergeant call the Essex squad.

The communication trooper at the farm picked up the call. The sergeant ran Morgan's name past him and in the background he heard muffled shouts.

'Hold please. Wait. Wait. No. Sorry, Sarge. He's not at this end'.

'Not dead or captured?'

'That's a negative' the trooper said positively.

'Check his possible location with the captured xrays' ordered the NCO.

'Wilco. Please hold.' After what seemed an age, the trooper came back. 'It seems that your man had a back up plan at the filtration plant, but the captured xrays don't know what it is.'

'Thanks. Out.' The sergeant turned to his CO and Alex. 'SAS confirm that he's not with them. The captured xrays believe he may be in the plant with a back up plan.'

Alex stood up and stared intently at the nearby building. 'Oh my God! He's probably got a box of capsules!' He called the Tower and spoke to the communication NCO. 'Where does the tracking chip that Amanda planted on him put his location at now?' He heard what he was expecting. 'Put the Colonel on fast' he demanded immediately. He waited for what seemed an eternity.

'Alex. What's the panic?'

'It's Morgan sir. He's not on any of the captured or dead listings. His buddies at the farm think he arranged a back up plan. They, and I, think he's in the plant. The tracker confirms it.'

'But why? What has he to gain now?' said the Colonel, starting to sound concerned. 'Surely *if* he is alive, he only has access to a limited supply of the weaker capsules? I can't see how he can infect the whole stadium. Any damage would be marginal.'

'Sorry to advise you Colonel, but Chekhov's wife confirmed to Tentacle's chemists the composition of the stronger virulent that they had been tweaking and Ibotu probably has a batch with him.'

'Alex. Put the Prof on will you?' the Colonel asked urgently.

He handed the unit over to the Professor.

'Lang here Colonel. If Tentacle has been able, via Morag, to modify just a small batch of capsules then you could have an unstoppable train crash waiting to happen.'

There was a deafening silence from the receiver.

'Colonel? Are you there?' the Professor asked.

'How can we tell if he's succeeded?' asked the Colonel, now slightly on edge.

'We can't, unless you stop him, or you sit back and watch systemic rioting and revolution take place right under your nose. The chemical is, as I've said, in capsule form, the safer of the two sealed in blue, the dangerous one in black. Within minutes, all those who are exposed to it will be affected.'

'How large are the packets that contain the capsules?' asked the Colonel.

'Let me put it this way Colonel. If you had a bag of sugar in your hand, you would have enough capsules to affect over fifty thousand people.'

'Bloody hell. What can we do?' snapped the officer.

'Find him and fast. He can only deliver the capsules through the filtration valves.'

'Give me Alex!' snapped the Army man.

The Professor passed the receiver to Alex.

'Colonel? Alex here.'

'We have less than an hour to find and stop this bastard. I'm sending extra help immediately. But until then, the clock is running. Find him and contain the capsules and whatever you do, stop him infecting the water supply.'

Alex called the commander across and, after briefing him, passed across the receiver so he could double check with the Colonel in the tower. Alex took back the handset while the commander briefed his troops.

'Good luck Alex' said the Colonel.

'Same to you Sir' and clicked off the line.

'Go!' ordered the commander, his troopers sprinting up the bank and entering the plant for the second time.

Morgan was sweating. He did not like confined spaces at the best of times and certainly not now, trapped under an air ducting grill in the main filtration room. The shouting, explosions and gunfire had given him just enough time to hide. He lay on his back staring upwards and trembling. Two black clad and fully armed men had blasted their way in raking the room with gunfire. He watched Helga inches above him pressing downwards on the ducting.

'Goodbye' she mouthed, reaching for her weapon and blowing her head off. She collapsed near him, her blood pouring through the grills onto his face. He shut his eyes and waited till there was silence. Pushing upwards, he managed to ease her body from the grill and carefully got to his knees listening intently. Scrambling across the room he wiped her congealing blood from his face, as he headed for the maintenance section of the plant. Ahead of him stretched a corridor of blue and orange stainless steel low-pressure pumps, mounted beneath rows of giant dealkalisers, humming constantly. He hobbled towards the entrance door, dragging his left foot, deadened with cramp from the confined space he had just left. Pushing the door open, he stepped in and limped over to the bright red emergency tool box on the wall opposite and removed a large spanner. To his right, four large nuts stood proudly above a pressurised water mains cover. Placing the spanner against the first and gritting his teeth, he eased the nut off, followed in slow succession by the second and third, as cold jets of water soaked him from beneath the flange. Gulping in torrents of water and with his vision impaired from the spray, Morgan unscrewed the last nut, which flew off with the speed of a bullet, just missing his face. Immediately, litres of water exploded into the room from the exposed pipe in a fountain of energy, throwing him backwards against a safety barrier. Getting up and rubbing the bruise that almost immediately appeared from this impact, he opened a large waterproof bag that he had secured around his waist. Pushing his hand into the opening, he withdrew all the capsules and with brute strength, forced them past the raging water into the outflow pipe. Within minutes he had dispensed of the entire contents and moved back across the soaking floor to a metal platform set three feet above the rising brew. Removing his phone, he made a quick call to the Ramada Hotel in the Docklands and then slumped wet and tired onto the soaking steps, trying to gather his thoughts. Suddenly the door behind him burst open, silhouetting two masked troopers, Alex and the Professor in the doorway.

The black clad marksmen pointed their weapons directly at Morgan.

'Don't kill him' ordered Lang. 'I must know what he's done.'

The troopers advanced on Morgan, red spot beams centred on his legs and arms. Alex and the Professor cautiously moved across the slippery platform above the turbulent rising waters.

Morgan slowly rose and grinned. 'You think you've won?' he mocked. 'I think not' smiling and nodding at the exposed pipe.

'You maniac!' shouted the Professor. 'Do you know what you've done? What colour capsules did you use?' knowing that Tentacle had probably re-engineered the genetic code.

'That's for you to guess and me to know' Morgan laughed at him.

'Search him' ordered Alex.

Morgan casually raised his arms. One of the troopers flung him forward against a wall and kicked his legs apart. A quick frisk revealed his communicator and the empty capsule bag. Lang searched the bag for an indication of the colour of capsule used, but couldn't see anything. He looked at his watch. One thirty.

'Morgan. For God's sake tell me what colour capsules went in' begged the Professor.

The wet man turned his head and smiled cynically. 'Good luck Professor! My job's done. You'll get nothing from me.'

He twisted his face and crunched his teeth together. Almost immediately his body tensed, dropped to the platform and rolled down into the churning waters two steps below, the cyanide tablet lodged between his back molars killing him instantly.

While one of the troopers kept his laser sight on the partly submerged body, his partner stepped down into the cold water and dragged the now inert body upwards and onto the steps. When he was satisfied that no pulse was evident, he looked up at his partner and nodded. He in turn clicked the safety back on his weapon and stood back, allowing Alex to carry out a more detailed search than they had just completed. Finding nothing of consequence on him, Alex turned urgently to the Professor.

'Whatever capsules he's inserted' he said 'the short term effect will still be the same; mass panic. He looked at his watch. One forty five. Fifteen minutes before the official opening ceremony. 'Is there *any* way, Professor, that we can still stop the water from entering the stadium?'

The big Scottish scientist furrowed his brow and rubbed his chin. 'Come with me!' he suddenly and urgently shouted. 'There may be a way!' The Chameleon inventor ran, arms flailing, through two twisting corridors, coming to a stop in the main control room, complete with large bright red valves and an illuminated flow chart displaying the entire pipe network to and from the plant.

As Alex and the troopers crashed through the open doorway, they found the Professor jotting down some rapid calculations on a nearby piece of paper. He raised his head and frowned. 'If we act quickly' he stressed 'we might be able to limit the damage.'

'What do we need to do?' Alex asked urgently.

'Do you see where this pipe divides?' asked the Professor pointing to the chart.

'Yes I do' Alex replied.

'Well. At that very point there's a divert valve, which an operator can control. It's located in the stadium's boiler-room. I've calculated that the infected water will take just over ten minutes to get to that point from here. If we move *very* fast we *may* be in time.' He looked desperately at Alex, who immediately called Leroy and Sandra, his CIA and SO15 contacts at the stadium. 'Get into the boiler-room fast and close that bloody valve. You've got less than ten minutes!'

DOCKLANDS

Jimmy Williams was the first to see it. From his 360 degree enhanced radar screen, the experienced air traffic controller watched the blip approach from the west, with the British Airways identifier of BA 412. He checked its altitude and bearing and established direct radio contact after accepting the handover from Air Traffic Control at West Drayton.

'London City to BA 412. Do you read me?' he mechanically and concisely asked in his best English accent, although he was well aware that his native South African tone could be marginally heard sometimes when he relaxed among friends.

'BA 412. We hear you clearly London. Could you give us our initial approach sequencing?'

With that, Jimmy conducted the routine patter with the co-pilot, allowing the Captain to bring the Airbus 318 into visual range of the Airport, located just two miles from the Olympic

Park and three miles from the skyscrapers of Canary Wharf. As the plane began its final approach, lining up for a steep angled descent onto the narrow concrete runway positioned midway between the waters of the Royal Albert and King George V Docks, the thirty two politicians who had slept soundly across the Atlantic on their flat beds from New York, peered out of their windows at the sprawling London vista spread out below them. To their left, the blue grey mass of the River Thames swam up-stream through the open flood barriers of Woolwich and swung westwards towards the bustling financial square mile of the City, with its political epicentre of Westminster another mile upriver.

Up ahead, in the cockpit, the co-pilot engaged the two Pratt and Witney PW 6000 engines, which screamed in defiance as the Captain slowed the plane and pitched the nose into a near suicidal dive through the few fluffy clouds that drifted aimlessly above the runway. As the ground rushed up to meet them, Blanco sat back into his seat and for a moment believed that the designer of this runway must have had military experience as a navy pilot on board an aircraft carrier, or he was just plain crazy. Either way, as the jet touched down with a thump and the air brakes increased the G force up to a count of three, the Harlem man watched with trepidation as the water on either side of the aircraft rippled in the slight breeze, shortening the distance to the end of the runway with every life preserving foot. From his portside window, he nervously watched the rescue crews in their red inshore safety boats roar past the strategically placed life belts in the dock waters. He silently prayed that their practice drill would remain just that and the plane would not overshoot and end up in the water. Trundling to an almost impossible halt, the plane came to a rest opposite the tower and almost immediately proceeded to slowly taxi off the runway, wheeling left and gently pulled up by the dedicated VIP stand adjacent to the Terminal Building. With a slight bead of sweat on his forehead and a trembling to his knees, Blanco looked down at his hands gripping for dear life the armrests and felt that he had aged years in the last few moments. Around him, the dignitaries representing some of the most evil states in the world started to rise from their seats as the doors opened and the steps were attached to the fuselage.

'You coming, Blanco?' said the Foreign Minister from Bulla, one of the world's worst countries on human rights, 'or are you getting ready for another hair raising flight?' he laughed menacingly at the New Yorker's noticeable discomfort.

'I'll be right with you sir. Just getting my jacket' he replied and exhaled deeply as he quickly regained his composure.

'Nice hands' another man said, referring to the six hour poker game that they had all played and that Blanco had been coerced into and expertly won. 'Good job we weren't playing for your life' he added 'as you would have been in the Atlantic by now!'

Blanco didn't know how to take the comment, but to his relief the swarthy man slowly smiled, revealing a shiny gold lower tooth in what can only be described as a film star set of dentures.

'Don't worry my friend' he added, grinning cruelly.   'If we wanted to kill you over a few dollars, we wouldn't be having this conversation now. After all, you could be of use to us all' he indicated with his hand to the rest of the departing occupants. 'We've got our eyes on you, my friend, so be cool!' and with that he put his arm around the Tentacle man's shoulders and squeezed him affectionately.

He waited for all the politico's to disembark ahead of him and only then, while grabbing his holdall and straightening his tie, did he walk down the steps and into the Jet Centre, where HM Customs and Immigration awaited him.

From his tower, fifty feet above Blanco's head, Jimmy trained his powerful Zeiss binoculars on the Harlem man as he crossed the apron and entered the Terminal Building. Ensuring that the other controllers were otherwise occupied, he removed a mobile from his jacket pocket and compared the forwarded image sent to him from Joe in New York. Mentally agreeing that both images matched, he slipped the phone into his trouser pocket and called across to the other three. 'I'm just going for a pee. I've got no other traffic on my watch.'

'No problem' shouted the big guy in jeans and red lumber checked shirt. 'Just bring me a large bar of plain white chocolate on the way back. But remember' he laughed, causing Jimmy to stop on the second step, 'make sure you wash your hands first!'

'In your dreams!' Jimmy quipped back and disappeared downstairs into the toilets.

Checking that no one else was in any of the 'traps', he quickly took his mobile out and hit the speed button. 'Jimmy here. Blanco's arrived.'

'Are all his *friends* with him?' Joe asked in a sleepy, but not altogether surprising tone, as it was still only three in the morning in the 'city that never sleeps'. 'Yes. All safe and sound and shortly about to leave for the hotel. Out.' He clicked off the handset, left the toilet and started back upstairs when he suddenly realised that he had forgotten something. Stepping across to the terminal, he walked over to the large, bright vending machine, dropped a two pound coin into the receptacle and pressed the dispensing button. With a gentle thud, the last white bar on display appeared in the cavernous mouth at the bottom of the unit. He reached down, ripped off the wrapper and bit two slabs off between his teeth. As he made his way back upstairs for the second time, he almost threw up, suddenly realising that he detested any form of chocolate and spat out a mouthful into a nearby waste bin, followed quickly by the remainder of the bar. Wiping his mouth clean with a grubby paper tissue from his trouser pocket, he re-entered the control tower and told the checked shirt man that only black's were left.

For a second it didn't dawn on him what he had said, but suddenly all the lights came on and he smiled knowingly.

The ten uniformed officers from Customs and Immigration watched with more than a passing interest all the passengers from the New York BA flight that passed through their channels on the pre-booked arrangements, while fleetingly displaying their UN passports. Although none, including Blanco, were stopped, the biometric scanners and photo imaging equipment set in strategic positions, captured every image and electronically matched them immediately with the extensive database held at the joint offices of the security services. To the sharp witted intelligence officer sitting alone and receiving the uploaded images on a bank of state-of-the-art plasma screens, every face and identifier triggered a recognition alert. Everyone, that was, except Blanco. Surprisingly, because of the company he was keeping, his profile rang no alarm bells as no-one knew what his connection might be to these high profile diplomats, but a case file was opened on him anyway.

To the rear of the terminal building and with its large, three litre diesel engine running quietly, stood a large black executive coach sporting a UN flag fluttering on its roof. The smart, bespectacled, liveried driver slipped the gear in drive and slowly, but precisely moved the three ton vehicle out of its designated parking bay behind the Fire Station and stopped adjacent to the Jet Centre. As the first of the UN diplomats boarded the blackened out windowed vehicle, two luminescent clad police motorcycle outriders swung their large Honda bikes ahead and to the rear of the bus, triggering their blue strobe lights. The driver checked over his shoulder that all the occupants were seated and eased the vehicle forward onto the airport's slip road. As they gently rolled out onto Connaught Road and the long spine of Connaught Bridge that divided the Royal Albert and Royal Victoria Docks, the leading bike blocked the road for all other traffic while his partner roared past, sirens wailing and stopped on the Ramada Hotel slip road adjoining a large roundabout ahead.

On the coach, Blanco sat alone at the rear of the vehicle and assessed the distance from the Airport to the hotel as being just over half a mile. Through the windows, he watched a three carriage train of the Docklands Light Railway arrive at Prince Regent Station, only a few hundred yards from the massive ExCel exhibition centre and a crowd of about fifty people disembark. Within seconds they had come to a halt outside the stunning entrance to the blue, steel, six storey hotel and the coach began to empty ahead of him. Only when everyone had left did he step out and follow them to the reception, where check-in was taking place. He spotted the sign for the Fitness Room and casually walked across to the large double doors, slipping silently inside. Beyond the entrance the atmosphere was religiously quiet and, looking around, he quickly found what he was seeking. With five long strides, he made the emergency door and checking carefully that it was not alarmed, pressed downwards on the bar and stepped out to the small patio that also doubled as the evacuation area in the event of an emergency. With the sun now locked into a slow, but steady, climb in the blue sky above him, Blanco moved out from the short, cool shadow of the building and bathed himself in the warming rays of the morning air. Ahead of him, in the large sheltered stone-walled garden stood a magnificent thirty foot Scots Pine by an ornamental pond and cascading waterfall. He moved unseen to the back of the tree and texted Joe in the Big Apple. Within seconds he received a reply.

'Keep them all there until contacted by the London operative. Negro is travelling alone, Hardeep with mixed group from India and Nandi with African Union. They will all be with you within 24 hours. Joe. Pics attached.'

Clicking onto his jpeg application, he viewed Hardeep and Nandi's smiling pictures with interest, casting both of their images to memory. For a moment he tried to guess what their reasons were for political change and quickly reasoned that it was certainly none of his business, except that they all wanted the same thing and were willing to put their lives on the line for it. After deleting all the messages and pictures, he slipped the phone back into his pocket and casually strolled around the perimeter of the building and re-entered for the second time that morning, from the front entrance. His fellow travellers had already checked in and were on their way to their suites.

Five hours later, Negro's Swissair flight from Geneva touched down where his twin had landed earlier. Jimmy, standing in the tower, watched his man leave the BAe 146 in the company of several smart suited financiers and head out of sight into the Terminal Building, where his luggage had already been cleared by HM Customs and Immigration under the auspices of the International Olympic Committee Headquarters. For the second time that day, the portly air traffic controller excused himself from the tower and contacted Joe, this time though by text. At passport control, Negro displayed his credentials to the impassive uniformed officials who, after cursorily noting his face and details, waved him through the low, stainless steel barriers and onwards into the small, smart arrivals hall. A suited driver, holding a sign for Hamilton, ushered him into a waiting car for the two minute drive to the hotel. Once again, the thin, bespectacled, intelligence officer who had opened a file on

Blanco a few hours before, studied the imagery being relayed from the airport and together with his electronic database, made a risk threat assessment based on the all the information to hand. On a scale of one to ten, ten being high risk, Negro fell into the passive group of two. His level would have been lower, but for the fact that the system flagged up an unpaid traffic violation given to him on the Queensboro Bridge in New York, by a bored bike cop, for speeding just before he left for Europe. To his left, a high priority red lamp blinked urgently. He reached across to the adjacent handset and placed the receiver to his ear and listened. After five years of monotonous surveillance operations, his face still remained deadpan as the caller imparted the information on Negro. The only outward sign that he was absorbing anything at all came just as he replaced the receiver. For a fleeting moment, he raised his right eyebrow and looked back at the images of this young black man on the screens around him. With his left hand, he tapped a series of codes into the ergonomic keyboard ahead of him and waited. Almost immediately the previous information held on screen changed and the risk assessment jumped to ten, triggering a visual alarm on all the screens. Then, with a cool and typically British professional manner, he lifted a different phone and passed on the information to the equally emotionless duty officer at the top of the Post Office Tower.

The following morning, a BA flight from Geneva touched down at London City Airport carrying forty state leaders and diplomats representing all those on Negro's list. Again, as on many of the flights pouring into London for the Olympics, these foreign dignitaries were afforded diplomatic protection and a police escort from the Met's Olympic Command. They all boarded a luxury coach and turned sedately out of the Airport gates en-route for the Ramada Hotel, a quarter of a mile away. Lowering a copy of that morning's Times to eye-line level, Negro watched from a discrete vantage point within the reception area, as the small entourage disembarked from the coach and registered at the large hemispherical guest desk. Travelling with them was a representative from the Olympic Committee, who faffed around the dignitaries like a mother hen proudly looking after her new-born brood. But, unlike docile, fluffy and adorable chickens, these birds displayed all the tenderness of vultures at a free-for-all buffet. In between the shouts, violent tantrums and general abuse to the hotel staff and each other, Negro observed that every one of them refused to compromise or give way on anything. In fact at one point, only the intervention of the hotel manager and several beefy security personnel stopped a queuing argument get completely out of hand. The Harlem man recognised the majority of the group from the portfolio that Claude had handed to him in Switzerland and his further research from the web, but he had to be absolutely sure that they were all here and he had not missed anyone. When finally the mesmerising, yet synthesised strings, of the Boston Pops orchestra could at last be heard again through the strategically placed ceiling speakers, did he rise and stroll casually over to the concierge desk, manned by a uniformed smiling youth and an older, more mature man wearing a small, powerful badge that read 'Head Porter'.

'Yes, sir?' said the latter, smiling emphatically beneath his neatly trimmed and waxed military styled, handle-bar moustache.

'I was wondering if there was any mail for me. My name is Hamilton. Negro Hamilton.'

'Just a moment sir' replied the Head Porter and disappeared through a swing door behind the desk, returning a few moments later holding a plain sealed packet with his room number written on it. 'There you are sir. This is all we have for you.' He sounded apologetic, as if he somehow felt that there should be more.

'Thank you very much' said Negro, dropping a two pound coin onto a small saucer at the end of the counter. He walked away, packet in hand, towards the lifts. Arriving outside his suite, he swiped the room card and entered, the energy saving lights automatically clicking on, while the door closed firmly behind him. Once inside, he took his jacket off and cautiously opened the padded container, tipping the contents onto the bed. It contained only one item; an unlabelled DVD, which he slipped into the suite's player and sat back into an arm chair while triggering the remote play button. To his total surprise, he was presented with a set of camera shots and sound recordings of all those on his list, as they passed through immigration at City Airport half an hour ago. He pulled the photos across and frame by frame, double checked them all again. Then, just as he thought the recording had finished, another suspicious looking group appeared, the camera following them as they boarded a waiting coach supported by a police bike escort. He counted thirty two individuals in total, whom he had never seen before, and then almost in a blur another image passed across the screen quickly, in a vain attempt to avoid identification. He slowed the imagery down and froze the screen. Gradually, like a heated volcanic fissure, his right cheek expanded and a thin but growing smile developed across his ever opening mouth, until he was absolutely sure who the grainy image was of.

Sixteen miles to the west of London, a fleet of transatlantic airliners hung like glowing marionettes in the early morning sky, their forward facing pencil beam lights punching a hole through the gloom of the early dawn as they followed each other to the south of the capital and wheeled gently through one hundred and eighty degrees over Crystal Palace, lining up for a final approach at Heathrow across Dulwich, Putney and Southall. The South African 747 and the Air India 777 spaced five miles apart and carrying Nandi and Hardeep with their respective groups, screamed precariously across the neatly tiled rooftops of Waye Avenue, near the Eastern Perimeter Road of the airport, each landing heavily on the long, bald concrete runway. Within five minutes, both planes had rolled round to their respective gates and connected themselves to the extended umbilical passenger bridges that reached out to meet them. While the economy passengers crowded their aisles like desperate shoppers queuing for the winter sales, Nandi and Hardeep remained in their Business seats until all were vacated and then casually disembarked much to the chagrin and annoyance of the waiting queues behind them. Terminal four is not as large as it's newly built sister T5, but it is massive all the same and because all First and Business passengers are given priority on arrival and departures, it did not take long for all of Nandi's and Hardeep's *guests* to clear immigration and customs. Although all those on Tentacle's lists were waved through on diplomatic passports, there were some individuals among them that also flagged up as 'potentials' and it was these that the security services took a close look at as they passed through the airport, en-route for their waiting transportation.

In the days that followed, SO15 and it's partners attempted to build a picture of those suspects that flashed up on their screens by risk level, but as of this moment, all they could do was watch and report. The trip eastwards through London to the Ramada was by way of the M4 and although both groups were motoring by six thirty, they still ran into the chaos that was the normal early morning rush hour traffic beginning at five. Under average motoring conditions the journey would have taken about an hour, but this was the week in which the Olympics opened and every road was choked with a plethora of extra traffic, extending the journey time to just under two hours. Bill Smith, who was driving the lead coach of four, cursed heavily as he followed the police outriders through the condensed, snarling traffic and onto the specially cleared lanes for official Olympic vehicles only. Only once on the journey did an unauthorised car block their route, but was moved out of the way by an unforgiving police bike rider, roaring up on its inside and signalling the driver to move across into the commuter lanes. It took the officer two attempts with lights and sirens to get the driver to move, triggering a flurry of comments from some of the passengers sitting behind Bill.

'Back home' one said 'we would have run him off the road into the nearest ditch.'

'No' said another 'that would have been too good for him. My men would have dragged him out the car, hung him from a tree and while still alive, set his body on fire.'

'But remember we are in England now and everyone has rights!' several delegates cynically shouted in unison.

This caused a general, but sinister laughter behind Bill, which for all his hard nosed military experiences in war-torn countries, still sent a shiver down his spine. The knowledge that some of the world's most vicious dictators and their cronies, protected by diplomatic immunity, were sitting only a matter of feet behind him was slightly unnerving, but was tempered by the fact that they were on his 'patch' now and subject to the omnipresent rule of British justice. Four miles and eight minutes ahead of the coaches, two black diesel cabs travelling along Victoria Dock Road entered the Connaught Roundabout and after completing an almost 360 degree turn, took the final exit down the gradient to the bleak tarmac car park that fronted the entrance to the

Ramada. From the first cab stepped Nandi, a small grey holdall over her right shoulder. She paid the driver, giving him a more than generous tip, walked the few paces into the reception area and checked in. Close behind came Hardeep, his gaze falling upon the reflected image of the hotel in the almost millpond waters of the Royal Victoria Dock, immediately to the left of the entrance. An immaculate lawn, formally arranged with a smattering of low backed wooden seats, faced the tranquil basin, dissecting the water from the clinical car park and adding a touch of peace to the surroundings. With the warm morning sun on his face and a case by his side, he watched his cab disappear under the fifty foot concrete structure of the Connaught Bridge, joining Royal Albert Way and the massive campus of the University of East London half a mile up the road. As he checked in and made his way to his third floor room, a mixed wave of nausea and jet lag suddenly hit him, sending him sprawling onto the Queen sized bed, unconcerned and unresponsive.

Three floors below in the reception area, the hotel personnel were enduring yet again similar scenes from the day before. This time though, although voices were raised, the guests did on the whole attempt to act in a more reasonable and conciliatory manner to each other and the staff, struggling to register and disperse them to their respective rooms. Agnes, the Business Development Executive, had noticed that among the one hundred and twenty new guests, there appeared to be a sharp personality demarcation between the African guests and those from elsewhere, including all the Afro-Americans. It was in general their aggressive attitude to authority that stood out. Equally she noticed that some of those from the South American and newly independent eastern block countries were also close to, as she said, 'losing it', but who was she to make judgements on others anyway, since several of her own Polish countrymen had blotted their copybooks by violently overreacting at F.I.F.A. football matches? Within the hour of the four coaches arriving, her team had, under great duress, managed to clear the reception area and calmly escort all the guests to their rooms and suites. Where sixty minutes ago, hotel security was totally stretched and highly compromised, with the very high possibility of calling for Riot Police to back them up, it was now amazing to see a calm, quiet reception, totally devoid of any other people bar the indigenous and exhausted staff. The hotel itself had one hundred and fifty three guest rooms, with seventy one suites and was now fully occupied. Bar Nandi, Hardeep, Blanco and Negro, all the occupants were Tentacle targets. That is except for the two last minute bookings made directly via the hotel General Manager and allocated the Penthouse suite normally reserved for visiting Heads of State. The staff were instructed that a Mr and Mrs Smith would be checking in and no identification will be shown or should be asked for.

'Their stay is with the compliments of the General Manager and they should be shown every courtesy without reserve.'

When Agnes received this instruction, she was intrigued as to whom this couple might be and pondered long and hard as to their possible identities. 'They must be publicity shy stars' she thought excitedly! She put her staff on notice and asked for the duty manager to contact her whenever they arrived, even if she herself was off duty.

She didn't have long to wait, as at just after midday, a couple identifying themselves as Mr and Mrs Smith arrived by taxi with very little luggage and checked in at reception. Agnes was immediately called to the front desk, but was perplexed at not being able to recognise them. She led the way to the lifts with one of the concierge team smartly wheeling their bags behind on a hotel trolley. Not a word passed between them as they arrived on the Penthouse floor, with the porter in close attendance. He wheeled the trolley into an ante-room and unloaded the cases onto a low slatted wooden bench, before waiting by the main suite doorway for any further instructions and of course the unspoken, but customary tip. Agnes pointed out the main features and drew their attention to the house phone and internal directory if they needed any help at all. She smiled pleasantly and bid them a good day, passing the porter by the open door. Mr Smith stepped forward and placed a twenty pound note in the lad's hand, smiling as he did so.

'Thanks' said Mr Smith, his strong New York accent just slipping through as he mechanically closed the door, leaving Agnes totally bemused and the young man twenty pounds richer.

'I think you've made a financial friend Mr Smith' said Sandra, his British counterpart, leaning against the closed door and smiling at her CIA colleague.

'Let's call it an investment' retorted Leroy, easing her away from the door and peering through the concave eyepiece.

'It's all clear' he said backing into the room and strolling over to the vast panoramic floor to ceiling windows, shielded by voluminous sets of expensive fine net curtains.

'I suggest we get some sleep right away,' he said, strolling over to where the raised Emperor double bed sat majestically overlooking the calm dock water sixty feet below them. 'If this operation is to be stopped' he turned and looked at his British SO15 partner, 'we are going to need all our wits about us, and if I've learnt just one thing in all my time in the Company, it is that sleep is the best medicine to a successful result.' He sat on the bed and casually kicked his shoes off.

'What *are* you doing?' she said, narrowing her eyes, and simultaneously striding across the suite with her arms folded.

'As I said' he responded, looking up at her standing menacingly over him, 'I'm going to bed.'

'Not in here you're not' she quickly countered. 'One of us will sleep elsewhere' eyeing the sofa 'and that is not going to be me!'

'Oh well!' he said whimsically. 'I thought I'd give it a try. You never know!' He winked at her and moved off the bed, picking up his shoes as he went.

She watched him stroll across and open up the sofa into the combination bed, arranging the sheets, blankets and pillows to taste. Then without a second's thought, he removed his fitted, white, cotton shirt, revealing a beautifully muscled black torso. For a second she held her breath at the sight of this Adonis and was really tempted to call him over, but somewhere deep in her psyche an alarm bell rang and she passed on the invite.

'I'll set the alarm for six pm' he said sternly, adjusted his illuminated diver's watch and closed the heavily-lined curtains, instantly drowning the room in semi-darkness. Unashamedly, he pulled down his trousers, slipped straight into the bed and fell instantly asleep.

'Huh!' she thought climbing alone into her bed, wearing just her underclothes and drifted off almost immediately into a deep, but welcoming slumber.

After several hours, she was woken by a soft continuous clicking sound. Her natural instinct would have been to sit up sharply, but something deep inside her urged caution, and she responded by slowly opening her eyelids and peering through the soft light at Leroy, interacting with the hotel's laptop. Without moving, she watched him, head down and totally focussed, his black face strangely radiant by the intense reflection of the large blue screen. 'What's happening?' she asked, noticing that he had already changed and reconstructed the sofa.

He stopped his input, turned and faced her across the thirty foot divide, his features now sharply contrasted between the translucent light and the gloom that pervaded the Penthouse. 'I've received a message from Pennsylvania Avenue which was forwarded on by your SO15. The operative who initiated the flash is Alex Mason. I've been advised you know him?'

Deliberately avoiding the question, she pulled back the soft quilt and reached across for the towelling robe supplied by the hotel. As she stood to put it on and traipsed silently into the bathroom, he courteously averted his gaze back to the screen. By the time she had freshened up and changed into a pair of white slacks, pink sweater and canvas trainers, Leroy had deleted the encrypted screen message and had pulled the curtains open, flooding the suite with the soft rays of a glorious early summer evening.

'What did he say?' she asked, as he poured out a steaming mug of Brazilian coffee for her.

Looking straight at her, he advised that according to all intelligence decrypts, the attempt to infect and overthrow a number of government leaders here at the Games will go ahead within the next twenty four hours.

Just after six that evening, Hardeep heard a light knocking on his suite door. Dressed only in blue denims and a soft short-sleeved cotton shirt, he padded across to the eyepiece in the door and waited until his focus adjusted to the darkened concave image of Nandi. He would have recognised her anywhere, her pretty features and great figure more than doing justice to the image he had seen of her via the split screen display with Joe, many weeks beforehand. She gracefully, but confidently strode in, her light perfume, combined with a strong sense of style and poise, immediately making an impression on him. The air of superiority that she emitted was further enhanced by the black-leather, tight-fitting jacket and trousers that snaked around her slim body. Contrary to his images of her, she had no pre-conceived ideas about him, except that he was as committed as she was to Tentacle and his appearance, as sloppy as it appeared, was of no importance to her. That suited her well, as being the cool and calculating individual that she was, only the job came first, personalities were irrelevant. He quickly slipped a pair of canvas shoes on and offered her a drink.

'Thanks, but no thanks' she smiled at him.

Not standing on ceremony, he poured himself a cold fruit juice and sat silently admiring her figure.

'Is there a problem?' she cynically demanded, staring right back at him.

Before he had a chance to reply, another soft knock greeted his ears and he gratefully grabbed the opportunity to check the eyepiece again. Carefully focussing and recognising the callers, he opened the door, revealing two smartly dressed men both in suits and matching ties. Elegantly rising, Nandi stepped forward to greet Blanco and Negro, as Hardeep checked the corridor behind them and re-entered closing the door securely behind him. He had only known one other set of twins from his childhood in Delhi, but apart from the fact that they were brother and sister, the most obvious difference was that they were both of the same colour, unlike the brothers in front of him now. After shaking Nandi's hand enthusiastically, they both turned to face him at exactly the same time, their synchronisation only bettered by the Olympic water ballet competitors. Unnervingly, they both shook his hand together, leaving him totally flummoxed and bemused.

'Please,' he indicated the other three vacant chairs.

The twins sat apart, leaving Hardeep uncomfortably between them and opposite Nandi, whose eyes seemed to bore right through him.

'Would you like a drink?' he asked each of them.

Blanco spoke for them both. 'Thanks Hardeep. We're fine. Don't let us stop you' he indicated the half glass of orange that the Indian had placed on a nearby coffee table.

The Delhi man suddenly raised his finger to his lips and walked over to the in house radio system, clicking on some background music, just loud enough to shield their voices from any prying ears. Then, purposefully, he opened the combination safe by the door, withdrawing a set of documents together with four black capsules and brought them all over to a large table by the window that overlooked the dock. Nandi, Blanco and Negro all joined him, as he spread the contents out equally, like a croupier dealing cards.

'Close the blinds please' he asked.

Negro, being closest to the window, duly obliged and brought the room into a semi darkened state, until Hardeep flicked on an overhead light, flooding the table with a soft yellow glow. He spread out beneath them a large topological map of the Olympic Park and the Village that housed the athletes, with certain areas prominently shaded in red. Overlaying this, he carefully placed a transparent sheet detailing the entire transport of the games infrastructure, that had been surreptitiously obtained by Agnes in return for favours supplied to visiting members of the ODA and the IOC while staying at the hotel.

'You will notice' stressed Hardeep, 'that the area designated in red is specifically reserved for our *guests* only. This concentration of our targets in one place, while being of immeasurable help in itself, also has a drawback.' He paused and looked around him, making sure they were all following. 'Unfortunately, the Olympic Police and the Olympic Security Officers have been given specific orders to protect special client groups like our 'friends' at all times and that means that we will not be able to get close to them. Further you can be sure and I know you've checked that in nearly all cases our 'friends' will have their own security people flown in with them. However, these 'heavies' will not be able to sit with their charges, but will be on call if needed and unlike in their own countries, none will be able to carry weapons in or around the Park.' He looked up at them again and continued. 'In addition' he added 'there is a security perimeter around all the venues, which is tightly controlled and monitored non-stop, particularly through the official checkpoints. Only valid games identity and accreditation cards or valid event tickets will allow the bearer through. Even then, the holders will still have to pass through pedestrian screening areas, akin to airport scanners. Further, all modes of transport must have vehicle access and parking permits before being processed through a screening area, where they will be thoroughly scanned.'

'This could create a problem if the scanner detected any capsules in your clothes. However, since they are considerably smaller than standard size aspirins, you can easily secrete them in your mouth with a minimal chance of discovery.' Hardeep pushed himself away from the table, stretched his arms vertically and cracked his finger joints. 'Now you can see the problem we have getting through this minefield of security.' He paused briefly for effect. 'Luckily' he smiled 'we don't have to tangle with any of these problems.' Leaning over the table, he pointed with his right index finger to the water filtration plant by the River Lee and then Stratford International Rail Station. 'Just prior to our 'friends' taking their seats, they will all be given an Olympic cocktail within their exclusive VIP bar. Our London team will have already infected the water specifically for that outlet and *our* bar staff are under orders to make sure that every guest consumes them.' Without waiting for any comments, he continued. 'Your part of the operation' he looked at them all 'is to shepherd your people en-masse onto the Docklands Light Railway at Prince Regent Station just behind us,' he pointed out of the window and to his right. 'The weather forecast is hot and sunny, so the two minute walk from the hotel to the station should be no problem. The nine station journey to Stratford International normally takes just under half an hour as it is an all-stopper. However because of the 'political' status of the travellers, a special non-stop service will be laid on and will depart sharply at one pm, taking just under fifteen minutes. The entire journey will be monitored by remote surveillance cameras on and off the train and will have a police and security presence door to door. In other words, the most sophisticated security system the world has ever seen will actually be assisting us in breaching its own impregnable walls.' Standing back from the table, Hardeep left the others to talk amongst themselves and strode over to the kitchenette, pouring himself a cup of freshly brewed black coffee.

'Are we to travel with them into the Park?' asked Nandi, having followed him and now pouring herself a mug of the same.

By now, Blanco and Negro had also joined them and hearing the question posed, waited for Hardeep's response.

'Of course' he smiled. '*We* must ensure that they *all* enter the VIP suite safely, so your presence will be needed right up to that point. None of us have the VIP clearance that they all have, so your responsibility ends at that point. I would suggest that you get out of the Park immediately and get back to your respective countries to help take control as the shock sets in. Your individual travel arrangements are included with each set of documents and it is vital that once you have memorised them, you destroy the evidence.'

'Where are our passes and tickets?' asked Blanco.

'Good point' said Hardeep, moving over to the still open safe. He withdrew three sets of tickets, together with matching sets of valid games identity and accreditation cards and handed them out. 'They're date-coded and can only be used for tomorrow' Hardeep added.

'You've all got *both* sets. Just in case' he smiled encouragingly at them.

'Have you all got sufficient funds to see you through?' he finally added, like a doting father to his children.

'I don't know about the others,' answered Negro, 'but five thousand dollars and everything else paid is quite ok for me.'

'Same here' said his brother.

'Me too' added Nandi, now cautiously smiling at Hardeep for the first time since meeting him, her initial and instant dislike of his eyes ogling her, now replaced by a healthy respect of a consummate professional in action.

'Good!' the man from Delhi smiled back at all of them.

'If there are no further questions, then I propose we all have dinner separately and get some sleep? Agnes, the Business Development Executive is to be trusted. She has arranged for all the guests to be at the station before one, but you all need to make sure and if necessary act like sheepdogs, rounding up any strays. That's it!' he summarised, standing upright and strolling over to the door. 'Except for these' he added, placing an extra capsule in each person's palm as they all filed past him and exited the suite. 'Just in case!' he whispered confidentially. Closing the door behind them, he walked over to the maps and ran them through the small cross-shredder supplied by the hotel, standing near the in house lap-top. Finally, he sent a text to Joe updating him, only to receive an instant 'Good Luck' response.

Six floors above, Leroy and Sandra left their suite and headed down in the private lift to the now busy reception area.

At the desk, Leroy saw the young bellboy who he had generously tipped earlier. 'Hello' the New Yorker said. 'You suddenly seem to be very busy?'

'Yes sir. All of these' he indicated the large groups, 'arrived earlier and are for the Olympics.'

'Who isn't?' quipped Leroy smiling amiably. 'I'll bet you'll be pleased when they check out?' he gently probed, noting some of the aggressive and threatening attitudes displayed around him.

'Couldn't come sooner' the boy confidentially whispered back. 'Thank God they're all checking out tomorrow' he confided further. 'I've been here two years and these are the most aggressive guests I've ever seen.'

'Really' said Leroy, trying to prise some more information out of his young informant, 'Where are they all going?'

'Oh. They're all being given a VIP escort to the opening ceremony on the DLR at one pm' he said quietly and furtively.

'Listen' said Leroy smiling. 'I've got a friend who's staying here. I want to surprise him with a present, but I don't know his room number and I was wondering if you could tell me so that I could give it to him personally. You know how it is? We're old friends from New York. His name is Negro. You can't miss him. He's the same colour as me' he smiled.

'Well. It's strictly against regulations. You know? I could get into a lot of trouble' he whispered, looking nervously at the hubbub around him.

'Could this help?' Leroy asked, proffering a twenty pound note almost hidden in a nearby hotel brochure that was resting on the counter.

The boy quickly grabbed the brochure and withdrew the note, sliding it unnoticed into his trouser pocket. 'Just a minute sir' he said loudly. 'I'll check for you' and stepped smartly through a doorway behind the front desk. Within a minute, he was back with a pamphlet of hotel excursions with a number scribbled on it.

'I think this will be what you are looking for' he smiled at his benefactor.

'Thank you' said Leroy. 'I'll see him tomorrow' he added.

'You should hurry then' the boy said quietly 'as he's also checking out and going on the same train with these morons' he nodded over his shoulder.

'I appreciate your help' said Leroy, now quietly turning to join Sandra waiting by the hotel entrance.

'Got what you wanted?' she asked, as they stepped out into the warm, sticky evening.

'Absolutely. Let's get some Chinese. I'll fill you in as we dine.'

Exiting the hotel, they turned left and strolled fifty yards over to an adjacent Chinese restaurant set by the warm glinting waters of the Dockside.

Dawn of the next day found Negro jogging steadily around the eight mile perimeter that encompassed the Royal docks of Victoria, Albert and King George V. However, unlike Lausanne, he wasn't alone, as Nandi also being a fitness guru, always stretched her legs at this hour of the day. For both of them, it was still inspirational to see the sun rise slowly and dramatically in the east, watching and listening to the swooping and screaming of sharp beaked seagulls congregating around the churning wake of the early morning Woolwich Ferries, as they slowly weaved their suicidal paths across the busy shipping lanes of the Thames.

'Magic isn't it?' said Nandi, as they both took in the open panoramic scene before them.

'Yep' replied Negro. 'Not as good as Lausanne, but better than the Hudson' he dreamily tossed back at her. He checked his watch. 'We better get a move on. It's almost five.'

'Race you back' she said teasingly.

'After you' he offered with his hand.

'I think I remember somewhere a phrase about age before beauty' she added, smiling. Her words suddenly tailed off as she looked intensely at a small mark on his left arm and brushed her hand over the minuscule bump. 'Keep *very* still' she said, withdrawing a fine blade from a small utility belt that always accompanied her and firmly gripped his arm.

'What the hell? Hey! That hurt! You've just cut me!'

'You've been tagged' she said. 'Someone slipped it under your skin, but not any more!' She held up an ultra-thin micro-tracker for him to see.

'My God! How long has it been there?' he said, dabbing the blood on his arm with his running shirt.

'It doesn't matter' she replied. 'What it does show' she added 'is that someone is on to us and we have to really watch out!' With that, she snapped the transmitter in half and kicked it into the dock waters.

Then, without warning, he sprinted off leaving her rooted to the ground. 'Come on if you're coming' he shouted over his shoulder at her.

By five thirty they were seated in the Oval Bar of the hotel, Nandi with a cold glass of orange juice, while Negro sat opposite her on his bar stool, fresh milk in hand, still dabbing the cut.

'You run well' she said admiringly.

'Just practice' he humbly replied. 'Thanks for this' he motioned to his arm.

'No problem' she smiled. 'It's par for the course. Just keep your eyes open!'

'I think we should get going' he said, downing his drink. 'Breakfast starts at seven,' he reminded her 'and we're going to be very busy today.'

She followed his lead and sank her drink in one gulp.

At eight, the breakfast area was manic with the 'diplomats' reverting to type as they shouted at each other in the vain attempt to curry favour with the waiting staff.

Nandi, Hardeep, Blanco and Negro had all eaten and left well before this and therefore didn't need to be further reminded about the people that they were going to 'take out'. Upstairs in their top floor suite, Leroy and Sandra were enjoying an in-house meal, well away from any prying eyes and ears. She had been in touch with Alex in the Post Office Tower since the break of dawn and together they had exchanged notes on the rapidly developing situation. At one point, Leroy took the handset from her, stressing in no uncertain terms, that his President, who was attending the opening ceremony, was to be protected all costs and that there was a very high probability that the Vice President was implicated with other senior members of the US administration. It was agreed that they just could not stop the diplomats on the floors below them attending the opening ceremony. Despicable as these so-called leaders and their abhorrent policies were, it was deemed by those in higher circles that to protect them would be the better of two evils, whilst also stopping Tentacle dead in its tracks and preventing an unstoppable mini-holocaust being unleashed on the general public.

By twelve thirty, almost the entire compliment of the hotel's guests were assembled inside the entrance hall with Nandi, Hardeep, Blanco and Negro standing outside. Agnes, resplendent in her navy blue manager's uniform, stood in front of them and politely called for their silence and cooperation while she explained what was about to happen as they made their way by foot to the station, three hundred yards away. Before they all left, she asked them to ensure that they carried with them their valid games identity and accreditation card, together with a valid event ticket. As soon as she was sure that all the guests were in attendance and that they held their documents, she led them across the large car park and onto the single footpath by the side of the Premier Inn. Within five minutes they had started to congregate on the platform, the Police and Olympic Security Officers blocking the entrance to all other passengers. Promptly at one, a three carriage, driverless train, bearing a destination of 'special' on its front indicator board, pulled into the platform, the doors opening with a quiet hiss. Thirty seconds later, the entire platform was deserted as the red and white liveried vehicle moved off on its non-stop journey to the Olympic Park. As the train automatically slowed at Custom House for ExCel and then sped up to the annoyance of regular commuters waiting to board, Blanco realised that everything appeared to be running exactly to their planned schedule and nodded slightly to Hardeep. This pattern repeated itself at Royal Victoria, Canning Town, Star Lane, West Ham, Abbey Road, Stratford High Street and Stratford before finally stopping at their ultimate destination of Stratford International. The nod, although hardly perceptible to anyone not looking for it, was definitely noticed by the controllers at the Main Operations Centre, under guidance from counter-terrorist officers with SO15.

As the doors opened and the diplomats immersed themselves into the maelstrom of thousands of heaving, yet orderly, visitors, Nandi, Blanco, Negro and Hardeep lost touch with each other and their 'charges'. For several minutes they searched in all directions, sighting small groups and solitary individuals as they themselves were carried forward amongst the sea of people towards the entry booths and scanners. Feeling inadequate and helpless, they realised that all they could do now was to go with the flow and try and form up on the other side of the security controls. However, unknown to them, their activities were now being closely monitored by a whole array of security enabled systems from CCTV to laser voice encryption beams. As each of them cleared security they all communicated by mobile arranging to rendezvous by the Olympic Stadium's VIP entrance. Within ten minutes, this motley quartet of would be sentinels realised that they could do no more than to direct any stragglers that they recognised in the direction of the VIP entrance, knowing that the majority would already be in there. After rounding up twelve more diplomats from their respective groups, they decided that it was time to call it a day and leave, before the panic and hysteria consumed all those around them.

Hardeep sent a brief report to Joe five hours behind them in New York, expressing his frustration at not being totally sure that they had corralled everybody.

A quick response flashed on his screen. *'Don't worry. We didn't expect to get them all first time. If we hit the majority then we've succeeded. Give the team my best, including Agnes at the hotel and make sure you all get out before the shit hits the fan! We will speak soon. Joe.'*

Hardeep checked his watch. One forty five.

'Joe says we've done well, even though we may not have got them all. It can work with the majority. He also says we should get out now and wait for his call, before things turn ugly.'

They all silently acknowledged him and, as unobtrusively as possible, turned away from the Stadium and headed towards the exit barriers.

BOILER-ROOM

One hundred feet above the International Broadcast Centre in the studio tower, Leroy and Sandra were observing the quartet far below them, when they received Alex's urgent order to drop everything and immediately get to the valve in the boiler room of the Stadium. Running like the wind, they made the ground floor in under a minute and, supported by local police, headed into the bowels of the stadium. With the help of two engineers who ran with them, they entered a maze of corridors until arriving outside the boiler room. Leroy checked his watch. One fifty. Only five minutes before the infected water enters. They ran inside, finding the large valve to their right and the electronic controls on the wall adjacent to it. Sweating profusely, Leroy lowered the grey plastic cover shielding the controls.

'Stop!' shouted both of the red capped technicians in unison.

'What's the problem?' Leroy asked, raising his voice in able to be heard above the whine and growl of the massive pumps and generators.

'Which area are you going to cut off?' they demanded, watching his hand hover over one of the two switches.

'What are you talking about?' he shouted back at them.

'If you depress the left one you'll cut off the entire VIP area, but in so doing you'll expose all the spectators, athletes and their trainers in the stadium. Conversely if you hit the right switch you'll protect the athletes, trainers and spectators, but infect all the VIP's.'

'Can't I depress both and stop the entire water flow?' he screamed at them again.

'No. The system won't let you do that. It is been set up to only operate either one or the other. Not both.'

'What if we kill all the power to the plant?' Leroy desperately asked.

'There's not enough time. It would normally take just over half an hour and I don't think you have that.'

He checked his watch. The sweep second hand took another minute off. Only four to go and counting. Desperately he called Alex and explained the situation.

'Wait. I'll check with the Prof' Alex said quickly.

In the background he could hear them assessing and debating the problem.

Alex came back. 'Leroy. We don't have time for anything else. The Prof and I both agree that you should press the ......'

'Alex? Alex? Are you there? Can you hear me? Which one should I press? Come in buddy. I can't hear you. Can you hear me? Alex, come back.'

Leroy desperately checked the handset, while Sandra tried her comms including her own mobile. Nothing! All radio traffic was out!

'It sometimes happens' said one of the engineers apologetically. 'Sod's law it has to be now!' he added.

'Yeah' said Leroy unimpressed. 'Do you have an emergency phone direct to the filtration plant?' he frantically requested.

'On the wall there' replied the engineer.

Leroy ran across and picked up the receiver. Nothing! Dead as a Dodo! He tapped the line hard. Still nothing! He checked his watch again. Only one minute left.

'What are you going to do?' Sandra asked.

'Try the line again to Alex' he ordered her.

As hard as she tried, there was no outside communications. They were on their own and time was not on their side. He closed his eyes and tried to work out what logical conclusion the Professor and Alex had come to and why.

'Leroy? We can't wait. There's only thirty seconds left' shouted Sandra.

With beads of sweat running down his forehead, he reached across, prayed to God for forgiveness and depressed the switch.

OLYMPIC STADIUM

The sun hung high in the bright blue sky, surrounded by a few wispy cirrus clouds and the sweeping dives of the summer swifts showboating on the thermals above the Olympic Village. Far below, over half a million flag waving people crowded the pavements behind miles of brightly-decorated grey crush barriers in and around Stratford Broadway and the Olympic Park. Nearby, an impromptu jazz band struck up in the old cemetery of a church, which stood in the centre of a large and normally busy traffic island set directly in front of the bustling Stratford Shopping Centre. Strategically positioned loudspeakers relayed a constant feed of information to the assembled masses, many of whom hoisted their children aloft on their shoulders. The fairground sights and smells of steaming hot-dog's layered with lashings of soft onions and yellow mustard were everywhere, as spectators, casually dressed in shorts and holding battery operated fans, sipped cold drinks from paper cups bearing the official 2012 London logo. Today though, the cars were noticeable by their absence, being replaced by a multi-ethnic, noisy sea of humanity, all eagerly awaiting the arrival of the Olympic torch and its penultimate bearer from the United Kingdom that had originated on its journey from Greece some weeks before and was now only minutes away from a momentous reception.

Adjacent to the stadium, the massed ranks of the 20,000 broadcasters and photo-journalists were strategically located in the sprawling 120,000 sq metres of The International Broadcast Centre/Main Press Centre on a 24-hour basis, relaying the Games to an estimated global audience of well over four billion. Directly above them and incorporating the latest state-of-the-art facilities, was a massive studio tower with incredible panoramic views of the Games site and beyond, while cruising at an even higher elevation floated the GOODYEAR blimp, casting its famous shadow over the stadium and its assembled masses far below. Just two miles away on the Bow Flyover and travelling in a fast moving convoy of flashing blue lights and Olympic Police outriders, the Colonel and his guests from the Post Office Tower eased their way past the gridlocked traffic on the reserved Olympic roads leading back from Stratford in the specially adapted Strike Range Rover. From behind them, two brightly clad officers riding powerful, adapted, BMW Police bikes roared past, the first clearing all vehicles immediately in front, while the other vanished half a mile ahead, into the distance. By the time the convoy had caught up with him, he had stopped and was sitting bolt upright and straddled across his bike in the middle of Stratford Broadway with both his arms extended outwards, halting all traffic. Following the Range Rover and also surrounded by Police outriders, came a blackened window Chrysler PT Cruiser. It had no visible markings save its 012 number plate, indicating to the casual observer that it had just rolled off the production line. If the same observer had the authority to check the plates, he would be surprised to learn that the registration details would come up as classified.

Since leaving the Tower, a running commentary had been patched through by Alex and the troop commander to the Colonel, as the situation quickly developed. Originally believing that they had everything well under control since the capture of Morgan Ibotu, this final twist, coming out of the blue as it did, was certainly nothing that any of them could have anticipated. The same radio traffic that the Colonel had received was also broadcast into the PT behind. Inside, the four plain clothed officers and their driver stared intently at the road ahead.

'Remember,' the team leader said, 'our job is to get the President out and safely away before he consumes anything. Our secret service guys are not aware of this latest news. All comms are down inside the stadium and we may have to force the issue.' He took his portable radio out. 'Let's do a radio check.'

As they tail-gated the Range Rover, supported and flanked by the wailing bikes, through the pre-opened security gates and onto the red emergency road leading to the rear of the Stadium, he put his hand ready on the door catch. Chekhov, sitting between Jenny and Karen, with the CRE Commissioner opposite him, looked through the rear window at the black PT Cruiser following them.

'Colonel' he asked 'who is in that vehicle behind us? Do they belong to you as well?' Karen, Jenny and the CRE Commissioner instantly followed the Staff Officer's eyes, as he glimpsed briefly in the wing mirror and smiled.

'The answer Mr Chekhov is yes and no. Yes, they are allied with us. No, I don't own them. They are' he chose his words carefully 'a US Kill-Team.'

In the stadium, eighty thousand seated people rose to their feet as they saw on the giant internal screens the approaching torch runner. The cheering amplified with every stride and as the runner emerged into the brilliant sunshine from the shadows of the massive tunnel, the triumphant and explosive voices of the massed audience drowned out any meaningful conversation. A blinding series of camera flashes around the stadium, together with a tumultuous applause from the ecstatic crowds, greeted the young British runner who, while holding this fabled burning torch proud and high with his right hand, managed to maintain an air of grace and serenity as he completed his final four hundred metres.   Down in the shadows of the stadium, seventeen thousand athletes sipped the water fountains strategically placed by their sides to keep cool and hydrated during the extended wait time, the flag bearers of their respective nations placed at the head of each marching team. A buzzer sounded and in time-honoured tradition, the Greek Team, heralding the Olympic flag, stepped out to a thunderous applause, as thousands of brilliantly coloured balloons drifted vertically above the heaving stadium. The two vehicles screeched to a halt by a set of bright red emergency doors. Before the PT had stopped, the team leader, followed by his entire crew except the black-gloved driver, were already sprinting up the rear stairs two at a time. Behind them ran the Colonel, his Captain and a Royal Marine Sergeant. Within a minute they were at the VIP floor and quietly entered the plush, but crowded, bar and dining area, containing over a thousand people. As they tried to get their bearings, a plain-clothed security officer approached them and asked them their business. The Colonel showed his high-clearance pass and demanded their immediate co-operation on the grounds of national security.

'I'll have to check this' he said, starting to withdraw his personal radio.

'Put that down' the kill-team leader ordered, checking his watch while simultaneously producing a gun and jamming it into the security man's ribs.

Offering no resistance, the Marine Sergeant quietly took the security man out through the emergency doors, returning within a few seconds.

'No permanent damage Sergeant?' enquired the Colonel, slightly concerned.

'No Sir. He'll have a donker of a headache though, when he wakes in a couple of hours.'

'We have two minutes max before the infection hits the water supply' the kill-team leader said quietly. He looked around.

'Where's the President?' he whispered.

'Over there' said the Colonel pointing to a small group 'talking with our Prime Minister.'

'Ok. Let's get them out!' said the leader.

'But we can't just leave the others. Think of the repercussions' added the Colonel.

'You're right' the American said. 'Jones and Brooker' he turned to his men. 'You two go with the Captain here,' he indicated the British Officer 'and get the President and Prime Minister out now.' He checked with the Colonel. 'Ok?'

'Do it!' snapped the Colonel.

The three men rapidly made their way across the crowded venue and after a brief word in their respective leader's ears, started ushering them quickly towards the emergency stairs. As he was just about to leave, the President, not wishing to appear to insult his British host, raised his glass in one last toast with his orange and lemonade squash. Just as he placed it to his lips, Jones wrenched the vessel from his hand and forcefully frogmarched his Commander-in-Chief across the packed floor filled with startled dignitaries and into the echoing stairwell, passing the unconscious security man slumped heavily in a corner by a glass encased fire-hose.

'What now?' said the Colonel.

'Let's shut the bar and hit the lights,' suggested the Sergeant.

The American spun on him. 'Brilliant!' he said.

'Anything else?' the kill-team leader asked, looking between the two men.

The Colonel rigorously shook his head. 'I'll take the bar' said the Colonel quickly. 'You've got the lights' he motioned to the American. 'You come with me Sergeant' the Colonel added. 'I may need your muscle!'

The American turned to his remaining men. 'As they shut the bar, we turn every light off. Let's go!'

Suddenly and to the bewilderment of the assembled guests, the Colonel went round to the back of the bar and ordered all the staff to stop whatever they were doing and leave. When one portly man particularly objected, the Sergeant physically yanked him out and forced him heavily to the ground.

'Ladies and Gentlemen' the Colonel announced standing on a chair for effect. 'We have a small security issue that we need your full cooperation with. You are all perfectly safe, but we need you to put all your drinks down and immediately clear this area. Please leave by the emergency doors.'

On cue, all the lights went out, except the small emergency bulbs that glowed softly above the doorways.

'There's nothing to be alarmed about,' the Colonel shouted above the commotion and heightened sense of panic that was starting to grip the assembled guests.

In the semi-gloom, amongst the shoving and jostling, some individuals had decided to nonchalantly finish their drinks, but powerful unseen hands had urgently relieved them of their glasses and pushed them unceremoniously towards the exit doors. With the bar now firmly closed and a dangerously growing number of guests starting to jam the stairwells, the kill-team leader considered it was now prudent to restore the lights. With a sudden flicker, the overhead bulbs in the ceiling sprang into life, illuminating the partially empty lounge and causing those who were queuing to stop and look around them. For a moment, as everyone's eyes attempted to re-focus on their immediate surroundings and assess any possible threat or danger that may still remain, the Colonel heard what could only be described as sharp gasps of breath amongst the crushed VIP's. For a moment, the sound seemed to fade, but within a moment it was back, this time with a growing intensity. Low moans were now turning into screams as those in the stairwells were sent tumbling downwards by the pressure from an ever increasing panicked crowd many steps above them. The guests that were originally queuing for the exits, backed away into the middle of the semi-empty lounge, motionless and terrified.

Within seconds, a few of the attendees from 'third world' countries were starting to experience a slight itching under their skins followed by a severe blistering and discolouration on their faces, hands and arms. The Colonel called the Americans over to the bar, where they tried to take stock of the situation.

'We're too late!' he said mournfully, as they watched some people fall screaming onto the floor in abject terror as their skin metamorphosed in front of them. In every direction, men and women, politicians and business moguls were being affected.

'Go and see what the situation is on the stairs,' the kill-team leader said to his men.

Within minutes they were back, detailing the injuries sustained in the fusion of crushed bodies falling onto each other. 'There are no deaths, but plenty of bruising and broken bones' was the consensus from all the exits.

'Here's a thing though,' said one of his men staring at the chaos reigning around them. 'Among the black and coloured people, a few are affected by this skin change. Maybe only ten per cent tops.'

A visual check of all the others suggested the same ratio.

'Maybe we've almost stopped them' said the American.

'Let's get the medics here' insisted the Colonel. 'Do your radios work or are they also down?' he asked the leader.

A quick test indicated a two-way available transmission.

'Ok' the Colonel said. 'I want you to call the Royal London Hospital and get hold of Dr. Steven Williams.'

Within a minute he was on the line. The Colonel explained as much as he dare without compromising himself. 'A medical convoy is on the way as we speak' the Colonel announced to the American team leader. 'By the way' he added, almost as an afterthought 'what's happened to your President and our PM?'

'I saw them get into the PT and drive off, police in attendance' said one of the kill team.

'Thank God for that' the Colonel said, relieved. 'In the meantime, let's contain what we have here and help some of these people.' He turned away and walked over to Fernandez Essonite, the brutal leader of a South American country, laying on the floor, gasping for breath, his skin lightening and blistering rapidly under the Chameleon effect now sweeping his body. Almost against the Officer's better judgment, he knelt down to assist this insatiable butcher of the poor and weak, advising him that help was on the way and he should just keep calm. Then, quite without warning, the Colonel felt a cold pointed object placed at the back of his head.

'Move away slowly' came a cultured masculine voice. 'No sudden moves or it'll be your last breath!'

Realising that this individual meant every word, the Colonel calmly rose and stepped carefully away from the injured man, the sharp point still against his neck until he was facing and touching the bar.

Essonite's eyes enlarged in fear, as he suddenly recognised the man behind the voice. 'You!' he gasped, terrified. 'You can't kill me!' he begged, mesmerized by the pointed implement now removed from the Colonel and held firmly against his throat. 'I'll give you whatever you want' he choked, as the assailant pushed the steel tip deeply into Essonite's skin, triggering the release of the contents from a black pellet through the hollow core of the stick into the dictator's windpipe.

'How about my country you murdering bastard?' his adversary replied bitterly.

Gurgling and drowning to death in the tweaked anti-Cancer fluid, Essonite's skin instantly metamorphosed to white.

Thud! The aggressor toppled heavily to the ground, blood surging onto the carpet from a small bullet hole at the back of his head. Some guests screamed. Others stood transfixed at this blood-fest. Behind the Colonel stood the sergeant, gripping a silenced revolver, his face calm and placid as he walked round to the inert bodies of Essonite and his assassin sprawled, dead next to him.

The Colonel looked around at the terrified crowd, grabbed a nearby tablecloth and reverently covered the faces. 'You know the Olympic Committee may sue us for the damage we've caused to their carpets, Sergeant!' the Colonel said quietly, but cynically.

Ignoring the comment, the Non-Commissioned Officer replied 'This is the same shit I dragged from the bar before! He's probably one of these revolutionaries.'

'Or an individual who has nothing to lose' said the Colonel, staring at the well-dressed torso of the small, chubby man, his torn cravatte and gold-topped walking-stick lying by his feet.

'Not your typical terrorist!' stated the Colonel, ruminating on where the chubby man had emanated from and what may have been his motive, since he knew he was bound to be caught and probably shot. It was almost suicidal.

Within minutes, a convoy of ambulances, escorted by armed police vehicles, whisked the affected VIP's to the Royal London Hospital for analysis and treatment, while security officers from the Diplomatic Protection Squad, MI5 and SO15 were debriefed in a private room nearby, by the Colonel. Several floors below in the waiting Range Rover, Chekhov, Jenny, Karen and the Commissioner could hear the muted screams in the stairwells, while observing through the darkened windows the curious spectators that always seem to gather like flies at any incident involving blue-light vehicles. They could also hear radio chatter between different units involved in the operation and it was on one of these that Chekov thought he heard Morag's name mentioned.

'Quiet!' he shouted, as the brief commentary between the farmhouse and the filtration plant crackled across. He leaned forward, squinted his eyes and cocked his ear, like a dog straining to listen for the tell-tale signature of a fox in deep cover. He heard the troop commander at the farm confirm that the female hostage was bruised, but otherwise unhurt and was being checked over by the medics before being taken to the Royal London Hospital for a more thorough examination.

'She's alright!' he beamed at his companions. 'My Morag's safe. Thank God!' Suddenly it seemed that the heavy burden he had been carrying for the last few weeks had instantly dispelled and his face, strained and lifeless before, now seemed relaxed and full of returning colour. He sat head down and unashamedly wept, not recovering his composure for a couple of minutes. When he eventually raised his head, he looked like a different man, but not just relieved. There was something else that he had been bottling up inside him for the last few weeks, waiting for the right opportunity to present itself. It was just discernable in his eyes and Karen, being the observant journalist, spotted the signals immediately and knew he was about to do something drastic.

The Range Rover was parked close to where Leroy had entered the bowels of the stadium with Sandra. Since there was no way of them knowing which cut-off valve they had activated, the pair emerged from the corridors into the bright sunshine full of trepidation and were immediately met by the Colonel, who updated them regarding the VIP suite. They both heaved a sigh of relief, but immediately expressed their concerns about the quartet they were observing before being diverted into the stadium.

'Where are they now?' asked Sandra quite concerned.

'Get in the car and we'll talk' the Colonel said, pointing to the Range Rover.

Although it was very cramped with six in the back and the Colonel up front, it was necessary, as the only secure place in the vicinity.

'Does Alex know about the VIP suite and these four?' Leroy asked, passing around the photos that he and Sandra had in their possession from the CCTV surveillance cameras.

'Yes' replied the Colonel. 'We're keeping him up to speed.'

As they discussed the best way forward, Karen's eyes for a moment glimpsed someone outside the vehicle that she vaguely recognised, but couldn't quite place. Then without warning, she was out and running through the crowds towards the exit barriers.

'I think' said Leroy, answering the Colonel's question 'that she's seen one of our targets (he held up a photo of Nandi with a deep fingernail impression of Karen's in it), and let her journalistic instincts take over.'

'Sandra' said Leroy, 'you better get after her, giving us constant feed-back.'

Without a word, she too was gone, hot on Karen's heels.

'Bloody journalists!' the Colonel shook his head in disbelief. 'Give them an inch....' he mumbled, not finishing the phrase. 'If she's right' he added, 'we'll have to focus on the other three'.

After a few minutes, a flash message came in from Sandra to say that Nandi was heading west on the tube, destination probably Heathrow, while Hardeep had accessed the Eurostar platform and the Hamilton's the Docklands Light Railway connection to the Royal Docks, leading to the adjoining harbour.

'Leroy', the Colonel addressed the American, 'you target the twins with your team leader, while I, with the Sergeant, tackle Hardeep. But be very careful. They may have some capsules with them intending to infect another mass of people!'

'You three' he addressed Chekhov, Jenny and the Commissioner, 'stay here. The driver will take you back to the Post Office Tower.'

Tullett got out with Leroy and electronically locked them all in, handing the keys to the driver.

'We don't want any more loose cannons whizzing around!' he stressed, updating the Sergeant, as they all sprinted to the exit barriers through the massed crowds.

EXIT STRATEGY

For Nandi, Hardeep, Blanco and Negro, the entrance to Stratford International Station couldn't come any sooner. They moved as a group with difficulty against the throng heading towards the stadium and, as planned, split up, heading for their own escape routes. Nandi, carrying her holdall, stood breathing heavily on the jam-packed Central Line train covertly observed by Karen and Sandra, reporting back when they could. The South African intelligence officer knew that she would be identified at some stage, but hoped that she could embark on the British Airways 747 before the hue and cry went up. 'Timing was everything' she kept telling herself, as she strolled beneath the myriad of cameras towards the left-luggage cabinets at Terminal Four where she had deposited a pre-packed airline bag on her in-bound flight. She wheeled the case over to 'check-in', keeping the holdall over her shoulder, which held her passport and open flight tickets. With the formalities over, she cleared passport control, followed closely by Karen and Sandra. The latter had alerted Special Branch and SO15 on their way in. Now feeling more confident by the minute, Nandi sat in Starbucks with a Cappuccino, carefully observing anyone displaying any unusual body language in her immediate vicinity. Her flight was not due to board for another hour so she took the opportunity to stroll around the shops acquiring some clothes with the dollars she still held. Time passed quickly and soon she noticed that her flight had been called and strolled, bags in hand, towards gate eighteen. Ahead of her she stepped into the queue for First/Business and waited patiently behind a tall, well-built man carrying a small leather attaché case. As he cleared the control point he stopped, barring her progress to the waiting uniformed ticket official. Behind, she felt a passenger press up close and turned to see a slim young woman casually smiling at her. Instantaneously the man ahead stepped sharply backwards, lowered his head and whispered in her ear.

'Please don't make a scene, Nandi. You are under arrest and have nowhere to go.'

Karen stood to one side and took copious shorthand notes for her promised post-games exclusive. Then the slim woman firmly, but unobtrusively, escorted her from the queue flanked by armed police to a secure interview room nearby and identified herself as Sandra, the tall man entering immediately afterwards.

'My name is Alex' he said informally, offering Nandi a glass of water.

Inside, a preliminary search produced, amongst other things, one unused black capsule which she admitted was hers. She did not tell them about the second, circumspectly passed to Agnes at the dockside hotel as a back-up plan.

From Hardeep's perspective, gaining the high speed Eurostar, destination Gare du Nord, Paris, with only two minutes to departure could not have been better timed. He boarded the first-class compartment and sat comfortably watching the milling crowds through a landscaped, double-glazed window. With the exception of three businessmen further up the carriage, he was alone, visibly relaxing as the train slowly eased forward on its cross- country rush first to Ebbsfleet and then the Channel Tunnel. From his inside jacket pocket, he withdrew an IPod and slipping the ear-pieces in, lowered his eyelids, immersing himself in Beethoven's Fifth.

'Can we sit here?' a strong voice asked, while a firm hand tapped him heavily on the shoulder.

He opened his eyes and saw a tall, senior, uniformed officer sitting opposite him and a very large, uniformed Sergeant by his side, hemming him in against the window. The officer lifted the ear-pieces out while Hardeep's hands were gripped in a vice-like embrace by the Sergeant.

'Hardeep isn't it?' asked the Colonel, leaning forward and comparing the photo in his hand to that of the man in front of him.

The Tentacle man sat facing him, surprised. 'How did you get to me so fast?' he asked calmly.

'Oh. You know. Information' replied the Colonel. 'I'm sure you can appreciate that?' he added.

'Were we sold out?' the Indian requested politely.

'Not to my knowledge' the Colonel answered matter-of-factly.

'My Sergeant is going to frisk you now and I would be obliged if you do not resist. I'm sure you don't want a broken arm?' he added firmly.

With an expert hand gained from body searches over the years, the Sergeant checked Hardeep and produced amongst other things, one black unused capsule.

'Do you have any more?' asked the Colonel warningly.

'No. This is it. On my mother's life' he stressed, knowing that he would be safe with this eulogy as his mother had passed away two years before.

'Very well' accepted the Colonel, knowing that there would be almost no way to prove otherwise, adding 'let's enjoy the journey together, until we get off at Ebbsfleet.'

'Could I have a drink?' Hardeep asked 'I'm very thirsty. It's been a long day!'

'Alright' said the Colonel and held his hand up for the steward as he was passing, whilst also indicating to the Sergeant to release his grip.

'A bottle of still water for my friend' he ordered.

A few minutes later the bottle arrived with a plastic glass. Hardeep reached out and broke the seal, pouring out the cold, clear water. He lifted the glass in a toast to his two companions. 'It's a pity' he said 'that I won't be joining you in Ebbsfleet. It was one of my ambitions to see the Garden of England!'

With that he swallowed the water and simultaneously bit into the plastic concealed in his mouth. Instantly, a black liquid ran out from his now blistering lips while his pigmentation changed from brown to white as the full effect of the undiluted liquid entered his bloodstream. His arms and legs thrashed silently in an uncontrolled death throw. Within seconds he was dead, the businessmen further down the carriage unaware of the incident. At Ebbsfleet, his lifeless body was escorted off the train by the two military men to a private ambulance, supporting him as if he was drunk and incapable of standing.

By the time Leroy and the 'kill-team' leader had made it to the DLR platform, Blanco and Negro were already well down the tracks and moving gradually out of their reach.

The Harlem man checked his watch. 'Damn!' he cursed loudly, drawing shocking glances from the passengers around them. 'Come on. Come on' he urged the train onwards as the doors opened and closed in what he perceived was extremely slow time. More objectionable glances were hurled at him as the train, now half-full, appeared to speed up.

The traditional silence of the British travelling public was interrupted by his radio bursting into life. 'We've lost sight of them both!   The tracker on Negro is dead! We believe they're headed for the marina. Support on way.'

Ignoring the alarmed glances of about twenty passengers, Negro looked downwards through the rails to the streets below and watched a convoy of fast moving police vehicles, sirens wailing and blue strobes flashing, heading towards the docks. Slowly, but surely, the train made its way via a network of stops until with no further passengers on board, the Americans stepped off onto King George V station. Ahead of them and across the calm waters of the dock, two planes were nose to tail on the roundabout leading to the main runway, the first punching its engines to maximum revolutions before releasing its brakes and hurtling down the concrete and lifting serenely into the air. To their right stood the pontoon road bridge that spanned the eastern end of the two Royal docks, in which a flotilla of ocean going ships and yachts lay at anchor. Across the bridge, marked cars blocked both ends, while armed police, under the orders of a senior officer from the Olympic Command, started a methodical search of all the boats.

A traffic-car drew up by the station entrance, the driver ushering Leroy and the kill team leader in, while his partner updated them on the search as they sped off, claxons howling.

'We believe that they are still in our cordon and have units on both sides of the Thames checking the Woolwich Ferry plus the surrounding roads, in case they try to slip out that way.'

Within minutes they were met by the tall, uniformed Borough Commander who greeted them both with firm handshakes. 'Your people *should* be in here' he waved his hand across a wide area, 'but the Tentacle men might have just got away. They had the edge on us. We've called in air support and the water units' he indicated Hotel 99, the police helicopter hovering above 'but if they were quick enough we might not pick them up. They *could* have slipped through. There is an unconfirmed report' he added 'that a DLR train was brought to an emergency stop just before City Airport and two individuals were seen crossing the tracks heading for the terminal. We are still checking this with the Special Branch unit based in the building.'

The frustrated Langley man gritted his teeth, kicked a nearby empty drinks can and silently cursed to himself. His exasperation would have been even worse if he had glanced across at the adjoining runway and seen the twins in a private jet lift off, banking between the clouds, on a bearing that would take them to a private airstrip not far from where Moses and Emmanuel were greeting Raj aboard their ocean-going yacht.

PRESS RELEASE –SEPTEMBER 2012

'A plot to overthrow many world leaders at the Opening Ceremony of the Olympic Games was recently foiled by the Security Services. A terrorist group had been closely monitored by the UK security forces for many months leading up to the Olympic Games and were stopped firmly in their tracks before any harm could be done. Officials have said that there was never any real threat, but the authorities had to ensure that they had caught all involved, which required waiting until the Opening Ceremony, watching every move of the suspects. Several people were arrested and charged.

Speculation has surrounded President Obama, since his illness following his visit to the UK. President Obama developed a slight skin rash while attending the Opening Ceremony, which medics said was due to the unusually *high temperatures and stressed that, contrary to unsubstantiated and baseless speculation, President Obama is now fully recovered and still black. Strangely, there had been numerous reports about skin conditions which had altered the way the President looked, including the colour of his skin. The Spokesperson for the President confirmed that his lack of appearances since the Olympics has been due to a wish not to aggravate the rash and not anything more sinister.*

On a lighter note, the Olympic Russian Team Coach's application to join his Scottish wife in the UK has been received and is under consideration.'

Karen Jones, Reporter

Lightning Source UK Ltd.
Milton Keynes UK
UKOW052048050312

188389UK00004B/10/P